Smokescreen

by

Lynette Prucha

Clothespin Fever Press
San Diego   1993

Cataloging information:
Prucha, Lynette
      Smokescreen
1. Title
2. Crime fiction

1993   ISBN: 1-878533-01-0

Cover artist: Merlyn Rosenberg
Cover Design: S.O.S. L o s Angeles
Photo of author on back cover: Scott E. Schwimer

Acknowledgements

Many people were kind enough to read and comment on versions of this novel.

I would especially like to thank Steven J. Wolfe, Scott E. Schwimer, Susan Phelan, Ann Bradley, Terry Press, Dr. Linda Lee Talbert, David Vernon, Dr. Sheila Namir, Robert Drake, Sandra Watt, Carla Hacken, Monica Torres and the publishers, Jenny Wrenn and Carolyn Weathers.

Doug Muir offered astute and invaluable editorial advice. Bronwen McGarva contributed an unyielding and ruthless final edit and provided creative stimulation and enthusiasm.

Susan Silton of S.O.S. Los Angeles captured the noir feel of the text with her stunning design and evocative graphics.

I am deeply grateful to have the emotional support and encouragement of my brilliant writing group, past and present: Noelle Sickels, Terry Wolverton, Wendi Frisch, Jeane Jacobs, Linda Higgins and Jacqueline DeAngelis.

And finally, thanks to my literary guru, Terry Wolverton, who offered me a room of my own at a Connexxus workshop six years ago. Her intelligent criticism and insightful vision provided a guiding light on my darkest of nights.

To Raymond Chandler . . .

    Down these mean streets a woman must go who is not herself mean, who is neither tarnished, nor afraid.

Strip away the phony tinsel in Hollywood and you'll find the real tinsel underneath
—Oscar Levant

Table of

Contents

ONE

BIG LEAGUE BLONDE

Los Angeles is a sprawling metropolis, a smog shrouded melting pot of crime, decadence and economic disparity.

Hollywood, its alter ego, a former "sixth class" patch of California land that went from farm to town to city of celluloid fantasies, is a cultdom of image-makers, the locus primi of a film state committed to the indecent exposures of our pseudo Americana culture. And when it isn't tapping into our dark pit of pathological obsessions, it spoon-feeds pablum to the masses and placates our ethnicity by allowing three or four African American and Latino filmmakers to call the shots—as long as the budgets are under ten million.

When Mercedes Martini received a call from her friend Mona Lisa begging for help late one night, it came as no surprise. After all, this was Hollywood and Mona Lisa was an actress. But this time it wasn't car trouble, girl trouble or money trouble. This time it was BIG trouble.

"I'm in a jam. I need your help." Mona Lisa's words were punctuated by fear.

Mercedes groaned and checked the clock. It was three in the morning. "Where've you been?"

"Around."

Mercedes hadn't heard from Mona Lisa in weeks, but her friend had pulled numerous disappearing acts in the past. Ambitious and just desperate enough to grab the town by its balls, no gig was too small. "Low budget cinema" she'd call it. Quick shoots south of the border where crews were cheap, or deserted little Northern pit-stops, a few days in Reno.

"I may be a dark horse," Mona Lisa said, "but I've got one hell of a kick and I'll come in a winner." From the tony shore of Malibu to the crack-filled streets of South Central L.A., a girl like Mona Lisa could always find diversions.

"Listen, it's hard to explain."

"Try me." Mercedes had to get up early for work. A docent for Conservancy West, an architectural society that had saved hundreds of historic buildings from demolition, Mercedes lived a neat, tidy life in a marginally safe part of the foothills of Hollywood. She didn't have time for drama. She wanted to go back to her dreams and meet tall, dark and wonderful. She stared out the bay window at the sparkling landscape below. Los Angeles stared back.

"I'm at the Clark Hotel, but I won't be here for long. They're after me."

"After you?" Mercedes knew Mona Lisa would never stay at such a seedy joint. An east-end hotel, a "no" star despite its proximity to the Biltmore, the Clark was a far cry from the New Otani where Mona Lisa stayed when pulling an overnighter downtown. "Don't pull the rehearsal bit on me again." It could be another Hollywood con job; Mona Lisa was inclined to be dramatic whenever she was in character.

"Christ, just listen," Mona Lisa begged. "Tomorrow you'll get a package, a very important package. Hide it. I'll try to meet you at Derringer at midnight. And Merce," she paused, only calling Mercedes that nickname when she really needed her.

"Yeah?" Mercedes' heart beat swiftly.

"Don't call the police. No matter what happens. If the press get hold of this, my career's ruined." There was an edge of terror to her voice.

A dark and perilous fear invaded Mercedes like an injection of speed in her veins. It was more than a premonition of danger. She swallowed hard.

"They're out to get me," Mona Lisa whispered, then fell silent as if someone had severed her vocal cords.

The line was dead, but before the annoying drone of the dial tone cut them off, Mercedes heard a click, as if someone had been listening.

Bolting up in bed, Mercedes threw back the covers. Mona Lisa was in trouble. What kind of trouble, this time, she didn't have a clue.

She switched on a lamp, reached over and yanked a serape draped around Gilda, an antique mannequin Mona Lisa had insisted on buying her one wild weekend in Rosarito Beach. She wrapped the warm cloth around her shoulders and called information for the number of the Clark.

She first met Mona Lisa opening night at an equity waiver play called *Lounge Lizards and Lies* at the Tiffany. Posturing for the paparazzi, sipping champagne insilly plastic cups with strangers , Mona Lisa, hamming up the big league blonde bit, hobnobbed with critics on the prowl for fresh fodder as they made the most of theater in a town slave to the screen.

"Hello," she said to Mercedes. "Haven't we met before?"

Mercedes was about to say no, but Mona Lisa was on a roll. She rambled on about how they'd got stuck at this party in Brooklyn. "Don't you hate signing autographs?" she asked, whipping a ballpoint from behind her ear and penning her signature to a young man's program, soaking in every minute. "They're so declassy," she drawled in the east coast "deli" lingo she used in the play. "You got a name?" Mona Lisa finally inquired, waving off her agent, Myron Lebowitz, whose sole claim to fame at the Majestic Talent Agency was booking a yodler on Arsenio Hall.

Mercedes smiled. "Mercedes Martini."

"Martini," the actress repeated, licking her lower lip. "Extra dry. Cool. Hip. A girl after my own heart."

Mercedes heard the last sentence echo in her head, one pungent memory in a potpourri of images, as the line at the Clark Hotel rang on. Finally a man answered. He sounded drunk, or half-asleep.

"Mona Lisa Selavy," Mercedes said hurriedly, swinging her feet off the bed. As she paced on the throw rug, she caught a glimpse of herself in the mirror. Average height, attractive, a crop of short, dark red hair, full lips and manicured fingernails. Her flannel jockey shorts exposed her well-toned legs and fit torso. Her face was pale and drawn, mascara smudged her lower lids.

"Who's calling?" the man grunted as if someone were poking him in the ribs.

"None of your business," Mercedes snapped as she attempted to remove the mascara with a wet finger. Her deep blue eyes, dark as India ink on a draughtsman's drawing board, flared up in the mirror. "Put me through to Mona Lisa." There was a long silence. Mercedes got the feeling he was smiling. She could almost hear his grin. Somebody must have been feeding him whiskey because his reply was filled with gravel and malcontent.

"Ain't nobody here by that name, lady." The line went dead.

"Damn it." Mercedes slammed down the phone on the receiver. She tried the number again, but no one answered. Grabbing the Yellow Pages from under the bed, she double checked the Clark's address. It was on Fourth and Hill, not a nice neighborhood to leave your mother in, even if you wanted to.

DEATH SHADOWS

Mona Lisa stared at her reflection in the speckled mirror. The dark shadows in the dingy room of the Clark Hotel stalked her like death. She shivered and applied a matte coat of Crimson Passion to her thin lips, then ran a finger around her weary hazel eyes, the left a tad off center. The nose at that angle was a little too big, the roots of her blonde hair in need of attention.

The tears welled and trickled down her soft cheeks. Losing connection with Mercedes felt like she'd cut the lifeline to salvation. Did their friendship stand a chance if Mercedes knew the truth about her? Was she willing to risk losing her best friend?

It seemed just like yesterday when Mona Lisa boarded a plane for Los Angeles, all her hopes and dreams neatly locked in her make-up case. It felt good to leave her past behind. Everything. Even her name. If she hadn't been seated next to this eccentric art professor on the plane, and hadn't seen a picture of this crazy French artist who'd painted a moustache on the Mona Lisa, she might have adopted a different name. It was somewhere over Kansas City that she lost her real name: Sydney Stein. She always hated it anyway. It was harsh, masculine, uninviting. It wasn't elegant, timeless. Not like the authentic Mona Lisa hanging in the Louvre.

And since she was heading for Hollywood, she needed a really clever, dramatic name. Something to catch the attention of casting directors and producers. And it worked! There she was standing outside American Airlines, wondering whether to take a bus or taxi to Hollywood (she had less than five hundred dollars on her) when Lou Lamont drove up in a shiny white BMW and offered to drive her to a posh party in Bel Air. If it wasn't for him, she just might have ended up a cocktail waitress. A thin smile etched her face, partially crooked, just like her namesake.

Lou, "big lug Lamont," she'd later call him after he got her the

Tampax commercial, with his perennial tan, even as a coat of paint, and a flashy pinky ring, signature initials LL dotted in diamonds. Lou's white teeth gleamed in the California sunshine. They chatted as they drove along in the convertible Beamer. He was one of those. A non-stopper. Didn't know what to do with a period. But producers talk that way and Lou was a producer. He never said what exactly he'd produced, but this early in the game, Mona Lisa wasn't about to look a gift horse in the mouth.

"Mona Lisa, huh?" he asked again, checking out her legs. "Catchy. Original. I like it."

Mona Lisa glowed with pride as they pulled up to this huge pink hotel on Sunset. Little men in green suits tripped over themselves to get to the door. Someone tried to take her make-up case from her, but she wouldn't let go.

Her first Hollywood shindig. A private party out by the pool. Some rock star *du jour* who was cool and hip. And the crowd even hipper.

The food passed around was alien. Nothing on the trays looked familiar to her. A native Brooklynite, she fancied expensive deli, pastrami and good provolone. She handled a California spring roll with suspicion, dipped a chip in this chunky green mixture that looked like clay left in the sun. A few minutes later, she started to unwind enough to put down her make-up case and enjoy a glass of chilled champagne. It made her eyes water it was so good. Soon she was having a ball.

Lou winked at her from across the pool and raised his glass in a toast. A guy wearing white tennis shorts, a shirt with a green alligator on his breast pocket and matching gators on his socks came up to her and introduced himself. He addressed his yelping Scottish terrier as "Junior."

"Hi, I'm Gillings Hedgeworth. And who might you be, my lovely?"

"Lovely what?" she thought to herself, waiting for him to finish his sentence, but he never did.

"Mona Lisa," she replied.

"Umm. Charming. Very bold." He signaled to his friend to join them. A handsome Latina made her way over, dark-skin as smooth as satin, her tongue as hot as chile. "Carmen, I want you to meet

Mona Lisa. Isn't she a charm?" Junior barked.

Carmen smiled. *"No me diga."*

"What's that?" he said, pointing to Mona Lisa's make-up case.

"It's a conversation piece," Mona Lisa said, feeling bold from the champagne, "when someone asks me a stupid question, I can fish inside for an answer."

Carmen grinned. *"Pendejo.* She's got your number, Gillings. Now let me get hers."

Slipping her arm into Mona Lisa's, Carmen drew her past the crowd, into a tiny cabana where they sat talking and drinking until the sun set. *"Diga me, mujer,* tell me a secret," Carmen said, moving closer to Mona Lisa. Closer than any woman had ever come before.

"I'll tell you a secret, but I'll lie about my past," Mona Lisa said.

"You've got no past, girlfriend. It didn't include me."

Before Mona Lisa could think of a response, Carmen pressed her against the wall and kissed her. If that was the way they did things in California, well then, Mona Lisa thought to herself, this was as good a place as any to lay her head for awhile.

Footsteps outside the hotel door jolted her out of her reverie. She didn't have time for nostalgia. There were things to prepare. What she was about to do, scared her to death, but her future was at stake.

A door creaked open. "You walked out on us." The voice was nasty.

Mona Lisa didn't have to turn around to discover the identity of the intruder. She could feel the man's hot breath on her back, the stale smell of Tingsao beer and street sweat.

"Look at me," he ordered.

Mona Lisa faced Redlite, an Asian American bruiser who made up in muscle what he lacked in height and intelligence. All four feet, nine inches of him, skin burnished red from too much sun, arms tattooed with busty women with names like Dora, Lora, and Marguerita. A chump short enough to be nicknamed "fire hydrant," he cracked his knuckles.

"Xuan didn't pay you fifty G's for nuthin'. You forgot, you were supposed to deliver the piece to her today. She sent me to collect," he barked.

Just then a light flashed from the Bath Building. JESUS SAVES. This neon messenger of God promised hope like a false prophet.

Mona Lisa tried to stall for time, but Redlite pushed her down on the bed, whipped out his pen knife and slashed an imaginary X across her frightened face. She winced as he toyed with the weapon. He shoved his knee in between her legs, planting her up against the splintered headboard.

His eyes were tightfisted and wild. His face was twenty miles of rough road, pock-marked, scarred and just plain ugly. The weathered cowboy boots matched an equally ridiculous hodgepodge of caballero poor taste. She couldn't help but laugh at him.

"I was listenin' to you gab with your girlfriend on the phone. Who is she?"

Mona Lisa kept silent. He slapped her hard on the cheek. She could feel the blood rush to the surface like a large ink stamp pressed against her face.

"A friend," she whimpered.

"Then let's go get it back, you little bitch. Xuan's waiting." He pronounced his boss' name American style, "swan." A small trickle of saliva dripped from the corner of his mouth. It fell on Mona Lisa's chin. He licked it off. She cringed as she felt his hot tongue, like wet sandpaper, dab her rice-powdered skin.

She tried to shift her body, but he was too strong. Whatever he did to her, she knew Xuan wouldn't want her number one girl to be damaged beyond recognition.

"Didn't we pay you enough? No hard labor there. Must have taken you ten minutes in the plannin' and fifteen in the takin'." The urban cowboy removed his hat and wiped his brow.

"Bullshit," Mona Lisa shouted. "You know how much that's worth. My cut's nothing."

How dare he minimize her brilliant scheme. It took weeks to worm her way into the confidence of Fletcher. And hours of secret "talks" with Mallory, Fletcher's latest "girl toy" just so she could hold the piece in her hands for a few minutes. Besides, she never got enough. Life had short-changed her. As soon as she had a taste of something good, she was hungry for more. Someone had to foot the bill, someone had to pay. The American dream in a bucket of champagne, only Mona Lisa hadn't counted on picking up the tab.

"I want more, damn it." She managed to push him off her and sat up.

"You're gonna choke on that appetite," Redlite snarled, cruising her smooth skin peeking from the V in the silk bathrobe. He carefully placed his Stetson on the night table as if laying flowers at a shrine. "Don't worry about my diet." Mona Lisa caught the direction of his gaze. She dropped her shoulder. The kimono slipped down her naked torso. The breasts were small, firm, slightly plump. Two question marks of possibility.

The display excited Redlite. His manhood was intact, at least as much as it could be corralled in a stump of a body like his.

"Get me a drink." Mona Lisa crossed her legs as if she'd been practicing for years and lit up a cigarette. The smoke came out of her dry mouth in tiny lassos.

Redlite never took his eyes off the legs as he called the desk. Five minutes later, the night man brought up a bottle of Wild Turkey with a bucket of ice and two filmy glasses.

"Keep your ear on that switchboard and don't let anyone know she's here." He slammed the door shut and walked into the room with the drinks.

First they drank to warm their guts, then Mona Lisa had Redlite pour her a second. "It helps clear my head," she said, holding out the glass.

Redlite hesitated before he helped himself to more booze. "You give the piece to me, keep ya fifty grand and go back to two-steppin' at Club Sayonara."

"I bet Xuan's cutting me out of a lot of dough. Think what we could get on the market." Mona Lisa planted a seed. At times like these she enjoyed lapsing into screen vernacular.

Redlite stared at her as he mulled over the thought. He took a healthy swill of the golden liquid, getting tighter by the minute, until Mona Lisa prodded him even further. "Let's you and me cash it in, split the money fifty-fifty and blow. *Sayonara* and *adios*. What'd ya say, Redlite?"

He took a little too long to reply so she turned on the water works, tears dripping down her cheeks. He put his arms around her and drew her close. She cushioned her head on his shoulder, dampening his shirt as she sucked in these tiny sobs of melodrama. She thought of Gloria Grahame in *Fear City* with Jimmy Cagney. Was that the one with the grapefruit? It didn't matter.

"Come on honey. A man like you's as brave as John Wayne."
He looked down at his spit polished, turquoise cowboy boots,
straightened his shoulders, reached up and touched Mona Lisa's
cheek. A shudder swept over his body.
His movements were rough and clumsy. The sash to her robe fell
to the floor. He pawed her small breasts. Lost in the heat of his need,
Redlite forgot what he was there for. "Yes, baby. Sure, whatever you
want, cookie."
Somewhere in that miserable excuse of a hotel, music seeped out
of the bricks: mellow, saxy blues accompanied by an indistinguishable
crooner. Redlite cued up to sing homage to the girl of all his wet
dreams, "Moan-a-lease-her, Moan-a-lease-her," he drawled on while
she cupped her perfumed breasts in his face.
While Redlite's mouth and hands were busier than those of a
campaigning politician, Mona Lisa grabbed a handful of his hair and
fisted him hard on the cheek. She got hold of a lead vase and knocked
him on the head. Bone cracked. His eyes gaped wide; his tongue fell
out of his mouth as if lost. Blood trickled down the side of his cheek
and his eyes shut. He was unconscious.
Mona Lisa jumped up and dressed. Tomorrow night she'd meet
Mercedes at Derringer and collect the antique she planned to have
delivered to her friend for safekeeping. Just in case. Then she'd tell
Mercedes everything. Well, almost everything.
She leaned over the inert body to grab her make-up case. A cold,
clammy hand shot out and clutched her ankle. She screamed.
"Move across the room," Redlite ordered.
Mona Lisa stared at the gun as she backed off. She was mumbling
something when she came up against the dirty wall of the room. The
gun went off and she felt a warm, wet heat as her body slumped to the
floor like a tired accordion, all played out.

CONSERVANCY WEST

The sun was an alarm of light over the city as Mercedes made her way through Pershing Square, one of downtown's green, cooler pastures, the sparse lawn littered with early morning risers. Men mostly playing cards, drinking their OJ out of brown paper bags, hanging out like they didn't have a care in the world. Lost pilgrims in the land of pigeons and pimps.

Mercedes was still hoping this ordeal with Mona Lisa was just a bad dream, but the anxiety in the pit of her stomach told her otherwise. And to add fuel to her apprehension, the sight of the ominous Clark Hotel, with its graffiti walls and garish neon sign, confirmed her worst suspicions.

She stopped at Hill Street and waited for the light to change. Although downtown was familiar domain, she didn't make it a habit to frequent places like the Clark. As a tour guide for Conservancy West, she'd walked and talked her way along these crowded streets for the last six months. A master's in art history from USC didn't qualify her to do much more than teach part-time — if she could even get the work; although the Conservancy supplemented her modest annual stipend from her grandmother's estate, she was way over her head in expenses, but that's one of the few things she never knew how to control. She still hadn't decided what she wanted to do with her life, and crossing the street and standing outside the Clark Hotel, she had the dreadful feeling she might never find out.

Five worn-out chairs, a chintzy upholstered sofa, a potted palm, and a thin, tired man sporting a buzzed crewcut, served as the welcome committee. "Excuse me," Mercedes said, drawing the man's eyes away from his tabloid. "I'm looking for Mona Lisa Selavy."

The man stood up from behind the front desk and rolled a tattered toothpick round in his mouth. There are those who drink and drink well and there are those who drink hard and it shows. His complexion was yellow and the broken network of veins around his reddened nose could have taken you anywhere you wanted to go. It was the Thomas Brothers of face maps, only you'd stop at the bushy eyebrows. You wouldn't want to travel any farther. The grease on the hair would kill you.

"And I'm looking for Madonna," he said. He scanned her navy, double-breasted Calvin Klein jacket, the russet turtleneck, pleated white trousers and smirked.

Mercedes took a deep breath. "Listen, if this is too much for you to handle so early in the morning, I'd be happy to call the police and have them answer my question."

"Umm." His eyes lingered on her flashy cinnamon hair, then moved down to the striking ornament pinned on her lapel. In the patinated torso of a woman, the face of an antique watch was set dead center. *Carpe diem* was printed on a flag held by a human hand that served as the large hand of the clock.

He took the chewed toothpick out of his mouth, pointed to the pin and remarked, "Nice gadget." Again the toothpick found its way back in his mouth as it rolled from side to side. He closed his newspaper, pulled out the registry and opened it. He flatly recited the names.

"Ms. Jenkins, Boom-Boom Madison, Dr. Leda Tolbern, Maggie Martin, Sydney Stein . . . no Mona Lisa." He slammed the book shut.

Nothing rang a bell. Mercedes looked disappointed.

"Maybe you got the wrong three-star hotel. Try the Alexandria over on Spring."

Mercedes leaned as close to him as she could stand. "Listen, mister. My friend was here last night. In this hotel. Blonde, brown eyes, two inches taller than me." Mercedes slipped him ten dollars.

"It's kinda coming back to me," he said, digging around in a large molar with his toothpick. He pocketed the money. "She's gone. Walked out alone, with a towel wrapped 'round her arm in a sling. Looked like she was hurt, bleeding."

"Bleeding?" Mercedes' heart was racing. "A gun wound?"

He shrugged his shoulders. "Blood's blood. Half hour later this Asian woman came flying in here. Went up the elevator. In less than fifteen minutes, she came down with this strange-looking dude holding a bloody rag to his head. Heard the woman call him `Redlite'. He was hooched-up and pissed off."

"Why didn't you call the police?"

He removed the toothpick from his mouth and laughed. Mercedes could see his yellowed teeth, stained with tobacco.

"Like I said, I didn't see anything, lady."

"Where'd they go?"

He shrugged his shoulders again. "They got into a black car and headed toward Chinatown or the moon, whichever's closer."

Mercedes put on her sunglasses. "Thanks for nothing." She brushed past a few lobby veterans as faded as old movie posters, and headed out the door. She was late for work.

* * *

Mercedes dashed into Conservancy West, a converted red brick fire house built in 1892, which the organization had fought hard to preserve from demolition. The corporate offices were upstairs, above a trendy restaurant called Engine Company 28.

Georgia Press was as plain and conservative as they come. A woman who carried her lunch to work in tidy, plastic containers, she was married to a dull certified accountant who wore three-piece polyester suits a half size too small. Georgia was the director of the architectural preservation society and co-chair of the Community Redevelopment Agency. She was just finishing the morning brief when she glanced at Mercedes. Surprised by her star docent's tardiness, she headed in her direction.

Mercedes was never late. She browsed the literature on the various Conservancy walks as Georgia approached.

"Mercedes, I hear you're making tremendous headway on the MDM project."

"It's really coming together." The Million Dollar Movie project was the Conservancy's attempt to solicit the film community's support in renovating and keeping alive the six or seven prominent theaters downtown, all built before 1930. Mercedes was in charge of getting pertinent films from the old MGM or Universal libraries for the Conservancy's premiere New Year's Eve "black tie" fundraiser in a few months, to be held at the stunning, art deco St. James Club.

"I don't doubt it. Your reviews have been consistently excellent, my dear. The best."

Mercedes smiled. She had been working hard and it was nice to get the compliment. She tried to move on, but Georgia had other plans.

"My brother Webster's in town. You remember, he was at our last reception on *Remaking America*. He was *very* impressed with your impassioned plea to save the Pan Pacific."

"A lot of good that did," Mercedes blurted. Still smarting over the *suspect* arson that reduced the 1935 historic Streamline Moderne auditorium to ashes, Mercedes had organized a major protest to restore this timepiece to the Fairfax community.

"I'd love you to join us for dinner this evening. Give you two the opportunity to get . . . better acquainted." Georgia winked.

"Get a clue," Mercedes wanted to say. "Thanks, but I'm totally booked this evening. Please give Warren my regards."

"Webster, you mean. Are you feeling okay, Mercedes?" Georgia pushed the frizzy, permed hair off her wide forehead.

Mercedes laughed nervously. No one had tried to fix her up on a blind date with a man for several years now. She was rusty. Losing it. Couldn't play the game. Not that she had to.

Georgia called after her. "Webster will be in town for a few weeks. He's on sabbatical." Pride soaked her voice.

"Wonderful." Mercedes opened the double doors and exited. Why didn't she say she wasn't interested, never had any interest. Not in Webster. Not in a million years.

*   *   *

The sky was a crisp patchwork of white, blue and yellow. Fall was in the air and the feel was like an old memory that crept up and sent its chilly fingers along the back of your spine. Mercedes slipped on her sunglasses and took a deep breath, trying to stave off the anxiety that had steadily grown since last night. Her teeth were on edge. She craved a cigarette, but she'd quit. Quit smoking maybe, but that hadn't stopped her from *thinking* about it.

Fourteen more grueling hours before Mona Lisa would meet her at Club Derringer. The suspense knit inside her, slowly took form and emerged as an intricate tapestry straight out of a scene from Bosch's hell.

Each passerby became a potential villain. Even the tourists and Conservancy buffs waiting outside the Biltmore for her to guide them on this peripatetic tour around skyscrapers, Chicago-style edifices and beaux-art theaters, appeared to be a menacing frieze of mobsters and gang-lords.

Mercedes' imagination was getting the better of her. She needed to put her personal trauma aside. She had a job to do and do it she would. She introduced herself, put a smile on her face and led the eager flock of spectators down to Broadway.

It was outside the Pantages/Warner Brothers Theater, then a showcase for the "talkies", now a showcase for diamonds, precious stones, gold and silver, that Mrs. Horn, a blue-haired matron who took all of Mercedes tours for lack of anything better to do, chose to share with the group.

"That imposing bust is Hermes, messenger of the Gods. Some say he was the patron god of thieves." Mrs. Horn smiled at a young man in plaid trousers and an olive green jacket.

Mercedes waited politely. Mrs. Horn had the most annoying habit of picking up bits and pieces from her lectures. Whatever she neglected to include, Mrs. Horn merrily interjected.

A siren wailed in the distance, reminding everyone that the days of old were indeed far away, now that the city had been looted and robbed of its former prestige and glory.

"Bitch," someone shouted. Mercedes turned toward the commotion. The crowd separated, people clutched their cameras, alarmed.

Mercedes was familiar with these "sidewalk" showstoppers, poor panhandlers who were *generally* harmless, but to the Beverly Hills housewife out for some Saturday morning culture, these urchins were nothing short of cold killers.

Mercedes tried to corral her group and keep them calm. A short, muscular man, a large white bandage wrapped around his head like a wounded revolutionary soldier, jumped in front of her, causing her to lose her balance. His eyes were wet, nasty and full of bad intentions. The chapped lips were curled in a permanent snarl — his outfit, a garish Western rendition of cowboy-Indian attire.

Holding onto a lamp post for support, Mercedes tried to stand her ground. "This is a private tour, sir." People were always barging in without paying. But this one really gave her the chills.

"I've got my eye on you," he growled, his left eye twitching angrily. He pressed into the doorway of Reed Jewelers and lit up a stogie.

Mercedes didn't know what to do, so she continued her commentary, surreptitiously eyeing the intruder. He could be the usual sidewalk schizophrenic, but the determination in his eyes frightened her. And what about that blood-soaked bandana on his head?

She stopped mid-sentence. Could this nut be the wounded man the desk clerk described at the Clark Hotel? If so, how would he know anything about her? Unless he was the one eavesdropping on the line. Or worse — he'd forced it out of Mona Lisa.

All eyes were on her, waiting for the infologue to continue. After a minor detour, she managed to get back on track and pick up where she'd left off. Then she rushed the group past Clifton's Silverspoon restaurant and the Quinby building on 7th and Grand.

The creep continued stalking like a rabid wolf, the puff of smoke from his cigar a small chimney ten feet away. She couldn't concentrate. In fact, she wasn't cognizant of what she was saying. She was slipping, leaving out the juicy architectural details, which thrilled Mrs. Horn to no end.

"My mother worked here in 1923." Pleased to have the spotlight, Mrs. Horn stood waving her hands in a theatrical gesture at the Robinson store.

"This store opened in 1915," Mercedes interrupted. "It reflected a period of affluence and commercialism in Southern California. White-gloved operators, writing desks, restrooms with chandeliers, a smoking room for men and an open-air cafe on the roof." She sounded like a tape recording. No inflections. The buzz in her head extinguished her usual theatrical flair.

The creep pushed through the crowd. Her forehead was beaded with sweat despite the cool breeze. What if he took out a gun?

"And they had underground parking for electric cars," Mrs. Horn added, oblivious to the potential danger. At least she hadn't missed a goddamn beat.

Mercedes wondered whether she should call over a cop, not that there were any in sight or that she'd know what to say, but before she could make up her mind she saw the creep disappear into a candy store.

She didn't lose a moment. She rushed the group to its final destination and was just about to cross the street when disaster number TWO arrived.

A pale intense-looking nun ran up to her and pulled her into an arched Flemish Gothic doorway. The sister, her eyes dark catacombs of sleepless nights, mad from too much prayer, or lack thereof, pulled out a small, wrapped package from the loose bib of her uniform and gave it to Mercedes.

"*Dominus vobiscum,*" she said, her raspy voice the stale evidence of a heavy smoker. The faded blue and white habit was two sizes too small, the Reeboks scuffed, blonde, bleached-out hair erupted from the loose-fitting headdress.

Mercedes grabbed her arm. "Who are you?"

The nun smiled and winked. "Special delivery. From Mona Lisa herself. Blessings, my child."

"Where is she?" Mercedes had a hard time soaking this in. Did Mona Lisa find God in a homeless shelter for errant nuns?

"All good girls go to heaven, dear." She yanked her arm free. "Me, I prefer to burn in hell." Then she rushed off into the street, disappearing around the corner.

"My, my," Mrs. Horn said to Mercedes as she strained to overhear this cryptic conversation. "This is better than going to the movies."

"Cheaper too." Mercedes quickly slipped the mysterious package into her leather bag.

*   *   *

Mercedes ushered her group into the Fine Arts Building, the final stop of the two hour tour. They meandered around the beautiful, high-ceilinged Spanish courtyard as the other docents arrived with their groups. The buzz of conversation, the flash of cameras, the thrill of discovery.

Mercedes needed a drink. The ugly pug seemed to have disappeared. She took a deep breath, but before she had a chance to exhale, she felt a fist shoved into her back. She swung around, catching sight of a mop of hair caked with a blood-soaked bandage.

The crazy man, his eyes enraged, was determined to get his way.

"The package is mine," he said, reinforcing his claim with a .22. The sight of the black gun paralyzed Mercedes.

"Where's Mona Lisa?" Mercedes tried hard not to show she was trembling.

"Lying in an alley with her throat cut, if you don't give me the package."

Mercedes' knees started to give in.

"We got a problem here?"

Mercedes swung around and caught sight of her friend. A fellow docent, Snapshot was a tall Teutonic with ash blonde hair and kind blue eyes that softened her imposing six foot stature. She crossed her arms and looked mean enough to scare an ex-convict.

The creep saw he was outnumbered. He stashed the gun in his pocket and ran away before Snapshot flagged over the security guard.

"You okay, Ms. Martini?" the guard inquired, not quite sure how to handle the situation. "I better go file a report on this, just in case."

Snapshot led a dazed Mercedes into the restroom where she splashed cold water on her pale face.

"Why do I feel like humming a few bars of *Goldfinger*?" Snapshot chided.

"Very funny," Mercedes replied. She looked up at her face in the mirror. She didn't know whether to cry, scream or break out laughing.

Snapshot slipped a comb through her cropped hair, opened her brown leather bomber jacket, lit a cigarette and took a long, deep drag. The sound made Mercedes groan.

"He had a gun," Mercedes said, trying to collect herself.

Snapshot shook her head. "Welcome to the real world, kiddo." She offered Mercedes a cigarette.

Mercedes grit her teeth. "I quit."

"Yeah, and I'm straight." Snapshot was a notorious womanizer with a penchant for girls low on morals. Her dry sense of dyke humor calmed Mercedes. "How long this time?"

"Few weeks." Mercedes opened her leather bag and removed the package. She shook the contents. Nothing ticked or moved.

"You quit every other month, then go back. Give up the fight. It's like me giving up sex. `The Surgeon General warns sex is hazardous to your health.' Well amen and thank you for that piece of advice.

Safe or otherwise, I'll always do it. So stop beating yourself over the head. Now what 'chu got in the package and who was Mother Theresa with the bad dye job?"

"You saw her?" Mercedes was glad to have someone corroborate this bizarre chain of events.

"Come on, she wasn't hard to miss. Seems like you're flirting with danger, Ms. Martini."

"Flirting, my ass. I nearly got shot out there. You're a witness."

"Witness I am, reliable, now that's another story. The sham sister wasn't hard to miss. I spent two years in a Catholic school and had my very first religious experience when Mary Louise Zagarella walked into the classroom and smiled at me. Somehow all that translated into a perverse reverence for women of the cloth. They made sex sinful. I'm grateful for their tutelage."

Mercedes grinned. "You're unbelievable."

"That's what they keep telling me, sweetheart." Snapshot pulled off her 35mm camera slung across her broad shoulder like a holster. "Got you some physical evidence."

Mercedes' face brightened. A professional photographer whose latest claim to underground fame was a *menage a trois* expose for *Out* magazine, Snapshot was a bold, arrogant artist, a cross between a Mappelthorpe and an Arbus. Her obsession with "mammary empowerment" hung on the walls at Little Frieda's coffeehouse on Santa Monica Boulevard. The panoply of pierced nipples caused quite a stir. Her real name was Bronwen Himmelfarb, but everyone called her Snapshot.

Mercedes slumped in a chair. "I thought I was losing my mind."

Snapshot laughed. "Join the human race, kiddo. Nuts, loonies, shell-shocked veterans and housewives, paranoid maniacs, schizos off their rockers, kooks, eccentric ladies who sew billfolds onto their faded slips. The old lady next door can't grasp the fact I drive around in a used ambulance. Every time I pass by, she howls and kicks at the air like there's a dead mule in front of her."

Mercedes smiled. "You're nuts."

Snapshot grinned and removed her jacket. Her muscular arms and taut body had caught the attention of many. "So what's up?"

"Mona Lisa's disappeared, some crazy guy's after her and now he's stalking me. I don't get it."

"There's nothing to get." Snapshot ran a comb through her hair again. "The world's a certified asylum and we've all checked in. Anyone out there could want to harm Mona Lisa. The mailman, an ex-lover — Cherie still sends me poisoned fruitcakes every Christmas — a fan, any slimy jerk sittin' on the sidelines who thinks he doesn't deserve his monopoly on misery."

"I'm going to the police."

"Good luck."

"They'll handle this."

"Sure they will."

Snapshot's voice echoed in Mercedes' ears. She turned and stared in the mirror. Her eyes were animated. Her teeth on edge. She hadn't felt this excited in ages. Hell, she couldn't even remember the last time she was so hyped-up.

The gauntlet had been accepted. The challenge was on. And whether Mercedes wanted to or not, she was about to play the game.

THE DANCE CARD

Mercedes tried calling Mona Lisa's apartment several times, but each time the phone machine picked up, she had to listen to Tony Bennett croon, "Mona Lisa, Mona Lisa, men have named you." And then, Mona Lisa's seductive voice, "I'm lost in the heart of La-La Land and can't return your call." **Beep** . . . Mercedes left one more frantic message and finished her paperwork at the Conservancy.

Mercedes hadn't fully appreciated the expression, "one for the road," until that moment. She headed for a little bar, a regular hole-in-the-wall, only this joint had something she really needed —a friend.

The Last Call was as dark as Hades and nearly as bleak. It didn't take long for her eyes to adjust, nor did it take long for her buddy to spot her.

"Yo, girl. What the hell you doin' here?" Good Friday cracked a hard-boiled egg against a Budweiser bottle; seated on a red stool lining the bar, his right eye catching an old rerun of the Dodger's game, he'd often sip a cold beer mid-afternoon and shoot the breeze with the bartender. Blind in his left eye, Good Friday managed to see what he needed to see. Sharp as a whip, with natty hair the color of chalk and eyes that matched, he carried a poker cane and could smell a corner before his feet ever reached it. He was her patron saint on these mean streets.

Mercedes patted him on the back, slid onto a stool. "A Scotch. Straight up," she told the bartender.

Good Friday chuckled. "That blue-haired biddy got ta' ya again, huh?"

Mercedes managed to smile. "Mrs. Horn was the least of my problems today. What do you know about a guy named Redlite?" Mercedes lifted the shot glass and downed her drink. Her eyes watered.

Good Friday arched his eyebrows and let out a sigh.

Bingo. Mercedes could always count on Good Friday to have his finger on the rolodex of players downtown. The crimelords, the street bums, the good sisters who were forever trying to save everyone's soul, the sweat shop owners near Palmetto, the Chinese gambling honchos, the sweet-smelling streetwalkers, the sex club proprietors and the dwellers of rat-infested tenements on Mission Road along the Los Angeles River.

Good Friday's head rolled back and forth. "That shouldn't be a name comin' from your mouth. I'll tell you why 'fore you ask. He's a mean son-of-a-bitch who's been in and out of the joint for years. Works for a sharp lady by the name of Xuan. Two peas in a rotten pod. Your turn."

"I think he's harmed Mona Lisa, maybe even . . . killed her."

"Whoa, Jesus, Mary Madonna. What's a nice lady like her mixed up with them for?"

"I was hoping you'd tell me?" Mercedes' pretzel snapped in half.

"You see a sign outside that door?" Good Friday pointed. "It say, `Black-As-The-Ace-Of-Spades-Fortune-Tellin'-Wizard' inside? No siree. It says, The Last Call. And darling, this is where you get off 'fore you get mixed up in somethin' you can't get outta."

"Too late," Mercedes said, growing more anxious with Good Friday's confirmation. The fact that he knew Redlite blew any theories of a theatrical hoax.

"Scram. Let me see what I can dig up 'round town. In the meantime, lay low. Can't you find anything to do on your night off? Try a date on for size, girl."

Mercedes couldn't help but smile. "You're doing it, Friday. Stop playing Daddy."

"I do it good when I do it, baby." He grinned ear to ear, his capped white teeth glowing in the dark.

He watched Mercedes walk out the bar. As soon as the door closed, his face grew serious. He got up, walked to the phone booth, slipped in a quarter and slammed the door shut.

* * *

The last slice of the big orange beast recoiled below the Western horizon, leaving behind a chilly October evening. In another hour the sky would settle under the cover of night. Mercedes, comfortably ensconced in her mint-condition '50 black Cadillac, raced to Mona Lisa's apartment.

The city was thinly veiled; lights winked and neon grinned like a mad hatter out for a good time. Los Angeles was an open invitation to everything worth doing, which meant everything worth staying away from.

Something in her gut told Mercedes to chuck the package out the window, disconnect her phone and move to Idyllwild. But Mona Lisa needed her. What could she have gotten involved in? Drugs? Espionage? Blackmail?

Mercedes made a left off Highland on Camrose and then a sharp right on High Tower. The apartment complex at 1502 was famous. Its "high-towered" elevator shot up from the hill and overlooked the Hollywood Bowl. A landmark, it was used as a bachelor pad for Elliot Gould in *The Long Goodbye* and in the more recent thriller, *Dead Again*. Mercedes liked to pepper her architectural acumen with snippets of media trivia. Tourists loved it.

She hadn't been at Mona Lisa's for nearly a year. Now that all this had happened, she wondered why Mona Lisa always seemed reluctant to have her visit. No matter what they'd planned for the evening, she had the best excuses to rendezvous at a restaurant, a bar, or the latest coffeehouse on the boulevard. Or they just hung out at Mercedes' house.

No one was in sight. Mercedes took the elevator with its grilled gate up to the seventh floor. She knocked on Mona Lisa's door. Silence. She pounded again. Silence. She even called out her name, but there was no reply.

Mercedes stopped at the manager's apartment on the way out. No one was home.

* * *

Ten minutes later, Mercedes' Cadillac heaved up the steep hill and made a left on Kings Road. She pulled into the driveway of her modest, gray and black-trimmed "streamline moderne" refuge, designed by Kesling in the late thirties. It was a mere two miles from a Scotch on the rocks at the exclusive, pink Beverly Hills Hotel and boasted a perfect view of the St. James Club, renovated to art deco perfection.

In fact, it was Mona Lisa who had encouraged Mercedes to buy the house. "Check out the view," she had said excitedly. "Take it, kid. If you get the creeps living alone up here, I'll move in and be your parlor maid. If Hollywood doesn't wake up soon and make me a star, it might just be the only thing left for me to do," she'd jest.

Maybe that was it, Mercedes thought, as she got out of the car. Mona Lisa was bummed lately about her stalled career. She'd had a small part in Roger Corman's *Body Chemistry*, but that was nothing more than seeing her frozen in a plastic bubble. And that they lost in the cutting room.

The scent of eucalyptus and cedar assaulted her. She walked up the few steps, opened her mail slot and pulled out a huge chunk of bills. She didn't even bother to worry about paying them. There was too much on her mind.

The interior was a clever ensemble of deco and nouveau offset with a few early American pieces, colorful Bauerware, a large wooden cross with painted nails she'd picked up in Mexico and an African mask.

She headed for the phone. No messages from Mona Lisa. No messages from anyone. She removed the mysterious package from her bag, laid it on the coffee table and wondered whether she should open it. After all, Mona Lisa hadn't given her permission to do so. She was simply to bring the package to Derringer and hand it over.

Mercedes was inclined to be suspicious. It could have something to do with her Italian heritage on her mother's side. She grew up under the influence of the "evil eye" — everytime she got out of hand, her *nonna* would put up two gnarled fingers, her black eyes would roll in her white-haired head and she'd mumble strange words in her native tongue. Behavior like that had had its impact. Not that Mercedes believed the package would unleash pernicious spirits, poisonous snakes or a miniature voodoo doll, she just wasn't putting anything past the whims of the universe. Or the curses of her deceased grandmother.

She decided not to open it. Whatever was inside was none of her business. She left the package on the table and went to prepare supper.

Her kitchen was recently remodeled: the bleached wood table

and four matching zebra-patterned chairs; the small black and white-tiled floor; and the colorful Italian ceramic counter tops designed by Cottura Galleries. Mercedes had them reproduce Botticelli's birth of Venus rising from the sea. "With the kind of money you spent," Mona Lisa chided as they had sipped chilled martinis to christen the maiden kitchen several months ago, "we could have high-tailed it to Greece, kissed the Parthenon and lived off feta and the goodwill of the gods for weeks."

Not the way Mona Lisa spent money, Mercedes mused as she heated some leftovers. Besides, the money had been part of an estate her grandmother had bequeathed a year ago. It was a lifesaver and helped make ends meet since her salary at the Conservancy was less than $30,000 a year. And it gave her the opportunity to do what she always wanted to do: own a home and decorate it. She had no brothers and sisters, her parents lived in a retirement village in Whiting, New Jersey. There were no kids, no animals, no lover.

She popped a stuffed artichoke in the Dutch oven, tossed a salad, opened a bottle of Merlot, heated some *penne* pasta with tomato and eggplant, put her supper on a tray and carried it into the living room.

* * *

R. Carlos Nakai's nose flute solo echoed off the wood floor. A fire crackled, jasmine incense burned, and Mercedes sat there, her dinner half-eaten, feeling the solitude of the room, the peaceful quiet of what could be her last moment of relaxation.

The package beckoned like a lodestar. The suspense was killing her. She had to know what was inside. She picked up a steak knife and cut the cord. She thought she heard someone whisper, "Remember what happened to Pandora."

She picked up the box and shook it. Again, nothing moved. She wished she knew some kind of prayer to bless the moment, but didn't think the Hail Mary appropriate and couldn't remember it anyway. She tore off the wrapping, took another sip of wine and opened the box.

The heady scent of Mona Lisa's perfume *Must de Cartier* wafted to her nose like a captive genie released from the confines of a bottle.

Wind chimes rustled outside. The tick-tock, tick-tock of the ancient grandfather clock on the mantle added to the tension. Mercedes trembled as she unveiled the contents.

Nestled in tissue paper was no ordinary trinket. Not your *faux* Dior cluster of gold, diamonds and emeralds. This was very real, expensive and rare. Someone had excellent taste.

An antique gold and silver dance-card, approximately four by five inches in diameter lay in the palm of her hand. Three sensual Muses in diaphanous robes were carved in relief, trapped in the past, whirling their last dance to a forgotten tune, imprisoned by bars of moonstones, diamonds and emeralds glittering around the border. Each woman had a tiny ruby chip in place of a heart.

This was a museum piece. Mercedes was stunned by its ephemeral beauty.

How could Mona Lisa have gotten hold of something like this? Not too long ago, Mercedes had seen a collection of late 18th-century jewelry and artifacts at the L.A. County Museum. Dance-cards were very popular in Europe. Jane Austen's crowd and the ill-fated Emma Bovary wouldn't have dreamt of going to a party without a delicate card hanging from their wrist. Men lined up to secure dances for the evening. Very civilized. Very democratic.

Mercedes flipped the latch on the right side of the holder where a thin gold pencil was fastened in a small attachment on the left side. Opened, the dance card revealed a scroll of rice paper. Scribbled on the paper in Mona Lisa's schoolgirl's script was a cryptic message.

red little fish, I kill you with the three-bladed knife that there may be an end to the silent circling of the past. This dark passage will be my guiding light.

Mercedes was puzzled. She'd always known Mona Lisa to be carefree, a party gal. What secrets was she hiding?

She fingered the delicate curves; held it up to the light. How many women had been captivated by this accessory? What stories could be told about their adventures? An international choir of forgotten women, their heartaches and struggles, the intrigue of love, the desperation of passion, the suffocation of their spirits.

There was a signature and date scrawled in the left-hand lower corner: *J. Hoffman, 1922.* She placed the object in the box, walked into her study and searched for a text on antique jewelry and the decorative arts. A large, dusty volume, it hadn't been used since her graduate days. She checked the index, found Hoffman's name and looked up the entry on page 246. There in full color was a picture of the exact same dance-card with minor variations. Designed by Josef Hoffman in Vienna, the caption read:

Hoffman was seduced by the erotic mysticism behind most of the painting of his contemporaries, Klimpt, Kokoschka and Schiele; however, unlike the twisted dark display of frenzied passion, Hoffman paid tribute to Eros in a most charmingly pedantic way. His limited edition dance-cards quickly became collector's items. While dance-cards traditionally were as common among the aristocracy as servants, these jeweled "passion pieces" symbolized the spirit of the dance, the joyous exultation of men and women.

Mercedes shut the book and slumped into a cushy leather recliner. It suddenly struck her how different she and Mona Lisa were. Mercedes wasn't starving for fame. Her destiny was amorphous. A dedicated dilettante, she didn't suffer from the malady of every aspiring actor, comedian, singer and artiste: a burning desire for universal validation. She was perfectly satisfied with her lifestyle. At least up until this point, she thought she was. But something was eating at her; she didn't know quite what it was.

Again that eerie stillness. Nakai's wind spirits had stopped. A final gasp before death. A few dogs barked. A cat meowed for Friskies Buffet. Adrenaline pumped through Mercedes' body in quick, staccato spurts. A nice, hot shower was just what she needed.

* * *

Mercedes sipped her cappucino and stared at herself in the bathroom mirror. The day's events had taken a toll on her thirty-year-old face. The dimples, which appeared when she smiled, seemed to have permanently disappeared. She looked a bit ragged, her eyes bloodshot. She smeared some cold cream on her skin, down along her neck, the way Mona Lisa had instructed her. If anyone knew about health and preservation, it was Ms. Beauty Queen herself.

"Two camomile tea bags for the eyes, a dash of eucalyptus in each nostril to help cleanse the lower chakras, mud mask for that oily T-spot, a ten minute cat nap and you're as good as new," she'd chirp.

Suddenly, last night's dream came back to her. A faceless woman had appeared with a gift. The gift was of no size, dimension or weight. It was as soft as a kiss and more powerful than evil. It held the future.

Mercedes shivered and stepped into the hot shower. As the water hit her back, relieving her aching limbs, she knew the dream was some sort of nocturnal premonition.

Like a death knell ringing out in the night, Mercedes realized that a chapter was closing and that a new one, mysterious and foreboding, was about to begin.

VENUS FLY TRAP

In another part of town, in a cozy gated enclave on the Westside called Bel Air, Flora Fletcher, a well-preserved woman in her mid-forties, laid a silver trowel in a bed of compost and glanced at a row of Venus Fly Traps newly arrived from South Carolina that morning.

She glanced at her Cartier watch. It was time for her meeting. She closed the glass door of her designer greenhouse and moved along a narrow path trimmed with hawthorn, a few laurel trees and a gurgling fountain. A wrack of gray clouds canopied the sky.

The figure she cut was admirable. Fletcher wore a cream two-piece suede suit, alligator loafers and emerald earrings. A woman who knew how to gamble with the clock, fastidious and compulsive, Fletcher had hired Noh, a young Asian American, to caretake her.

Skilled in Oriental medicine, Noh practiced acupuncture, dabbled with herbs and vitamins and knew everything there was to know about balenology, the art of bath. She supervised Fletcher's ablutions with sea salts, herb scrubs and exotic oils. Paraffin wraps, eucalyptus mists, Hungarian clays and Swedish creams, the ingredients extracted from sheep embryos, were all used in one measure or combination thereof each day.

As much as Fletcher hated this battle with the clock, she knew she was winning. She detested losing—losing in poker, in business, and most importantly, in love.

Since the dance-card had disappeared, her lover Mallory had grown cold, distant and unaffectionate. Given all Fletcher knew about the checkered history of this relic, she shouldn't have been surprised about the outcome of things. But being in love, as she was in love, didn't mean being clear-headed. The sooner Fletcher retrieved the antique, the sooner things would settle down and life could return to normal.

She entered her Tudor Estate through the pantry. Cinnamon and apples and a simmering beef stew created a fugue of piquant smells. She added a pinch of thyme to the stew swimming in a sea of pearl onions and baby carrots.

Fletcher didn't have any intention of inviting Samantha to dinner. A Lothario by heart and swindler by nature, Samantha's reputation, no doubt, far exceeded her exploits. The community thrived on gossip the way her lovely Venus Fly Traps feasted on juicy insects.

Before entering the study, Fletcher smoothed back her dark brown hair. Her brilliant eyes were sharp and cruel. She glanced up at an oil painting bequeathed to her by her father. It was a Hogarth. A rather ugly painting, it was a scene from the Rake's Progress, a poor raving maniac ended his days in Bedlam. It wasn't the sort of picture one hangs in the living room, nor anywhere for that matter, but Fletcher was superstitious about family possessions and refused to sell it, even though her ex-husband, Max Pitts, claimed it could fetch millions.

* * *

Samantha Mann sipped her chilled martini and waited for Fletcher in the study. She lit a cigarette and checked out her appearance in a gilt-framed mirror. Despite the long trip from Rio, she looked pretty good.

Wearing a Versace leather jacket, man-tailored pants, silver-tipped suede shoes, her hair as dark as a raven, cut blunt across her shoulders, with bangs slicing her thick, dark eyebrows, Samantha realized South America had changed her for the better.

The Latin sensibility and fiery emotionalism tempered her Nordic, hard-edged personality. The year away provided a ritual cleansing. A perfect detoxification from the shallow theatrics of West Hollywood, a microcosm with all its queer ramifications of the larger and more global superego of Hollywood.

This cultural odyssey from the Andes in Peru, to Caracas and Sao Paulo, Brazil, reacquainted her with a promising career in archeology, one she'd forsaken for a quick buck. Not that she was about to re-enter the world of academe, nor was she about to embark on some third-world archeological dig, but she knew that between a life of "crime" and a life of earnest poverty doing what she loved, some middle ground must exist. All she had to do was find it.

But like any addiction worth the trouble, there was still the lure of lotus land where dreams are manufactured and boxed daily. An open jewelry box waiting to be pilfered, this town sparkled under a dazzling rococo of neon.

Someone once told her Los Angeles was a place where ice was loot, ice was murder and ice was cold. And as Fletcher walked into the room, Samantha knew what they meant.

*   *   *

The two women were seated apart from each other, separated by a tray of caviar and ten years.

"So how was Brazil?" Fletcher asked, not really caring. "They say the women are very beautiful. Did you bring home a . . . souvenir?"

Samantha smiled. The comedy of manners was about to begin, only no one had given her a program. She glanced around the olive green library filled with antique books, orchids and tiger lilies. A stab of jealousy wrenched her gut. She had had to work hard for everything she earned, even if she stole it. Fletcher, on the other hand, had inherited all this from her family.

"Naturally," Samantha replied. Well, not exactly, she thought. A flight attendant she'd met on the plane could hardly be considered a cross-cultural catch, but Samantha couldn't resist the blatant flirtations, the extra consideration. "Do you need another pillow, Ms. Mann?" Besides, the woman was only in town for a few weeks. Long enough.

"How's business?"

Fletcher recoiled. Samantha could feel the middle-aged woman's hair bristle on the nape of her neck. She knew mention of Fletcher's "boutique collection" hit a sore spot. Fletcher got her kicks transforming waifs into elegant call girls to entertain the rich and the very bored rich. Sell a little art, pander a little flesh. Came down to the same thing: merchandise and money.

"Look who's calling the kettle black," Fletcher shot back. The Queen Anne chair she sat in was strategically placed in front of a Shoji screen. "A girl with your talents, pedaling ice from country to country. A once-famous archaeologist digging for treasure in obscure places like Chiriqui, Almeria or Chalton. Clearly the fact you appropriated your findings didn't sit well with your esteemed colleagues. Your days at Berkeley were numbered."

Samantha stabbed out her cigarette. The reference to her former career stung like a poisoned arrow. Fletcher was exaggerating. It only happened once. With an Indian statue, a beguiling piece Samantha had unearthed. The owl goddess of regeneration. Time and space—everything contained within her. Such power. A tangible possession of immortality. She had to keep it. At least for awhile. "Let's leave the past behind. Deal?"

"Deal." Fletcher nestled in the Queen Anne chair. "Possessions in this town are all a matter of semantics, as I'm sure you'd agree."

"That depends on your vantage point."

Fletcher ignored her rejoinder. "Someone's stolen something very precious from me," she said, twisting her fingers, "and I want it back." Fletcher's lips were tight, the eyes feverish.

At that moment, the wall housing the bookcase slid open. A shadow crossed the rug before the figure appeared. And then a man emerged from the wine cellar carrying a bottle of *Pouille Fuisse,* his Doberman at his side. It was Max Pitts. He seemed surprised to find the women there. He came over and kissed his ex-wife on the forehead and coolly glanced at Fletcher's guest.

"Well, look who's back in town," Max said, his voice thick with condescension.

Samantha was never crazy about Max. He was one of those borderline sociopaths she'd met up with too many times, a disaster waiting to happen. The twisted network of braces on his lower teeth glinted like the polished blade of a serrated knife. Such a steely prop. Ever one to indulge in the latest fad to improve his image, Max was a stickler for perfection. His narcissism went beyond the accepted Sports Connection "Adonis" breeding ground. And the designer steel-rimmed glasses lodged on his aquiline nose was as jarring as a delicate instrument of torture. The eyes behind the lenses were rabid and predatory.

Watching the ex-paramours was an exercise in theater of the absurd. A warped Punch and Judy. They'd been married for five years in London and in those five years they'd colluded on a number of scams and art hoaxes. They finally had to leave the country and settled in Los Angeles. By then they were divorced.

From the half-opened door, a waft of the evening's dinner punched Samantha's nose. Her stomach did a flip-flop. All this melodrama had stirred her appetite.

Fletcher pet the Doberman who never took its eyes off Samantha. She cleared her throat. "As I was saying, Mona Lisa stole a valuable antique and won't give it back. I've done everything I can do . . . within reason . . . to persuade her to return it. I want you to find her and bring it back to me."

A dark fog descended on Max. The Doberman looked at him as if sensing his shift in mood. The canine moved over to Max and licked his hand.

Samantha took his silence for anger, not complicity. She remembered he had given the antique to Fletcher as a gift. No doubt her giving it away didn't sit well with him. She was impressed that a two-bit actress like Mona Lisa was able to pull off such a stunt. Samantha suppressed a smile.

"My dear partner in crime," Max patted the dog's head with obvious affection, "has lost her head, giving away . . . ."

Fletcher cut him off. "Yes, yes, I've heard this a thousand times—really Max, *do* get sentimental over something else."

"I've lost my taste for cheap drama," Samantha said, getting up.

"Perhaps, but I know you haven't lost your taste for money." Fletcher smiled, a lean cuisine of frozen fare, it disappeared in seconds.

She was right. Samantha was pretty low on cash. "What about Mona Lisa?"

"Bring her to me. Ten thousand dollars—but," she pointed her finger, "I want the antique and the girl."

Samantha drew out the moment. "Make that twenty grand, plus expenses, and you've got yourself a deal."

Fletcher looked at Max. He nodded. The Doberman barked. Neither of them were too happy but they acquiesced.

The double door opened and in walked five feet three inches of pure beauty. Fletcher quickly moved to put a protective arm around her lover.

"Samantha, this is Mallory. Mallory Archer." She made the obligatory introduction with about as much relish as someone entering a morgue.

"I hope I'm not interrupting anything," Mallory said, her voice soft as a rose petal.

Samantha grinned. There are blondes and there are *blondes*.
Ms. Archer was one of the latter. Her corn silk hair, marcelled in
waves, scalloped a Pre-Raphaelite face. A shy nose and slender lips
seemed to smile over nothing in particular. The blue eyes appeared
to recognize you and then tried to place you as if you were an old
friend she'd forgotten years ago.

Slim like an ivory poker and curved in all the right places, Ms.
Archer wasn't a day over twenty-two. Her pale pink, two-piece
Chanel suit matched high heeled *poie de soie* pumps. Fletcher clutched
her hand. It was apparent the little display annoyed Max.

The double strand of South Sea baroque pearls around the girl's
neck were authentic. Although Samantha had no loupe, she had an
excellent eye for these things. These were strictly Tiffany's. The
antique must be a pretty heavy piece of sentimental artillery. Who
said money couldn't buy love?

Fletcher ushered Samantha out into the hallway. "Mallory's my
new . . . secretary," she said.

Samantha laughed. What an epilogue. Such a flourish deserved
a curtain call. That neo-noir knockout never struck a keyboard in her
life. Why the added pretense?

"Don't overplay a good hand." Fletcher's menacing voice came
from a place dark and evil.

"We'll play the game your way, Fletcher. We always do."
Samantha slammed the door behind her.

*   *   *

Once outside Fletcher's estate, Samantha zipped her jacket. Fall
was settling in, leaves rustled behind her in the garden. She heard the
patter of footsteps nearby, turned and caught a glimpse of a fleeing
figure like a large bat, dressed in an oversized black coat and felt hat.
It was headed for a small cottage.

Samantha caught up and grabbed hold of an arm. The figure
whipped around. She was a pretty Asian. A single, perfectly braided
strand of dark hair hung down between the center of her left eye and
ended in the middle of her pale cheek. A hangman's noose of Eurotrash
design, in the moonlight it appeared to be a deep red gash that had

healed into a nasty scar.

"Who are you?"

"Noh," the girl replied, her black crow's eyes full of determination.

"And what do you do for the lady of the house?"

"I mind my business."

"And I mind Fletcher's." Samantha nodded toward the estate. "What do you know about Mona Lisa?"

Noh's eyes were implacable. "She's gone."

"Tell me something I don't know."

Noh glanced at the house. A servant turned on the chandelier in the dining room. "Mona Lisa's . . . dead." Her voice was pitched in a key of sorrow.

She let the line settle. At that angle, the girl bore an uncanny resemblance to someone Samantha knew. "You're Xuan's kid, aren't you?" Samantha had met the young girl at a party Xuan had thrown for her daughter's sixteenth birthday. At the time, Samantha had some jade and precious stones that Xuan was exporting for her.

"So she tells me."

"Does your mother know what you do for a living?"

Noh's eyes flared with anger. "It's not like that."

"It's never like *that*, it just always is."

Noh thought a few seconds before responding. "If you want to know more about Mona Lisa, ask Carmen." She quickly turned on her heels, opened the door and disappeared inside the cottage.

Carmen Machado. Probably still hooked on Mona Lisa. So we play a little ring-around-the-rosy. Samantha shook her head. Some things never changed. She walked down the cobblestone path, got into a black Jeep and peeled away down the empty street.

KGAY

The night was wet and slippery. But Sydney wouldn't escape. Felony had a vested interest in tailing the elusive girl and it wasn't just for the money. This was emotional blackmail and the night suited her mood: cold and calculating. The sky, a clearly defined road map of stars, glittered above Felony's head like a halo, only she didn't feel so holy tonight. Vengeance had killed charity. She was motivated by despair and not the calling of her trade. The life of a private eye was lonely indeed, she thought as she made her way down the silent street. Felony stood in front of Sydney's apartment. Pendants of shadow hung in the air like doom. Inside a red light illuminated the sweet cheat's bedroom. Felony stood there under the lamplight and dragged on a cigarette. The big pay-off was only a few feet away.

Carmen Machado, a dark-skinned Latina with short, spiky hair, sat in the glass-windowed booth. Her hazel eyes, usually full of sparkle and wit, were tired. It'd been a long night. Her voice, though, was in top form. All sax, a bit scratchy and deeper than a well-buried secret, Carmen's words poured out over the sound waves like warm brandy mixed with cream.

"You've been listening to DAMES, broadcast live from K-G-A-Y, the only gay and lesbian sponsored radio program in the city. And for those newcomers, I'm Carmen Machado, your host, bringing you the best in jazz, swing, salsa and R&B. Don't forget to check out Jezebel's in Venice for some bad R&B."

Carmen stretched her long legs. The faded Levi's and cowboy boots fit her mood this evening. She was on edge; if she went home now, she knew she'd never go to sleep. While Derringer was off-limits—running into Fletcher was not her idea of a good time—there was still Girl Bar, Encanto or the Palms. But that would only mean temptation. And she wasn't in the mood for a "quick pick" and she didn't have the energy for yet another getting-to-know-you encounter. She packed up her stuff and was ready to head out when she spotted Samantha Mann.

Her stomach knotted. She knew then no matter how hard she tried to bury her past, it would always come back to haunt her. Samantha wasn't here to pay a social call. She was here to dig in the knife on behalf of Fletcher. While Carmen didn't have a grudge against Samantha—they'd done their share of partying—she wasn't about to be manipulated by Fletcher via proxy.

Carmen shook her head, ran a hand through her hair. It wasn't as if she owed Mona Lisa any kind of protection. Mona Lisa had lied, cheated and broken her heart. *And* defected to Fletcher's fold. It was one slow burn and the scars had never healed.

Carmen opened the door for Samantha. She had long admired Samantha's cool charm, her quick tongue, her ability to work both sides of the street. "When did you get into town?"

"Yesterday." Samantha gave her a hug and looked Carmen over.

*   *   *

Carmen's small office was lined with posters from the movies, *Flamenco Argentina*, *Naked Tango*, and *Sunset Boulevard*, the only splash of color and culture in the dingy room.

Samantha spoke first. "You're quite the storyteller."

"A little fact, a lot of fiction. As long as it works, that's the ticket."

"It works."

Carmen smiled weakly. At least something in her life was working. She had always been drawn to the idea of reinventing a language spoken by men, but told from a woman's point of view. She liked keeping the sharp edge; after all, she'd walked it like she'd talked it in this town. *Pueblo de Nuestra Señora la Reina de Los Angeles.* An archipelago of low and high brow dreams. The lesbian detective as outlaw.

Carmen tapped her pencil on the desk. She waited a few seconds and then decided to push the conversation. "Looks like Mona Lisa's got everyone in a tailspin. I'm surprised. . ."

"Surprised?"

"Yeah, surprised you're still angling for Fletcher. You dumped this shit a year ago. South America was supposed to be the great purifier." Carmen leaned closer, her disdain challenging Samantha.

Samantha shrugged her shoulders. "Times are rough, money's

lean, and some things just don't change, do they?"

"No, some things don't change, but let me tell you this. I'm out. Not playing her game, so if you came to me to help you find Mona Lisa, you can forget it."

"I better find her before Fletcher does," Samantha said, looking Carmen straight in the eye.

Carmen arched her eyebrows. She fingered a yellow pencil. "Even if I knew where she was, what makes you think I'd tell you?"

Samantha lit up a cigarette. "Judging by that narrated smokescreen, I don't think you've gotten over her. In fact, I'm starting to think you may know exactly where she is."

A nasty smile curled on Carmen's full lips. The eyes as cold as ice.

"Fletcher's not a stupid woman. If she can plant a murder or disappearance on someone else and get away with it, she will. You two didn't part on the best of terms."

"I've still got the knife in my back." Carmen scratched her neck.

"Then I suggest you cooperate." Samantha's voice was harsher than intended.

"Are you threatening me?"

Samantha smiled. "Come on, *guapa*. I'm just laying it on the line."

This encounter was starting to dredge up some loathsome memories from the past. Carmen thought she'd done a pretty good job of burying her pain, but Samantha's comments were like a salve, drawing the poison to the surface. But more than pain, there was that spasm between her legs. That slow, treacherous stab of lust. As sharp and potentially deadly as a serrated knife.

Her past opened like a trapdoor and she plunged into a dangerous pit filled with hissing snakes. Call it bad conscience, guilt, karma. Managing Derringer and doing a little extra leg work on the side for Fletcher had brought nothing but misfortune. Sure, the job paid handsomely, well enough to keep Mona Lisa happy. But money earned cheaply is hot. Franklins burn a hole in the palm of the hand if you keep them long enough. Carmen never did. After all, this town was one big slot machine with a healthy appetite for slugs.

Months after Carmen's first encounter with Mona Lisa—this native waif from Brooklyn—she found herself in love. She was hooked. Slowly her obsession grew. Carmen had always been a woman in control, but with Mona Lisa it was different. She was out of control.

Call it santeria, black magic or bad luck, Mona Lisa was a snake charmer.

Sure it was sexual. But then it went beyond sex. It became a challenge to keep her girlfriend's unruly behavior in check. The need to control overtook her again.

They both liked the danger of game playing. Mona Lisa's vagrant behavior became more and more exaggerated. White lies turned into big fiction and there were these strange friends who appeared and disappeared in the blink of an eye. The hot and cold theatrical displays of devotion drove Carmen crazy.

It gave her an excuse to feel rage. Rage against her own weakness. Rage against a woman who represented the other. It wasn't as much personal as it was generic. A masochistic war dance, her heartbeat accelerated by the sting of argument, the erotic dialectic of two bodies drumming different beats.

As Mona Lisa slipped farther behind the curtain of Hollywood and ingratiated herself with Fletcher's hip lesbian crowd, the more Carmen tried to control her and the more Mona Lisa insisted on her freedom.

"I can't breath, Carmen. I need to be trusted," Mona Lisa screamed. "I love you, isn't that enough?"

It wasn't. Her Latina friends didn't understand why she was so *loco* about this white woman. Sometimes, Carmen didn't get it either. It had nothing to do with a perfect fit, nothing to do with ethnic identity, nothing to do with doing the **right** thing. Mona Lisa was a drug, as lethal as crack, as sweet as opium, as mind-altering as LSD. Addiction was addiction. It went beyond color, sense and sensibility.

The obsession she could deal with. Hell, it would pass. But when a friend of hers snitched, told Carmen that Mona Lisa was working on the side for Fletcher, Carmen nearly killed her. It would have been easy to do. Her hands around Mona Lisa's soft neck. A seeming embrace, then a quick snap and it would all be over.

Well, for a short time it was. Carmen grew sullen. She was drinking heavy. Using. Losing herself in a stew of rage. She had Mona Lisa followed like some common criminal.

Some things are better left in the dark. It turned out Fletcher was matchmaking her girlfriend with some Westside friends, a charming coterie of wealthy housewives out for a little fun. When Carmen confronted Mona Lisa about her "side" work, she denied it. "I'm not guilty of anything," Mona Lisa insisted. "It's you, you're jealous and you're punishing me." So instead of taking it out on Mona Lisa, she made Fletcher the scapegoat.

Carmen realized Mona Lisa's metamorphosis was complete and final. She would never be the sweet, innocent young girl she was the day they first met at the Beverly Hills Hotel.

Mona Lisa was hooked. Addicted to the handsome women vying for her services, ensnared by the promise of fame and fortune, reeling from all the attention, she became spoiled.

A pang of guilt shot through Carmen. She hadn't really set the best of examples. She was an accessory. Working Fletcher's club, keeping her mouth shut about her boss' wheeling and dealing, playing the game. So if she had a gripe about anyone, it ought to be with Fletcher. She called it quits with Mona Lisa, told Fletcher to go fuck herself and started to get her life back on track. She tried to forget Mona Lisa, but it wasn't easy.

And now here was Samantha, soliciting her help. Carmen's eyes were tundra cool, her face implacable. "Looks like you've hit a dead end."

"You don't walk out on Fletcher without paying a price. You know that, Carmen."

"I know Mona Lisa's nobody's fool." There was a rancor underscoring her voice, a razor sharp recitative that cut to the quick.

Samantha stiffened. "Is Xuan protecting Mona Lisa?"

"Xuan's a shrewd businesswoman who runs a lucrative dance hall, panders on the side, dabbles in contraband and isn't past putting a bullet in anyone's chest if they stand in her way. She protects her own interests."

Samantha took out a card, wrote a number on it and gave it to Carmen. "If you change your mind about helping me, call. Mona Lisa's in danger. Fletcher's not playing this time."

Carmen got up and walked Samantha to the door. "And neither am I," Carmen remarked, her voice all barrelhouse and just plain bad.

COLD SHOULDER

Night brushed the shoulders of the urban landscape like a black cape on the back of a masquer's costume. It was one of those evenings only a New Yorker could appreciate: the dark sky was illuminated by the moon; the air was forest fresh and chilled like a dry martini; and the wind blew stray litter along the dusty sidewalks of West Hollywood. Traffic roared up and down La Brea Avenue. Headlights flashed, horns honked, and a few pedestrians, heads bent, darted into Derringer where a blue neon pistol glared above the doorway. The urban refuge, more than just a hangout for chilled, lonely hearts, was a haven for the faithful, the nucleus of women who vanished below the surface of the cathouse each night to seek their own.

Mercedes' black leather heels clicked along the pavement like muffled rivets from a machine gun. Wearing a two-piece chestnut Agnes B. suit, a 1940s cut with a single strand of pearls, she suddenly felt her confidence falter.

A few minutes before Mercedes left the comfort of her home, Snapshot showed up with pictures of the nun. When Mercedes revealed what she'd found in the package, Snapshot was speechless. And concerned. "Not such a good idea to run around town with that in tow," she advised Mercedes. Mercedes agreed. Snapshot was happy to be of service and took a few Polaroids of the dance-card, just in case. Then Mercedes carefully sealed the antique in a large Ziploc baggie and slipped it into a huge jar of Pond's cold cream.

Footsteps fell into place behind her, drawing her back to the moment. Someone whistled. Mercedes stopped, whipped around and saw Regan Hawk, Derringer's watchdog, or to put it more politely, manager of the joint.

Regan smiled coolly. Wearing faded 501's and a black leather jacket that hung on her broad shoulders with arrogance, Regan's brown, spit-polished boots, nearly knee-high, crushed against the sidewalk as if the body she'd inherited from Gold's Gym were too much for the street to handle.

"How's it going?" Regan asked, walking along with Mercedes. Her chiseled features, framed by thick black hair, slicked off the side of her head, axed short and blunt at the base of the neck, had always attracted Mercedes, only she'd never admitted it. To anyone.

"It's going," Mercedes replied. Regan always flirted with her, but Mercedes never picked up the cue. Regan had a reputation for liking women who were well-seasoned, classy and mean. She fancied breaking spirits. She was a tamer of hearts.

"You shouldn't be out walking alone," Regan pressed, her voice rich and deep.

"I'm a big girl," Mercedes replied.

It was obvious Regan couldn't take her eyes off Mercedes. The cold shoulder wasn't cold enough to send her on her way. Mercedes would have to try harder. She didn't have time to flirt. Not this evening.

Regan brushed a strand of hair off Mercedes' face. The neon sign above the doorway flashed provocatively on her skin. "Beautiful, too," Regan said as Mercedes walked inside the club.

* * *

Regan had a hunch Mercedes was here to look for Mona Lisa. She'd gotten wind of the details from Fletcher. Maybe she could help out. Fixing things came easy to her. It was amazing how grateful women could be in the face of danger. If Regan had to create a little of that danger herself—what the hell, it all washed out in the end. If anyone forgot the favor—few did—she had a way of making them remember. Gratitude could be a very beautiful thing.

Regan surveyed the women waiting to pay the cover charge. It promised to be a busy night. She lit a cigarette and nodded to a few women entering the club. She knew if she tried hard enough, she'd get to Mercedes. A smile creased her handsome face.

In a town that opened and closed lesbian bars like venetian blinds, Derringer hadn't yet hit the mortality list. As clubs for women go, it was tidy, a bit on the dreary side. The drinks were cheap, the women, well, they weren't cheap, but a damn lot of them were easy to be had.

At twenty-seven, Regan had cultivated a saloon philosophy suited for this stone-hearted town. She never mixed business with anyone's pleasure; she was careful to separate the Dos Equis of this world from the Dom Perignons; she never touched a mixed drink and made it a point to keep her nose clean during working hours. She kept her back to the door, never letting anyone push her up against a wall, the only tips she took came from the top and once she stepped on someone's toes, she never looked back.

Fletcher had already warned her to keep her eye out for Mona Lisa. Regan didn't think Mona Lisa would be stupid enough to show up here. But you never knew. A pink champagne-haired checker derailed Regan.

"What's up?" Regan said impatiently.

"I'll tell you what's up. It ain't me," the gum-chewing rock 'n roller said. "I'm suffering from a serious case of claustrophobia." She blew a bazooka bubble in Regan's face. There must have been thirty women jammed on line. "On top of it, they forget their card and give me a mouthful about not paying."

Regan turned to a tall, tough-looking brunette with an earring pierced through her nose. "This isn't supposed to be hard. You got your card?"

The girl shook her head no, annoyed.

"Seven bucks. Now let's move it."

The girl threw down a wad of crumbled bills.

"Like they say on TV, don't leave home without it," the checker drawled, cracking a big smile.

"Let's keep this line moving," Regan shouted, turning toward the door. The words were hardly out of her mouth before someone caught her attention.

At first she didn't recognize her because of the round, dark glasses, but upon closer inspection, she remembered quite well. It was a hard face, but attractive all the same. The woman stood there, agile, self-assured like a statue of Artemis. Only this wasn't a marble statue, it was all steel. Samantha Mann was back in town.

TROUBLE IN MIND

       Mercedes had disappeared like Eurydice into the bowels of the subterranean den. Crushing through the frieze of women, she made her way to the long narrow bar.

"What can I do 'ya, doll face?" the bartender asked. A tall brunette who tended bar on weekends and a quality control inspector for Anheuser Busch the rest of the week, she was a recovering alcoholic with the initials VSOP tattooed on her right arm. No one completely buried their past.

"Tanqueray and tonic." Mercedes settled in to wait for Mona Lisa. It was nearly midnight and the bar was packed with the regulars, the not-so-regulars and a few downright new faces, like the copper blonde two seats away who sipped a strawberry daiquiri like a seasoned professional.

As bars go, the decor at Derringer was borderline tacky, but not half as garish as the Palms with its perennial Christmas tree lights and neon Budweiser signs. The lights here were soft enough to disguise the chipped walls, the faded posters, the spotted, thin carpet, but bright enough to make sure the woman leaning against the wall was someone you wanted to bring orange juice to the next morning.

Mercedes and Mona Lisa had often talked about opening their own bar. A first-class intimate lounge, with an eclectic variety of music, South American, African, jazz and blues. A place where you could get a glass of Pinot Grigio without the waiter saying "huh?" A place to go after work, to take a business meeting, to hold fundraisers and parties. The thought of this unrealized dream plunged Mercedes into depression.

Was Mona Lisa the same person who'd tended to her when she was sick with the flu? The same good-natured pal who was never without a word of encouragement? Wasn't she always at her doorstep with Sweet Lady Jane brownies and Haagen-Dazs to cure a broken heart? This was no fair-weather friend . . . a little eccentric to be sure, but certainly one to rely on in a jam.

Mercedes checked the crowd for familiar faces. In the center of the lounge area, on top of a circular table draped with fishermen's net, the white-faced, lugubrious Morac danced to Madonna's latest hit. A Corona in one hand and a cigarette in the other, this go-go dancer shut her eyes, lost in the myriad gyrations of her body. Not one for chitchat between sets, she sat pushing limes in her beer while she read *Mondo* magazine or the *Wall Street Journal*.

Derringer was a place to be seen and a place to hide. Depended on what you were up for that evening. Being partial to anonymity herself, Mercedes enjoyed hiding in the shadows of whispered come-ons, sweet plea-bargaining and your basic old-fashioned, "Haven't we met somewhere before?" But tonight, tension was in the air like a stick of dynamite ready to explode. No one was safe. Safety wasn't the name of the game in this hide-out.

"I feel lucky tonight," a dark-skinned beauty said to Mercedes.

"I wish I could say the same," Mercedes smiled weakly. The smile froze when she felt a hand on her shoulder. She prayed it was Mona Lisa, but when she turned around, Snapshot loomed over her.

"Don't look so happy to see me," Snapshot teased, ordering a Coke. She had on a pair of jean overalls, a v-neck t-shirt and a denim jacket with Marilyn Monroe painted on back, the ubiquitous camera hanging off her left shoulder.

"No sign of Mona Lisa," Mercedes said, catching sight of Regan in the mirror over the bar.

"I'll check upstairs." Snapshot squeezed Mercedes' arm, then moved off.

Regan slid in between the bar stools. "You ready for another?" She pointed to Mercedes' half-empty glass.

Mercedes shook her head.

"What's that you got in your pocket?"

Before Mercedes could do anything, Regan's hand shot out and plucked the Polaroid from Mercedes' breast pocket. She didn't bring the dance-card, but she brought the picture Snapshot had taken earlier.

Regan's eyes gave away her surprise. "Pretty expensive present. Who gave it to you?"

"I took you for many things, but not a pickpocket." Mercedes snatched the Polaroid from Regan's hand and put it in her purse. "You got a little show, now I'd like a little tell."

A thin sneer stretched Regan's full lips. The eyes, lashes black and long, tried to go neutral but Mercedes guessed Regan knew more than she'd let on.

"Mona Lisa told me she was doing some volunteer work for your boss, Flora Fletcher. What exactly was she doing?"

Regan winced. "Use your imagination." She ran her hand through her hair. "If you have something that doesn't belong to you, I'd suggest you give it back."

"Even if I did have it, which I don't, why would I give it to Fletcher?"

"It's hers."

"Why should I believe you?"

Regan's eyes were hotter than the red neon number hanging above the bar. For a moment it looked as if she would expose something, but then, just as quickly, she shut off. Like a malfunctioning traffic signal, sometimes flashing green, but mostly red, Regan seemed on the blink.

"Why don't we talk about this later. I've got to get back upstairs."

Mercedes watched Regan walk away. She breathed more easily. Fletcher was tied up in this and now Regan knew Mercedes was on to the antique. Why would Mona Lisa have suggested this spot to rendezvous? Perhaps because she never had any intention of showing up. Mercedes climbed off the stool.

"Mercedes!"

She looked toward the balcony. Ariel and Eve waved to her. The latest newsome twosome, their ashy brunette hair spilled over their shoulders like wild weeds in an otherwise perfectly groomed and manicured garden. Clad in matching Vittadini jackets, they stood arm in arm, the new Lady Sneerwells. Sentinels above the crowd, they gossiped and flirted, proud to be loving their sisters, proud to be doing it in public; seditious, rebellious, stubborn, these two lovers seemed to shout above the music, "Yes, look up here at us, we are a new generation of lipstick lesbians, we proclaim a different litany of freedom, watch the way we kiss and coo, we've taken narcissism to its extreme and slapped the faces of convention that mock us."

Mercedes waved back, momentarily distracted by the sight of her friends. She wondered how long that relationship would last. A few weeks, months? Keeping up with the square dance of lovers was practically impossible in this town.

It was twelve-thirty. She polished off her drink, then noticed a pack of cigarettes unattended next to her. She slipped a cigarette from the pack. The temptation was too great. She had no will power. Stroking the cigarette as she would a long-lost love, Mercedes weakened. A box of matches lay next to her empty glass.

Mercedes stared at herself in the mirror across the bar. Her cinnamon cropped hair looked as though she'd been caught in a windstorm. She tapped the cigarette against the formica surface.

From out of the stairwell, shielded by the shoulders of the crowd, Mercedes caught sight of a woman, dangerously self-assured, as she muscled her way through the cacophony of chatter.

"You look like you could use a light," the woman said behind Mercedes. The music pounded with congas, steel drums, a Latin pop band.

Mercedes whipped around and faced a raven-haired beauty. She was dressed in black, save for a leopard silk scarf draped around her neck and shoulders, twisted right above her heart and pinned in place by a striking quartz and emerald brooch, the kind your mother wore in the fifties, if she were that kind of lady. The kind who envied the real thing and thought she could get away with wearing imitation jewels at a cocktail party. Only this didn't look like a fake.

"I don't smoke." Mercedes tried to hide the cigarette she still had in her hand.

"Looks that way to me." The stranger flicked a tortoise lighter under Mercedes' nose.

Mercedes flipped up and dragged on the cigarette like a criminal reacquainted with a crime. For a second she thought of stamping out the cigarette, but took another drag instead.

"I'm Samantha. Samantha Mann."

Mercedes said nothing. She was too busy staring at her. And she was definitely worth a stare. Her eyes were the color of seaweed, the full lips demanded attention. Dark crimson, they appeared bruised, slightly swollen, as if too much blood had rushed to the surface. They were thirsty lips.

Samantha put on a pair of tinted, designer steel-rimmed glasses. She had expensive taste. "It's the lights," she volunteered. "My eyes are sensitive."

In the mirror above the bar, Mercedes watched, unnerved, as Samantha downed the better part of a Scotch and soda, then leaned close. She gave off a scent remote and foreign, an aromatic wet and dark like a jungle in the midst of a downpour.

"You'd better stop staring at me," she teased. "I'm beginning to feel like a Christmas present."

Mercedes was mortified.

Samantha ordered another round of drinks for them. Mercedes didn't even remember drinking her second. What the hell was going on tonight? Felony, magic, witchcraft, Mercury retrograde?

"I could ask your name," Samantha spoke. "But I already know that."

Mercedes looked surprised.

"And I could ask if you're waiting for someone, but I know that too." She placed a twenty on the bar and told the bartender to keep the change.

A generous *bruja* to boot, Mercedes thought. "Since you know so much, Samantha, maybe you can fill me in."

"My name sounds good in your mouth," she said, running a finger along Mercedes' pearls.

Mercedes' head was spinning. She'd forgotten the taste of the first cigarette, so Mercedes let the woman light her another.

Samantha loitered a moment, the smoke a gray-blue veil between them. "We have something in common."

"We do?"

"Mona Lisa."

Mercedes choked on her drink.

"She's in a bit of hot water at the moment. I'm here to fish her out. I think you can help me."

"Thanks for the drink, but I don't discuss my affairs with strangers." Mercedes started to move off the stool, but the stranger held her in place.

She leaned in and whispered in her ear. "I like a woman with backbone. We belong on the same team."

Mercedes reeled from the pressure of Samantha's fingers on her arm. She shook loose from the siren's clutch.

Samantha smiled, then looked down at her Gucci watch. "Before you disappear, check out that ugly little excuse of a man next to Ms.

Pelvic Thrust."

Mercedes turned, glancing in the direction of Samantha's nod. Standing a mere four feet, nine inches short was Redlite, looking like he needed to blow off steam.

"He's having an awful time trying to be inconspicuous in the middle of this perfume warfare."

Mercedes felt sick. The color disappeared from her face faster than a blush on a whore.

Samantha caught Mercedes' discomfort. Her eyes were no longer shards of obsidian charm. There was a warmth behind the stone. The woman was human after all.

Redlite tried to make his way over, but got distracted; he was too busy brewing a boil watching Morac gyrate her hips.

"What's going on with Mona Lisa?" Mercedes demanded.

"Now's not the time nor the place." Samantha's eyes darted around the room like someone was pointing a gun in her direction, a double-barrel shotgun, and it only took a second to realize who she was looking at.

Flora Fletcher, dressed in a DKNY pant suit, was engaged in a heated conference with Regan. Mercedes hadn't seen Fletcher in several months. And while she still looked every bit as *haute couture* as she always did, there were signs of wear and tear etched on her face.

"Looks like we got plenty of company." Samantha put a hand on Mercedes. "You've been stood up, sister. How about a nightcap?"

Mercedes hesitated. Was it wise to drink with the enemy? Could she trust her motives for going off with tall, dark and dangerous?

"Sure." Mercedes played along.

"You could be asking for trouble," Samantha warned.

"What kind of trouble." Mercedes was soon sorry she asked.

"The kind you look like you need." Samantha's eyes were a crack of lightning as she gave Mercedes the once-over. She slipped on a pair of black leather gloves, softened her voice and pressed closer. "Seems to me you might enjoy it." Samantha blew the words in Mercedes' face like a cloud of smoke.

Mercedes took a deep breath. It didn't help. She needed to take about ten thousand of them, but there wasn't time. There was something wild and underhanded about Samantha, something about her that made Mercedes hope she'd stick around longer than a hangover.

They tried to cut through the crowd, but Regan grabbed Mercedes' arm. Samantha stopped her.

"Isn't that Fletcher signaling you, Regan?"

Regan turned around. Fletcher easily stood out in the crowd of jeans and lycra. She motioned to Regan to steer clear.

Mercedes' head was spinning from those double Tanqueray and tonics. Tomorrow she'd give up booze, cigarettes, bad women and every reason for living. Tonight, she'd learn to live with herself.

Redlite pushed through the crowd, his eyes livid with revenge.

"This is the end of the line, bitch." Redlite reached in his pocket, but before he could do anything, Regan, pissed off that Samantha had outdistanced her with Fletcher and more importantly, Mercedes, slammed the punk against the empty fish tank. His head crashed into the glass. Regan pinned his arms behind him and kneed him in the groin.

He howled in pain.

The security guard came up and slammed handcuffs on his puny wrists.

The scene was all the distraction Samantha needed. She pulled Mercedes toward the stairwell. Mercedes turned around. A brilliant white flash of light blinded her as Snapshot aimed her Minolta at Regan and Redlite as if they were the evening's honorary couple.

Two fugitives on the lam, Samantha and Mercedes ran across the street, the full moon casting a mustard hue on the empty street.

A COUPLE OF JIGGERS OF MOONLIGHT

At least Samantha didn't wear the dark glasses while driving. But maybe it would have been easier for Mercedes to concentrate without the surreptitious stare, the rascal smile etched like a proposition on her beautiful face.

They must have been traveling sixty miles an hour. Swept away, more like abducted in Samantha's jeep, Mercedes felt as if she were suddenly transported into a different world. Familiar signposts zipped by: Director's Guild, Gaucho Grill, Greenblatt's Deli, La Toque, the invincible Marlboro Man had now become part of an alien terrain. The glare of neon and the shafts of traffic light were all warnings from extraterrestrials. "Go home, hide under the covers. We'll let you know when it's safe to come out."

Mercedes blinked. She knew her old life was safe, a bit predictable, but she was in the driver's seat, in control. But now with Samantha at the wheel, an expert navigator, this fetching amazon careened along Sunset Boulevard, jackknifing around curves, the moonlight on their tail like an undercover agent, Mercedes felt out of control. And she wasn't sure she liked the feeling.

"Home, sweet, home," Samantha said as the vehicle heaved up the faintly lit alleyway of the gothic-looking Chateau Marmont, a hotel-cum-castle on a bluff noted for its illicit assignations.

A vintage Hollywood hostel, which in its heyday lured celebrity guests like Jean Harlow, Howard Hughes and Greta Garbo who'd check in as Harriet Brown, the cosy hideaway was built in 1929 and had recently added John Belushi's tragic death to its repertoire of resident gossip.

Mercedes caught a glimpse of herself in the side mirror. Her hair was windswept, cheeks rosy and eyes glazed, but that had less to do with the night air than the booze.

"I hope you don't mind a little quiet conversation in my room,"

Samantha said, helping Mercedes out of the Jeep. "I just got into town."

Mercedes looked at her suspiciously. No apartment and the first thing she does when she comes into town is hang out at Derringer? There was no doorman to welcome them. Vaguely conscious of gliding through the small lobby with its beautifully painted ceiling and deco chandelier, Mercedes rode up an elevator and walked into a large, two-bedroom suite with a magnificent view of the Strip. It was all so obvious what was happening, yet she felt propelled by an overpowering, mysterious force. Part of her wanted to believe she was investigating Mona Lisa's disappearance. And the other part was going along for the ride, the adventure. The thrill of the chase.

"Make yourself comfortable. I'll order us some coffee. How about scrambled eggs and caviar?" Samantha torched a cigarette and reached for the phone on the marble bar.

Mercedes nodded her approval. While Samantha was on the phone, she walked into the restroom. A quick inspection revealed Samantha's expensive taste in creams, shampoo and perfumes. Mercedes felt a little woozy. She splashed her face with cold water, pinched her cheeks and applied some fresh lipstick. What next? An interrogation scene. But who was interrogating whom?

Now that everyone in town was looking for Mona Lisa the stakes were higher. And time was running out. If only she could be sure Mona Lisa was hiding out till the heat died down.

Mercedes had what everyone wanted. The dance-card. She'd never been so popular. Nor had she ever been the target of so much attention. Had Mona Lisa purposely arranged it so? To deflect attention from what she was doing? If this was her friend's idea of being in the limelight, Mercedes would rather take a bow and get off center stage.

Mercedes ran a brush through her hair. If she took any longer, she might never leave the safe confines of the bathroom. She was making a terrific impression.

She took a deep breath, opened the door, and was just in time to catch Samantha laugh, then say, "Don't worry. It's under control."

When Mercedes stepped into the room, Samantha stood up, smiling. The food was arranged beautifully on a silver cart. A bottle of chilled champagne sat waiting in an ice bucket. The smell of steaming hot coffee wafted over to Mercedes.

"Nice, very nice," Mercedes thought. Who was this mysterious woman with excellent taste in midnight snacks? She was having a hell of a hard time staying on track. If she was going to be any kind of competent sleuth, she'd better put aside this gnawing temptation to fling herself into Samantha's arms.

Mercedes moved toward the window to admire the view, to take a few deep breaths, to stall for a few seconds, to think of something clever to say, but Samantha's hand shot out and pulled her close. Mercedes struggled.

Samantha kissed her. It wasn't your friendly sort of kiss. More like erotic thievery. Mercedes' knees turned to silly putty. The sensation of the kiss, the arrogant, abrupt gesture, split her heart. She couldn't breathe. Her temples throbbed. She felt Samantha's strong hands caress her back. Her neck tingled. She felt faint. Mercedes pulled away. She was swimming, spinning. And then suddenly everything went black and the room closed in on her. Without warning, the four walls collapsed, the floor gave way and she plunged into a deep, dark pool. It had no bottom.

Mercedes felt herself flagged by thick ribbons whirling in concentric circles like the huge brushes of a carwash. She plummeted deeper and deeper into this bottomless pit until she fell like a feather into Samantha's outstretched arms. The room was full of smoke and fear. Somewhere in the distance, maybe over the rainbow, a lone sax, filled with heartache and remorse, wailed the blues. The room glowed from an orange neon sign, the words indistinguishable.

Samantha made her stand up and gave her a drink that tasted like a warm kiss. Smoking a thin Havana, Samantha marched around the desk. Her outfit was all guerilla warfare—skintight loden and khaki jumpsuit, knee-high brown leather military boots. Part bounty hunter, part soldier. She could ride the wind out of an Arabian stallion or a water buffalo for that matter. Anything for the sport of it.

Mercedes spotted the dance-card on the desk. She grabbed it, but Samantha slapped her hand with a riding crop. The outfit was complete.

"Don't touch what doesn't belong to you," she commanded in a stiletto voice. Then a razor-thin smile slashed her face. She rang a bell. "Soup's on," Mercedes thought, but what came through the door was nothing like beef stew, pasta primavera or a peach cobbler. It was a blonde, bad and beautiful. It was Mona Lisa. Wearing a velvet merry widow, thigh-high fishnets and pink·slippers, Mona Lisa's devil-may-care face was partly obscured by a

jewel-specked mask. Her sun-bleached hair fell on her naked shoulders as she sat on the desk, crossed her legs with slow deliberation and leaned over to kiss Samantha. She paid no mind to her best friend.

Mercedes was infuriated. Even more so when Mona Lisa started moaning with pleasure. The murmur grew in proportion to Samantha's caresses; first her neck, then the pale breasts peeking out of the tight lingerie. Samantha's eyes were filled with a malicious glee only a bride stealing a husband from his childhood sweetheart could understand.

Mercedes tried to move, but her feet were stuck in black tar. An arctic breeze swept across the room as the two women walked off with the antique and closed the door behind them. Their hollow laughter hung in the air like a witch's curse.

Bolting up in bed, her head reeling from too much booze, Mercedes looked around the empty hotel room. Samantha was gone. A window had blown open and the thin white curtains billowed like a diaphanous wing of an angel. Only she doubted it was heaven she'd just visited.

She jumped up and steadied herself against the dresser. Her head was still spiraling in that black pool of unconsciousness. Samantha had removed her sweater, but was kind enough to leave on her pearls.

Mercedes caught a glimpse of her half-naked body in the mirror. There was a bruise on her left breast. She moved closer. Her mouth dropped opened. It wasn't a bruise—it was a souvenir of Samantha's lips.

Mercedes pulled on her jacket. Her driver's license and the photo fell to the floor. Terrific. Samantha was probably at her house this very minute, combing for the antique. Why didn't Mercedes give her the key before fainting?

She finished dressing, but all that moving around made her dizzy. She had to lie down for a minute. Just until the room stopped spinning.

Her body quivered with rage. There seemed to be a twelve-piece marching band in her head. The temples throbbed. She touched her mouth. She fingered the imprint of Samantha's lips on hers. Desire overcame her. She tried to fight it, but the more she did, the more she savored Samantha's tongue stabbing her mouth. She knew then that this woman would definitely stay around longer than the very worst of hangovers.

"Samantha". The name slipped from Mercedes' mouth, echoing like a dangerous incantation in the silent night.

TWO

SUCKER

Regan buttoned the fly of her 501's, sat at the edge of the queen-sized bed and put on her boots. The room was dark, the only light coming from a luminous clock face jammed in the mouth of a mock Cro-Magnon relic.

It was 2:30. A body stirred next to her. A thin, white hand reached out from beneath the down comforter and fingered Regan's thigh. "What'd ya know," thought Regan. "Ms. Daiquiri turned out to have a master's degree in anthropology." She watched the pretty woman drift back to sleep.

Regan couldn't sleep. She was pissed that Fletcher solicited Samantha's help and not hers. Retrieving the antique was a choice assignment. In the year she'd worked at Derringer, there'd been no double-crossing, no slip-ups. In fact, until this point, life had been damn easy. And Regan liked it that way.

Working in a club filled with women was better than cruising the filthy sidewalks and bleak landscape of the warehouse district downtown.

As a cop, she'd had her run-ins with tough truckers and fishnet-stockinged transvestites trolling outside El Caribe bar on Seventh and Ceres—those transient prowlers who masquerade as society's forgotten, the stingy hustlers, the rent boys, the jive drugged-out dudes, eyes bleary from crack. On hot summer nights, the traffic was so congested along these dank, inner city blocks, it was like a freeway jam. She had grown tired of kicking scavengers on their cement beds as they clutched bottles of booze to their sunken chests. And she had become sick of watching them jerk and shake like wind-up dolls as the nightmare they'd wake up to in the morning hit them.

It was the cold, distilled light of dawn, the wintry breath of bus fumes and patrol cars, the stale smell of cheap Mexican cigars and foul-mouthed pedestrians that Regan opened her eyes to every morning for two years. Being a cop, a plain flatfoot along this "tenderloin" beat held no glamour and little excitement. It had taken its toll.

It seemed like yesterday. The day Miles Malone, Captain of the 77th precinct downtown, invited her to "choir" practice one evening. Regan had heard rumors about Malone, but she didn't care. Her curiosity had gotten the better of her.

Five of them met that evening in a tiny gin mill in Little Tokyo, a dark bar decorated with red velour wallpaper and crushed velvet seats spotted with stains. The smell was old, stale and a little garlicky, like a leftover salami sandwich. Seated at a round table, a cone of light hanging over the consortium of sharp-edged cops, Regan was positioned next to Malone.

"You're doing well, Regan. It seems a shame," Malone said, popping a handful of nuts into his mouth, "You're too good a cop for this beat." His white eyebrows were spotted with a few black hairs that had refused to turn white. He had a large nose, only after the last fracture you couldn't really call it a nose anymore. It seemed to melt into his lips. And he had a screwball face. It made Regan want to laugh for no good reason.

"I can tell you're one of us, one of the *boys*, so to speak." He winked at a sergeant who nodded his head in agreement.

"There's a little club two blocks away, just off Central, called Club Sayonara. Now we know it's a dance hall and the Japs from Glendale hang out after work before they go home to their wives and kids. It gets pretty crowded, the saps buy tickets so they can dance with the broads. During the war—the big one that is," Malone continued, talking while popping peanuts into his mouth, "We used to pay a dime for `stag' dances. Yep. The Roseland Roof on Spring." His eyes misted with the memory. "Now they charge *ten* bucks," Malone sneered. "Inflation's killing everything."

A short waitress with no chin shuffled up to the table and placed icy beers and shots of whiskey on colored napkins. Malone waved her off like a fly.

"Now on the surface, everything's on the `up and up,' you know what I mean?"

Regan nodded her head.

"I can't go in there every week and bust them for doing the

tango." Malone laughed. A wide gap between his upper front teeth caused it to turn into a whistle. "Can you picture that? A skinny little Jap, his face pressed to some doll's tits, tangoing across the dance floor?" The guys laughed along.

"The Japs like to drink alcohol. The Chinese stay away from the stuff, they're too busy running the gambling casinos in Chinatown."

Malone eyeballed Regan. "The long and short of it is we can't infiltrate these clubs. On the surface, the girls are paid to dance. We know about the contraband, the stolen gold and jade. The mastermind behind the operation," he paused, his eyes darting back and forth like a nervous clock, "is Madame Xuan." A pained look cracked his face like the oiled surface on a counterfeit canvas.

"Madame Xuan?" Regan questioned.

"Yeh. Part white, part Asian. Fifty. Only you'd never know it from looking at her. "Five years ago she bought a new face, tits, ass, God knows what else. That's America for you. All that money can buy. She's every plastic surgeon's dream." Malone moved his face close to Regan's. "I want her nailed." He slammed his fist on the table. "Even her fingerprints have been changed."

Regan asked what she could do.

Malone smiled. "If you agree to take the job, I'll pull you off your beat."

Regan swallowed the rest of her beer. Eight eyeballs were glued to her. It was time to cue up. She chalked the stick.

"I'll set you up in a West Hollywood detail. You'll report to me. None of this gets out." Malone looked around the table at the boys.

"What's in it for me?" Regan said, the question hitting all eight balls, scattering them north, south, east and west around the table.

One made the pocket. Malone looked as if he was going to slug her. "Don't fuck with me, and you'll get plenty. The sergeant here will be your contact. Use the rest of the men as muscle." He shot an envious glance at Regan's well-developed arm. "Not that you ain't got that department covered," he jeered. "Anything it takes, even if that means putting on a skirt and showing a bit of leg."

Malone squeezed her thigh to make sure she had one. She did. Regan also had a hand that moved quicker than his. She grabbed his thick wrist and twisted it under the table till his shit-eating grin turned into a dirty scowl. One swift move and his wrist would snap like a stalk of celery.

Malone grunted and let go. It was getting late. His wife would have dinner waiting.

Regan had her first assignment. So what if it appeared shady? Captain Malone had been on the LAPD for thirty years. If she couldn't trust him, who could she trust?

A siren wailed outside in the distance, then the noise died down and the night was still. She looked over at Ms. Daiquiri who was fast asleep.

She should have known it was a set-up, but working "undercover" was a challenge. And infiltrating Club Sayonara, run by Xuan, the *mama san* of the house, was easier than she'd thought. Especially when two people spoke the same language. Money has a way of uniting the most disparate of people. Greasing the palm of Xuan's hand helped to break the language barrier in a matter of minutes.

"No trouble," Xuan warned, her voice as soft as sandpaper. Possessing the eyes of a Gorgon, Xuan was always in black, a silver dagger pinned above her heart. She canvassed her club with authority, striking fear in the occasional riff-raff and culling respect from her girls.

Redlite, on the other hand, packed a rod the size of a small nightstick and was less keen on her being there. But Xuan brushed him away. Business was business. And she wasn't going to discriminate if some dyke wanted to party with her clientele.

And party she did. Club Sayonara was the swankiest of dance halls downtown, not that that was anything to put it on the map. In the vicinity of the Mayan Theatre, a previous X-rated hang-out, the club drew a steady stream of men into its dark pit of promise.

Filled with pretty girls with big dreams and empty pockets, oddballs, society's forgotten, mostly runaways, they came to bury their troubles in a speakeasy decorated with Christmas lights.

Regan would sit on a naugahyde couch with the "regulars" behind a glass shield, waiting for just the right girl to parade by. Some of the men were attractive and they paid well for the top girls. But the rest of the taxi-dancers were stuck with beefy jerks, slimeballs and pimple-faced nerds. These were the girls she targeted to get her information about Xuan. A few drinks and they were more than happy to share what they knew.

"It's all a confidence game," Captain Malone had said to her at lunch over a bowl of spaghetti and meatballs at the Italian Kitchen on 7th. "You get in good with the girls, they open up."

Regan decided not to share all the information she'd gotten with the Captain. At least not right now. When she found out that Xuan had an exchange program going on with a rich woman on the Westside, an operator by the name of Flora Fletcher, she pricked up her ears. There were lots of lonely, rich housewives looking for a little action, a few kicks. Fletcher's girls were discreet, educated and willing to cooperate. For a price, that is. Everyone had their price.

Regan soon discovered that there was only one girl suited for a Westside exchange and that was Mona Lisa. Carrying a fistful of bad faith and a mind lacking all conscience, Mona Lisa always knew where to find her next bottle of Cristal. Men like Mr. Yamamoto, a big-time banker, who was soon to cash in some chips as his corporation took over the fourth largest bank in the country. He paid for her time double, triple. "Name your price, baby," and she did.

A counterfeit in the middle of a regular Barnum & Bailey's Circus, Mona Lisa was mistress of ceremonies in that danceland of cha-cha-chas and thin, brittle tangos.

"What's a nice girl like you doing in a place like this?" men would ask.

"Looking for the man of my dreams," she said, her voice a dull rustle like a sheet blowing in the wind.

As soon as Regan got wind of a shipment of jade, she blew the whistle. It was a Tuesday night. The club was crowded, the usual fog of smoke hung in the air. She nursed a Scotch to calm her nerves.

Then Fletcher arrived unexpectedly. One of the girls Xuan had sent over to the Westside had robbed and beat a client in her Beverly Hills home. An incident like that could ruin Fletcher. To show her irritation, she lured Mona Lisa to her kennel full-time. "Just to even the score," she said to Xuan.

Regan thought there'd be a vicious cat fight, but Fletcher had the protection of the police on the Westside and Xuan couldn't afford that kind of confrontation.

Fletcher left, and no sooner did Xuan have time to stew over the loss of Mona Lisa, than the wail of sirens blared outside.

Regan ran out. Six car loads of law blockaded the exits. A dozen cops raided the joint. There were even smoke bombs. Captain Malone barreled into the bar, his eyes darting around as if they'd been in solitary confinement for years. It was that look on his face when he slapped the steel on Xuan's slender wrists that gave it away for Regan. She guessed, but had nothing to go on, that Malone's obsession was more than professional. Xuan was busted for prostitution and possession of over a hundred thousand dollars in contraband gems and thrown in jail until her attorney got her out on bail.

Regan learned from one of the girls that Xuan thought Fletcher had set her up. "I'll get my revenge," Xuan swore.

Three days later, Captain Malone called Regan to his office and shoved a file in her face. The tables had turned and not in her favor. All it took was one poor sucker, someone had to be the fall guy and that someone had been Regan.

"Is this your signature?" Malone questioned.

Regan reviewed the paper. "Yes."

Malone peered up at her before looking over at the sergeant and a federal stooge. "You disappoint me, Regan." He pressed his intercom and in walked a reporting officer and three FBI agents. They read Regan her rights, then told her what she'd done wrong.

They nailed her on a couple of traffic violations, not hers, but a few she'd pulled from the computer for a friend. It just so happened this "friend" was the daughter of Malone's new girlfriend and she didn't approve of her daughter hanging out with Regan. And since Malone hated Regan, it was the perfect set-up.

Malone threw a picture of the two girls on the desk. A flattering pose—under other circumstances—it showed Regan in her best light. On top and in control. Somehow the girl's mother didn't see it that way.

"I want my attorney," Regan said, grinding her teeth so hard they hurt.

"Sure, sure," Malone chuckled. "You know your rights," his eyes twinkling with malevolent glee.

Regan was suspended. It was a felony to tamper with the computer, but that was nothing compared to the scams that went down at the 77th. The murders, set-ups, extortion, not to mention the kickbacks that greased the palms of haggard cops sitting around with nothing better to do than walk the streets with a bad attitude. Malone ended up taking all the credit for the Sayonara scam.

Luckily, Regan had withheld the information about Fletcher. That was her calling card to West Hollywood. Direct dial.

This time the same hand reached out and rubbed Regan's thigh more insistently. Something called lust stirred in her.

"Will I see you again?" the voice whispered in the starkly furnished room, the fingers drumming a seductive riff on Regan's thigh.

"Sure," Regan said, ripping off the bed covers as she leaned down to kiss Ms. Daiquiri a long good-bye.

JUST THE FACTS

There was morning gray in the sky when the taxi dropped Mercedes at her house. Weary, yet unsettled and shaken from the night's events, she opened her front door with the spare key she kept in her cosmetic case.

She felt as if someone had socked her in the jaw. Everywhere, everything was out of order. Her neat, beautifully decorated little haven was in complete shambles. A veritable war zone of books, sofa cushions, papers, opened drawers and scattered linens. Mercedes had been burglarized.

She raced upstairs to check on the dance-card. It was still tucked in the jar of cold cream. Mercedes let out a sigh of relief. Her ruse was fool-proof. Better than taking the chance and bringing it to her safety deposit box at the bank. Suddenly she was so wide awake, it felt as if she never needed to sleep again. Bluejays chirped outside and in neighboring homes, husbands and wives, bachelors, lonely-hearts and God knows who else prepared coffee and bacon and eggs and spread the *Los Angeles Times* on their kitchen tables.

Mercedes had been hoodwinked. She went to call the police, but stopped short of dialing. "Please, whatever you do, don't call the cops," Mona Lisa's terrified voice echoed in her ears. Mercedes slammed down the phone and looked around her room.

The bedroom fared no better than the rest of the house. She made sure none of her valuables were missing from her jewelry box. Her grandmother's antique brooch, two Christian Dior pins and her mother's diamond and onyx ring were still there. Everything was accounted for. Everything that is except a picture.

It was a photograph Snapshot had coerced her into taking. It was gone. Stolen. Mercedes slapped her palm against the dresser. Anger seethed and swelled. She had never been taken advantage like this.

"I want you to meet your doppelgänger," Snapshot had said during the photo shoot, "to draw out the dark side, the one you're afraid to reveal. Everyone has two sides." Mercedes attempted to find hers wearing a sheer black lace body stocking. But that was just ornamentation. There was something incomprehensible, more frightening about the way she was feeling now. Samantha had triggered a small avalanche. And like an ancient diviner searching the rich, black earth with her rod for the wellspring of life, she had dug beneath the bedrock, tapping into this darkness, causing this spontaneous combustion of emotion.

Mercedes got a hold of herself. She dialed the Chateau Marmont and asked for Samantha Mann.

"Sorry, no Ms. Mann."

Mercedes slammed down the phone. Her heart was racing. She couldn't go to the police even if Mona Lisa told her not to. This whole story was too bizarre. Too embarrassing to report. She'd be laughed right out of the station.

*   *   *

Regan arrived after Mercedes had had a second cup of espresso. "Your car's still at Derringer." Regan took one look at Mercedes' home and whistled. "Somehow I figured you for the neat and tidy type."

"The maid's in Cancun."

Regan's eyes twinkled as she took off her Ray-Bans, helped herself to a cup of coffee and listened to Mercedes' story.

"What happened to Redlite?" Mercedes hoped he'd been hauled away by the police.

Regan shook her head. "Nothing. He ran off licking his wounds. He'll be back. And so will the black widow."

Mercedes stiffened.

"If she broke in once, she'll break in again. And maybe this time you won't be so lucky. You might be home. Get the locks changed."

Mercedes had already called the locksmith.

"Let's get down to the facts. Redlite's nuts. He belongs to Xuan, a woman who runs a dance hall downtown. And she's after this dance-card—the one you seem to insist you've never seen—in person—because she fronted Mona Lisa fifty G's to steal it from Fletcher. The two women have an old bone of contention between them. Regan examined Mercedes' face. "But the antique belongs to Fletcher. Apparently Mona Lisa stole it from Mallory."

Mercedes lit one of Regan's cigarettes. "Who's Mallory?"

"Fletcher's lover."

Mercedes looked exasperated. "What did Mona Lisa have to do with these women?"

Regan stretched out her long legs, pulled a cigarette from behind her ear and placed it on the table. "First off, Samantha's just got in from Rio and already she's working for Fletcher. She's a regular scam artist."

"Thanks for telling me after the fact."

Regan put up her hands in protest. "I tried to pry you away, but her fingers were glued to you." She finished her coffee. "Second, Mona Lisa may have been your friend, but she kept pretty strange bedfellows. She fucked up with Fletcher and she double crossed Xuan by keeping the antique she was supposed to return to her in the first place." Regan's eyes were clear and calm.

Mercedes got up and walked to the window. Her hands were shaking. There were many times in the past when Mona Lisa would dodge her questions. Sometimes she'd disappear for days on end. Or call from Santa Barbara. It was always this producer or that casting agent. Or a location scout who was introducing her around. Or she was back again with Carmen and laying low.

Mona Lisa had been leading a double life she could never even begin to suspect. This was the stuff of Hollywood movies. But then again, Mercedes thought, turning to look at Regan, if anyone was a product of her environment, it was Mona Lisa.

"Are you after the dance-card too?" Mercedes asked.

Regan smiled. "Right now I've got one interest and that's making sure you stay out of danger." Regan got up and poured herself another cup of coffee. "Can you cook, or are all these gadgets just for show?" She moved closer.

"I can handle a spatula pretty well." Mercedes backed off.

Regan's shoulders were broad, strong. Aggressive. She grew serious. "Can we discuss this over dinner?"

Mercedes hesitated. "I'd like to hear more about Mona Lisa, if that's what you mean."

Regan put a hand on Mercedes' shoulder. "Sure, but let's not have Fletcher get wind of this. I still work for her.

"I'm going to find Mona Lisa . . . ."

"Find her and convince her to return the antique to Fletcher.

Otherwise your friend . . . ." Her voice trailed off.

Mercedes got the point and nodded her head.

Regan slipped out a card from her pant pocket and handed it to Mercedes. "He's the best. His name's Pinkerton and he runs a Detective Agency on Broadway. He'll help push you in the right direction. Tell him I sent you." Regan kissed Mercedes' cheek, put on her Ray-Bans and left her to clean up the mess.

* * *

Less than a half hour later, Mercedes had showered, put on jeans, a t-shirt, boots and was making her way through the lobby of the Chateau Marmont where Samantha "claimed" she was staying. She remembered the floor and room number like the date of her birth.

Mercedes pounded on the door. She heard a woman singing in Spanish. She pounded again.

"Ah, *dios, un momento*," a voice floated into the hallway.

The door opened. Mercedes held her breath. Standing before her was a stunning brunette with topaz eyes and a button nose, clad in a floral white silk dressing gown with less than nothing underneath. The garment was half opened.

"*Si*," the woman said, hardly surprised to see a stranger before her, not moving a muscle to conceal her semi-nakedness.

The sight threw Mercedes off-track. "Samantha. I'm looking for Samantha Mann." Nothing registered on the woman's face.

"Apparently she's checked out. I'm here now. My name's Rita. Perhaps you have the wrong room." There wasn't a trace of Spanish in the woman's diction. She eyed Mercedes with approval.

Mercedes' forehead grew moist. "No. This is the room."

"You can check under the bed if you like. I usually do keep track of my guests." She smiled.

"I bet you do," Mercedes said.

The woman threw back her shoulders and laughed. Her breasts were smaller than a 36C, but not much. They were the kind of accessories every girl dreams of growing up with. Firm, golden brown with hard nipples, perfectly shaped.

"Well, I hope you find her." Her eyes twinkled with pleasure as she slowly closed the door.

"You're damn right I will." Mercedes' palms were hot and sweaty. It was time for another shower.

DICK FOR HIRE

Mercedes parked her Chevy two blocks from the Bradbury Building and pushed her way past the Million Dollar Theater on the corner of Hill where the movie *The Mambo Kings* drew a steady crowd. The district was primarily Latino. Cumbia blared from record shops and the chatter on the streets was diced with rapid-fire salutations; the exhaust from lumbering buses and broken tailpipes added to the haze of the day.

Mercedes darted into the Bradbury Building. A century old, the sky-lit Victorian central atrium was a striking rococo of wrought-iron, open-cage elevators and ornate gates that traveled to a high glass ceiling. It's dark wood and pink marble staircases lent atmosphere to the filming of the original *D.O.A.* and Ridley Scott's futuristic *Blade Runner.*

She found her man on the third floor. Pinkerton's Detective Agency was stenciled on the opaque glass door. She glanced at the card Regan had given her. What harm could come from asking a few questions?

She entered and walked up to the receptionist who never took her eyes off the keyboard in front of her. "I'd like to see Detective Pinkerton."

"You and everybody else in this town. What's the problem?"

The woman wore twin plastic sheaves that protected her white silk blouse. Her hair was the color of wheat, braided from her temples and pulled back; the eyebrows were heavily lined and the lipstick tangerine. She looked like she stepped out of a 1940s movie sans the horn-rimmed glasses.

"I need to find someone."

"How long's he been missin', sugar?" she said, finally looking up at Mercedes and shaking her head.

"He's a she," Mercedes replied, impatient. "Look, is Pinkerton in or isn't he?"

"Put a lid on the steam, sister. I'm just doing my job." She sat back in a swivel chair and slipped a yellow pencil behind her left ear. Her earrings were two small lion heads. She eyed Mercedes' black wool pantsuit, forest green turtleneck and the red mop of hair, and gave a nod of approval. After taking down the necessary information, she buzzed her boss. "A Ms. Martini to see you."

Mr. Pinkerton's office was like any Mercedes had seen and soon forgotten. An oversized wooden coat rack was adorned with an umbrella, a raincoat and a black beret. A water-stained certificate hung on the wall behind the oak desk. An old glass and wood curio, empty except for a bottle of Chivas and two tumblers, hugged the wall.

Mercedes sat across from Mr. Pinkerton. His tanned complexion, dark hair and thick eyebrows made him handsome in a rugged, sneaky sort of way. He was either very good at what he did, or not to be trusted at all. His "trouble-is-my-business" cockiness matched well with the cleft carved in the middle of his chin. It was deep enough to serve as a small ashtray.

He knew how to wear a suit. His was a Kenzo, pinstriped, black with a white shirt and blue speckled tie.

"What can I do for you, Ms. Martini?" He lit a cigarette and slipped a hand into his imported pant pocket. A finger picked at a curl of tobacco stuck on his lower lip.

"Regan Hawk recommended you, Mr. Pinkerton."

"Skip the formality. Call me Dick." He smiled and bared his nice, white teeth.

Mercedes opened her purse and pulled out a picture of her and Mona Lisa. She slipped the photo across his empty desk and watched as he examined the two women.

It was a picture taken the previous summer at Two Bunch Palms when they sported healthy tans. Mona Lisa was on a liquid diet. "Nothing like a good colonic and carrot juice to irrigate the system. Think of all those toxins just lodged in every Motel 6 of your pores. Disgusting." Her alimentary regime didn't stop her from drinking plenty of wine and Margaritas. The purification stopped short of nirvana. Mercedes' cotton shorts and tank top were hardly appropriate for this watering hole of the rich and infamous. It was a ruse on Mona Lisa's part to treat her to a weekend away, pretending they were just going to the Marina to "catch some rays." Mercedes was still in "mourning" over her last affair, one that ended in tears. Her lover Syn left her to return to a former lover in New York. How plebeian. She swore off relationships for at least a year. So far, she had been pretty successful. A few side trips, but no obligations. Mona Lisa knew that two nights in the desert's hippest, "healthiest" arid retreat with its mineral baths, Shiatsu massage and clay facials would help assuage some of the heartbreak. And Mercedes knew Mona Lisa couldn't afford to blow five hundred for the weekend. "Don't worry. I'm still getting residuals from a Quaker Oats commercial I did two years ago. Besides, I'm likely to run into producers and directors. All of La-La town hangs here on weekends."

Mercedes searched Pinkerton's face for a reaction to the photograph, but there was none. "Her name's Mona Lisa Selavy."

Pinkerton looked up. A slight cloud, matching his five o'clock shadow, eclipsed his face, but disappeared just as quickly. He touched Mona Lisa's face with his finger, then pulled his hand back as if caught on fire.

Mercedes gave him a preliminary run-through and when she was finished, Pinkerton leaned back in his chair.

"This year the National Crime Center listed 60,000 Americans who'd disappeared without logical explanation. And those are only the ones reported missing. I've got wives, girlfriends, husbands, parents, cops, crooks, you name it, coming in here like I'm Houdini, hoping that somehow, magically, I'm gonna make their loved ones appear out of thin air. And seven times out of ten, they're in trouble."

"And the others?"

"Dreamers with small visions and big appetites for change. They leave behind successful lives to lose themselves on the high seas. Or they join a circus and end up a year later with new spouses in some small town like Peoria sporting a different name and identity. They're dumpers running away from the squeeze of their miserable lives. Maybe your friend Mona Lisa joined them."

"Maybe. And maybe not. I won't stop looking for her until I find her. I can't afford to waste any more time."

"Very noble, Ms. Martini. That's how they all sound when they come through here, but you'd be surprised how quickly they give up when their hope and money run out."

"I've got plenty of both, Mr. Pinkerton," Mercedes fibbed. "Can you help me?"

Pinkerton got up and moved closer to Mercedes. He sat on his desk, pulled up his pant leg so that it creased just right.

"In a town like this, you find trouble on every street corner. What's her angle?"

Mercedes hesitated. "It seems she's stolen an antique."

His ears pointed and his eyes darted around the room like they were lost. "Antique? What kind of antique?"

"A dance-card. They were very popular, especially in Europe." She slipped him the picture Snapshot took of the antique.

Pinkerton reached inside his desk and pulled out a loupe. He pressed it to his eye and inspected the photo. "Moonstones, diamonds and a few rubies. It looks expensive." He ran a hand through his dark hair. "So who's got the goods?"

Mercedes shrugged her shoulders. She watched Pinkerton ground out his cigarette. The sun started to slant through the window. His face seemed less kind in the natural light.

"So your Mona Lisa stole it, the owner got sore, as owners are wont to do when double-crossed, the heat's on and she's taken a powder."

Mercedes shifted uncomfortably in the chair.

"This could take time."

Pinkerton's mind appeared to whir like the soft, smooth drone of machinery, only his intellectual gadgetry wasn't quite that fine tuned.

"I don't want to seem mercenary, but taking advantage of my experience, will cost you $75 a day, plus expenses."

Mercedes swallowed. "If you're as good as Regan says you are, then I guess I'm getting a bargain."

Pinkerton smiled. "My normal rates are $200, but I owe her one," he said humbly. He looked down at his manicured fingernails.

Mercedes managed a weak smile. "It's comforting to know some detectives have charity at heart. Rather softens a dangerous and unscrupulous profession."

Pinkerton grimaced. "No more unscrupulous than a cop, sweetheart. It's a business loaded with risk, danger ... and adventure." Pinkerton moved closer to Mercedes. She wasn't terribly comfortable with the proximity nor his after-shave. A little too *rat d'eau*.

"I like my adventure as well as the next, but thievery, fraud, extortion and foul play are not my racket. Or Mona Lisa's."

"No? Then what's her sport?"

Mercedes didn't reply.

"Drugs, extortion . . . prostitution?"

Her eyes widened. She wanted to say no, but the word just didn't come out.

"Professionally . . . what'd she do to earn her dough?"

"She's an actress . . . a very good actress," Mercedes said defensively. The smile in his eyes irritated her. He raised his brow like someone had lit a match under his nose. He laughed out loud.

"She and every sister in this town. Now tell me what did she do for dough?"

Mercedes crossed her arms. "She was a dancer." Her confidence was starting to fail. Mona Lisa had after all auditioned to perform with Feld's internationally acclaimed dance troupe.

"Next I suppose you're gonna tell me she dances for The Joffrey? Even that wouldn't keep her in moonstones, now would it?" Pinkerton sneered and threw the picture across the desk at Mercedes. "Let's start over, but this time, let's cut the pledge of allegiance and try a little good old-fashioned truth. What's Mona Lisa to you?" he pressed.

"She's my friend."

"Sure. You stick your neck out in the middle of some heavy shit just in the name of friendship? Come on, honey. What's in this for you?"

Mercedes smiled. It was obvious Pinkerton didn't have a friend in the world. He didn't have a clue. What did men understand about bonding? They were too busy soaking their egos in a pool of fellow sharks. "I don't think we're on the same wavelength."

"The last time someone took me for a ride, Martini, they came along. I need all the facts if I'm gonna help you. I'm a busy man."

The silence of the room belied his statement. He picked up the phone and told his secretary to hold all his calls.

This guy should be in show biz himself, Mercedes thought. "I think I'm all you've got for the moment, Pinkerton."

"Don't flatter yourself, Wisenheimer," he snapped, loosening his Dior tie. "So where's this dance-card?"

"I may be new at this, but I'm no fool." Mercedes lit a cigarette.

Tomorrow she'd quit.

"So you got this phone call, she didn't show and now you're worried. Nice. Very nice. Well, you want to know what the nicest thing about all this is?"

Mercedes took a deep drag on her Marlboro.

Pinkerton rolled up his sleeves inch by inch. "The nicest piece is your so-called *friend*'s pulled the wool over your eyes. I hate to be the bearer of bad news, but Mona Lisa was nothing but a smart operator. She's come to me more than once to bail her out of jams. Jams you don't want to know about."

Mercedes stared at him, incredulous. Was he bluffing? Trying to rile her even more than she already was? "Jams, maybe. A parking ticket, some crazy guy following her around town, a picked lock. Cut her some slack."

"Slack? Mona Lisa's a whore who was smart enough never to get arrested."

Pinkerton's words cut deep. Mercedes couldn't process all this information. She had to get out of there. Away from his accusations. She stood up and grabbed her bag. Her face was red. She needed air. Lots of it.

"Sit down. You don't look so good." Pinkerton pulled a bottle of Chivas off the shelf and poured her a drink. "Have some lunch. It's on me," he said softly.

Mercedes downed the alcohol. It burned her throat, made her eyes water.

"This town's smaller than you think. Every morning I wake up with someone else's garbage at my doorstep. You just got a special delivery. Don't look so amazed."

Mercedes tried to speak. But the words wouldn't come out. She was stunned by Pinkerton's allegations. Could there even be an ounce of truth in what he was saying? She felt hurt, betrayed and more determined than ever to get to the bottom of this. She cleared her throat. "Give me facts. Dates. Names."

"Sure, sure. The fact is you need me now more than you care to admit. Time to get off of that high horse of yours and trot down here with the rest of us."

"You're wrong."

Pinkerton shook his head. "You're not too smart, are you Martini?"

"I'm smart enough to know you're just a shamus." Mercedes moved closer to the door. "Men like you make your own trouble. That's your business. I'll attend to my own."

"You don't have a prayer of a chance of finding that little lady without me." His voice rose, cutting through the room like a buzz saw. "This town's ugly and your Mona Lisa ate with some pretty dangerous thugs. You pick up chopsticks with the wrong crowd once too often and suddenly you find you ain't got such an appetite for life. Sounds to me like someone's been shanghaied." He put a thin cigar in his mouth and chewed on his words.

Mercedes had taken all she could for one day. "You're beginning to feel like a wad of gum on the bottom of my shoe."

Pinkerton sprang toward her, putting his face in hers. "Enough with the insults."

Mercedes smiled. "You're not so tough, are you? You're just a two-bit dick in a poor excuse for an office."

Pinkerton's eyes leered. "You like bringing the best to their knees, don't you Martini?"

"Only those who deserve to be there, Pinkerton." Mercedes turned on her heel and marched out, slamming the door behind her.

* * *

"So Pinkerton's a little rough around the edges," Regan remarked to Mercedes. They were at Gold's Gym in Hollywood. A few years ago Gold's had taken over a section of the block-long Art Deco building, now part of the Hollywood Television Center, which up until 1975 had housed Technicolor, Inc., the company responsible for developing a three-negative process to colorize film.

The gym was packed as usual. Musclemen and a few women who had elevated the grunt and groan of bodybuilding to a fine art. Mercedes hadn't worked out in weeks. But for Regan it was a regular hangout.

Regan lifted the hundred-pound barbell in a steady curl from the middle of her muscular thighs to her chest. She did ten repetitions. Red boxer shorts with bold, black stripes cut high up Regan's thigh and a white ribbed muscle t-shirt fit snug against a pair of firm breasts, her dark nipples visible.

Mercedes did a half hour on the treadmill at a clipped run. It helped sweat out some of her frustration. She wore black lycra biker shorts under a black danskin. Her hair was a bonnet of wild red curls. "I didn't hire him. I didn't like his accusations."

"Whether or not you liked him, he'd get the job done. You asked for help; I sent you to the best. I don't need to remind you that your friend's in danger." Regan dropped the barbell on the floor and wiped her forehead with a blue towel.

Mercedes winced. "Listen, Honey West I'm not, but I could do a better job than that self-centered dick."

"Hey," Regan moved closer. "Watch the language." Her wet, black hair was slicked off her face. Sweat dripped down her neck. "Anyway I take it you're sore 'cause he told you things you didn't want to hear. I wanted you to get it from the horse's mouth, just in case you thought I might have my own agenda. You wanted facts, Martini, you got 'em."

Mercedes knew she was right. "This town breeds gossip. People love to dig up dirt, dish, gather round the lesbian campfire and tell tall dark tales of love and lust. A little emotional extortion. But all that talk doesn't necessarily add up to the truth. I'm not letting some idiot who doesn't even know Mona Lisa talk that way about her."

Regan took a long sip from her Evian bottle. "Whether you let him or not, sweetheart, he's just the beginning. When's the last time Mona Lisa told you how she got her money?"

Mercedes searched her memory. "You know, commercials, my God, she worked. Odd jobs to make ends meet. Half of my friends work two jobs, have day jobs that have nothing to do with what they really want to do in life because they can't get paid for it. Besides, I don't interrogate my friends."

She realized she was defensive about Mona Lisa, still clutching to what she wanted to believe. It would take some time to process this new information. So far it was just talk.

Regan shrugged her shoulders. Two herculean heavyweights barreled past. The whir of pulleys, the clang of two-hundred pound weights hitting the floor, the steady grind of the Lifecycles joined forces with the heavy rock score—a real symphony of aggression.

Regan pulled Mercedes over to the bench press, away from a frieze of brawn. "I'll help you."

Mercedes shook her head. "I can handle this."

Regan moved closer. "I'll dig around, see what I can come up with." She wiped the back of her neck with the towel. "Fletcher knows Mona Lisa was set up by Xuan to steal the dance-card. I think Mona Lisa double-crossed them both, made off with the goods, the money and, as we speak, she's probably sipping a piña colada in some briny little Mexican resort while five guitarists strum "*La Noche de Ronda*" and she gets to have the last laugh."

"You should write fiction, Regan. You've got one hell of an imagination." Mercedes picked up her towel and darted into the women's locker room.

She opened her locker and pulled out her dufflebag. For a second she thought it was sweat pouring down her face, but when she looked in the mirror, Mercedes realized it was tears.

JANUS II

Max Pitts slammed down the phone in his Melrose gallery. Butch, his Doberman pinscher, licked his lips, then yawned. The animal had a calming effect on Max, his presence helped him think and after the call from his friend Pinkerton, he needed to put things in perspective.

"Don't look at me that way," Max said to his dog as he rubbed him behind the ears. "I'll show Fletcher."

Butch barked in agreement. His master wouldn't let him down.

"And as for her sweet little Mallory, such a ridiculous distraction at her age."

Max looked at himself in the mirror. Both he and Fletcher were equally vain—one thing they always had in common and always would. He removed his steel-rimmed glasses and rubbed his eyes. His long hair, usually pulled back in a ponytail, touched his broad, tense shoulders.

Someone once told him he looked like the Greek hero Ulysses. He appreciated the larger-than-life mythic comparison, having had an affinity for Hellenic culture. After all, his grandmother on his father's side was Greek.

Bruxism. He was grinding his teeth again. A week after he stopped taking his Xanax for "anxiety disorders." The drug was mild, but it still took the edge off.

The exercises his Western doctor suggested, a series of stretching, humming, extending his tongue as far as it would go, made him feel ridiculous. It was the braces, put on to correct a slight overbite, that made him really miserable. Luckily, they'd be off in a few more months.

Insomnia. He was having problems sleeping. In his nightmares he'd come close to retrieving the dance-card. Seemed all his ailments disappeared once the treasure was in his safekeeping. And then some shadowy figure would pounce from the wings of his subconscious and threaten him with a jagged knife. He'd wake in the middle of the night, sweat pouring from his forehead, his own teeth gnashing against each other.

He would consult an ayurveda specialist in Malibu next month for his maladies. He'd heard the warm oil enemas and aromatherapy treatments were the elixirs *du jour*.

Max eased himself into a soft leather chair, Butch's chin obediently propped on his knee. Max loved his dog. Butch was the most uncomplicated person in his life. Their relationship seemed miraculously ordained from the start. Max believed Butch could read his mind. The dog knew how upset he was when Fletcher gave Mallory the dance-card. Max nearly struck his ex-wife across the face. But he held back. Kept it in and now he was paying the price.

Max rubbed his dog's head. Whenever Butch lay like this it was to soothe his harrowed master. These days, riding the crest of the latest trends and keeping as quiet about his counterfeit sales was draining. And to top this, his prized possession he'd given to Fletcher was floating somewhere out in the city; he wouldn't put it past Mona Lisa to have hocked it for a few thousand dollars.

His stomach churned, burbled: acid indigestion. Fortunately, art theft was a low priority for the police department and the FBI, too many nasty serial killers on the loose to worry about retrieving stolen goods from the rich and famous.

Max rubbed his temples. Still there were plenty of back-stabbers who'd love to see him fall on his face. It was a very competitive business. Just last week Manntucket Museum offered a million dollar reward for any information regarding the whereabouts of twelve paintings stolen from their premises two years ago. Clever job. And the museum had no insurance!

Art heists were usually bloodless with no fatal casualties and with the right international connections, it was easy to hide the booty in a diplomat's wine cellar somewhere in Prague or the French countryside.

His temples throbbed. He was feeling cagey. On edge. A cross between wanting to have sex and wanting to punch someone in the face. Lately the only intimacy he craved was infiltrating as many elite echelons of the community as possible. He prided himself in belonging to disparate social circles.

"We're pretty popular, aren't we?"

Butch blinked his eyes.

Max's engagements with Fletcher and her ilk satisfied a growing sadomasochistic yearning to place his masculinity in a position of vulnerability with his ex-wife and her female lovers.

He hardly even had time for "physical engagements," as he liked to call them. In fact, the last time he got laid he insisted the girl not tell him her name. He made one up in his head. It was fast, hot and extremely impersonal.

Max checked the clock. He didn't want to be late for dinner. A new client. Word on the street was this dealer had a flawless reproduction of an early American *trompe l'oeil*. "After The Hunt."

He was a member in good standing of the California Society of the Avant-Garde. His hip gallery, Janus II, was a hotbed of activity. With a collection that boasted contempo L.A. artisans, ethnic pieces from Africa and Mexico, Italian ceramics, bauhaus furniture and neo-dada objects d'art, it was the site specific of social fund-raisers. His two-faced preoccupations saved him from leaning too far to the right or too far to the left.

Balance was important to Max. He never liked to wallow in one extreme or the other. That's why he had executed this ruse with the antique and agreed to loan Xuan the money so Mona Lisa would grab the goods. He wanted to make Fletcher suffer. To even the score.

He was stymied by Fletcher's obsession with Mallory. There was something off about the way the young girl stared vacantly every time Max entered the room. He could swear Mallory had no cognitive recollection of his presence. It was unnerving. And it infuriated him that Fletcher's fetish caused her to cave in to whatever the girl wanted, after she'd given him such a hard time during their short-lived marriage.

Max had his pride. And he wasn't going to be shortchanged in business, nor in his long-standing relationship with Fletcher. Fifteen years were a big investment and they jointly owned several businesses.

But his damn swindle backfired. The fifty thousand he had lent Xuan to front to Mona Lisa, her star taxi-dancer, more than generous compensation for pilfering the dance-card, was now in Mona Lisa's greedy hands. Sweet little cheat.

For that kind of money, he could have nailed Smith's *Men Seldom*

Make Passes At Girls Who Wear Glasses, a large collage he'd been hankering after for years, that was in the artist's private collection. And for slightly less than fifty grand he'd just bought Yerman's *Cave Canem* (Butch's favorite).

He wasn't going to throw good money away for nothing. But more than the money, although that sum in today's economy certainly wasn't negligible, he wanted the dance-card back and he wanted to be sure *he* retrieved it. It would humble Fletcher, embarrass her, and that's what he intended to do.

Little by little Mallory's charm, undetectable to him as it were, would no longer be such an intoxicating decoy. Max would be restored to his rightful place of favor in Fletcher's eyes and they'd go on looting and loving in a town filled with nubile treasures.

The fact that Max had given her that antique ten years ago, the fact that it was worth in the neighborhood of a million dollars on the market, had nothing to do with Fletcher's motivation for retrieving it.

This lubricious phase of her adulthood caused a temporary snap in her personality. Did she really believe returning the dance-card to Mallory would somehow restore the girl's love for her?

Max laughed out loud. Butch joined him in a bark that turned into a long yawn.

This neurotic delusion must be the result of some unresolved need rising to the surface of forty-plus. She was out of her mind in love. If Max had anything to do with circumstances, Mallory soon would fare no better than Fletcher's prized palomino gelding. A minor accident had rendered the poor creature out of commission.

Max stood up and stretched. Butch followed suit. The bell rang over the door to the gallery. A man walked in, smiled at Max and started to browse. Surely just a looky-loo. Max could smell a buyer. Something about the scent of the skin, an inevitable excitation in the eyes, the casual saunter of steps, the coy maneuver of the fingers.

A browser to be sure.

Max pulled out a phone directory and looked up the address of Mercedes Martini. At least she was in the neighborhood. If Martini had the dance-card in her possession for safekeeping, then he'd just have to use his charm and persuasion on her. He fancied a little cloak and dagger. He'd enjoy shaking the tumbler. He liked his martini dry with a twist of lemon and one pearl onion.

Max clucked his tongue. Butch stood erect. A Doberman warrior. Max felt a swell of pride. He moved to an African mask from the Uribe tribe hanging at the farthest end of the gallery. He removed the mask and there hidden in the wall was a small safe. He jiggled the tumbler, opened the secret enclosure and pulled out a .22. It was a collector's item. It also worked. He closed the safe, slipped the gun in a velour pouch and replaced the mask.

His next move would be to call Xuan and put the squeeze on her. He would refuse to pay her the ten thousand he had promised if she pulled this off. After all, it had turned into a fiasco and he was out fifty G's. It was Xuan's headache. Her point in this charade was resecuring Mona Lisa as an asset to her work force and leaving Fletcher high and dry without her best girl and her antique.

Then on to Martini. It was almost too easy. She'd be a piece of cake from what Pinkerton described, and Max suddenly had a sweet tooth.

Women. Max laughed out loud again. Butch barked in unison. No wonder Ulysses ran away from home.

"The male lion may be the king of the jungle," Max whispered into Butch's ear, running a hand through his animal's shiny coat, "but it's the female who hunts and kills."

MARTINI UNDERCOVER

Mercedes checked her rear view mirror again to see if the ominous black sedan was still following her. It was. Instead of heading up Highland on her way to Mona Lisa's apartment, she swung a left on Cahuenga, zigzagged north of Hollywood Boulevard and came out at Highland off Franklin. The car was nowhere in sight. The dodge was successful.

Midge Williams and her Jazz Jesters bellowed the blues on the radio, *Oh love is like whisky; love, love, love, makes you walk on air. Somebody touch you on the shoulders and you turn around and there ain't nobody there.* Ain't that the truth.

She arrived at High Tower Apartments a little after four. The sky was dark, cloudy, a hint of rain in the air. She felt keyed up and tense. She cut the ignition, got out of the car, and walked up the sidewalk. The black sedan pulled up and parked across the street in front of a Craftsman-style home four doors down—a bad paint job and a row of sunflowers lining the porch. A newspaper shielded the driver's face. Whoever it was, coincidence or not, didn't care to be seen.

The lobby was quiet, the pervasive odor of fried fish lingered in the air, a leftover scent not particularly offensive or pleasant. It just reminded Mercedes that she was famished.

She knocked on the manager's door. Feet shuffled inside. A "who is it?" whined nasally on the other side. An eye glued itself to the peep hole as Mercedes explained her mission. A chain scratched the door, a few locks clicked and the door opened to reveal a face and body that were attached by coincidence. One had nothing to do with the other. The face was framed by hair all too well-acquainted with peroxide. The make-up was Kabuki. The body, however, belonged on a fifty-year-old in good standing, the unfortunate victim of a mug yearning to be buried in sand. Quicksand.

"How do I know you're a friend of Mona Lisa's?" she queried.

Mercedes insisted it was a matter of life and death. The manager sneered slightly. "For starters, she owes two months rent . . . she's always late. One thousand bucks."

Pulling out her checkbook, Mercedes offered to pay the tab. There went at least six outstanding accounts she could have made payment on.

"Maybe I should call the law, seeing as you think it's a matter of extreme consequences," she said slyly, waving the check in front of Mercedes as if waiting for the ink to dry.

"The key," Mercedes said through her teeth, then smiled.

The manager strutted over to a cabinet, found the key and handed it to Mercedes. "Bring it back. Nothing's to be taken from the premises. I'm not responsible."

Mercedes nodded her head and was about to leave when the manager called her back.

"Who does your make-up?"

Mercedes arched her eyebrow. "I do."

"Try a little more cheek accentuation. Takes away from the nose," she said, closing the door in Mercedes' startled face.

Someone yelled in the corridor. Mercedes turned around but no one was there. She walked to the elevator and heard the heavy thud of footsteps coming from round the north side of the elevator, but they stopped as soon as the elevator hit the lobby. The grilled gates opened and Mercedes stepped inside.

As the door creaked shut, a hand thrust inside, preventing the gate from closing. A man clambered in. He was wearing dark sunglasses, a raincoat and looked and smelled as if he hadn't shaved or bathed in days.

The elevator heaved slowly from floor to floor. The man hadn't pressed a button. Mercedes heart beat fast. His eyes were clamped on her until they reached the twelfth floor. The rusted gate clanked open and Mercedes stepped out. The man was behind her.

Mona Lisa's apartment was at the end of the corridor. Two lights were out and the hallway was dark and dreary, muted patterns of chiaroscuro. Just as Mercedes approached the door, the man tapped her on the shoulder. She whipped around. He held a piece of paper in his hand.

"Joe Franklin, apartment 1298. Am I heading in the wrong

direction?" he asked. He wiped his mouth with the back of his hand.

Mona Lisa's door flew open and a young girl, carrying a leather suitcase, knocked Mercedes over as she rushed past. Mercedes hit the floor. She looked up at the figure, dressed completely in black, a bolero hat covering her head, a thin braid hanging down her face. She ran down the corridor.

"Hey!" Mercedes shouted after her, trying to get to her feet as the man stared in a daze, proffering no assistance. She got to her feet and ran after the girl, but her ankle gave way and pain seared her leg like a hot iron. The girl flew through the emergency exit and disappeared. Mercedes had never seen her before.

The strange man peered into Mona Lisa's apartment. She pushed past him and slammed the door in his face. Her heart was pounding. What was that girl doing here?

Hopping to the window overlooking the front of the apartment, she watched the girl get in the black sedan across the street. The car screeched off toward Highland. At that angle, again, it was impossible to make out the driver.

Her ankle pulsated with pain. She tried to get her bearing. A quick look around Mona Lisa's apartment and suddenly the absence of her friend settled in.

Apartments are meant to be lived in, surely, but Mona Lisa's pad, a compact studio, tastelessly decorated, was part five-and-dime, part Maxwell's of Beverly Hills. It certainly didn't appear to be ransacked; it was obvious whoever was there came for a few particular items.

She bumped into a water-stained placard hanging on a flimsy chain from one of the bedposts. GIRLS! GIRLS! GIRLS! FIFTY BEAUTIFUL DANCE HOSTESSES. Her friend had awful taste in memorabilia.

The kitchen wasn't *House & Garden* material either. Empty, save for two coffee cups on the counter, muck settled over the liquid remains. An empty bottle of prune juice and a rotten carrot sat between a bottle of Stolichnaya and a box of Arm and Hammer baking soda in the fridge.

The phone rang, startling Mercedes. The machine came on. Then the message. A man's deep voice echoed in the room. *"Doll, Mr. Yamamoto wants you. That rub did the trick. Daddy-O'll be in town Saturday. Told him you were **dying** for more of the same. Sayonara's at* *eight."*

Mercedes sunk into a chair. Was Pinkerton telling the truth? Had Mona Lisa been picking up chopsticks with the wrong crowd? She rewound the tape and listened to the litany of messages.

"Kitten, kitten, purrty pussy. See you 'round ten, baby."

"Jimmy Lee here, what say you and I tango in Tokyo?"

In the middle of this barrage of callers, Mercedes heard her own voice on the machine, pleading for Mona Lisa to respond. It put the situation into perspective. She felt so naive. She was devastated.

"Hello?" This time a woman's voice. *"Mona Lisa this is Eileen calling for Dr. Flesch. Your appointment has been confirmed. Sunday. 1:00. Bring the rest of the payment. Call to confirm."*

"Ms. Mona? Divinity herself. DaVinci's finest creation? Suck this one, baby."

"Yes," a woman's voice, deep and sexy. *"Last week. At the Bel Age Hotel. My husband'd like to see you again . . . so would I. We'll be waiting. Same room. Nine o'clock. No need to bring your own toys this time."*

Mercedes was hyperventilating. Mona Lisa's past was closing in on her. Her lips were parched. She couldn't move. She listened to the tape again and again until she'd memorized every message. Her fingers grew numb and all she could do was try to hold on to the unsullied image she had of her friend. But it was getting harder. She staggered to the fridge, her ankle throbbing with pain, pulled out the bottle of Stoli and took a swig. She returned the bottle. Talk about a double life. No wonder Mercedes hadn't seen her friend for weeks with an itinerary like that.

Mona Lisa always avoided talking about sex. She never went into details. Men she dismissed with a wave of the hand. "Rote mechanics," she'd tell Mercedes.

Women, well, there was Carmen and a few others. "Let's not make a mountain out of a mole hill," she'd say whenever Mercedes tried to get a little more graphic in conversation. She had a knack for turning the conversation around to Mercedes' affairs. Now she knew why.

One mixed metaphor after the other hit her as she glanced around Mona Lisa's apartment. A dozen xeroxed 8x10 pics of DaVinci's smiling lady were glued together in a Warhol grid, the eyes and lips magic-markered blue and day-glo orange. The last in the line of repetition was a pic of Mona Lisa's audition glossy posted next to a cheesy pinup girl from a fifties girlie magazine.

Ballroom dance albums were lined up by the dozen on the floor. An album cover of Tina Turner's "Private Dancer" posted on the wall by darts. A big X drawn across Tina's figure.

She dug through dresser drawers. Mona Lisa's lingerie fetish ran the gamut from Dior to Frederick's. Crotchless panties, nippleless bras, sheer body hose, fish net stockings, garter belts, you name it, she had it. Not to mention a plethora of sex toys. Latex gloves, a leather hood, nipple clamps, three dildos—small, medium and large; pink, black and purple. Handcuffs, leather mask with silver studs around the eye holes, and lodged in between several porno magazines, a red leather diary. Like most journals worth reading, it was locked, the key nowhere to be found.

Mercedes searched for the key. She opened the closet door. An avalanche of high fashion came tumbling down on her. Garments, shoes, coats, a silver gown, kimonos, exercise gear and a pair of skis were crammed inside the louvered storage area. She searched pockets, rummaged through the lining of jackets; business cards, ticket stubs, gum wrappers, phone numbers and a card for Club Sayonara (down by the Convention Center) *"where the customer never says goodbye."*

She pulled a picture from the breast pocket of a red leather jacket with a black dragon embroidered on back. It was a shot of Mona Lisa and an Asian girl. The same girl who ran out of the apartment a few minutes ago. Scrawled on the back was *"My two blossoms. Mama san."*

Mercedes slipped the photo in her pocket, grabbed the diary and was about to leave when she heard the doorknob twist. Someone keyed the lock.

Mercedes moved into the closet, closed the door and wedged her body in between a stuffed row of clothes, side-stepping shoes littering the floor.

The front door opened. She arched her neck as she peeked through the tight slats in the door. All she could see at that angle were black leather pants and cowboy boots. She held her breath. Her heart was pumping like mad. A hot, electric pain shot up from her ankle making it even more difficult to stand in that awkward position.

The door slammed shut. Mercedes watched a pair of hands as they flung open dresser drawers, parachuting lingerie across the room. Finally she had a bird's eye view. The intruder was no stranger at all.

It was Carmen Machado, Mona Lisa's ex-lover, and she didn't look like she'd dropped in for tea. Her hair was disheveled, her dark brown eyes darted around the apartment in search of something. Then she charged in the direction of the closet. This was it. The final showdown. But she stopped midway and disappeared from Mercedes' range of vision.

"*Cabrona. Puta.*" A rip. Boots kicked the dresser. A vase thrown across the room. The shatter of glass.

Carmen picked up the phone, tears streaking her face. "Samantha . . . changed my mind. Meet me at Jezebel's in an hour." When she hung up, she stretched out her hand and placed her palm on Mona Lisa's photo. But it wasn't the talisman she'd hoped for. She took one more look around the room, then left.

Mercedes counted till ten, then burst out of the closet. There, laying on the floor, sliced in two pieces, was Mona Lisa's silk nightshirt.

Carmen was on her way to meet the enigmatic black widow herself, Samantha Mann. Mercedes opened the door and made sure she wasn't too far behind.

CHUCK A LUCK

"Who are you?" the voice asked Mona Lisa, cutting the silence of the room. It was a quick, clean incision. She couldn't get away from the voice; after all she was strapped to a table. All she could do was talk. And that, barely.

"I'd prefer to remain a mystery," she replied weakly, unsure of where she was or whom she was addressing. It wasn't a good idea to trust strangers, anyway, she reasoned.

"You're no mystery," the voice said acidly. "You lost at chuckaluck. We know you cheated at the game. We've got your number, sister."

But the person was bluffing. She was sure of it. "Yeah? I ain't no loser and you ain't got my name. People should change their names every few years," she whimpered in pain. Her lips were dry and her tongue felt like fur.

"So what's in a name. I got you tagged," the voice said, gaining confidence.

"Impossible. I never give my background," the girl replied, "and anyhow, if I did, I'd make it up differently each time you asked."

"So one of those, *one of those, one of those*," the voice hammered in her head like a migraine.

Then everything went black again, her past escaping like a swirl of smoke into her subconscious. For a moment there was nothing standing between Mona Lisa and death. It was as if she were in a giant plastic bag and someone yanked open the zipper to let in a sliver of light, until, bit by bit, she was able to make out an overhead lamp, a few pieces of furniture and an abstract picture on the wall. Mona Lisa didn't care whether or not she liked the surroundings, as long as she was alive, it was as good as anything. Red headlights, a chariot from hell, had arrived to deliver her to an inferno. The heat was unbearable.

Pain seared through her swollen limbs like electric currents. She couldn't move a muscle, barely able to keep her eyelids open. This was it. The moment before she would close her eyes forever on the world. She thought about her dream, thought about the art professor who'd named her on her first flight to the west coast nearly three years ago. There was nothing like taking stock of your life when there were no more pages to turn.

Mona Lisa's head continued to throb. For a second she was back in time, back in a place where everything was green and exciting and she wore her new name like a prom corsage. A time unfamiliar with Little Tokyo, Xuan and Fletcher, all that was rotten in her life. Whoever thought, standing there with Carmen under that first California night with a thousand stars shining promise, that she'd be lying here, a few feet from death.

Mona Lisa started to fade. She closed her eyes, tears welling beneath her purple lids. She was in too much pain to sob. Her last thought was of Mercedes. A pang of guilt and an ache in her heart so acute it was bound to kill her. Then a hand swept across her eyes and she heard that zipper ripping over her body till it covered her face, shutting off the only light she'd see for a long, long time.

JEZEBEL'S GIN MILL

The sun had already set and the sky was spotted with clouds. Traffic was heavy on the Santa Monica Freeway. Normal for a Monday night. Mercedes would have preferred to have had a second to shower, wash her hair, get the day's grime out of her system, wrap her swollen ankle in an Ace bandage, and have a good cry, but there wasn't time. Not if she intended to catch Samantha and Carmen red-handed.

Despite all she'd uncovered about Mona Lisa's secret life, she felt compelled to continue her search, elusive as it might be at this point. She hated giving up on anything. And while these unplanned maneuvers didn't suit her Virgo temperament—spontaneity made her uneasy and left her feeling overpowered—she liked being in control. And right now everything was totally out of control.

Were these renegades after Mona Lisa or the dance-card? Carmen had just cause to be pissed off at her ex-lover. Mona Lisa had dumped her, but who doesn't get dumped? The lesbian casualty list was in the thousands; you don't hang out in this town for long without someone or something interfering in your domestic bliss. Carmen was sharp enough to know that.

It was after dark by the time she reached Jezebel's, a hip, crowded cozy dive of a restaurant club off Main Street run by a charming black woman, Eva Wise.

Mercedes knew she'd have no trouble getting a table. "Give my pal here a drink," Eva ordered as she ushered Mercedes up to the bar.

"The place is packed," Mercedes said, happy to see Eva doing so well.

A grin of self-satisfaction ironed the woman's face, a face that refused to allow the lines of age to crease her firm skin. Looking ten years younger than her forty-plus, she teased, "What are you doing here at this hour, girlfriend, without a reservation?"

"I didn't really come to eat . . . ."

"You not eat!" Eva opened her mouth wide and laughed good-naturedly. There was a small space in between her white upper teeth. Her lips were outlined in red, the eyes dramatically made up.

Mercedes scanned the room for any sign of Carmen or Samantha. The smell of Cajun and Belizean cuisine made Mercedes' stomach growl. Eva looked down at her tummy and gave it a good pat.

"You come here and sit down at my special table and tell ol' Eva what ails you. You got that dog-eared look about you, make me want to weep." Eva pushed away a young man with a tattoo on his cheek, a red bandana on his head, and set Mercedes up at a small table in the corner.

The evening's special hung in the air, thick and heavy, an aromatic fish stew with sweet potatoes in a tomato and onion sauce, piled high over boil cakes—sweet, chewy dumplings. "My mouth's watering," Mercedes said, as Eva put down a cold beer in front of her.

"Special for Ms. Martini," Eva ordered to the waiter who nodded, then dodged another waiter carrying a steaming hot tray.

"I've missed you." Mercedes looked into Eva's large brown eyes, wishing she could hide there. "I feel like I've spent the last few days on a rollercoaster."

"Yeah, well, nothing wrong with that. Last I heard, the way you been burying yourself in work and fixing up that house of yours, your life could use a little shake 'n bake, if you know what I mean." Eva winked. "Come on, what's the bellyache?"

Mercedes admired this powerhouse of a woman. With a few thousand bucks, a lot of sweat and patience, she'd turned this little shack into one of the trendiest spots at the beach. After the fabulous food review in the *Los Angeles Times*, a pack of hungry hounds invaded the premises and no one went away disappointed. It put her on the culinary map of Los Angeles.

Eva had been bowled over, never expecting that kind of overnight success. "You think I single-handedly invented conch the way that food critic crooned over my fritters. Here give me my glasses, let me read the quote to you," she had said, proud as could be. "A calibrated interplay of finely ground conch meat, onions, flour and habanew chili. A poor man's meal fit for a queen."

But it wasn't just the food. Together with Gin "Ray" Robinson on bass, Mingo on sax and Beryle Booker on keys, Eva's music made folks forget who they were. Her back-up was a perfect counterpart to her voice—dark and rich like a garden in bloom. All power, provocation and balm, she lorded over her listeners, making them slaves to a sound part ethereal, part damp earth. Her lyrics reached in and massaged the soul and left you begging for more. It was a laying-on of hands all over the body.

Mercedes canvassed the joint one more time. The crowd was thinning. Eva was watching her closely. "Who you scouting for?"

"Carmen. She's supposed to meet Samantha, a dark-haired woman about my age. Very attractive."

"Suppose you tell me what's going on before I stick my nose into your business." Eva signaled the waiter to bring over another coffee.

In between bites of the scrumptious meal, Mercedes poured out some of the details to the story. Mona Lisa's strange disappearance and the meeting with Samantha. She neglected to mention that the dance-card was safely hidden in her home and that she'd appropriated the diary. That she'd keep to herself for now. "I feel as if I'm trying to surface from my own nightmare."

Eva nodded her head. "Behind every truth, a lie's just waiting to be discovered."

Mercedes nodded her head. "I keep returning to the beginning, before I knew any of this. Her biggest fear was being rejected. I guess she couldn't balance both identities and keep me as a friend." It sounded like a neat explanation, but deep down Mercedes felt betrayed by this double-life.

Eva scrutinized Mercedes' face. "What else you got on your mind?" she asked softly.

Mercedes sighed, reluctant to go any further. "Samantha."

Eva smiled. "Hum, I'm listening."

"I hardly know her," Mercedes said thoughtfully. No matter how hard she tried to annihilate Samantha's image, it came back, harder and stronger. She lit a cigarette. "She appeared out of nowhere and then disappeared."

"Don't need to know anyone to fall in love. It's all one big puzzle anyway, you know that," Eva said. "Listen to this song."

She moved to the piano on the small stage close to their table. Eva eased her attractive body onto the bench, then rubbed her smooth fingers along a pair of brown suede pants and did what she did best. Someone whistled from the bar as she played. A few people clapped.

When she finished, Eva returned to their table. "Lena first recorded that in '41. 'Out of Nowhere.' That's where love hides."

Mercedes caught a glimpse of Carmen coming out of the restroom. She had on a pair of round dark shades and the same boots she wore when she broke into Mona Lisa's apartment. Eva caught Mercedes' preoccupation.

"Now Carmen's just hot steam from a kettle. Go on, see if she knows where Mona Lisa's hiding."

Mercedes squeezed Eva's hand. She walked over to the bar where Carmen was seated. "Looks like you've been stood up."

Carmen turned around surprised. "Yeah, in more ways than one. I'm sure this isn't a social call."

"I think we're after the same woman. I have my reasons, now suppose you tell me yours."

Carmen knocked back her Corona. "I don't like being followed, it makes me edgy."

"And I don't like being led round in circles. Where's Mona Lisa?" Was it only six months ago that the three of them had dinner and Margaritas at Cha-Cha-Cha, a little box of a restaurant on the corner of Melrose and Virgil?

Carmen lit a cigarette. She took off her glasses. Her eyes were tired, bloodshot. It looked as if she'd been crying. "You won't believe what I've got to say. *Solamente locos y ninos dicen la verdad.*"

Mercedes nodded. "I'm listening."

"Go home and wait for Mona Lisa to blow back into town."

"No. I want to hear it from you."

Carmen toyed with her beer bottle before replying. "If you think me telling you the truth with a capital T's gonna set things straight, let me tell you something, sometimes, ignorance is fucking bliss. She kept you in the dark because she wanted it that way. She manipulated everyone." Carmen took a drink before continuing. "Right before we split, I was out of town up in Barstow. I came home early. My little darling didn't expect such a swift return. Well, there she was, doing some striptease for this dried out money-bags. No she wasn't that old, but she was rich and I hated her. And Mona Lisa pulled her number. Turned the tables. She was pissed off at me! Said she had a right to use her body any way she saw fit. That she wasn't even having `sex' with the woman, just showing her a good time. It didn't `mean' anything to her." Carmen laughed; a hard, bitter smile etched itself on her handsome face.

Mercedes felt the pain on Carmen's face. "Why'd you stay with her?"

Carmen took a drag of her cigarette. "You know why I stayed. Look at you. Trying to put together the pieces. Believing some things, not believing others. Trying to justify the shit. Defending her against other accusations. And she's just your friend. I was in love with her."

Mercedes nodded her head. What was Carmen searching for in Mona Lisa's apartment? The diary? Mercedes burned with curiosity. "But she betrayed you. Mona Lisa never let me down. She was all I could ever expect from a friend."

"Sure. But she's a hoax. She's not for real. Maybe she was kinder to you than the rest of us."

"She was."

"Then you're one of the lucky ones."

Mercedes could only wonder. "Samantha. You're supposed to meet her here."

The surprised showed on Carmen's face. "How'd you know?"

"Sometimes I happen to be in the right place at the right time." Mercedes locked eyes with Carmen.

Carmen shrugged her shoulders. "I thought I'd help Samantha find Mona Lisa. I made a few calls, but came up dry. Anyway, she didn't show up and I've got to get to work. It's time to put this shit behind me."

Carmen slipped the bartender a few bills and got off the bar stool. "A word of caution. I just gave you a fair shake. Don't keep tailing me. I'm not in the mood."

Mercedes stared into her angry eyes. Carmen brushed past her and exited the club. A chill ran down Mercedes' spine. She knew she hadn't gotten the whole story. But then she doubted she ever would.

*   *   *

Mercedes listened to Eva play. It had a soothing effect on her. She'd spent the last half hour watching the door, waiting for Samantha to show up. She was ready to call it a night, when Eva sat down and joined her for a nightcap.

"Let me tell you something. I grew up in the bayou. It gets hot there, very hot, especially at night. And quiet. Someone once said you could hear the lightning bugs talk. As a child I'd listen to the silence of the night. And I learned. There's a power out there and I use it. You use it, girl."

"I'm doing my best," Mercedes said, leaning in closer, hoping some of her common sense and calm would descend on her.

"You've got to listen with your eyes and see with your ears. And taste with your heart. Take my music. Those notes I play? Opens the darkness. Now most people just get lost, even if you open the door for them. You know Mona Lisa's lost out there.

Eva was right. Mercedes had played private eye of the heart enough times to be an expert witness. She'd been privy to the thrills that sandblast boredom and send sanity to the cleaners. To wonder, "Who is that woman?" and then spend days, weeks, months, even years investigating the paradox of the other. And once every little secret is divested and laid bare before your very eyes, the lover is no longer shrouded in mystery. Exposed, the inevitable disappointment sets in. Disillusioned by the familiarity of the stranger, the exotic becomes commonplace. Love prepares for its own disappearance and escapes out the back door. Another case closed. But she didn't want to close the door on Mona Lisa. She had to keep digging even though disillusionment had started to set in. She felt compelled, driven to investigate the truth.

"Only you know whether she's worth the fuss or not."

Mercedes nodded her head. She stalled before asking the next question.

"And what do I do about Samantha?"

Eva smiled. "You ask questions like I've got a crystal ball in front of me. Samantha's smart. Never stays in one place too long. Then again, maybe she's tired of running. Lots of people 'round here get into trouble like the world hasn't offered them enough of it. Everybody thinks everyone's bedroom is their own. Some'll even claim the sheets, but in the morning, the sun has a way of reminding us where we belong."

*   *   *

Eva stretched out her legs. She was alone. The place was empty. The door behind her opened and shut. Footsteps came her way. A hand squeezed her shoulder. It belonged to a familiar face.

Samantha sat down. "You've been telling those bedtime stories again."

"Where were you hiding out? Shame on you for turning that poor girl's head. Now don't you go messing where you don't belong."

Samantha pinched Eva's cheek. "You know what they say about love and war, don't you Eva?"

"Hum. Any luck with Mona Lisa?"

Samantha's face darkened. "I'll find her by the end of the week. Let's just hope she's in one piece. If Max or Redlite get their hands on her, she's dead. Once I get the antique, this mess will settle down."

"I hope that little scenario *includes* returning it to Fletcher."

Samantha smiled. It was a dry, thin smile. "What did you tell Mercedes about me?"

"I told her you were a no-good, two-timing womanizer and she should have her head examined for even talkin' to you."

"Come on. You told her I was charming."

"Yeah. A snake charmer's more like it."

Samantha put her hand on Eva's. "I know your kind of black magic. You're a dangerous witchwoman conjuring tales."

"Take care I don't put a spell on you. Might make you *human*."

Samantha laughed. Her pretty face lit up.

"Now tell me what kind of design you have on Mercedes."

"I like her. You know how it goes, Eva. If I wasn't who I am, maybe we'd get married and have babies. But that's not how it goes for me."

"Well I didn't hear any proposals from her. And I'm not talking 'bout housekeeping, smart ass. It's high time you took stock of your life. Been on the lam too long."

"Don't know any other way to live. It's in my blood." Her voice carried the weight of her conviction.

"Blood! What do you know about blood? That's ice water you got in those veins. Look at me, an old bag of bones, falling in love. Feel like I'm twenty again."

"Good for you." Samantha meant that genuinely, she just didn't believe it for herself.

"Your heart gets old and shrinks. You need to exercise that muscle." Eva smoothed back her hair.

"I get plenty, believe me." Samantha stood up.

"I'm not talking south-of-the-border exercise," Eva snapped, playfully.

Samantha patted Eva on the back. "You enjoy it for both of us. I got business to tend to. You know where to reach me," she said and left.

* * *

Fifteen minutes later Eva climbed the stairs to her apartment, lodged above the restaurant. When the night was good to her she had no other choice but to give it back.

She stopped outside the bedroom and peeked inside the candle-lit room. The smell of burning wax and jasmine made her shiver. And the sight of Noh, serene, still like Buddha, provocatively poised in the middle of the bed, legs folded in the lotus position, her usual braid of hair now carefully combed behind her ears, was all the nightcap Eva needed.

THE LADY VANISHES

Wind chimes rustled in the still of the night. A siren wailed down Sunset Boulevard, the moon was half asleep and Mercedes wide awake. Home never looked so good. She was exhausted, but juiced. The red diary lay on her bed, beckoning her to purloin the pages, to uncover the layered secrets of her friend. And although it was private property, she had to read it. She had no choice.

She retrieved the dance-card from the Pond's cold cream jar and held it in her hand. The jewels sparkled with secrets. Why did it give her such comfort? Because it was expensive and beautifully crafted? Was she hypnotized by its power to transform the lives of so many people? Or had it been the only tangible thing connecting her to Mona Lisa? She placed it on her night table, got into bed and propped her ankle on a few pillows, the swelling not nearly as bad as before.

Her room, its familiar belongings—Gilda, the mannequin—didn't do much to reinforce her sense of place. Beyond any identifiable reef of normalcy, Mercedes was adrift on a dangerous course without a compass. Mysterious and powerful like the pull of the ocean, her emotions had been buried in the sand until she met Samantha. Sucked into an undertow that would inevitably dash her onto jagged rocks, she had become increasingly more excited by the prospect of breaking out of her complacent shell. No matter what the future held, it certainly wouldn't be predictable.

Mercedes jimmied the diary's lock with a screwdriver. The book snapped open, but before she could dig into the contents, the phone rang. She picked up the receiver. Who would be calling at one in the morning?

There was silence on the other end of line. Then the unmistakable sound of breathing. Deep and raspy. She threw a protective glance at the dance-card and was just about to hang up when a man's voice broke the silence like a short-lived fast.

"Ms. Martini? I've got a proposition."

"Who is this?" Mercedes had double-locked her doors. In the morning she'd have an alarm installed, buy a German shepherd and hire armed guards.

"My name is Max. And I want you to know how well I can play the game. Rumor has it you have an antique. I want it. I can be a very persuasive man."

Mercedes heard a dog barking in the background. She grabbed the antique and held it protectively in her hand. "I don't know what you're talking about."

The man took a deep breath, exhaling slowly. The dog had stopped barking. "I know how to fix it so you'll never see Mona Lisa again."

"What do you want?" Mercedes asked.

"To look at you from your bedroom window."

Mercedes' eyebrows furrowed. She looked at the window, the moonlight slicing through. "Juliet I'm not."

The man laughed. "I like a woman with a sense of humor. Come to the window."

Mercedes got off the bed, pulled the phone cord behind her. Parked in front of her house was a beautiful black 500 SL Mercedes.

"I drove my Mercedes in your honor."

Mercedes couldn't make out the man's face, shielded in the shadow of the expensive car. But she could see the teeth of his Doberman seated next to him.

"Meet me tomorrow night. Ten o'clock. I'll be waiting for you in the back room of Revolver."

Revolver was a popular hang-out for boys and girls on the northwest corner of Santa Monica Boulevard and Larrabee. "I'm calling the police. They can meet you." Mercedes had no intention of meeting this man, whoever he was.

The man laughed. "I'll be watching for you." The phone went dead. The headlights gleamed; the car moved up the street, disappearing from sight.

Mercedes ran downstairs, made sure all the doors and windows were locked, came back upstairs, checked the window to make sure no one was there, then got into bed once again and opened the diary. Any reservations about peeking through someone's personal belongings disappeared after the mysterious phone call.

First pages clue you in on what to expect. Mona Lisa's diary was prefaced with the inscription: *I am the grand coquette living in the tower of babel. Those who listen to my lies are blind.* Certainly more poetic than Mercedes had expected from Mona Lisa. What ever happened to "Dear Diary, today I kissed my girlfriend in the back of my Dad's Corvette . . . . "?

Mercedes settled in. Deciphering Mona Lisa's handwriting would be a task in and of itself. She grabbed her glasses and put them on.

Under the Brooklyn Bridge a girl lost the only thing she had to give one night to a man who was mean and ugly and sharp. He speared her. The lights twinkled on the bridge. They laughed. Mocked the girl with her skirt up over her face like a mask.

NO ONE MAKES ME DO WHAT I DON'T WANT TO!!!

I am an imitation of a perverted imitation of a work of art. Flesh not oil, my heart is canvas. Paint me red.

Monday, crack of dawn. Couldn't sleep last night. Had those dreams again. Someone's after me. I wanted to tell Mercedes, but I didn't. I can't ever tell her. It's my secret.

Mercedes was as equally mesmerized by the diary entries as she was the voices on Mona Lisa's phone machine. But the diary revealed another layer to her friend's personality. It became more apparent that Mona Lisa had harbored a lot of pain and rejection. Not only was she fascinated by Mona Lisa's flair for description, but she realized she was part of the story, a character in the pages of her sordid existence. How could she have been so blind to her friend's inner life?

BARGAIN BASEMENT BABES. Step right up. These goddamn cheap shoes are killing me. Women get the short end of the stick. Sometimes I wish I were a man. I could lose my heart behind the fleecy hair on my chest. And my muscles would keep out the fear. And that pistol between my legs. BAM BAM. You're dead. Now leave me alone. My feet ache. Dance is going to be the death of me yet. But, baby, oh baby, what a way to go.

Sunday night and the L.A. river is red with tears. Someone got knifed and they dumped the body. I threw rose petals in the water. Noh wants to leave. But I can't. My big break is just around the fucking Hollywood corner. Besides, how can I leave without telling "her" I love her?

Mercedes was puzzled. Was Mona Lisa in love with Noh? The strange young girl with the braid . . . or were they just friends? Did she mean Carmen?

The moon had disappeared behind clouds. The night was silent with an occasional overlay of wind. Mercedes needed to sleep, but all she could do was turn the page.

Who turned out the lights? Hey, this is supposed to be an audition. "Come here," spoken in the dark. I did my thing. It was expected. Next time I'm bringing a poker with me. Beat their goddamn arrogance down. So the job's mine. I earned it. FUCKER . . . .

Yes . . . breathe deeply. High-heeled hen lays the golden egg. You're sitting pretty on top of the world. Wrap those honey thighs tight 'round ambition, baby. You just done birthed a nation.

Not to forget. Dr. Flesch. Sounds like one of my lousy movies . . . ha ha ha . . . 1:00 Sunday. I'm afraid. But I can't look back now.

Mercedes recalled the message on Mona Lisa's answering machine confirming the appointment. Could it have been for an abortion? Mercedes called information, but there was no listing for a Dr. Flesch in L.A., Beverly Hills or the Valley. Was it a *nom-de-plume* or some quack, a white-cloaked fanatic who rallied 'round the flag pole of the social dis-eases of the season? Dr. Flesch, body not spirit. Mercedes read on. She wasn't confused enough.

Car. MEN. Take me for a ride. Night slaps my face and I slap yours. We're even, steven. Let's say it backwards, take it from behind, ok, the way you like it. NEMRAC . . . my carmia, no flower you said was too sweet to describe my taste. But don't go quizzing me like that. Here's a towel, just wipe that look off your kisser, you ain't got me wrapped around your finger.

So here's the wrap up. One night in a dream, a real one, god came to me and said, little girl, why did I make you so pretty? And I said, because almighty god, you have the good taste to make me in the light of your image. Then he said, so why did you blaspheme me by your tawdry acts. I take my cue from you, the little girl said. God took a break. He needed one. When he returned he called her Eve. She said, You got the wrong gal, god. She's down the block polishing an apple. But god said Eve was too busy fucking Adam to worry about polishing apples. You're making me hungry, the little girl said. Have a tart, god said. What's a tart? A tart's a tainted woman. Now why, the little girl said, would I want to eat a woman. Man is bitter, god replied, all knowingly, woman is sweet.

Dear Mom: I'm sorry I didn't turn out the way you wanted. I forgot what you wanted. But now things will be different. I'll be different. I think about who I admire the most. You see I have this friend who loves me unconditionally. You'd like her Mom. She's smart and cares about what happens to this godforsaken town. Her name's Mercedes. Maybe you'd like her better than me.

Mercedes closed the book, picked up the dance-card and rested it on her lap, touched by Mona Lisa's candid feelings about their relationship.

She shut her eyes, tried to capture the woman she knew and loved, but it was hopeless. Her friend had vanished in more ways than one and in her stead, a new Mona Lisa emerged, hard, bitter, with a dark sense of humor to mask her pain.

Mercedes slipped the dance-card under the pillow, a sacred yet profane charm linking her to her friend, and slowly drifted off to sleep.

HARD, FAST & BEAUTIFUL

For the last five years, Fletcher had kept her horses at the Griffith Park Equestrian Center. Riding was the one outdoor recreation Mallory seemed to get excited about. But even today, knowing that she would be several hours in the company of her favorite horse, Aeolus, a gray Arabian stallion she had named because "he travels as swift as the winds," Mallory's spirits lagged.

Fletcher was convinced it was due to the absence of the dance-card. Last night when she passed Mallory's room, the girl was in a stupor. Her jewelry box lay open on her vanity table, the velour pouch that once contained the favored dance-card lay there forlorn and as lonely as Mallory. The sight tore at Fletcher like a unhealed wound.

Clouds loomed overhead, ominous shapes stamped against a drab background. If they could forecast the future like tea leaves on the bottom of a cup, danger was definitely in the air.

Fletcher watched Mallory jump on her horse. Dressed in tight, beige riding pants, a swatch of brown suede down the inner thigh to the calf, her hair braided off her beautiful face, Mallory seemed happy to be on her own horse, alone, riding with the wind at her back. It made Fletcher crazy. She had to restrain the urge to climb in the saddle with her.

The two took off down the dung-strewn path, a few riders nodding an early morning greeting. Mallory seemed lost in her own world. Fletcher noticed her lean down a few times to whisper to Aeolus. Even her words Fletcher coveted.

"Darling, don't ride too far, now." Fletcher caught the girl's body stiffen at the sound of her voice. Just as she'd suspected. Mallory had done it again. She had this deplorable habit of pretending people didn't exist. Something about retreating into this Alice in Wonderland world. But the sound of Fletcher's voice forced her to come back to reality, forsake the Mad Hatter and re-engage in the land of the living.

Mallory turned around and smiled weakly. It tore Fletcher's heart and a tiny wail escaped her lips, drowned by the adjacent freeway traffic. Fletcher pulled down the zipper of her leather jacket. For although the air was appropriately chilled, she was burning inside.

Fletcher looked at her Rolex. There were still ten minutes to go. Whatever reservations she had about her plan were dismissed and duly discharged. Something drastic had to be done. She'd tried everything to restore Mallory's interest, but as each day passed, she knew the girl was slowly slipping away. And nothing slipped away from Fletcher unless she wanted it to.

Suddenly Mallory quickened her pace, digging her booted feet deeper into the stirrups. Her thighs hugged Aeolus' flanks as she rounded a bend in the muddy road, swerved left and cut across a field of dried, yellow grass and mown hay. Fletcher's heart raced along as she followed suit. Sometimes when they rode like this, she liked to imagine Mallory an outlaw she pursued with a vengeance. Fletcher was there to tame the girl, break her unruly habits. The thought agitated and provoked her as she watched Mallory canter along the empty path.

Six months ago Mallory walked into her life on a day not unsimilar to this. The rain was falling and Bach's "Concerto for Violin, Oboe and Strings in D minor" filled the room. It had become "their song."

She had come to apply for the job as executive assistant and personal secretary. The fact she didn't know Microsoft from Word Perfect or a Mac from an IBM made Fletcher want her even more. And the fact she'd never experienced love with a woman had Fletcher crawling out of her skin.

Mallory was an orphan. Raised by a nanny who was deaf and couldn't speak, her adoptive parents seemed to have forgotten they had a child in their care. Mallory had arrived a *tabula rasa*; Fletcher was there to fill in the blanks and create a life for her. Mallory hit a sexual chord Fletcher hadn't fully exercised.

There was something inscrutable about the way Mallory responded (or didn't respond) to her. Mallory's eyes, deep blue and dotted with black specks, sometimes frightened Fletcher, wore at her heart, tore down the defenses of a ruthless career at love. It didn't take hours, days or weeks to erode Fletcher's moxie. Just a steady diet of Mallory.

Max thought her obsession with Mallory odious. Ridiculous. Of course he was jealous. Max had no illusions about Fletcher's sexual inclinations, however he craved her solicitude and loathed her attentions to others.

Mallory dug her heels into the animal's meaty flanks. Aeolus broke into a gallop. The two took off, rider and horse, one.

Fletcher grit her teeth. Her horse was bigger and faster, but she needed to keep some distance for a few more minutes if this was going to work. Rain drops fell on Fletcher's face. A dark cloud moved across the sky.

She longed to recapture the joy on Mallory's face when she opened the gift. Fletcher wasn't generous with her ex-lovers, as Max would attest. But Mallory was growing restless. Fletcher knew she loved trinkets. Certain the girl had no idea how valuable the token was, Fletcher knew Mallory was taken by its magic charm.

"Women used to write the names of their boyfriends in the dance-card," Fletcher told her.

"Why?" Mallory had asked, her eyes wide and happy, fingering the treasure.

"So they could keep track of their admirers."

Mallory thought this practical but unnecessary and when Fletcher pressed farther she responded, "If you were in the room, there'd be no one I'd dance with but you." The remark devastated Fletcher. Her soul had been kidnapped. Her heart was in Mallory's possession weeks ago. She knew she was lost.

"Now I belong to you," Mallory had said, clutching the dance-card in her hand. She jumped up and spun around in balletic circles, a graceful silhouette against the moonlight. Pirouetting on slipperless toes, Mallory floated to the antique Chinese bed with its engraved wooden partition and lattice grill and laid the dance-card on the pillow.

As she turned to Fletcher, she opened her white silk robe. She had nothing on underneath. Fletcher felt a fever come on, a hot yellow flame scorched the edges of her brain and black smoke greedily sucked the oxygen from the room. Bach's concerto in D Minor swelled and the dance-card was imprinted with indelible ink on Fletcher's heart: Mallory in love.

Fletcher felt the stab of that memory. It gave her courage. Out of the corner of her eye, she saw a figure in black riding gear on a gray horse. She pulled the reins tight. Mallory was less than an eighth of a mile ahead of her.

A gunshot cracked the air like a boom of thunder. Fletcher felt the impact. Her cry echoed in the park. Her arm dropped to her side, the horse, startled and unsure, followed Aeolus.

By the time Mallory turned around, Fletcher was hanging off the chestnut horse, slumped over like a sack of grain. Barely conscious, the blood oozing down her arm, staining her suede jacket, she remembered Mallory shouting out her name, terror mixing with concern.   A small smile etched her lips. The dark, damp earth never looked more beautiful.

*   *   *

When Fletcher opened her eyes, she saw Mallory leaning over her. She tried to move, but Mallory wouldn't let her budge. "I've got to get help," she said.

"What happened?" Fletcher liked the fear on Mallory's face. It made her look even younger, more vulnerable.

"My God, some maniac shot you. I saw a horse ride off toward the freeway, then it disappeared from sight."

Fletcher shook her head weakly. She looked around her. They were in a small shelter, the rain tapping against the roof. Fletcher thought she could spend eternity there. Mallory had tended to her wounded arm, wrapping it with her Anne Klein scarf. She liked lying in Mallory's lap.

A crack of thunder punctured the stillness and a bolt of lightning pierced the sky. "I'm dying," Fletcher said, her lips dry, her voice filled with just enough pathos to extract the appropriate amount of pity.

She could tell Mallory was scared. After all, the assailant could still be lurking around. They were about three miles from the Center and there was a good chance it would be awhile before someone came to offer assistance.

Fletcher's arm throbbed with pain, a red hot poker singing her flesh.

"Oh, you're in pain," Mallory soothed, cradling Fletcher in her arms like a baby.

She pulled Mallory closer. "Don't leave me to die alone," she begged, her steely eyes gray with terror, a fiendish glint tinging them with madness. Mallory pulled back, but Fletcher couldn't let her go. The pain exploded in her body.

"We've got to get help." Mallory listened for the sound of people, but the downpour drowned out any nearby noise.

"Kiss me," Fletcher pleaded. "Kiss me and tell me you love me."

Mallory obeyed. Fletcher thrust her tongue in the girl's mouth. Her bloody fingers left a trail on Mallory's ashen face. The girl was marked.

THE MAJESTIC TALENT AGENCY

The sirens in Los Angeles grow louder each year. As she jogged along the pavement, Mercedes could hear the wailing, whining cry of a wounded vehicle. And it was only seven in the morning.

She pulled up the zipper to her Adidas jacket, hoping to sweat out the last few days of alcohol, caffeine, nicotine and negative karma. She swallowed the sodden morning air as an asthmatic would suck the oxygen deep into narrow bronchioles. This was it. No more smoking.

The rain yesterday had kept her in most of the day. Absorbed by Mona Lisa's diary and its surreal revelations, she was surprised there were no ominous phone calls, no threatening letters, no break-ins, only the rain beating on her roof. She'd had no intention of meeting Max at Revolver and expected him to show up outside her house again, but he didn't. She'd made a broccoli, onion and gruyere quiche and a baked apple with cinnamon and walnuts for dessert. Usually nothing short of death killed her passion for food, but for some reason, she'd lost her appetite.

Her run today was a stretch from Sycamore, one block east of La Brea, along Beverly Boulevard to Pan Pacific Park where she ran three laps around the green playground. The remains of the spectacular Pan Pacific auditorium, three charred, melted pylons sticking out of the ground like tombstones, was the only evidence that this Angeleno exhibition hall existed.

She was planning to pay a visit to Mona Lisa's agent, Myron Lebowitz, at the Taft Building on the corner of Vine and Hollywood. A sleazy part of town, it still housed some magnificent buildings. The lavish Art Deco Pantages Theater which opened its doors in 1930 with MGM's *The Floradora Girl*, the Palace with its Spanish-baroque facade, the Max Factor Building on Highland and of course, Grauman's

Chinese Theater built in 1927 and renowned worldwide for its clever ploy of imprinting the hands and feet of cinema giants.

It was nine o'clock by the time Mercedes pulled into the parking lot behind the Taft Building. She had changed into a pair of Levi's with a matching denim shirt, a brown leather jacket and shoe boots.

The security guard in the faded art deco hallway looked tired and the day was just beginning. In a nasal voice that sounded as if she had cotton wads in her nose, the guard informed Mercedes that the Majestic had moved. Gone south. She wasn't sure of the address.

Mercedes walked to the nearest phone booth, grabbed a hankie from her pocket and reached for the receiver and dialed. She hated using public phones, but couldn't afford the luxury of a car phone. In all probability, the booth was crawling with germs. The operator told her the Majestic was located in West Hollywood. Melrose Place off La Cienega.

Fifteen minutes later, Mercedes drove down an elegant stretch of a street lined with expensive antique shops, a block north of Melrose Avenue. She parked in front of the now defunct Le Restaurant, and walked a few steps and entered a gated stairwell.

The agency shared a building with Dr. Eric Scott Pearl, a chiropractor, a healing gay veteran of boy's town. Mercedes checked the gold-plated directory. Next to Sneak Preview Productions, in Suite 204 was the Majestic. Myron must have moved up in the world.

Mercedes climbed a flight of stairs. Next to a potted palm was the Agency. A few good-looking boys with arrogant smiles and clear eyes, pushed past her, gesturing emphatically, excited over something. Probably just got parts in a new Van Damme movie. Or a gay porno.

The office was busy. There weren't the expected cattle call of tacky gals with bad skin and short skirts. Fresh-scrubbed farm girls and all-American jocks. A tall, elegant black man, bald, wearing a white shirt and crisp jeans asked if he could help her.

"I'd like to talk to Myron." Mercedes looked at the pictures on the wall. There was one of Mona Lisa. She looked so pretty and fresh. Full of hope and promise. Mercedes lost her bearing. She sunk into a plush red leather chair. The nice man brought her over a glass of water. She gobbled it down. Low on electrolytes. She'd forgotten to drink her Gatorade.

Mercedes explained her mission. The man listened in between

juggling three ringing lines. He left her and went back to talk to Myron.

Five minutes later Mercedes was seated in a green room with brown leather sofa and chairs. Pictures of all his "stars" hung on the wall, a collection of memorabilia on another. Then there was Mohammad Ali's boxing glove, signed and sealed behind a plexiglass box.

Myron had one phone in his hand and was yelling into a speaker phone. "What'dya mean she don't do nudity? She's got it in her contract and if I have to come down there myself, she'll work the part and work it well. Don't worry, Mark, I've never let you down, now have I? Listen, Norman's on the other line. Let's lunch." He disconnected, winked at Mercedes and kept the other guy on hold.

"So, you say you haven't seen Mona Lisa in over a week?"

"I think something may have happened to her. She'd check in with you, wouldn't she?"

"Yeah, normally she'd check in with me. But her contract ran out and I offered to renew for two, she's getting a little heat, as they say, but she felt she was too big for my britches. Me, raised her like I would my own brats. But that's the show, baby. Gotta love. Can't cry as they say over spilled sherry. No siree."

Myron held up a finger and depressed the hold button. "So you son of a bitch. We negotiated her contract and now you're tellin' me it ain't a play, so you gotta pay."

Myron winked at Mercedes and put an unlit plastic cigar in his mouth. It was about two inches in diameter. "My lawyer'll call yours. Let them work it out. I'm a busy man."

With that Myron hung up the phone. "You're not the only one after my little traitor. Some real looker came in here a few minutes before you."

Mercedes stiffened. "Who was she?"

Myron snorted and rolled the fake cigar from one side of his mouth to the other, then back again. He got up and did a one-two punch in front of Ali's gloves. Then he sat at the edge of his desk, rolled up the left leg of his pant and glared down at Mercedes. "Names don't mean shit in this town, honey. I got clients change their name to suit the weather. She had dark brown hair, wore a purple leather jacket and smelled expensive."

Mercedes wasn't surprised. Samantha always seemed to be two steps ahead of her. She coaxed Myron into sharing whatever information he had about Mona Lisa. He'd vaguely remembered meeting Mercedes before.

"Got a soft spot for that girl," Myron said. "She's screwier than hell, but she's got the chutzpah to make it in this dog-eat-dog town."

If she ever comes out of this alive, Mercedes thought. "You've got to help me."

Myron scratched his groin while thinking. His phone was ringing. He gave her the 411. "Try Favored Artists." He'd gotten wind she was being wooed by the latest crop of talent-meisters in Century City. It was just a rumor. But in this town, he reminded her, as she got up to leave, "truth is stranger than fiction."

CLIFTON'S SILVERSPOON

There were two places to go for a real breakfast downtown. One was the Pantry, open twenty-four hours a day, every day, and the other was Clifton's Cafeteria. Always packed and noisy, the only venue with its own newsletter, Clifton smelled like breakfast, lunch and dinner. About a million of them. The Seventh street old-fashioned emporium was a staple since the 1930s.

Mercedes removed her sunglasses and scanned the sea of hungry faces for Good Friday. She had wanted to pay a visit to Favored Artists, but she had promised to meet Good Friday. He had some info on Redlite.

"Tuna melt on rye. Hold the mayo," a perky waitress barked to the short order cook. Lured by fried eggs, bacon and sausage sizzling on the griddle, customers were chomping away in the wood-paneled diner.

Patsy Cline's "Cheating Heart" blared from speakers. Mercedes took a seat just as Lois, a Clifton veteran, set down a mug and poured some coffee. "You look like something the cat dragged in." Her forest green uniform was more scorched earth than verdant woodland from the kitchen heat.

"Save the compliment and keep pouring," Mercedes quipped.

"Just telling it as I see it," she said, clucking her tongue. "Are we being healthy today or sinful?"

"Sinful." Mercedes poured some cream into her coffee and took a sip.

Lois barked out, "Slice of pig, bull's eye over easy." She looked over at the door. "You got company." Lois stood there tapping her foot while Good Friday made his way to Mercedes' booth.

"Mornin' ladies. Fine day, fine day." His clean-shaven face emitted a trace of lime-scented cologne. With the dark shades, he looked like Ray Charles. Lois stood there, holding the empty pot of coffee.

Good Friday scowled. "I been comin' to this joint every Tuesday for as long as I can remember and I've been lookin' at your face longer than I'll ever want to remember, and still a man's gotta ask for his coffee. There oughta be a law," Good Friday said, flipping open and hiding behind his paper. "Lox and bagels."

Lois walked off in a huff to get some fresh brewed java. Mercedes took another sip of her coffee.

"Witch gone?" Good Friday peered over the top of his newspaper.

Mercedes grinned. "Coast's clear. Now tell me what you found out."

Good Friday folded his paper. "Before I tell you anything, I want you to listen to me."

Mercedes nodded her head, knowing she was in for a lecture.

"Go to the police. Tell 'em what you know. Let them find Mona Lisa."

Mercedes remembered Mona Lisa's final plea. "Don't go to the police." She didn't want any publicity. Leave it to her friend to worry about her image over her life. Mercedes told Good Friday everything she'd learned and explained why she had to do this herself.

He looked at her skeptical. "Now tell me what you're *really* after, girl."

Mercedes wasn't certain. Of course she wanted to find Mona Lisa, but her pursuit had more to do with this unnerving obsession to push herself to the limit. To break out and explore this dark layer of emotional duplicity she'd discovered. She needed to take things to the end of the line. "I'll tell you once I get there."

Good Friday shook his head and before he could offer any criticism, Lois returned with their food. "Called a buddy of mine. Redlite's wanted for murder," he slathered a generous portion of cream cheese on his toasted bagel. Turns out he offed a drug-dealer, made out with the loot, sold it on the streets. He's crazy, man. Did some time at the Detention Center on Alameda. Jailed in his own backyard. Xuan keeps him around 'cause he scares away the riff-raff. Plus he knows too much to be off working for someone else."

Lois shuffled by, catching drift of Good Friday's warning. She tapped her finger on their table. "Two things I can smell inside a hundred feet. Even in this joint," she sniveled, looking over at the cook, "and that's Glenn's burnt pork chops and trouble." She walked off satisfied that she knew something was going down.

"That gal needs a vacation," Good Friday scolded, piling lox on his bagel. "A nice long walk off the Santa Monica Pier."

Mercedes toyed with her eggs. She was just about to cut into her ham, when someone entered the restaurant. Someone she recognized. "It's her," Mercedes said, wiping her mouth with a napkin.

"Her who?" Good Friday replied, his mouth full of food.

"The nun. Without her habit and the convent crewcut."

"Here we go again, might as well be talkin' to myself." Good Friday puckered his lips and flapped open his newspaper.

Mercedes bounded across the room to the woman's table. She was startled at first, but quickly settled back into indifference. As long as she got a cup of coffee, she'd didn't quite care who joined her. She lit a cigarette, daring Mercedes with stony eyes.

Mercedes took the cue. "Mona Lisa. Where is she?"

The woman shrugged her shoulders. "I don't believe we've met. My name's Merle." She slurped her coffee, making a gurgling sound.

"Unless you tell me what's going on, I'm going to have you tailed morning, noon and night." Mercedes didn't realize she was tearing the paper placemat into pieces as she talked.

"And you listen to me," Merle replied, defensively. "I did your friend a favor. I owed her one. No questions asked. What's the big fucking deal? Jesus. You'd think there was a ticking bomb in that package. She said it was just a gag."

Mercedes didn't believe her. But then again, she did deliver the package. If Merle knew how valuable the contents were, wouldn't she have made off with it herself? "When did you last see her?"

Merle took a long deep drag of the cigarette. Her other hand she tapped on the formica table. "Thursday night. After class. I'm an acting instructor. She told me what to wear, what you looked like and where you'd be. That's it."

"She didn't tell you what was inside?"

Merle looked bored. "Nope. Listen, I gotta get some food in my stomach. Are we through with the interrogation?"

"No. What class?"

"Improvisation. She's the best. Only she didn't show up for class last night. She never misses class."

"Her agent. Who's the new agent she's with?"

Merle smiled. "Finally dumped poor Myron. She got herself a class act over at Favored Artists. One of those young, snooty Ivy Leaguers who thinks she knows talent from a hole in the wall. But she's got clout. Her name's Carla Simpson and if you can get her on the phone, my hat's off to you."

Mercedes looked over at Good Friday, in another heated argument with Lois.

"Listen," Merle said, lowering her voice a bit. "One night this crazy Latina comes hanging around outside. They have a fight. Real nasty. Girls will be girls, but honey, this woman almost clawed Mona Lisa's eyes out. I broke it up, shit, this stuff isn't exactly great for my business. And this Carmen, yeah, that's her name, says to Mona Lisa, right in front of me, mind you, `I'm gonna kill you.' Sent shivers down my spine."

Mercedes was starting to like Merle. Despite the rings around her eyes and the world-weary sighs, the woman seemed to be telling the truth. "What do you know about Club Sayonara, a guy named Redlite and a woman named Xuan?"

Merle sighed again. "You ain't going away, are you?"

Mercedes shook her head. She called over Lois and let Merle order breakfast. By the time Merle was breaking into her perfectly cooked egg with a slice of rye, Mercedes had found out plenty. How Redlite used to chauffeur Mona Lisa around town. How Mona Lisa was fast friends with Noh, the young woman who'd broken into Mona Lisa's apartment. And how they both hated Xuan. For someone who had nothing to say, she opened up as easily as her runny egg.

Mercedes paid for Merle's breakfast. She was starting to get the knack of this. Maybe once this puzzle was solved and Mona Lisa found and given a good spanking, she'd put in a stint as a private investigator. Take one of those six month trainee courses with a retired cop and snap pictures of errant husbands having trysts at fancy hotels. Or maybe she'd just move to another town, as far away from Hollywood as possible.

Good Friday was all ears when she returned to her cold breakfast. Lois took the dishes away while Mercedes filled him in. And then she dealt the final blow. "You've got to get me into Club Sayonara."

He rolled his eyes, put on his sunglasses and picked up his paper. "Now what you want to be tap dancing like some fool. They're gonna spot you a mile away."

Mercedes had heard about these dance clubs, had past the Savoy on Sixth off Broadway when she was taking her tourists to the State Theatre. But she'd never been to one. Private dancer. Tina Turner's song suddenly popped into her head. The album cover in Mona Lisa's apartment.

"This joint is a cut above the rest. Most of them are third-rate and draw a fourth-class crowd. The parking lot is packed with lots of rich cars. Japanese bankers. No surprise since three of the largest California banks are Japanese owned. Xuan sure knows how to pick her clients."

Mr. Yamamoto. The phone message. The urgent plea to see her again. "That's it," Mercedes said. "Saturday night. You with me?"

Good Friday scowled. He got up and stretched his legs. "I suppose I'm not talkin' you outta anything, so I guess I better tag along."

Mercedes smiled. She knew she could count on him. At least someone in her life was reliable. "One more thing," Mercedes said as they exited the restaurant, her arm linked in his.

"Oh lord, I feel it comin'."

"You still got that gun of yours?"

Good Friday stopped in his track. "Jesus, Mary 'n Joseph."

Mercedes pulled her arm free and stepped off the pavement. "Load it," she said as she disappeared across the street.

A BRUSH WITH DEATH

Forty-eight hours after Fletcher had been shot by some mysterious sniper, she was at home, recovering with the help of Noh who had applied a herbal ointment of thyme, Valerian root, seaweed and calendula to the gun wound. Luckily the bullet had grazed her flesh and not hit bone. But it was a shock nonetheless and such an ordeal. Poor Mallory. Fletcher never saw her look so worried. A lone rider had spotted them in the shelter and run off for help.

The police were called and there were endless questions and of course nothing was solved. Max insisted on hiring Pinkerton, but Fletcher had her reservations. Why drag him into this? But Mallory was adamant.

"The killer could still be after you," she exclaimed. The two-piece brown Chanel suit she wore was dotted with tufts of wool. She looked as gentle as a doe.

There was a knock at the door. It opened and in stepped Detective Pinkerton. If Fletcher was going to have a man in her bedroom, he'd better look as good as Pinkerton. He whipped off a handsome Valentino raincoat like a toreador would a cape, draped the garment over a chair and pulled out a pack of cigarettes from his gray houndstooth suit.

"I'm not sure you're going to do any good," Fletcher said, joining him in a smoke. Mallory sat graceful by her side.

"I get results . . . when results are to be had." His eyes twinkled with dark humor. "There are many things in the air nowadays. Smog. Pollution. Dirt. Ultraviolet rays from a sun that used to shine pretty. Now everyone's going undercover with a bottle of SPF 30. We've all got our protective devices." Pinkerton looked at Mallory with keen interest.

"Yes, well, do you think it was a random shot. A gang member?" Fletcher tried to pull his attention away from Mallory, back to the subject at hand.

"Gangs don't ride in parks on horses." Pinkerton examined Fletcher's face. "Why do you think some trigger-happy cowboy would want to hurt you?"

"Kill me, you mean," Fletcher said, for effect.

Mallory's eyes grew wide as a tire. Pinkerton caught the fear and put it in his pocket. Out of the same pocket he took a pad and slim gold pen. "Then why don't you let the cops handle it?"

"I'm allergic to cops. They wear polyester, don't they?" Fletcher smoothed her dressing gown, the ends of her lips curling with satisfaction.

Pinkerton threw his eyes to the ceiling just as the door opened. Regan walked in carrying a box of chocolates. Fletcher thought that nice. Mallory took the box, smiled and placed it on the table for Fletcher to nibble, then walked over to open the window.

Fletcher didn't like the way Regan and Pinkerton watched her walk. She was happy when Pinkerton stood up to leave.

"I'm going over to Griffith Park and check out the area. Might turn up something interesting. I told Regan to keep an eye on you. Stay inside for a few days. Lie low." He picked up his rain coat and started to leave. "One more thing."

"Yes," Fletcher said, impatiently. She popped a nut cluster in her mouth.

"This wouldn't have anything to do with a missing dance-card?"

Fletcher nearly choked on the candy. Mallory moved away from the window and grabbed Pinkerton's arm.

"Dance-card? Oh, Detective Pinkerton. Can you find out what happened to it?"

Fletcher managed to get up, but the room was spinning. "Don't poke your nose where it doesn't belong," Fletcher said, trying to swallow the goddamn piece of chocolate.

She noticed Mallory looking at Regan and didn't like the way the girl took an interest in her hired hand. And she didn't like Pinkerton.

When Max walked in, the whole thing had turned into a charade. He was wearing a ridiculous new outfit, a trendy blast of colors and short pants that would only look tolerable on a young boy on the cover of *Spin* magazine. If he were a moving target, a bullet wouldn't have a chance.

The two men shook hands. Fletcher thought their eyes lingered on each other longer than appropriate. As if they were communicating some secret. Her temples ached. Maybe it was the vicodin she'd been taking to kill the pain that was inducing all this paranoia.

Fletcher swooned. Max moved over to assist her. "Out, out, *mes amis*," he ordered, clapping his hands. "The lady needs her rest."

Fletcher reluctantly allowed Mallory to leave. It was insufferably warm in the room, even with the opened window.

"Did he buy the random shot theory?" Max asked, petting Fletcher's hand. She snapped her hand away and grabbed another chocolate.

"He didn't buy anything, but it looked good. For chrissakes, who told him about the dance-card? What is it, all over town?" Fletcher rolled the candy around in her mouth.

Max lit a thin cigar and smiled. "Your business is everyone's business, darling. You keep forgetting that."

She examined his face and wondered how they managed to remain friends for so long. Who else could she trust to pull off such a scheme? She looked down at her bandaged arm. "Such a crack shot. A few inches more and the bullet would have gone straight through my heart."

Max laughed. "I thought you traded yours in for an interactive gameshow."

Fletcher knew he was jealous of Mallory. But Max was a big boy. He'd just have to get over it. "Your sense of humor tires me, Max. See to Mallory."

"Sure," he said, his voice cold. He clipped his cigar tight between his teeth. "Get some sleep. You look like hell."

*   *   *

Hallways are good for two things: eavesdropping and trouble. Regan couldn't deny her attraction to Mallory. However, she wouldn't step over the line of duty. Not with Fletcher. Not when her boss was so nutso over her lover. She was at the head of the staircase when a door opened.

"Over here," Mallory whispered, sticking her head out.

Regan knew the only way to get downstairs was to put one foot on the step below and then the other would follow. But her feet felt implanted like the roots of a Sequoia.

"Please," Mallory pleaded.

Instead of down, Regan moved up.

Mallory pulled Regan inside her room and locked the door behind her. She put on a tiny Cinderella lamp, the kind you'd find in a child's room. Only Regan wasn't there to play.

She slipped a green envelope that smelled of jasmine and moonlit walks along the ocean into the breast pocket of Regan's jacket. "That will explain everything."

Regan peered into Mallory's blue peepers, clear and guileless. They transported her to a place where the sand was hot and the water cool and the earth pregnant with life. She heard the call of the wild. It was repeating her name:"*Stooge, sucker, shithead.*"

"Regan," Mallory implored, bringing her out of her stupor. "Please, you're the only one I can trust."

"Hey, listen. This isn't my trip," Regan replied, not sure what Mallory proposed in the letter. She didn't want to guess. She turned to leave, but Mallory pulled her back and planted a warm kiss on her lips. Regan broke away, startled. She liked what she was feeling and she knew she shouldn't. She slapped Mallory across the face. Not hard. But a slap all the same. Something about knocking some sense into the girl.

"Why'd you do that?" Mallory's voice quivered, her eyes dilating from the feel of Regan's palm on her hot cheek.

"That's for you as well as for me." Regan noticed the raw emotion behind those tranquil eyes. "If you're in trouble, I'll help. But let's not make any mistakes about why."

STORMY WEATHER

Mercedes had a mountain of paperwork on her desk, bills to pay, twenty unreturned phone calls, a major fund-raiser to organize for the Conservancy, and all she wanted to do was hit the streets and explore the underbelly of this town.

She pulled out Mona Lisa's diary from her dufflebag and flipped through, absorbed by the book's secret thoughts and nasty scribblings. This mounting distrust about her earnest intentions in this wild goose chase was exacerbated by Mona Lisa's strange entries. Did she have a right to dig into Mona Lisa's personal affairs? Was she becoming a Peeping Tom?

Mercedes was addicted. She turned a page. She had earned the privilege.

The world is a dangerous place for someone who plays by the rules.

And then I rushed into the dance-hall and Xuan was there, her eyes like a smoking gun, and Mr. Yamamoto all smiles. I wanted to shoot her. She made me mad. She needed me more than I needed her. Had to remind her of that. That's why I kept it. Payback is cruel. So I sang this song, right there in the middle of the club. Yeah, I was a little drunk. But damn good. Can't resist Fletcher's champagne. Drives Xuan crazy. So it goes like it goes and I fall on my knees, belting out, 'Xuany, oh Xuany how I love you.' Blah, blah, blah. Everyone in stitches. Ha.ha.ha. A few claps. Encore. So I do a little stand-up. Remember, I'm good on my feet.

You've been on your feet too long little sister, the man said. Don't know any other way to stand, I replied. Take a load off, wash down a few, let me tell you 'bout myself, the nice man said. Sure, I replied. I got nuthin' better to do. We sat down and chewed the fat. He shot his wad and I got an earful.

The dark passage is only a few weeks away. Dare I?

Mercedes closed the diary. She wondered what Mona Lisa meant by the dark passage? She had come across something similar scribbled on a piece of rice paper in the dance-card. "The dark passage will be my guiding light." Mercedes pressed her temples. Her head ached. It was hard to focus on work when she was pulled in so many directions. She hoped crossbones and skull wouldn't await her as laurels at the finish line.

After placing calls to several studios and independent producers, she managed to compile an impressive roster of films to highlight during the Million Dollar Movie series. RKO was contributing *Beyond A Reasonable Doubt*, a terrific film noir by Fritz Lang, his last American film, starring Dana Andrews and Joan Fontaine. For the opening event, she had selected David O. Selznick's *What Price Hollywood*, directed by George Cukor.

Mercedes called Carla Simpson at Favored Artists. She quickly learned it was easier getting through to the President of the United States. After fielding questions from the receptionist, the secretary and a voice mail, Mercedes got Carla on the line. Miracles do happen in Hollywood.

"I'm walking into a meeting." Ms. Simpson gave new meaning to the word cool. And arrogant and smart.

"Yes, Mona Lisa's being considered by the agency. Who did you say you were?"

"I'm her manager," Mercedes lied. "Martini & Associates."

Carla had never heard of her or her agency, and she was skeptical when Mercedes kept asking for Mona Lisa's whereabouts.

"I understand she was up for a very exciting part in Spielberg's next movie." Silence on the end of the line. "Ms. Simpson?"

"Listen, you manage your client, you find her. And I can't discuss the picture. It's too early. Script changes are being made."

Maybe Mona Lisa's disappearance had some bizarre connection to a deranged director on a rampage against the system. Never receiving his back-end cut from a sweet deal-making producer, he was on a kidnapping spree, torturing young starlets by forcing them to sit through ten years of his student films on super eight. In black and white, no less.

"Do you think I can come by and discuss—"

"I can't discuss anything until we sign your client. I'm walking into my meeting. Thank you."

Dial tone replaced a civil good-bye. Mercedes could picture Ms. Simpson in a two-piece suit entering a beautifully decorated office where a plethora of suits sat waiting for her as she handed her portable phone to her assistant.

* * *

Outside, the sky was murky and the first drop of rain hit Mercedes on the nose. Her calf-length raincoat covered black stretch pants and a brown sweater. It was nearly four o'clock and she needed to pick up some groceries from Central Market.

She pushed along Broadway, the mass of humanity swirling past her, caught in the peripatetic pace of survival. Who had time to stop and admire the Chicago-styled buildings, Beaux-Art landmarks and the Million Dollar Theater? The locals were too busy scrambling from the pressures of life. Survival was killing them.

Mercedes glanced over at the Bradbury Building and wondered if Pinkerton was hard at work? That was probably a contradiction in terms. A movie crew had blocked off the historic location. Maybe they were doing a remake of *Smiler With A Gun* and Pinkerton was hamming it up on camera. They could use his five o'clock shadow as a prop.

It started to pour. Mercedes slipped into the Grand Central, an airplane hanger of a market, a shopper's heaven awash in funky neon signs. Jones Grain Mill, Eastern Smoked Meats, Del Rey Food, Grand Central Pork Kitchen, and Avalon Sea Food. Designed in the shape of fish, fowl or game, there was a blue swordfish, a large obscene pink weenie and succulent *cabeza del puerco*, all lending marquee value.

Mercedes bargained with vendors, the pulse of primary appetites carried her like a wave along counters stuffed with sliced meats, mounds of whipped butter and vats of creamy *quesos*, pig's heads, *chiles secos*. She was just about to reach for an eggplant, when from the corner of her eye, she spotted a man leering at her. She dropped the eggplant in her basket and steered in the opposite direction.

She could feel the man's eyes on her back and instinctively knew he was following her. Casually, she stopped at Ana Maria's to get a lemonade and turned her head. Sure enough there he was. But this time she noticed a companion by his side. A dog. No, rather a beast. A Doberman the size of a small ship, make that an ocean liner. Mercedes wasn't too fond of dogs. And she wasn't too crazy about the menacing man stalking her every move.

Then the pieces came together. Man and beast. The phone call.
The Mercedes outside her window. Her pursuer had to be none other
than Max Pitts, pissed, no doubt, because she never met him at
Revolver. He probably knew where she worked, how much she
didn't get paid at the Conservancy and the color of her underwear.

The famous fast food stand was packed. It emitted the greasy, but
succulent odor of *carne asada*, *salsa* and deep-fried *pupusas*, a Mexican
medley of edibles she didn't have time to enjoy as she shielded herself
between the ravenous eaters.

She pushed past a gold-toothed Chinese man mumbling to himself
in native tongue. The man with the switchblade eyes and locked jaw
was coming her way. The dog didn't look so happy to see her, but the
man was an avalanche of charm.

Mercedes scrambled past the China Cafe, rounded a corner,
scurried down a short flight of steps and stopped at Howard's Quality
Meats. Dark slabs of liver swam in a pool of blood next to pork
kidneys and beef brains the size of a man's fist. It wasn't a pretty
sight. But far nicer to look at than Max only twenty feet away. His
supercilious grin took on a life of its own as he drew closer and closer.

Pinned against the meat counter, her heart hammering against
her ribs, Mercedes watched his legs cut across the floor like sharp
blades of a scissor. He was inches away and directly under a pink
neon sign, *Cabeza de Puerco*, when his Doberman spotted a seeing-eye
dog in the next aisle. The dog barked and growled at the German
shepherd. Max turned around. In that split second, Mercedes got her
feet to work again and dashed for the exit.

One, two, three more steps and she'd be home free but her black
boots skidded over a thin puddle of water and sawdust and she took
a backward dive. Her coat flapped open, the bag of groceries
suspended in mid-air. Her arms flailed about like a drunken sailor.
Her butt hit the floor right at the tip of her spine.

Blue-jeaned workers lined along a twelve foot bar, Corona-fisted,
raised their arms and voices and shouted, "*guapa, mujer*." So much for
gallantry.

Mercedes tried to move. She was used to waking up from bad
dreams. This one felt awful and it wasn't over. Her groceries were
scattered, the fruit bruised and battered. She managed to stand. The

room swayed, she swung around and bumped into a nasty gray column with nothing better to do but stand there.

The floor was beginning to feel like home the second time around. Only now her head was pounding with a marching band and she could feel her forehead swelling with blood. She was waiting for the nightmare to slip around a dark corner, when a flash of neon snarled at her like a rabid wolf.

She heard a voice, a pretty soothing sound, asking if she was all right. A friend, someone to save her from the market stalker. Her eyesight was fuzzy. Overhead, the pig's snout chortled at her clumsiness. The swordfish was ready to shish-kabob her with its pointed rapier nose while the pink weenie snickered lewdly above her, pleading to have his way with her first.

Clearly she was hallucinating. She allowed herself to be lifted off the floor.

"Drink this," a kind man ordered, putting a paper cup in her hands.

Mercedes did as she was told. The grapefruit juice was cool and sweet. She started to come to her senses. Her head still throbbed, but she could see.

Unfortunately she didn't like what she saw. There, next to her, was the stalker.

"Good to meet you in person. I'm Max," he said. "Max Pitts. You stood me up the other night at Revolver."

Mercedes looked down at the dog before she looked over at the man. She had no choice but to confront him. "I don't like blind dates," she said, surprised to find her voice had returned to her.

Max smiled. His braces were visible. "That's a pretty nasty bump you've got." He shouted to the waitress behind the counter, "*Dame, por favor, un poco de hielo.*" He took the scoop of ice she'd placed in a cup, pulled out a linen handkerchief with the initials MP embossed on all four corners. Dumping the shaved ice in the center, he rolled the cloth in a ball and gave it to Mercedes. She hesitated.

Max pressed it against her swollen forehead. Mercedes closed her eyes for a second and hoped when she opened them, he'd disappear. But he didn't.

"Why are you following me?"

"I like following beautiful women," Max said. "I want that

dance-card." The request was flat and final.

"And I want a million bucks." Mercedes heart was racing.

"I've a short fuse, isn't that so, Butch?" The dog woofed as good dogs woof.

Max slipped a steady hand into the breast pocket of his Lagerfield camel hair coat, drew out an antique silver cigarette case, offered Mercedes a cigarette, lit hers then his, snapped the case shut and returned it from whence it came.

Mercedes examined his outfit. He had good taste. Everything he wore was spotlessly clean, pressed and tailored. He looked as good as a man should when he had the money, time and taste to doll up on a Tuesday afternoon to go shopping.

"Once upon a time," Max recited, blowing out the smoke in staccato beats, his teeth whistling like a tea kettle, "there was a pretty little fox by the name of Mona Lisa. She knew how to sniff around for trouble and she found it. Foxes are clever animals. Keen and crafty. And very adaptable. She's an actress, after all," Max sneered.

"Well this fox appropriated a very valuable antique that happens to belong to me. I paid dearly for it—in more ways than one—and I want it back. Rumor has it that she's given it to you for safekeeping." Max ran a finger along Mercedes' arm. "And I'm sure you have it hidden in some clever place."

Mercedes tried to yank her arm free, but Max wasn't letting go. Butch growled.

"If you cooperate and give it to me without a fuss, I could make it worth your while." Max smiled, his eyes shifted to the left and right.

Mercedes laughed. "You're wasting my time. I Fed-Xed it out of state and it'll stay there until Mona Lisa returns, unharmed."

Max was thoughtful. "You're bluffing."

Mercedes shrugged her shoulders. "Where is she?"

"She's making a date with an angel and if I don't get what I want, she'll find herself necking in the back seat of heaven." There was a sick grin on his face that matched his tone of voice. "You realize that for the sake of dramatic effect, I'm mixing metaphors. Mona Lisa wouldn't know what an angel looked like if she bumped into a pair of wings."

"Mona Lisa's not a saint? That's a revelation. I'm shocked and you're a lousy storyteller." Mercedes ground out her cigarette on a tin ashtray.

Max twisted his lips from side to side as if he were exercising them. Then his face grew grave. He tightened his hands, the knuckles turned white, and when he spoke his voice was colder than winter. Mercedes stared into his dead gray eyes, the color of a Bonito fish.

He grabbed her arm and squeezed hard. "Your little angel came whining to me once to help her out of a jam. I put her in touch with a buddy of mine. Took care of this creep, a movie producer who promised her a part in exchange for a preview of her talents; when he didn't deliver she arranged to make sure he wouldn't walk for a few months. All she had to do was nod her pretty head and it was a done deal."

Mercedes refused to believe him. "*Quid pro quo*, Max. Six months ago Mona Lisa threw me a surprise party for my birthday. Made me feel like a kid again. We rode bumper cars on the pier."

Max sneered. "How precious."

Mercedes was furious. "She had a special birthday cake designed for me, in the shape of the Pan Pacific. But you wouldn't understand these things." Mercedes' head throbbed as all these emotions crammed to the surface.

"You realize how ridiculous you sound?"

Mercedes reached for the glass of grapefruit juice and flung it in his face. "Not nearly as ridiculous as you look."

Max winced. Butch barked wildly.

Mercedes heard a clap of thunder and tried to wrench herself from his iron-clad grip, but he held tight.

"Don't yell," he ordered, wiping the residue of the fresh squeezed juice from his face. He shoved her toward the exit.

Rain hit the sidewalk on Hill like a sheet of bullets. It was angry rain. Rain that knew the world's troubles couldn't be washed away with water, but tried all the same. It streamed down the street like a river, carrying along debris, cans and soiled newspapers. It wouldn't give up. Neither would Mercedes.

She was soaked. Her head ached and her back throbbed. At the corner she could barely see two feet in front of her. The screech of a car. Max grabbed tight. Pain seared through her body.

"Mercedes," a woman yelled above the din. A horn honked.

Mercedes wiped her face with the back of her hand to get a better look.

"That bitch," Max said. Butch barked.

Stopping traffic was a black Jeep. A door opened and out jumped Samantha. She was dry, confident and as beautiful as the Taj Mahal.

"I'll take over from here," Samantha yelled out to Max as she escorted Mercedes to the jeep and pushed her inside.

Samantha jumped in, rolled up her window and took off. Butch barked, Max leered, the rain against the Jeep's window giving his face the inhuman grid of a computer graphic.

"Wait a minute." Mercedes felt like a doll thrown from one con man to the next. But Samantha wasn't waiting. She peeled down Fourth, swung a sharp right on Broadway, came up round Fifth and hung a left on Hill.

Mercedes was a wreck. Her hair was plastered to her swollen forehead, her eyes runny with mascara. Samantha looked like she stepped from the pages of a new wave comic strip, dressed in a slick black rain jacket, black leather gloves, not a hair out of place. Her lips a pale shade of melon.

"Where are you taking me?" Mercedes held her hand over a bruise that felt as large as a golf ball.

Samantha turned and smiled. Steadily, the rain beat against the windows, the roof of the Jeep, echoing the staccato hammering in Mercedes' head. Actually it was more like a choir of demons bellowing and howling as Max, Butch and the outside world receded into the distance, disappearing all together until Mercedes was lost in the reservoir of Samantha's smile. Sinister and haunting. Brutal and beautiful at the same time.

STRAIGHT THROUGH THE HEART

Lambert and Summers, an architectural development firm, acquired the Biltmore Hotel in 1973 and sunk about forty-five million dollars to refurbish and restore the spectacular landmark to its former glory.

The Gallery Bar was dark and intimate, the cherry and mahogany furniture newly polished. The Baroque Cupid painted on the ceiling had an obscene smile curled on its lips as it floated above in that haven of old world elegance. It would have been a perfect afternoon to sip an aperitif before dinner, had Mercedes not been taken there against her will.

And although Mercedes had no business sitting at the bar in the Biltmore Hotel with her kidnapper, she admired Samantha's taste in watering holes.

Samantha clicked her glass of Glenlivet, no ice, against Mercedes' cognac. Her face was a study in contrasts. The lips were tight, withholding, but the eyes were available, hungry. Their intensity frightened Mercedes.

"We need to talk." Mercedes tried to run a hand through the tangled mess of wet hair on her head. A single strand refused to cooperate. It fell over her left eye like a question mark.

"About what?" Samantha looked lovely and every bit a part of the surroundings.

"About that charming man back there. About murder. In short, about Mona Lisa." Mercedes crossed her legs.

Samantha frowned. "And I was hoping you just wanted to say thanks."

Mercedes felt her temperature rising. "How did you know I'd be at the market?" She suspected Max and Samantha had rigged that little performance.

"I know everything I need to know about you."

"Then tell me what was Max planning to do with me?"

Samantha popped a glazed Brazil nut in her mouth. "Put the scare in you. He's after what Redlite's after. Mainly the dance-card. And since he knows how close you are to Mona Lisa, he thinks you may even know where she's hiding out."

Mercedes didn't reply.

"Or maybe he just has problems picking up girls. This is his way of getting friendly."

"And yours?" Mercedes voice was thick with sarcasm.

"What's on your mind?" Samantha scrutinized Mercedes.

Mercedes' spirit crumbled. She was thinking about the thousands of luminaries who had graced the Biltmore. And she thought about Mona Lisa. A woman who belonged in an elegant place like this, but who made her last phone call from a dump like the Clark. About the double life, the lies, and alibis. And then she thought about how she felt when Samantha was around. She felt charged, energized, more alive, as if she were on the threshold of some exciting discovery. These feelings frightened her. She wasn't sure she wanted her neat life shattered by this tempest.

"I'm wondering whether I like you." Mercedes hadn't given the words permission to escape her mouth, but they did.

"Don't wonder too hard." Samantha put a damp napkin on Mercedes' throbbing head. "You're in bad enough shape as it is." Samantha squeezed Mercedes' thigh. "But, off the record, I could like you . . . more than I'd care to." Samantha looked at herself in the girandole mirror above the bar.

"But I could get over it. I always do." The voice was a cool, cozy drawl full of insolence.

Mercedes tapped her cigarette on the table. "You're pretty sure of yourself."

Samantha pulled the cigarette from her fingers, lit it and returned the smoking stick to Mercedes. "I've earned my ego."

"And your reputation, no doubt."

Samantha threw her a stone cold look.

"You broke into my house." The memory of her vandalized home infuriated her.

Samantha shrugged. "Believe what you want to believe." She polished off her drink.

She was incorrigible. Mercedes pictured Samantha blindfolded. A pair of sheer black stockings binding her brazen eyes, hands tied behind her back, a cigarette dangling between her parched lips. The heat, unbearable: the high noon sun on their backs. Mercedes carried a derringer. As she neared Samantha, she untied the blindfold, plucked the cigarette from her lips and threw it to the ground. She snaked her body up against her prisoner and kissed her. A deep-throated moan broke the silence. Mercedes moved her hand over Samantha's breasts, along her belly and down between her legs, then she left and walked off into the dying sunset.

"Why did you leave me there?" Mercedes snapped out of her daydream.

"You were out cold. I had some business to tend to."

"At two in the morning?"

"I'm not a nine-to-fiver." A faint smile curled her lips.

"Who's the Carmen Miranda in your room?"

Samantha smiled. "My, you're just full of questions, aren't you?"

Mercedes stood up. "And you're wasting my time." She started to leave, but Samantha wouldn't let her.

Mercedes stared her down. "Give it to me straight."

"Straight through the heart? You don't want it straight. You just want to hear what you want to hear about me. I'm not so bad. I used to work. I had a profession. I was as legitimate as you."

Mercedes laughed. "You're a regular girl scout."

Samantha grew quiet. She lit a cigarette and let the smoke waft between them. "At least I tried. I used to be an archaeologist, a damn good one. But I got tired of reconstructing a past nobody appreciated."

"The stakes were just too small for you."

Samantha smiled sadly. "Yeah."

"You sold out," Mercedes voice was softer now.

"I decided to do what made sense to me," she said, her voice regaining its edge. "I like dealing with tangibles, expensive tangibles. I decided to buy a future."

"So you invested with Fletcher. You'd better fire your broker."

Samantha shrugged her shoulders. "I'm sorry about the other night. Next time I won't leave you alone."

Mercedes felt her stomach knot. "There won't be a next time."

"Oh yes there will." Samantha slipped her warm hand into Mercedes'.

Waves shot through Mercedes, huge breakers, white-capped. "How do I know you haven't hurt Mona Lisa?"

"That's not my style. It's Fletcher's, but I'm prepared to help you find her, before she does."

Mercedes hesitated. "What's in it for you?"

Samantha paused a few seconds before replying. "You. And the satisfaction of getting my hands on something Fletcher's dying to have."

"You're planning to double cross her?"

"I don't think I'll have any problem sleeping at night . . . not with you around."

Mercedes wished her heart would stop its obstinate pounding. This woman was all her very worst nightmares rolled into one. The overhead Cupid aimed its poison-tipped arrow and was shooting her way dead center.

Samantha broke the silence. "I'll find Mona Lisa for you. All you have to do is give me the antique."

"You take me for a fool, don't you." Mercedes felt like an emotional yo-yo.

"I'll take you anyway you want me to, as long as you're good. And somehow, I know you'll be good." Samantha brushed the question mark of hair from Mercedes' eye.

Mercedes stiffened.

"You're still mad?"

"I've been mad ever since I met you." Mercedes got up, the arrow in her heart smarting like hell.

Samantha grabbed her hand. "Good."

* * *

Walking into the shabby lobby of the Clark Hotel after coming from the dark, cool splendor of the Biltmore had its impact. Like a jackrabbit shocked out of its wits in front of a semi going seventy miles an hour.

"I'll pay in advance," Samantha told the desk clerk. It was the same thin young man Mercedes had interrogated before.

"I want the room . . . ." Mercedes didn't finish her sentence.

"Yeah, yeah. Room 46. They oughta rope it off and make it a historic site."

Samantha looked at Mercedes and smiled. "I'm not afraid of a little blood." She took the keys from the manager and headed for the elevator.

The corridor was dark and drab. Mercedes needed a good hot bath, about a two hour soak, a massage and a nice, clean bed with a fluffy pillow that manufactured pretty dreams.

They arrived at 46. Samantha slipped in the key and they entered. The room was threadbare and the walls, once green, were now a depressing shade of mustard. It was a room for the lonely of heart and empty of pocket.

Samantha stood in front of the large window. It was still raining, but not as hard. They had a clear view of the rooftop of the red-brick building below whose neon sign, JESUS SAVES, flashed intermittently into the room.

Mercedes navigated the room. Next to the chipped dresser she noticed a large water stain. Moving closer to inspect, she lifted the carpet that smelled like ammonia and vomit. Luckily the cleaning service didn't do a good job cleaning up. There, encrusted on the ancient molding, Mercedes saw what was unmistakably blood stains.

She shivered. Samantha moved over to inspect. Both women looked at each other. The impact of their quest hitting them hard. This was no game. Someone was out for the kill.

The two women sat on chairs facing each other. It felt like the final showdown. A small lamp glowed with ancient dust and dead hopes.

A slumming angel, Mercedes pulled off her raincoat and let it fall to the floor. By now her hair had dried and the humidity caused the loose curls to frizz.

"So Mona Lisa was in this room. She got shot, escaped and you haven't any idea where she is?"

Mercedes nodded her head. "I don't have the full story, maybe I never will."

Samantha looked out the window dotted with rain drops. "I like your loyalty. She's lucky to have you as a friend. She doesn't have too many."

Samantha removed her coat, then slipped off her wet boots and made herself as comfortable as she could on the heap of a lump called a king-size bed. Her hair was dark and shiny, strong like twine. "You want to know about Mona Lisa?

Mercedes took a deep breath. "Yes."

Samantha lit up a cigarette and started her story. "Before I skipped town, about a year ago, Mona Lisa was working some gig, I think it was a low-budget movie up north in Menlo Park. She'd come in for the weekend and I ran into her at one of these underground sex clubs."

Mercedes arched an eyebrow. She'd heard about these clubs, even tried finding Orgasm one night, but got lost and never made it. She guessed she really didn't have the appetite for that sort of thing.

Samantha continued, modulating her speech with careful glances at Mercedes.

"She'd had a bit to drink, and now that I think of it, I'd guess she was coked up. She had that edgy nervousness. I remember thinking she was scared. I wasn't sure of what. And then she started babbling on. At first I didn't really pay too much attention, there was much to catch my eye, but I sensed the quiet desperation in her voice. I knew she was in danger."

"What do you mean?"

Samantha looked at Mercedes before replying. "I thought, here is a woman who could kill herself if she thought about it for more than a minute. I suspect Mona Lisa was too possessed by her infatuation with Hollywood to give in to the inevitable."

"The inevitable?"

Samantha took a deep drag of the cigarette before answering. "Dozens of starlets have gone off the deep end with drugs, booze, bad men, lousy publicity. We only hear the occasional Rita Hayworth and Monroe tale of woe. Probably too many to count. Anyway, there we were, drinking and smoking and checking out the action when I noticed Fletcher walk into the bar. Mona Lisa darted to attention like some well-trained dog. Suddenly she wasn't so morose. She didn't even put out her cigarette, just left me there to nurse my drink."

It was highly unlikely Samantha was alone for long.

"I watched them talk to the owner of the dive and then a man came in, a very good-looking man. He checked out Mona Lisa, nodded and the four of them disappeared behind the manager's door. I was a little bored. And I knew enough about Fletcher's `deals' to be concerned Mona Lisa might be getting in over her head."

Mercedes removed her sweater. Her white t-shirt stuck to her skin. She wanted to tell Samantha to stop, but she had to know what happened that night.

Before Samantha continued, she ground out her cigarette and cushioned herself in the bed. Her eyes traveled over Mercedes' body, lingering on her breasts. She ran a dry tongue over her lips. There was a war going on behind the eyes.

Mercedes felt the heat rising in her face and jumped up to open the window, but it was painted shut. The rain had picked up. A crack of lightning bruised the darkened sky.

"It didn't take me long to find another way to get back there." Samantha drew out the words. "I came up quietly behind this red curtain. I heard someone whimpering in pain. Not pretending to be in pain. But someone really in pain. I remember I got this sick feeling in my stomach. I knew this was a sex club and that the sex was rough and wild, if you wanted it that way, but something always sets me on edge when a woman gets beaten by a man. And I didn't think Mona Lisa was in it for the pleasure. She'd already complained how broke she was so I knew Fletcher had set up the deal and Mona Lisa was there to put out."

There were beads of sweat on Mercedes' face. She looked around for an air-conditioner, a portable fan, a breeze. But the air was as still as death. "Go on," Mercedes said, her voice sounding as if it belonged to someone else.

Samantha's body was now bathed in the soft, hellish light from the JESUS SAVES sign. Her face took on the features of one of Matisse's odalisques. Or maybe Mercedes was trying to place her in a more aesthetic context. And by extension, herself.

"The room was dark. A few candles burned and S&M accoutrements hung on the wall. The man had been stripped naked and he was kneeling between 'Mistress' Mona Lisa's legs. She had removed her skirt and wore nothing but a white lace bridal garter around her thigh. She was shaved. And he was kissing her knees."

Mercedes walked to window again and looked out at the downtown landscape. The pounding in her bruised head seemed to drown out some of the thunder in the sky. Everything she thought familiar about the city now appeared foreign, haggard, in need of a facelift. She turned around to look at Samantha on the bed, but she was right behind her.

Mercedes felt herself weaken all over. When their lips met, it was as if warm blood gurgled from their mouths. Their tongues were hot and wet and the room exploded with secrets of the damned. Samantha smoothed her hands over Mercedes' body. A crack of lightning illuminated Samantha's face. Suddenly, it appeared harsh and mean.

Mercedes broke away. "Then what happened?"

Samantha returned to the bed. Mercedes lit a cigarette, the rain lashing against the window as she sat on the chipped radiator.

"It went on like that for quite a while. And then she whipped him. But this wasn't the kid stuff they did outside in the other rooms, you know with fake whips and smirks on their faces and bored S&M masters saying 'Eat shit, dog,' while flossing their nails with that vacant expression in their eyes like they'd loaned their brains to science."

Mercedes felt her heart thumping. "Yeah," she whispered hoarsely. The darkness crept in the room uninvited.

"This was a whip with small gold nails tied to the end. And I remember the look of pain on this man's face and I saw his bloody back and the glint in Fletcher's eye as she watched. I guess I forgot to look at Mona Lisa, 'cause when I did, our eyes caught; she knew I was there behind the curtain. I felt a chill. I knew that had he asked, she would have beaten him to death."

Mercedes ground out her cigarette, moved into the room and crumbled on the bed. Samantha kneaded her back with her strong fingers. Again, their lips met. But this time Samantha could taste the tears.

They lay there, quiet for what seemed hours, but was only minutes. Flashes of the story played in Mercedes' head like an old movie reel.

Thunder rumbled in the distance and the night brought a new smell to the room. Samantha yanked off Mercedes t-shirt and pulled Mercedes' face against hers and kissed her hard.

Sweat trickled down Mercedes' forehead. Samantha was a thousand pounds of flesh crashing down on her; her head throbbed, blood rushed to the temples and all around the room's walls grew closer and closer.

Belt buckles flew open. The sound of whips cracked in Mercedes' imagination. Her eyes closed. She saw Mona Lisa kneel in prayer, then rise, grab a whip and crack it hard across a man's shoulders.

That's when the floor caved in. She felt her own nails dig into Samantha's naked back and heard herself whimper in the dark, blood-stained room.

FULL MOON, EMPTY ARMS

The martini was dry. Very dry. The way martinis are supposed to be. Just the exact ratio of Bombay Gin and Cinzano Vermouth. Four to one. And cold. Cold enough to put a smile on the pimento in an olive.

Mercedes sat in her living room, drink in hand, waiting for Samantha to arrive. She looked around her neat and orderly environment. Everything was as it had always been, only something was missing. She felt restless, edgy. Complacency no longer suited her. Before all this started, she had no problem sitting home on a Saturday night, watching videos, reading, painting the study, listening to Enigma, Cole Porter or Patsy Cline.

Now she felt as if she were crawling out of her skin. It was as if someone had invited her to a peepshow and she'd gotten a real taste of life on the edge and she found it hard to go back to her old way of living.

There had been a lot to digest and she was trying to integrate the story Samantha had told her about Mona Lisa. Hardly a prude, Mercedes had had many lovers, male as well as female. She'd experienced the yin and yang of both species. Women were her companions of choice. Yet she'd never really pushed to the edge, the way Mona Lisa did. Her love life had been as consciously designed as her home.

Samantha, on the other hand, was as wild as Mona Lisa. A she-devil, a creature predestined to live out a life on the sly, artful dodger of hearth and home, she was a vagabond, a petty criminal with the soul of a parasite.

If only she wasn't so goddamn infectious. Mercedes sipped her martini. The fire roared, the flames licked the air like dozens of whips. They would be her handmaidens on this journey to hell.

Mercedes studied her reflection in the window. Her lips were matte red and her eyes were etched with bister. The hair was an unbridled magenta. The black dress she wore was tight with a scalloped neckline. Fishnets escaped into a pair of black-bowed heels. She was ready to take on the night.

The full moon, 238,857 miles away from the earth, smiled complicity. It knew she was there, dressed in ceremonial garb, lying in wait for her prey.

Samantha was an hour late. The memory of their lovemaking seemed like a dream, a wonderful hot, dangerous drag along a hairpin road that knew no waking state. Mercedes grabbed a cigarette to keep her hands busy. Anything to stave off the full throttle of desire. She took a deep drag, pulling the smoke in her lungs, the taste of tobacco mixing with the sting of gin.

She pulled out Mona Lisa's diary, hungry to absorb any details she may have overlooked. She flipped through the pages and read the words that burned like a brand on her heart. Images seemed to disintegrate into ashes on her fingers. Her mouth was suddenly dry, even the gin couldn't quench her thirst. She read on as the clock ticked on the mantelpiece.

Sing the traffic of never getting there. Rush hour, caught in a jam. The hot air rises from the belly of the city and suffocates the corporate townhouses, fingering the windows of success, leaving behind a thumbprint of evidence. Sleep city under your blanket of ambition. I will cover you in my arms and cradle you like a newborn child. I have bitten the umbilical cord that connects you to my womb. The blood is bitter.

The 24th district has been evacuated. Women and children must run for their lives. Little Tokyo lies under the ashes of burnt money. Will all my dreams be scorched under the raging fire of the sun?

Leaves rustled outside. Mercedes thought she heard a noise. She looked out the window. The street was empty and dark. She took another sip of the martini. Hoping the alcohol would relax her, she found it had an energizing effect.

Mercedes closed her eyes. Swimming in her imagination Mona Lisa stalked the streets, larger than life, like the Fifty-Foot Woman. Between skyscrapers, glass towers and terra-cotta hallmarks, Mona Lisa high-heeled it along Broadway, passersby gaping at the magnitude of her form as she ran her white-gloved hand along the dirty rooftops, in search of herself. Who was this woman? A friend, an enemy, a thief, a hooker, an imposter? And where was she?

I sleep in the bed of one night stands, holding on to a pillow the size of a ravioli, my heart shriveled like a prune. I wait for the man behind the Shoji screen to charge full steam ahead. Instead, he walks out calm and naked, his modesty draped over the screen like a silk stocking, a 35mm Nikon camera strapped around his neck. He insists on taking my picture. They are snapshots of the impossible. He is a worm on the sheets, crawling inside me. I want to kill him off. I run for a Singer sewing machine before he crawls out. Sitting by my mother's slippered foot on a warm, rainy afternoon on Avenue P, I watch as she pedals for a living; the thread bobs up and down, the needle stitches and I beg her to sew me a new life.

The doorbell rang. She quickly slipped the diary in its hiding place under the sofa and ran to open the door. She was banking on Samantha being there, but it was Regan. Annoyance stitched across her handsome face like a mended sleeve.

"You stood me up." Regan brushed past and entered the house.

Mercedes suddenly remembered they'd agreed to meet last night, but by the time she'd returned from Jezebel's, it was too late and she hadn't bothered to call.

"Sorry." Mercedes peered outside, but there was no one in sight.

"You look as if you're expecting company," Regan said, eyeing Mercedes' outfit and the empty martini glass.

Regan accepted a drink. "I'm getting mixed signals from Fletcher's house. I think something's goin' down and I'm not sure what to do. I do know Samantha's been at the house."

Mercedes took a breath. "Max came after me today. She got me away from him. I'm probably as mixed up as you are."

Regan smiled. "She's stringing you along, sweetheart. Trust me. It's a set-up and it looks like you've taken the bait."

Mercedes knew she was right. It was midnight. Samantha wasn't going to show up.

Regan sensed her restlessness. "Did I mention how beautiful you look?"

Mercedes shook her head.

Regan moved close and scooped Mercedes in her arms. The kiss was confident and warm.

Mercedes liked the solicitude and almost caught herself enjoying the foreplay, but now wasn't the time. She pulled away.

Regan cocked her head, picked up her glass and polished off the martini. "I'll let you off the hook for now, but I'll be back, gorgeous." She squeezed Mercedes' arm.

As soon as the door closed behind Regan, Mercedes knew she couldn't go to sleep. She waited till the engine from Regan's bike died, then killed the lights, locked the door and got into her car.

With the moon to guide her, she drove down part of the twenty-six mile stretch of Sunset Boulevard, the wind cooling her hot cheeks. She pulled into the driveway of Sunset Plaza, drove down the ramp and parked in the back of a half-empty shopping center. She shut the engine and watched the city from the precipice.

The view was magnificent. The night was clear. And the city sparkled below. But not for long. Mercedes saw a nest of vipers, hissing and sucking at the city's bosom. There before her in the moonlight drenching the city like acid rain were madmen, Madonnas and murderers.

The city had betrayed Mercedes. It was a greedy, hungry town feasting on its own tail. She wanted the beauty back. The innocence. She wanted to deny the knowledge she had of Mona Lisa. She wanted Samantha to come after her, but she hadn't.

Mercedes rolled down the window to let in some air. She starred into the barrel of a revolver. Redlite's stubby finger coiled against the trigger.

At first her mind went black with shock, followed by a second of lucid reality. Her head snapped back. She was scared.

"Open the door and slide over," Redlite growled. "We're going for a little ride." He was wearing a cowboy hat.

Mercedes didn't budge.

"Let's move it." Redlite stuck his hand in the window and unlocked the door.

Mercedes' hand shot out and rolled up the window, catching his wrist between glass and steel. She thought she heard bone crack.

"You fucking bitch, let go." His face contorted and his lips puckered like he'd swallowed something dirty and foul.

She turned on the ignition. His fingers groped for her face, the nail of his pinky, long and sharp, lashed the skin below her eye. She felt the sting of a cut and again the blackness was swimming before her eyes. Outside, his arm flailed around in the air, the gun attached like a vise to his hand.

Mercedes slammed the car in reverse, dragging him along for the ride, then floored the gas pedal and took off about twenty feet. She screeched to a halt and opened the window. He pulled his hand out and toppled to the ground, his face scraping pavement as he spun like a top.

She sped out of the parking lot, hung a right on Sunset and peeled down the boulevard. The moon seemed to howl and the stars were bullet holes in the sky. Sinewy clouds cast a net like concertina wire over the blackness and in less than four minutes Mercedes had pulled up in front of her house.

Next time she'd check her rear view mirror. Next time she wouldn't go out alone so late. Now she knew what it was like to live like a criminal. Someone always watching her. She wanted excitement. And goddamnit, she'd gotten it. Now maybe she could sink into her bed, pull the covers over her head and pretend all this was a bad dream, a dream that would go away as soon as she closed her eyes.

She locked the doors, closed the blinds and tried to calm down. Her teeth were chattering.

The moonlight was ruthless, it poured in through the Venetian blinds. Suddenly a shadow, heavy and solid, cut across the room. Mercedes swung around. Her arm shot out and grabbed the poker by the fireplace. This time she wasn't taking any chances. She swung blindly, but the intruder was too quick and blocked the blow.

Samantha stood there like a con fresh out of prison. "You should get in the habit of closing your blinds. People might get the wrong impression of you." Her voice was cold.

Mercedes glared. She couldn't see straight. Her mind hurled back to the Chateau Marmont, to the Clark, to Samantha's irreverent knack for showing up at the right place at the wrong time.

"Get out." Mercedes voice was clear and strong, nothing like the mush she felt inside. "I'm calling the police."

Mercedes walked to the phone, but Samantha was right behind her.

"You don't want to do that." Samantha clutched Mercedes' hips and pulled up her dress a few inches.

"What happened to you?" Samantha ran her finger along the bruise on Mercedes' face.

"It's a paper cut." Mercedes didn't want Samantha to know more than she did already.

"You're lying."

Mercedes laughed.

"Listen, I'm sorry I barged in." Her voice was deep and husky. "It's just that seeing you kissing Regan like that. I didn't like it. I drove away, thinking I'd leave you alone, but I couldn't, so I came back. And you were gone."

Mercedes tried to pry her hands off her body, but it did no good. She whirled around. "So you break into my house again?"

"You changed the front lock, but not the back. You make it too easy." Samantha pressed up against Mercedes. "Regan's kiss," she said softly, "was counterfeit."

Samantha pressed her lips to Mercedes neck. She held her in place, allowing her to fold into the strength of her arm. Their eyes locked.

Samantha's eyes were serious, filled with ancient longing. "One kiss," she said, grinding her hips into Mercedes, "but this time make me believe in love." There was an ache in her voice.

The attraction between them was as real and tangible as the city outside. Mercedes could wallow in it for a few centuries. She could feel the sinews and arteries of this thing called love.

No matter who Samantha was, or what she had done, no matter how Mercedes had been violated, she knew that if they made love tonight their fate would be sealed. She still had a chance to escape. To be free.

Mercedes never gambled. She let Samantha kiss her. Her heart pumped and beat like hot hands against a conga and blood coursed through her arms to her fingertips. Getting out of this would be a long shot. Ten to one.

Make that fifty.

*　*　*

From inside the bathroom, Mercedes could make out Samantha's naked silhouette on the bed. The bedroom flickered with candles and the scent of night blooming jasmine lingered in the air. She fingered the Pond's Cold Cream jar, knowing the dance-card was hidden inside. She smiled. That was her trump card. Something Samantha couldn't take from her.

"What are you looking at?" Samantha's voice broke her meditation.

"Nothing," Mercedes replied, as she closed the bathroom door behind her and stepped into the glowing room. She warmed to the game. Her recently acquired taste for deceit and deception had less to do with any desire on her part to do the wrong thing. It was the charge she got. It set her teeth on edge.

Mercedes moved closer, her naked feet slowly dragging along the cold wooden floor. She unzipped her dress and just let it hang there loose on her body like an invitation she wasn't sure she'd send.

Samantha's eyes narrowed and she patted the bed. "Don't make me beg." Her body was long and elegant and as a sleek as an ivory-carved statue.

Mercedes lit another candle, tall, tapered, white. The flame shot up along her pale face, the three inch scratch visible, the illumination as vibrant as a Georges de la Tour canvas. The dress slipped further down her arms. The straps to her black lace corset were visible. Her perfume rose to the surface of her skin.

"Tell me that again."

When she shifted the weight of her body, Samantha's taut breasts were like armor on her chest. "Don't make me beg." She shot up and lunged for Mercedes.

The hot wax from the candle scorched Mercedes' hand.

Samantha grabbed the candle and doused it in her drink. The thick, gray smoke smelled like the inside of a church.

Mercedes swallowed hard. With both hands Samantha ripped off the dress, pitching it across the room. It landed on the mannequin's head.

"Keep on the corset."

The body on the bed was a wild animal, her claws raked Mercedes' hair. She pulled her down on the soft bed, pushing her shoulders into the sheets, pressing them hard as if trying to leave an imprint in cement, mud or clay.

A dark and nasty storm swept through the room and along with it the dried leaves, the twigs, the emotional detritus of the past. Mercedes was an amnesiac. She forgot the dozens of faces, a veritable frieze of ex-lovers. She forgot everything worth forgetting, even her own name. It was a pleasure excursion down a bank of water simply for the sight, smell and feel of a city.

The miniscule beads and worsted cotton on the corset roughed up against Samantha's skin, sloughing the thin layer of epidermis as blood rushed to the surface and left crimson welts along her stomach, thighs and chest.

Samantha bared her teeth. "You're beginning to like this, aren't you?"

Mercedes moaned. "No."

Samantha kissed Mercedes hard, but not as hard as Mercedes returned the kiss.

The low modulated sounds of a tenor sax and the cool blue notes tore across the room, picking up speed, growing louder, horns joining in the syncopated play of hipster jazz.

Samantha bore down again like some powerful vulture, nibbling the ear lobe, sucking the neck and all the while Mercedes knew that this was the moment to stop, to put an end to this rabid passion and get away scott free. But Samantha's hand slipped down her corset and then there was that feeling of invasion. Her nipples hardened and the sound advice receded as all good intentions usually do.

"You love this, don't you?

"No." The word again slipped out of Mercedes' mouth like a painful groan.

"Yes, come sit like this. *Mijita, rica.* You want it, don't you? Here, kiss me here." Her hands stroked Mercedes' thighs as if they were a good luck charm. Arcane words spilled from her mouth in another language, maybe three.

Her words were blades pricking the skin. There was a swelling in Mercedes' womb. Her body contorted, her head moved from side to side and her red hair shot out like a starfish on the white pillowcase.

Samantha slithered on top of Mercedes, scraping her body against the rough material, a human pumice. Her hand traveled down between Mercedes' legs and ripped apart the three snaps hooking her corset. She clutched onto the land of milk and honey, her forefinger rigid, then she pulled away and looked down at Mercedes.

Shadows snaked in and out of Samantha's eyes and her face grew hard and mean. Intimacy had a way of doing that. She wrapped her hands around Mercedes' neck and tightened, the thumbs pressing against each side of her Adam's apple.

A flicker of fear drafted across Mercedes' eyes, but then the grip loosened.

"I'm crazy, you know that . . . ."

Mercedes swallowed the rest of Samantha's words like a communion wafer; she gnawed at her mouth as her lover's hands dragged along the length of her body, then the two of them rolled over on the bed.

Mercedes' legs wrapped tight around her Samantha, but she wouldn't be constricted like that.

She tore off the corset and created her own map as she licked her way from elbows, to stomach to knees, till she buried her face between Mercedes' thighs. A rash of wild strawberries, her fingers picked at the ripe fruit, plundered her field, demarking the territory as her own.

Mercedes ripped the sheet and tore the pillowcase with her teeth.

"Oh God," shot through the room like shooting star.

Then a profound silence. The deep wheezing of breath in starved lungs.

Somewhere a murmur of love? Or just a siren wailing outside in the florid counterpoint of city noise.

"Kiss me again." She was begging.

Samantha leaned over and caught Mercedes' warm breath in her mouth, as if coveting her life force in a ceramic jar to be buried in a sacred tomb deep beneath the earth.

The two women lay there, waiting for the moon to orchestrate their next move, their bodies swollen from desire, their lovemaking, one long sob in the night.

THREE

CLUB SAYONARA

　　　　A moon half gone hung in the sky, reluctant to disappear behind the few clouds lumbering nearby.　It was nine o'clock on a Saturday night and Mercedes was headed downtown to Club Sayonara.　She felt clear-headed and confident.

　　Her red hair, rinsed a deep brunette and slicked back off her face, was gelled in place.　Her oxford shoes matched a charcoal gray suit. A high-collared green and white striped silk shirt and thin, black worsted knit tie completed the masculine ensemble.　She wore no jewelry, no make-up, no perfume.

　　She was dressed as a man.

　　If she was going to play the part, she had to dress the part. Infiltrating Club Sayonara wouldn't be easy as a woman; as a man, it'd be that much simpler.

　　Stopping at a light on Sunset Boulevard and Vine, her window half opened, Mercedes spotted a few streetwalkers, painted daisies of the pavement, as they swung their purses, stood on four-inch heels and eyed the cars passing.　A foot-stomping pimp gestured in anger over his girl's take for the evening, his stale breath rising like Lazarus on this streets of misfits.

　　A pretty Latina came up to the car window.　"*Hola, guapo*. Fifty for you tonight."　Her eyes were coated with a purple liner and her lips were hot pink.

　　Mercedes could smell liquor on the woman's breath.　Her eyes were tired and bored.　She was no older than twenty-two.　"Not tonight," Mercedes replied, dropping her voice a few octaves.　The light changed; she turned left on Vine and headed south to Olympic.

　　Caught between the gridlock of poverty and affluence, Mona Lisa had struggled to surface above the muck of her past.　Yearning to escape from a life on the streets, she was just one more victim lost in the shuffle.

Mercedes felt a pang of loneliness. A week had passed without a word from Samantha. A few roses would have been nice, maybe a card. She stared in the rear view mirror and caught the smile in her eyes. To expect *anything* from a woman like Samantha would be plain stupid.

* * *

Mercedes swung past the Convention Center, Club Paradise and the Latin Lady where low rent cantinas and flea bag hotels marked the area. Pedestrians took on the complexion of the streets. Shabby, tired, worn-down like most of the buildings in the district, they walked along Olympic Boulevard blending into the nightscape, stalkers with no place to go but around in circles. When the sidewalk ends, the street only leads to another dirty sidewalk and soon they've got the cement beat down pat.

Club Sayonara wasn't hard to find. A small trail of cars pulled into a parking entrance off Nagoya. The lot was packed. The smell of tarmac from the sidewalk and cheap booze wafting from exhaust fans in the back of the club, made Mercedes queasy. Her nerves were reved up and she was keyed for action.

Good Friday was easy to spot, wearing a three-piece suit he'd outgrown about five years ago. The pants a little too short, the jacket a little too tight, he pursed his lips as if to say, "You sure you wanna go through with this harebrained scheme of yours," but before she could push him through the doorway, someone caught her eye.

It was a man, a man she'd seen before. A man who looked good standing under a street lamp with a cigarette burning between his fingers. If the face didn't give him away, the black trenchcoat and beret did.

Pinkerton was all dressed up with no better place to go than Club Sayonara. Something didn't compute. He looked straight at her and there was no sign of recognition. Mercedes could like this a lot.

A burly, bald-headed muscleman clad in a polyester suit the color of butternut squash blocked the entrance of this watering hole for the thirsty who never missed the last call. The expression behind the eyes was as putrid as his attire. He wasn't moving.

Good Friday glanced at Mercedes. She took a twenty dollar bill out of her pocket and passed it to the human bulldog. The man smiled and moved to the side to let them pass.

As soon as they pushed inside, a pretty girl in a green taffeta dress greeted them. "What's your name, handsome?" she asked Mercedes.

"Nick Charles," Mercedes replied, as she caught a glimpse of the black trenchcoat slip into the men's room. She knew she couldn't hold her liquor as well as her namesake, but if she was lucky there'd be plenty of Noras to feed her information.

The girl checked her out. "Two first names. Double your pleasure, huh?" Marci clutched a small beaded bag in her hand. "And you?" She looked at Good Friday with less interest.

"I'm Good Friday."

The girl smiled. "Go on, you're pulling my leg."

Good Friday eyed the ample cleavage that spilled from her dress like tasty stuffing. "Used to be a preacher man, used to preach me up a sermon every Friday night in a place you're too young to remember. Pretty ladies like you would hang on every word. I caught the sweetest gal a man could ever want with words," he said, digging into his pocket for some money.

"Yeah, well see if ya can catch me. Ten bucks a dance," she said, chewing on a white chiclet she'd just popped in her mouth.

Mercedes kept her eyes peeled on the men's room.

"Hum, yeah, well, anyways as I was tellin' you, I'd be preaching into the night and outside my apartment, the wind'd carry the words of my girl 'round town. I was `good.' Her good Friday night," he said with relish. "'Nough about me. What's your name?"

"Marci. With an `i'. But I ain't got such a story to go with it."

"Excuse me, I need to go to the men's room." Mercedes walked off.

"So?" Marci looked disappointed by Nick's hasty departure. "Your friend's kinda pretty."

Good Friday coughed. "Let's dance." Good Friday paid for his ticket, took one more look at the men's room and headed for the dance floor.

*   *   *

Mercedes entered the men's room and spotted Pinkerton at the end of the room. Stalls of yellow-stained urinals gave the impression of a military latrine. The cracked white and black tiled floor smelled of ammonia and Lysol. Mercedes turned on the water and held her hands under the cool trickle.

She heard him talk in low whispers to another man, a Latino with the side of his head buzzed and an earring in his ear.

"I hear you, man, I ain't dumb. I'm takin' care of business, shit." Pinkerton zipped his pants and walk toward her. The Latino brushed past, mumbling to himself and exited.

Pinkerton ran a comb through his hair, eyed Mercedes and nodded with interest. He liked the cut of her suit, surprised to find such a well-dressed young man, no doubt. He winked.

That threw her off. It wasn't exactly a "hey-bud-aren't-we-cool" wink. But a "hey-guy-what-say-you-and-I-shoot-the breeze-get-acquainted-have-a-whiskey-and-come-to-my-place-for-a-nightcap" type of affair.

Her hands dripped with water and she had to reach past Pinkerton to get the khaki paper towel. He tore a few out and handed it to her. She didn't want to open her mouth, afraid to try her new voice on someone who might recognize her. She nodded her head, dried her hands, threw the towel in the trash and left the unsuspecting dick behind in the john.

As she watched Good Friday and Marci finished their dance, her heart sank. The treasured dance-card should have had nothing to do with a place like Sayonara, but it did. And Mona Lisa did and that was harder to swallow.

The club was crowded and smoky. Good Friday came up. "So Nick, this here Marci's one hell of a dancer."

"Marci, that's spelled with an `i,'" she reiterated, sucking down a Mai Tai.

Mercedes nodded her head and turned on the charm. "I'm looking for a girl."

Marci snorted and popped a bubble. "That's original. So go on."

"Her name's Mona Lisa."

At the sound of Mona Lisa's name, Marci stopped chewing. She looked over at the exit sign flashing in neon.

Mercedes detected a streamline of worry behind the heavily made-up eyes. "Can I buy you another drink, Marci?" Mercedes said, leading her as far away from Pinkerton as possible. Good Friday followed.

Marci swung her eyes back and forth from Mercedes to Good

Friday before answering. "Maybe."

"Maybe's good," Mercedes said, paying for another Mai Tai. Marci didn't remove the pineapple fruit stick as she sucked the straw.

"Try putting a little kick in this, Diego," Marci said to the bartender. He grudgingly poured out a thin trickle of cheap rum.

"So back to Mona Lisa," Mercedes said, nursing a club soda.

Marci plopped down her drink, took Mercedes' arm and led her to the dance floor. "You wanna talk, let's do it dancing."

Mercedes paid for her ticket and the two of them crushed between the cheap suits and gauzy dresses. Music blared from speakers. Couples danced out their pipe dreams to a rhythm one third swing, one third rock and one third tuneless as if everyone were hearing a different beat and moving to the bump and grind of need.

Marci clutched onto Mercedes, but Mercedes put some distance between them. She didn't want the girl to feel her breasts, didn't want to tip her off. Didn't want her running off at the mouth. They sort of two-stepped it with a beat. "So when did you last see Mona Lisa?"

"You're not the only one looking . . . for chrissakes can't a girl blow town for awhile without everyone gettin' so crazy?" Marci tried again to snuggle closer, but Mercedes held her at bay.

"Hey, lighten up, baby. You're as stiff as a corpse."

Mercedes was having a hard time leading. She relaxed her shoulders. "Anyone asking you questions?"

Marci realized this conversation wasn't going away. "Yeah, yeah, some creepy detective, the woman who runs this joint, a few of her steady customers, Mr. Yamamoto, don't know why he's so high on her. I'm not so bad to look at what'dya think?"

"She hardly lights a candle to you."

Marci stopped dancing. "You wouldn't just be giving me a line?"

Mercedes smiled and pulled her a little closer. "You're too smart for that, Marci."

Marci sniffed, her eyes flashed with approval. "Yeah, well that Yamamoto dude was really pissed she didn't show. Xuan had to calm him down, and that ain't so easy to do." The dance was over. Mercedes led Marci to a dark table where they had another round of drinks. Couples around them played Mah-Jongg.

"You're not gonna ask me why I work here, are you?" Marci flashed her compact out of her purse and applied an even coat of fuchsia lipstick.

Mercedes looked her in the eye. "Nope. Just need to get some information about Mona Lisa.

Marci leaned in and fingered Mercedes' sleeve. "Now you know the policy here at the club is not to talk serious with the customers. Turns them off. What I'm about to tell you, is what they call precious information."

Mercedes assumed she meant privileged information.

Marci sucked on her straw and polished off her glass. She slid the glass to the edge of the table and flagged a waiter.

"Whatever I tell you, didn't come from me, you got that?"

Mercedes nodded her head and lit up a cigarette.

"OK. let's look like we're making nice-nice, so's the dragon lady won't get suspicious if she sees me talkin' to you." Marci had a way of draping her body over Mercedes in two seconds flat. It was as if they were attached by Velcro.

Mercedes scanned the room for Pinkerton and Good Friday, but they were nowhere in sight.

"Mona Lisa put in a year in this dump, don't ask me why, but dragon face was real sweet on the money she brought in. The last couple of months, I noticed Mona Lisa didn't dance as much. She would come in a couple times a week for clients like Mr. Yamamoto, but my guess is she had somethin' goin' on the side. Rumor had it she was into heavy stuff, you know."

Mercedes didn't know and didn't want to know, but she'd come this far and there was no use turning back. "Like what?"

"Nothing illegal, just kink, I mean just doin' what the customer wants."

Marci pulled the pineapple out of the fresh drink and laid it in the ashtray. She took a sip and licked her lips. "Now, me I'm into a little B&D," she looked over at Mercedes to judge her reaction. She got none and continued. "I say there's nothing wrong with harmless fun and it's safe, man, the safest sex you can get out there." Marci waved her hand over the crowd. "Guys like that humiliation shit. I got one loves to lick my dirty heels." She slapped her hand on the table. "One dude makes me watch while he pees into a potted palm his mother sent him from Florida. And one jerk—."

"Marci, do you know where Mona Lisa might be hiding?"

Mercedes had enough of the litany of perversions for one night.

"Well," Marci sucked the sweet, pink liquid, her eyes lapping Mercedes' expensive suit, "she was reading this book one night when I came in, you know, in the dressing room and she got a little nervous and everything, so she put the book in her make-up case—she carries that goddamn suitcase everyplace she goes, you think her eyes and nose were in it—so anyways, she goes to take a pee and I take a peek, mind you, nothing wrong with some healthy curiosity. And what'dya know. There's a book in Spanish, like those Berlin crash courses in language, you know what I'm saying."

"Berlitz," Mercedes said, wondering why Mona Lisa was so secretive about learning another language.

"Yeah, yeah, that's it. Can I bum a cig?"

Mercedes shook out a cigarette, lit it and handed the stick to her. Marci enjoyed the attention and the company. Her eyes darted around the room to make sure no one was watching them.

"Mona Lisa didn't hang out and gossip like the others, you know her breaking into film and all that. I think she was scared shitless some producer would find out how she earned her extra dough and she'd be blackballed."

"What about her buddy, Noh?"

Marci sighed. "She was quiet, different from the others and nothing like her mother."

"Her mother?"

"Yeah. Xuan's her mother. They fought like cats and dogs, every day."

Mercedes grilled her a few more minutes, but it was evident that Marci had given her all she had. Mercedes stood up, slipped a fifty out of her wallet and slid the bill across the table. Marci gently laid her palm over the money and smiled up at Mercedes.

"Gee, Nick, that was real nice of you."

"One more thing. Point me in the direction of Xuan."

Marci clutched at Mercedes sleeve. "You know I could point you in another direction," her hand slipped seductively along Mercedes' arm. "My place isn't far from here."

Mercedes suppressed a smile. "Maybe some other time, Marci."

Marci's eyes closed with disappointment. She fluffed up her hair and pointed to the exit sign. "Go through there and you'll find her office. But be careful."

"I'm always careful."

"Get a load of the guy with beret. Wonder what he's after?" She smoothed her dress and headed in his direction.

Mercedes felt her stomach churn. The club seemed to swallow her up as she moved closer and closer to the exit. It was insane. How could she ever pull this off? Her breath burned in her throat and suddenly she was thirsty, parched; she needed to drink a gallon of water.

But there wasn't time. She parted the curtain and walked down a dim corridor that smelled of limes and bad aftershave. Her shoes echoed on the wooden floor. She stopped just outside a door marked private. Her hand was steady as she reached for the knob, but her heart was doing the watusi.

SHOW DOWN

The room smelled of jasmine incense and wax from burnt candles. Chairs were covered in chintz and lace. An oil painting of an attractive young woman with just the right amount of innocence in her eyes to fool you with her smile hung over an Edwardian sofa.

Behind an oak desk, a tall-back chair swiveled around. Seated on a plush cushion was the very same woman in the picture, only older and meaner.

"Do you like the portrait?" The woman's voice was as soft as an alligator's back.

"Charming." Mercedes closed the door behind her and moved into the room.

The tone should have alarmed her, but the woman was used to attitude. "My name's Xuan, but my girls call me Mama san. What can I call you, pretty boy?" She was wearing a tight black dress with a high collar and a silver dagger pinned over her heart. The eyes had lost some of their ethnic contours, but the color was an implacable black.

"Nick." Mercedes lit a cigarette and watched the smoke trail in front of her.

"Nick, Dick, Ric. You Americans." Xuan laughed. "So you're here to negotiate one of my girls?" She pushed an ashtray to the edge of the desk.

"Yeah, Mona Lisa."

Mercedes enjoyed watching Xuan's face turn to stone. Her smile vanished beneath the smooth, cold skin.

"She's gone. Doesn't work here anymore. I got lots of pretty girls." The voice became more acidic.

"They won't do." Mercedes tapped Xuan's desk, impatient. "If you don't know where she is, maybe the police will be happy to find her."

At the mention of police, Xuan's eyes were firecrackers. "Who are you?"

"Nick. That's all you need to know, for now. Where is she?"

"She took a powder on me, and I'd suggest you do the same. I've got business to tend to."

"And I got a witness says he saw you at the Clark Hotel the night she disappeared. The night your man Redlite shot her. What do you think the police will do with that bit of information?"

Mercedes could hear Xuan grit her teeth. "If you want the dance-card, Xuan, then I'll expect some cooperation."

Xuan jumped up out of her chair. She nearly lunged across the desk. Mercedes moved back a few steps out of her reach. "What do you know?" she hissed like a rattlesnake. "That belongs to me. I paid for it."

"It's worth about a cool million. How much change did you give Mona Lisa?"

Footsteps approached. Xuan looked toward the door. Mercedes reached in her jacket pocket where Good Friday's gun was comfortably lodged. Her hands were still steady; it was the knees that were shaking.

The phone rang. Xuan's hand shot out, but Mercedes pulled the gun and pointed it at her. Xuan's hand froze in mid-stream.

"Cash is cash," Xuan said, falling into her seat. Suddenly her smooth face was cracked with wrinkles. She looked old, tired, used up. The phone stopped ringing.

"How much cash?"

"Fifty thousand." She practically spit the words out.

"Did Noh play her part?"

Xuan's eyes shot upwards. Her fingers rapped the desk so hard she split a nail. She refused to answer.

"She probably made it easy for Mona Lisa to slip in and steal the dance-card from Fletcher. After all, she worked for her, had access to the house, to Fletcher's personal belongings. That must be kinda rough on you. Not as bad as sleeping with the enemy, but close." Mercedes let the words settle. The gun gave her more confidence than she could ever imagine.

Xuan's face lost what little color it had.

"I guess a pretty good case could be made to establish your

daughter as an accessory to fraud, theft and . . . prostitution." She leveled the gun at Xuan's heart, knowing how the woman would be affected by the accusation.

Xuan jumped up again and slammed her fist on the desk. "Don't you play with me."

"I caught your daughter breaking into Mona Lisa's apartment. Maybe she's the one playing games behind her mother's back?"

Xuan let out a growl. "Leave my baby out of this."

"Baby." Mercedes laughed. "She's old enough to go to Sybil Brand. I hear the individual cells are really comfortable."

"What do you want from me." Xuan's voice was shaky and had lost most of its vinegar.

"I want you to pick up that phone, call Fletcher and tell her to keep her watchdogs off Mona Lisa. Then you'll bargain. If Mona Lisa returns, unharmed, Fletcher will get the dance-card and you'll get your money back."

Mercedes had no idea where the fifty thousand went, no doubt to South America with Mona Lisa, but she had nothing else to go on. It was a stall and it would buy her time. Time to find Mona Lisa and wring her little neck.

Xuan was just about to reach for the phone, but something stopped her. It was a man's voice, a voice Mercedes had heard before and liked even less this time around.

Xuan smiled. Before Mercedes could turn around, she felt a cold, sharp object at the base of her neck.

"Put the gun down."

Mercedes dropped it on the desk. Redlite came round and gave her the once over. He held a silver daggar with a five inch curved blade in his hand.

"It's about time. Where the hell were you?" Xuan snarled.

Redlite's eyes narrowed as he examined the young man in front of him. Then he snapped his fingers and started laughing. He slapped his knees and did a little jig.

Mercedes wondered if he was drunk or just an insane cowhand in a footloose emporium for the degenerate of heart.

"Well, look who's in drag. You fucking dyke." He pushed her down in the chair.

Xuan's eyebrows knitted. "What's going on?"

"This here's Mona Lisa's buddy. She has the dance-card. We almost went for a little ride, but she fucked me over and nearly broke my arm in her window. Who the fuck did you think you were playing with?"

Redlite slapped Mercedes across the face. It hurt. She'd never been hit before and she could feel the blood swell to the surface. He slapped her again. This time harder. Now she could taste the blood in her mouth. Her hands started shaking.

"That's enough, for now." Xuan tapped her fingers on the desk, trying to figure out the next move.

Redlite picked up Mercedes' .22 and held it on her.

Mercedes prayed Good Friday would burst in with ten cops, all armed with UZIs. Instead, the lights started to flicker and dim and then the room went dark. Shouts echoed outside the door. People seemed to be running in all directions. The music was still playing, but something was terribly wrong.

The door opened and closed. "Who's there?" Redlite shouted, letting go of Mercedes' arm.

Mercedes hit the floor and crawled as far away from the center of the room as possible.

"Gimme a light, Xuan."

Mercedes heard Xuan rummaging in her desk. "What's this all about?" Xuan demanded, unsteadily.

A flashlight cut across the room, brushing Mercedes' foot. She had just enough light to hide behind a stuffed chair and stay there.

"You fucked me over, Xuan and now you're gonna pay." It was a man's voice, frothing with hate.

The light was focused on Xuan's face. It seemed she'd aged twenty years. Fright would do that to you. The tension was unbearable.

"Shoot him," Xuan ordered. Redlite aimed Mercedes' .22 and fired, but of course, Good Friday was smart enough not to load it. Mercedes couldn't make out the man's face, hidden in shadow. His frame appeared huge, like some giant in a fairy tale. He laughed.

Everything fell apart at once. There was a sudden burst of light like a flash-bulb going off and then the sharp report of a gun as a bullet tore through the air.

Xuan took the bullet through the forehead. Blood spilled down her face and in that blinding strobe of light, Mercedes watched in horror as the woman toppled over on the oak desk. Her eyes were wide open. Not even in death did the anger leave those eyes. Any minute now, a snake would crawl from between her lips.

Redlite ran over to her. The door opened and the beam of light was killed. The room was dark again. The door slammed shut and Redlite wailed with grief, making these desperate sucking noises as he fought to get his breath.

Mercedes jumped up just as the lights came on and she bolted for the door.

Minutes later, the hallway was filled with cops and dancers and drunks. Mercedes was swept up in the frenzied crowd like a swarm of locusts. A sailor tossed a chair through a window and there was a shower of glass and everywhere the stomping of feet and the screams of women.

Someone grabbed hold of Mercedes' arm. She turned around. It was Good Friday. "Lord what happened to your face?"

"I slammed into a wall."

Good Friday yanked her past the bulldog in the polyester butternut squash-colored suit only now his sleeve was torn and a large splash of red wine stained his back. They crushed through the exit. Marci followed them and they exploded through the door out into the parking lot.

Mercedes doubled over; she couldn't breathe. Good Friday slapped her back.

"What'd I tell you, what'd I tell you?" Good Friday's brow was beaded with sweat and he was wheezing himself.

Mercedes lifted her head just in time to spot a black Jeep zoom out of the lot. It was Samantha's Jeep and seated next to her was Pinkerton with his goddamn black beret.

"Let's blow," Good Friday said, leading a bewildered Mercedes to the Cadillac.

"Hey, what about me, you guys?" Marci asked, holding her high heels in hand. Good Friday looked at Mercedes, then flagged Marci over. She let out a squeal and joined them.

* * *

On the polished wood bar inside the Gallery Bar at the Biltmore Hotel, three shots of whiskey stood in line. The hour was late and the place empty. Mercedes, Good Friday and Marci sat there waiting for their nerves to calm down.

"I don't like any of this," Good Friday said, shaking his head. "You better go to the police with this shit." He polished off his whiskey in one gulp.

"I can't identify the man," Mercedes said, rimming the shot glass with a finger. "He was big, though."

"Maybe it wasn't a man," Marci chimed in between popping fistfuls of cheddar fish in her mouth. "The way you were dancing. Tipped me off. Besides, you're not the only one hangs out in drag 'round there. Could have been your friend in the Jeep or Noh. Maybe they disguised their voice. No tellin'."

"Noh?"

"Yep. I caught her running outta the club ten minutes after you went in to grill Xuan."

Mercedes didn't think Noh would kill her own mother. No, more likely it was Pinkerton. Did Samantha put him up to it? Did the two ride off into the sunset together?

Mercedes slipped off the stool, paid the tab and said her good-night. Her face was smarting like hell and her head was in the early throes of a whopper of a migraine.

Marci handed her a piece of paper with her phone number on it. "Anything I can do, call."

"Thanks. Just one more thing. Noh's last name, do you know it?

"Yeah. Same as her mom's. Kishimoto."

"Kishimoto," Mercedes repeated as she walked out of the bar.

* * *

In less than ten minutes, Mercedes had parked her car on the north side of the Bradbury Building. She knew about the rear entry because on Saturdays, if the building was closed, she would arrange for the guard to keep the door open. If the cleaning crew was still there, chances were the door would be open. It was. She didn't know if she was lucky or just plain stupid.

A single shaft of moonlight sliced through the ornate skylight. She moved steadily through the lobby of the Bradbury, and up the stairwell to the second floor. Music pealed from Pinkerton's office, the only one illuminated on the floor. It was the kind of music you play at 2:00 in the morning if you're not alone. The kind that makes you want to be alone with a certain someone, uninterrupted. But Mercedes was in the mood to party crash. Especially when the life of the party was Pinkerton.

Mercedes opened the door. It didn't squeak. She moved past Charlotte's desk, neat and tidy, her twin plastic sheaths laid out nicely on a white blotter. A low cross-fire of voices played against the music. She tiptoed to Pinkerton's door. It was opened about two inches, wide enough for her to take a peek.

And what a peek it was. Pinkerton's back was to her, his leather suspenders hanging by his side, a stiff drink in his right hand as he sat on the edge of his desk. He was looking down at someone kneeling between his legs. His left hand clutched a nice clump of brown hair.

Mercedes held her breath. Her knees turned to rubber bands when the thought flashed that it could be Samantha between his legs. She felt dizzy. Her head was pounding with the migraine.

Pinkerton moaned. As he lifted his head slowly, his face arched to the left, a smile stretched on his lips. He didn't look like a man who'd just ordered someone's funeral. Or did he?

A hand came into frame. A man's hand. It found its way along Pinkerton's shoulders. The body followed and moved behind Pinkerton as he rubbed up against the shamus' muscular back. The well-dressed body belonged to none other than Max Pitts.

Mercedes backed away slowly and knocked into a stack of magazines. They crashed to the floor, the thud reverberating through the office into the inner sanctum. The woman bolted up from between Pinkerton's legs. It was Charlotte, Pinkerton's secretary. She was completely naked, drunk and didn't seem to appreciate the interruption.

Mercedes dashed out, not bothering to slam the door behind her. She heard Max and Pinkerton shouting to each other as she raced down the steps two at a time. When she hit the lobby, she looked up and spotted them leering down at her. But she was out the door and into her car before Pinkerton had a chance to zip his fly.

RED HERRING

Mercedes had a fitful night of sleep. She dreamt she grew a moustache she couldn't shave off and Samantha had tricked her into giving up the dance-card. The last thing she remembered was Mona Lisa returning from Brazil with a terrific tan and a heavy Spanish accent and Max and Pinkerton eloping to Las Vegas.

Over a cup of coffee, Mercedes' head started to clear, the surreal residue of the chaotic dreams faded. She examined the *Los Angeles Times* for news of the murder.

It had made the front page. It turned out Redlite was being held as the primary suspect; the motive still unclear. Captain Malone of the 77th Precinct was the investigating officer.

Mercedes wondered why everyone seemed to be at the scene of the crime last night. Was this a collective plot to overthrow a successful taxi-dancing joint? Did Xuan stick the knife in everyone's back? Was there more to this than just a missing dance-card?

Mercedes knew all along she was crazy keeping the dance-card at home. She again weighed the idea of putting it in her safety deposit box at First Interstate Bank, but why take any more chances in removing it at this point? So far, she'd been clever enough to deter everyone from getting their hands on it. Maybe Max really believed she Fed-Exed it out of state. Besides, she had grown possessive about it. After all she'd been through, hadn't she at least earned the right to have it on loan for a few weeks? In addition to the value of the piece and the powerful aura it seemed to exude, Mercedes appreciated the fine craftsmanship. She felt it almost belonged to her. And although it had brought nothing but trouble, and everyone in town was doing their own dance around it, she was captivated by its presence.

It was raining outside. Gray massive clouds floated against a black sky like a Georgia O'Keefe abstraction. There were no messages on Mercedes' machine. She'd called Regan to tell her what had happened at the Club, but she was nowhere to be found.

Mercedes opened Mona Lisa's diary and scanned the journal for any reference to Xuan or Noh. There were so many words crammed in her little book, but one paragraph in particular caught her attention.

My little sister Noh/Big Daddy's done gone/away. Did you ever think about the color of his eyes? Wouldn't it be nice to see our daddy-O's now/ show them how we've fucking adjusted/they fill the void of our past with the death of silence.

Was papa the missing link? Who was Noh's father? Was Kishimoto her mother's maiden name or her father's name?

Mona Lisa had told Mercedes that her father died of a heart attack when she was ten. "He loved me, his last words were for me," she'd said. Mercedes suspected it was a lie.

She scanned another page.

Everybody's somebody's fool and you were mine. Or was it the other way around? Let's play a game you and me. I'll be Sydney Stein and you be Carmen Miranda. Hey. Not so fast, sister. Be careful. That's not my watch you're holding, it's my heart. Ring around the rosy. A pocket full of doughsy. Pull up a chair, big daddy, and I'll sit on your knee and tell you who I'd like to be.

Sydney Stein. Mercedes had heard that name before, but where? It clicked. The Clark Hotel. Could Mona Lisa have used her real name when she checked in? Mercedes grabbed the phone and called information for the area code in Brooklyn, N.Y. 718. She called the operator and asked for a Sydney Stein. Maybe Mona Lisa's mother could tell her something.

There were probably one thousand Steins in Brooklyn. Luckily there were only twenty-seven Sydneys. Mercedes was prepared to call every single one of them. On the sixth number, a woman answered the phone. Her voice was vaguely familiar, as if the daughter had inherited her mother's voice. Mercedes felt chills run down her spine.

"Hello, Mrs. Stein?"

"Yes, this is Mrs. Stein, who's calling?"

"Mrs. Stein, this is Mercedes, a friend of Sydney's."

Silence on the other end.

"I was wondering if you knew where I could find her?"

"She's away."

"Away where, Mrs. Stein?"

There was a long pause before she replied and when she did, she sounded very nervous and confused. "Who's this calling?"

"I'm a friend."

"She don't have too many. Why don't you know where she is? You should know if you're her friend."

Mercedes detected annoyance in the woman's voice. She didn't want to upset her. "It's just that she's up for this part, Mrs. Stein, and she's disappeared and I'm worried about her."

"Ain't seen her in any movies yet. She lives in Hollywood somewhere. I can't help you. She was never one for calls, you know. When I got the postcard, I nearly . . . ." Silence.

Mercedes was careful not to push too hard. "Wow, you got a postcard. From where?"

More silence on the other end.

"Could you read the postmark, Mrs. Stein?" Mercedes pressed the phone so close to her ear, it hurt. Her heart beat fast and seconds seemed like hours.

"Well, Rosary Beach, Mexico."

"Mexico?

"Yep."

"You mean Rosarito Beach?

"Umm, let me put on my glasses, just a minute."

"Would you mind reading the card to me, it's really important. She could be missing out on a big opportunity."

"I been hearin' 'bout this big break now . . . ." Silence again. "Says, 'Weather's great. Big break coming up. Miss you moms. I'll be home soon.' That's it. Listen, I gotta go, dinner's in the oven." Her voice sounded sad and far away.

"Sure, one more thing. I was wondering, Sydney's dad . . . is he dead?"

There was a long silence. "Might as well be. He ran out on us years ago." Her voice was bitter. "My dinner's burning." Mrs. Stein hung up the phone.

So Mona Lisa was somewhere in Mexico, no doubt brushing up on her Berlitz Spanish. And her father ran out on her. Mrs. Stein sounded as if she were hiding something. She was so abrupt. It didn't make sense.

Mercedes scoured the diary for additional information. Searching for her friend south of the border would be crazy. There had to be an easier way to get to her. She nursed her cold cup of coffee and read on.

Can't forget Carmen's birthday. Sunday, October 21. I got her something to wash away the bad taste I left in her mouth. I hope she'll take it. I hope I'm still around to give it to her.

Mercedes glanced at the newspaper. It was Sunday, October 21. Could it be possible that Mona Lisa was planning to make an appearance? She shouldn't cancel any possibility. She had to go on what little she had.

She grabbed a black trenchcoat, slipped on a pair of flat boots, left a light on and locked the front door behind her.

*   *   *

Mercedes pushed open the doors of the publicly supported, KGAY radio station and asked for Carmen. A woman directed her to a small office where Carmen was seated on a stool, talking into a mike. Carmen glanced over to see who had entered. She shook her head as she continued her show.

There was nothing to do but settle in the only chair outside the recording booth and listen. Carmen's deep voice rang out with deft precision, drawing even the most reluctant listener into the suspenseful narrative.

Felony pulled the Sky Buick into the garage and cut the motor. She got out of the car, came round the back way and listened to the sound of the ocean. The smell of brine, seaweed and wet sand drifted off the black liquid carpet.

She reached into her faded leather jacket and pulled out a pack of Camels. Felony lit a cigarette and started walking toward the back porch.

A light was on in the beach house and a shadow moved about behind the open Venetian blinds. It was a shadow she'd seen before. A shadow in search of a body, only nobody would have her.

The weathered steps creaked as Felony climbed to the door. The shadow stopped moving. Maybe she heard the footsteps, but Felony didn't care.

She flicked her cigarette in the cold sand, took a deep breath and kicked open the door. The only thing between her and the shadow was nothing. The girl was an easy mark, a drink in hand, her dress crumpled up around her middle in some cheap, fashionable knot.

Desperate to find a quick exit, but knowing there was none, the girl's

*eyes were wild, her hair a coil of snakes and too much hairspray, the outfit,
something out of Frederick's of Hollywood. The girl did the only thing she
could do given the situation, given the rotten timing, given everything the
world had taken from her without permission.*

*She leaned her pretty head back and started laughing. It was a mad,
hysterical cackle, like a crazy witch whose drunk too much crushed lizard,
chicken blood and dried bones. "You bitch," she said when the laughter died
down. "Why did I come to you for help?"*

*Felony winced. "Don't bother to play up the sympathy. I've had my
fill," she said, pulling out a gray .22 pistol that felt good in her hand.*

The girl's clear eyes went electric with fear.

*"You little fake," Felony said, getting madder by the minute. "You
goddamn liar. Go on. Tell me your name. What's it today?"*

*The girl stopped laughing. She looked at Felony with those racetrack
eyes, eyes made for betting, for losing your shirt, for going around in circles
and coming in last. She whispered, "I've lost it."*

*Felony snickered. "You don't lose names, sister. You lose wallets,
girlfriends, suitcases, teeth. Names you get to keep whether you like them or
not."*

*The girl's eyes glared like red-hot pokers. Little bubbles of saliva escaped
from her dry lips the way soap effervesces when wet. "Sydney," the girl
muttered, pacing up and down.*

"Sydney what?" Felony prodded, cocking the gun in her hand.

*"Stein." Her lower lip quivered. "Sydney Stein . . . Sydney Stein," she
repeated, shrieking louder and louder, her hands muffling her ears so she
couldn't hear herself.*

*The empty words sailed out of the beach house to the sea where Neptune's
carrier pigeons crested the huge breakers to deliver the news.*

"Out of the mouth of babes," Felony jeered.

*Sydney was still screaming her name, tears melting away the face paint
when Felony cocked the trigger and put her out of her misery.*

Mercedes' feet had grown cold and her fingers were numb.
Carmen had just pulled the plug on a girl named Sydney Stein, alias
Mona Lisa.

Carmen was out of the booth and into Mercedes' face in a flash.
She was wearing a pair of high-waisted jeans, a denim shirt and an
attitude you couldn't remove with turpentine.

"I told you not to bother me." Carmen dug her fist into her thigh.

Mercedes backed off. "Looks like a guilty conscience to me, Carmen. Why don't you cut the crap and tell me what went down with Mona Lisa. This way I'll leave you to lick your wounds, and you won't have to see my face anymore."

"I told you I don't know where the fuck she is and I don't care."

"If you don't care, then why did you break into her apartment and rip her underwear to shreds? Just a gesture for old time's sake?"

Carmen's eyes were flares. How did Mercedes know? How could anyone unless they were in the room?

Mercedes watched Carmen decipher her options. Option number one: tell Mercedes nothing. Option number two: get this shit off her chest and be done with it. Carmen opted for the latter. It just seemed easier.

"I need a drink," Carmen said, grabbing her jacket. She looked at Mercedes, then opened the door. "You buyin'?"

Mercedes nodded and closed the door behind them.

*   *   *

Santa Monica Boulevard was all decked out for Halloween, two weeks in advance. The bars were getting ready to celebrate and boy's town buzzed with a surplus of testosterone.

Mercedes followed Carmen into the Palms where it took a minute to get adjusted to the dark interior. They sat at the bar and Mercedes ordered a beer. Carmen needed something stronger. She downed a shot of tequila, crushed a lime in her mouth and fingered a cold bottle of Tecate.

Mercedes lit a cigarette and waited. She ordered another round, this time toasting Carmen. "Happy Birthday."

Carmen seemed surprised Mercedes knew it was her birthday. "Thanks."

Mercedes figured this was tough for Carmen, but she was running out of time and running out of information. If Carmen had received a gift from Mona Lisa today, it wasn't apparent.

The bar was nearly empty. It was too early for the nightclub to have more than a dozen or so women who nursed drinks, smoked cigarettes and no doubt watched the clock for the first arrivals to enter. Mercedes tapped her finger on the bar. Carmen took the cue.

Carmen opened her shirt and pulled out a silver cross. It was beautiful, intricately carved with a black opal in the center. "You'll never guess—"

"Mona Lisa?"

Carmen looked at Mercedes, impressed. "How'd you know?"

Mercedes didn't want to tell her that she'd purloined Mona Lisa's diary. Carmen would want to see it and Mercedes didn't think she was ready to read it. At least not yet.

"Intuition, I guess," Mercedes replied. "When did you get it?"

"It was on my doorstep when I left for work. I have no idea who delivered it. There was no card. Nothing. Just the cross. I knew it was from her. She always told me she'd get me one, an antique."

Carmen fingered the cross, then put it inside her shirt, leaving the few buttons open. "You know, she still fucking gets to me. Even now, when I know everything she goes and does this."

Mercedes nodded sympathetically. "What about Xuan?" She wondered if Carmen was in any way connected to Xuan's murder. She took a long drink, watching Carmen's face as she waited for an answer.

"I didn't kill Xuan and I didn't hurt Mona Lisa. Now I'm not saying I wouldn't want to see something happen to Fletcher, but I wouldn't be responsible, directly that is, I'm not stupid." She sipped her drink. "Before all this came down, I gave Mona Lisa some money." Carmen laughed. "I'm crazy, what can I tell you. She said she was going to invest the money for me, but I knew she was in trouble. I gave her three thousand, not much, but plenty for me."

Carmen's shoulders seemed to cave in and Mercedes realized how tired she looked. She decided to trust Carmen with some information. "I think Mona Lisa's in Mexico."

"Mexico?" Carmen's eyes narrowed. She polished off her beer, then shook her head. "If she's in trouble down there, I think we can just kiss her good-bye, man."

"I think she's just hiding out for awhile." Mercedes hoped this was true.

Carmen shook her head again. "I'm not so sure. She was messed up with so much shit, for all I know she's running guns and ammo south of the border. She had this illusion, you know, of doing something really heroic with her life, once she became a big star. I think she was starting to believe her own fairy tales." Carmen took one of Mercedes' cigarettes, started to light it, then threw it down on the bar.

Mercedes smiled at her. "Do you know if she has friends in Rosarito Beach?"

Carmen shrugged. "She's got people all over." Carmen looked across the bar at a small woman with bleached-blonde wavy hair and blue eyes. They locked eyes for two cold seconds, before Carmen broke the stare. "Wait, there was this guy called a few times, about a couple of months ago. Had an accent. I tried to speak to him in Spanish, but he hung up on me. When I asked Mona Lisa who he was, she said some producer in Mexico. Wanted to launch an American star in one of his epic productions. Maybe it was just a john."

"Did she mention his name?"

"She never mentioned anyone's name."

Mercedes paid for their drinks. "One more thing. What about Noh? Were they lovers?"

Carmen laughed. Her eyes lit up and suddenly her face looked pretty again. "Shit, no. I think Noh was the only person who knew the real Mona Lisa, everything, all the dirt and still cared, God knows why. You, me, everyone else, even her agent, most of us got fed little bits and pieces of the truth."

Carmen watched the blonde again. This time the woman smiled suggestively, but Carmen returned nothing. "Let me tell you something, though. Noh doesn't say much, but she's got this mean streak. Xuan couldn't control her and the girl hated her mother. One time Mona Lisa and Noh came home, I was just getting out of the shower, they didn't know I was there. Well, I heard Noh say she was fed up with her mother and that if she could get away with it, she'd have her killed."

Carmen fingered the cigarette. "Funny, now I remember, Mona Lisa didn't try to talk her out of it, didn't even brush it off, just said, `If there's anything I can do, Noh.' Carmen got off the stool. "That should have tipped me off, huh?" Carmen shook her head. "Man, never again." Carmen's eyes swept across the bar, now lined with a number of attractive women. The blonde was up against the cigarette machine, smoking. Carmen started for the door, then stopped. "There was someone, though. Someone she really cared about."

"Who?"

Carmen shrugged her shoulders. "I can always tell when my lover's got someone else on her mind. Another one of her dark secrets I suppose."

Mercedes followed her outside. She zipped her jacket. The two women stood under the lamp light. Cars whizzed by on the boulevard of Saint Monica. Carmen put her hands in her jean pockets. "You should go talk to Eva."

"Eva?"

"Yeah, you know she's been seeing Noh?"

Mercedes held on to the meter for support. "Noh and Eva? Come on, you're kidding?"

Carmen caught Mercedes' shock. "*Chica,*" her voice grew serious, "in this town anything's possible."

Mercedes shook her head. Why didn't Eva say anything to her the night she was at the club? The night Mercedes poured out her heart about Mona Lisa and Samantha?

Carmen noticed the dejection on Mercedes face. "Listen, sorry I was so hard on you earlier. Mona Lisa's still such a sore spot." Carmen looked west, the anger momentarily dissipated.

A transient passed by, a woman wearing slippers, a distressed hat and baggy sweatshirt too big for her sunken chest and purple polyester pants too small for her fleshy rump. Her face was cracked by the constant exposure to sun, smog and life's disappointments. Her vacant eyes were behind lensless designer throwaways. One hand pushed a Mayfair cart stuffed with Brillo boxes, rumpled blankets and plastic bags, the other hand held a tattered cigarette, no doubt retrieved from the gutter.

Carmen and Mercedes watched the woman maneuver her portable home toward La Cienega Boulevard. "That was Mona Lisa's biggest fear," Carmen said softly. "That someday she'd end up like that. She said she'd do *anything* just so she wouldn't be a nobody."

Carmen ran a hand through her thick hair, put on her dark glasses, even though the sun had long since disappeared and walked down the street.

NOH DEAL

Jezebel's was empty and quiet as if even the tables and chairs and the well-tended plants were holding their breath, afraid to exhale, afraid to draw attention to their inanimate forms. Eva and Noh, likewise, were as still as death. And Mercedes was tired, angry and ready for a fight.

"The girl's had a hard time of it," Eva said, gently, hoping to placate Mercedes' temper. "The police have been at her all morning."

It didn't work.

"*She's* had a hard time. We've all had a hard time," Mercedes snapped. "Why were you at Club Sayonara last night?"

Noh stood up. She was wearing a black kimono with a pair of white karate pants. Her hair was pulled back in a pony tail, the ever-present braid dangling in front of her left eye. Under the circumstances, considering her mother had just been murdered, she seemed as calm as a Buddhist monk who's subsisted on a diet of meditation and goat's milk somewhere in the Himalayas.

"I came to Xuan to tell her that I was leaving Fletcher. And that I wouldn't be going off to school, like she'd planned. My mother worked hard to save enough money so I could study music in London." Eva nodded her head, urging her to continue. "But I met Eva and decided to stay here. This is my home now."

Mercedes cross-examined Eva. "Why didn't you tell me about the two of you?"

"It wasn't the time, not with all you had on your mind. Besides, you never even asked. Had you asked, I would have told you."

Mercedes didn't skip a beat. She addressed Noh. "I was in the room with your mother when she got shot."

Both women looked startled. Noh paced nervously, the calmness drained from her like bath water from a tub. Eva cracked her knuckles.

"I think there's something you're not telling me." Mercedes relayed the details of her disguise and how Redlite gave her away. "Nobody knows that, except Redlite, and he's keeping his mouth shut for the time being. You were seen fleeing the premises. If you didn't kill your mother, maybe you hired someone to do it."

Noh was about to explode. "You've got no proof."

Eva jumped up. "Listen, Noh meant no harm, it's just that her mother was threatening to . . . ." She cut off and stared at the burgundy carpet, then continued, "to get rid of me, if she didn't cooperate."

Noh corroborated Eva's statement. "My mother always gets what she wants, but I was prepared to do anything, just so she wouldn't run my life. I guess I'm lucky someone beat me to it."

The words poured out and Noh slumped on a chair and started sobbing. Eva held her lover in her arms, rocking her gently.

"Did you know," Mercedes said, addressing Eva, "that your girlfriend helped herself into Mona Lisa's apartment and stole a suitcase?"

Noh's eyes reached out across a great gulf of heartache, but Mercedes was implacable.

Eva seemed surprised. Noh dropped her head and sighed. The girl couldn't have been a day over twenty but she seemed as old as Methuselah.

"Mona Lisa and I were very close. I wanted to keep some of her things, just in case," her voice lost its trail and stopped. Noh's shoulders caved in and she started to sob again. Big, wet tears fell down her clear complexion as Eva wrapped the girl in her arms. Eva implored Mercedes to go away, but instead, Mercedes lit a cigarette and stared out the window at the ocean.

Mercedes thought of Carmen's radio detective, Felony and realized how lonely was the plight of the private eye. There was always some woman to muddy the picture, to pull at your heartstrings. Mercedes watched the two women and felt a stab of jealousy.

Minutes dragged by and she ground out her cigarette, having given Noh adequate time to emote. The girl's face was red and blotchy. Mercedes pulled up a footstool and sat close to the women.

"I'm all ears," Mercedes said coolly.

"My mother had a lot of enemies," Noh said bitterly. "It could have been anyone."

"Anyone by the name of Samantha Mann?"

Eva spoke first. "Now come on, Sam's caught up in all this shit mostly to get back that damn dance-card and save Mona Lisa's ass, though I don't know why she's sticking her neck out for her." Eva folded her arms. "Guess you have something to do with that."

Mercedes sneered. Still she felt a pang of hope in her belly. Maybe Samantha was on her side? Or was Eva feeding her what she needed to hear?

"She and Pinkerton zoomed out of the club less than five minutes after the murder. I know Pinkerton's voice. I've had the pleasure of hearing him pontificate. It wasn't him. But they were there. And so were you."

Noh took a gasp of air as if she'd forgotten to breathe for the last five minutes. Maybe holding her breath caused her to be more loquacious. "My mother set up this trust fund for me . . . and now I'm the legal owner of Sayonara." Noh looked over at Eva. "But I'm selling the place and starting over. Too many bad memories."

"Yeah, well one of those memories killed your mother." Mercedes was about to light another cigarette, but her throat was dry. She was tired and hungry. She missed her quiet home and the job she hadn't been to in days. And she missed the dance-card. It was time to leave.

"And Mona Lisa is gone. Why did your mother trust her to deliver the goods? I don't get it?"

Noh blinked. "I made Xuan do it. I lied. Told her I would move to England and go to school if she gave the money to Mona Lisa. Once Mona Lisa got the money, I knew she'd kick Sayonara like a bad habit. And she'd steer clear of Fletcher's crowd. I was counting on her making a go of her career. I knew someday, someway, she'd pay me back."

Mercedes stood up. Noh seemed like a loyal friend. "One more thing. How does Max fit into this little picture?"

Noh stretched her legs. "Max lent Xuan the fifty thousand. My mother would never use her own money. If she procured the dance-card from Mona Lisa, she would get a $10,000 bonus from Max. He figured Fletcher got what she deserved by giving the antique to Mallory. Max wanted to rub it in his ex-wife's face, return it to her, play the knight in shining armor."

"And it backfired in everyone's face." Mercedes pulled on her raincoat.

"And now my mother's dead." Noh stood up. "I need some sleep. Tomorrow's my last night at Fletcher's. She's having one of her parties. Samantha's going to be there."

Mercedes stiffened.

"If you want, I can get you in, maybe you can figure out what happened. If your disguise fooled my mother, it'll fool Fletcher's crowd."

Mercedes liked the idea of being in the thick of things undetected. Nick Charles was growing on her. And she especially liked the idea of seeing Samantha again. "I'm game."

Noh nodded her head.

"There's still something bothering me," Mercedes said, as she moved toward the door. "What did you do with the suitcase?"

Noh sighed. Her face was gray and you could see she was about to go to pieces. "She swore me to secrecy, but seeing all you're going through, I guess it's OK. She was heading for Mexico, a beach resort, she didn't say where. She was going to phone me when she got there and give me instructions . . . but she never called." Again Noh's voice seemed to fade out to sea.

"What about this Dr. Flesch? I checked Mona Lisa's machine. His office left a message, but there's no one by that name in L.A. county."

"She never mentioned a doctor. I don't know, maybe she was pregnant. It happened once. The last thing she needed was that."

Why wasn't Mercedes surprised to hear this? She glanced out at the gray weather. The sea was churning, mimicking the emotions swimming inside her. The women walked Mercedes to the door. There was one final question. "Who's your father?"

The sound of Noh's breathing was labored. Her eyes were frosty. She was as cold and stiff as an icicle. "I don't have a father."

Mercedes looked at Eva, but she was equally cold.

"Everyone has a father, like him or not."

"Can't like or hate him if you never met him." Noh walked up the stairs to the bedroom.

Mercedes looked over at Eva. There was nothing in the eyes, no more wise advise to dish up over a plate of stew.

She left in silence. One thing the two girls had in common was absentee fathers. But at least Mona Lisa's stuck around long enough to earn her hatred.

* * *

By the time Mercedes got home, she was bone weary. The sight of a large white rectangular box wrapped with a big red bow on her doorstep was enough to revitalize her.

She could only think one thing. Samantha sent it. She was working in her inimitable fashion, doing nothing by the book. Sending flowers after days of silence. Samantha's riff was effective. And like music to Mercedes' ears, she knew if Samantha was in the picture, no matter how sordid her past, there'd always be a refrain she'd want to hear over and over again, just the way she'd never grow tired of Samantha's vagrant kisses.

Mercedes didn't bother to remove her raincoat. She ripped off the ribbon, opened the box and was about to smell the gorgeous bouquet of white roses, when a shiver ran down her body.

A huge, hairy tarantula with a leg span of six inches, lay feasting on a dead beetle. Mercedes screamed. She lost her head for a minute and imagined the eight black legs, as thick as a monkey's fingers, crawling up her arm, along her neck, till the poisonous spider worked its way into her hair. She shuddered, grabbed the small card at the base of the bouquet, slammed the box shut, ran outside, opened her trash can and threw the "say-it-with-flowers" gesture in the dumpster.

Her hands were trembling as she read the card and all over she was itching as if her veins were polluted with the creature's venom.

"Mona Lisa will be dead by midnight Tuesday, if you don't deliver the antique. Arrive alone at M.O.N.A. at ten. Alone . . . or I will kill her."

Of course it was unsigned. It could be a bluff, but then again it could be the only way to save her friend. She went inside, closed the door, and walked upstairs as if in a trance. She removed the dance card from the Pond's jar, dropped her raincoat on the floor and sat on the edge of her bed. It was growing dark and the hills were as quiet as death.

Mercedes fingered the antique hoping to draw out some answers, a secret, a clue. It felt as if it belonged to her. If she followed the instructions, she could lose it and still never see Mona Lisa. Hell, she could lose her life and never see anyone.

LOVE ME TENDER

Mallory heard the double glass door open as the hot water streamed down her naked body. The voice outside the shower had a harsh baritone quality. She knew it was Fletcher.

She turned off the faucet and watched the water drain out of the tub, wishing she could go with it. Instead, she grabbed a thick white towel, wrapped it around herself and stepped outside the tub onto a gray rug.

Fletcher was leaning up against the marble wall, a terry cloth robe thrown casually over her shoulders like a cloak as if she'd just come from a performance of *La Boheme*. Only she was naked underneath, a clean white bandage wrapped around her left arm, lest Mallory, or anyone for that matter, forget her recent brush with death.

"Let me dry your back." Fletcher's tongue was coated with a nasty veneer of a woman who liked to do things just for spite. She'd been drinking and that was always worse. There was never a way to placate her. Only give in to whatever she wanted. Mallory couldn't play possum. Couldn't pretend not to know what Fletcher needed from her. Mallory knew the ropes.

Mallory sighed involuntarily and caught a glimpse of Fletcher in the bathroom mirror.

Fletcher's lips tightened with disdain and her dilated pupils were as dark as a raven's coat, the eyes sparked incandescent rage. She grabbed the towel and yanked it off Mallory's body.

Mallory hated her own nakedness, the vulnerability of her femininity under such close scrutiny.

The fire in Fletcher's eyes turned into the leer of a degenerate school girl who's been caught pulling her friend's panties to her ankles. She ran her nimble hand down Mallory's spine, blotting the drops of water from the shower.

Mallory shivered from the touch of Fletcher's icy fingers.

"Lean against the sink," Fletcher commanded, her tone a drill sergeant's.

Mallory did as she was told, but stood as stiff as a statue. In fact, she pretended she was winged and armless like the beautiful marble statue of Samothrace Mona Lisa once showed her. Mallory concentrated on the flecks of black dotting her iris as Fletcher cupped her right breast and tugged on her nipple.

The images of the two women seemed to merge in the convex mirror, the steam from the shower a veil between them. The silver rods on the towel rack were twisted and tortured into some nouveau design and the air was as heavy and solemn as Mozart's "G Minor Symphony."

Fletcher's bathrobe fell to the floor. She didn't bother to pick it up. Instead she pressed her face against Mallory's back and breathed in her skin, patchouli-scented from the bath. Mallory felt her tongue work its way down her spine until Fletcher disappeared from sight in the mirror. She was alone with her image. At first Mallory recoiled, but then she went to a place that was warm and safe, to a white room where there was nothing but calla lilies and swans and she was a marble statue.

Fletcher's probing fingers brought her back to reality. She tried to force Mallory's thighs apart, but Mallory was again the statue. And statues didn't move.

"Spread your legs."

Fletcher's breath came hard. Mallory knew how Fletcher liked to push her own games. Sometimes they became an effort, even for her.

"No."

Fletcher slapped her hard.

Mallory shivered. No doubt Fletcher thought it was from pleasure, but it was from hate.

"No." Mallory said, knowing full well the word would incite Fletcher even more. "No," she repeated, biting her lower lip. She saw her nipples harden without the help of Fletcher's fingers. She knew how her disobedience instigated her mistress' rage. A thin smile pursed Mallory's lips, but she wasn't quick enough to remove it. Fletcher caught it, stood up and walked over to an art nouveau vanity table.

For a woman Fletcher's age, her body was in relatively good

shape. No more than twenty pounds overweight, with large breasts that were firm and thighs a little fleshy, she had no doubt showered care on a body that hundreds of women had sampled.

Mallory heard the drawer open and slam shut. She didn't have to look over to know what Fletcher was after. She heard the crack of the whip before it hit her back.

"No?" Fletcher queried, pulling back her good arm, sending the thick, black leather across Mallory's trembling thighs.

Still Mallory did not move. Her fingers gripped the pink marble sink. "Please don't, please don't punish me." The words spilled out of her mouth hard, yet plaintive.

It was Fletcher's favorite. The whip. Imported from England, sturdy and intricately crafted, the dozen leather strips knotted at each end to procure the striped welts like small slugs that raised the surface of her tender skin. Mallory saw the pleasure this was giving Fletcher, knew her mistress enjoyed this solemn ritual of master and slave. Enjoyed reducing Mallory to her lowest common denominator. With each crack of the whip she felt vandalized.

And yet there was undeniably a slow burn across her loins as if sharp talons were locking into her flesh. Even her toes were plagued with a malarial heat. And that brutal rip in her abdomen as waves of pain melded into pleasure and then stopped, leaving her cold again.

Fletcher took her time. The boundary between them had been temporarily eradicated.

"Please," Mallory choked, a thin spittle seeping from between her dry lips.

"Please, what?" Fletcher interrogated, her eyes flickered with rabid pleasure as Mallory's atonement beat out her own demons.

"Please . . . take me." Mallory's voice was a deep whimper, her legs like rubber bands, the blood rushed to the surface of her penitent back, as pink as the marble sink.

Mallory tried to hide her face in the fold of her arm, but Fletcher had caught the look of pleasure on her face in the mirror. That half-hearted moment of ecstasy Veronica experienced when visaging the image of Christ on a blood-stained cloth. A holy moment, a second coming when all resistance and disbelief vanish.

Fletcher swelled with triumph and love. She dropped to her knees and worshiped her little sinner, pushing her nose into the soft folds of Mallory's flesh like some common hound.

Mallory cried out. The punch of Fletcher's fist inside her was like giving birth, that total feeling of consumption and expulsion. Her eyes rolled back in her head as if gripped by a seizure and the beating of her heart pumped the blood into that warm, black edge of darkness, that salty, wet spray of prenatal liquid dripping down her thighs.

Mallory's mouth opened in a silent scream, the whites of her teeth suddenly jagged edged and razor sharp. Her fists pounded on the marble counter.

It was a stiff, hot madness that grazed their faces in the mirror and the steam from their breath seemed to scorch the glass.

"You love me, don't you," Fletcher gasped, her own pleasure dodging Mallory's.

"Yes, yes," Mallory screamed.

"Show me." Fletcher's voice ached from the strain of her devotion.

Mallory's breasts arched in the air as she spread her legs as far apart as they'd go and dug her hips into the cold inert marble sink.

"Yes what?" Fletcher was weak, her breath coming in gasps now, her senses lost in the smell of leather and pachouli and the taste of victory sweet on her fingers.

"Yes, I love you." Mallory whimpered, her breasts heaving from the exertion and there behind her Fletcher's own sob of pleasure drowning out the manic drumming in her head.

THE BIG COMBO

The suit looked even better this time around. The dress rehearsal at Sayonara had prepared Mercedes for this evening's undercover assignation. Maybe being greeted by a deadly insect as a token of love gave her personality more of an aggressive edge. And she'd need it because as she pulled into the back of Fletcher's house in a beat-up, rented Ford, Mercedes knew she was calling on trouble.

Noh opened the back door, nodded and ushered Mercedes into a kitchen that made hers look like a short-order cook's from a greasy spoon. A young woman with red hair and plump breasts smiled coyly at Mercedes as she carried out a tray of puff pastry stuffed with salmon and beluga caviar.

"So this is the kind of deal Mona Lisa got used to," Mercedes thought. "Hard to say no to such temptations."

Noh introduced Mercedes to Albert, tall, gaunt, with fingers knotted by arthritis and lips curled by forty years of service. "Albert, this is my friend Nick Charles. He's filling in for Tony."

Albert looked Mercedes up and down with sour disdain. "Umm," he replied, glancing at the chef as if to get her approval. A bleach-blonde, thirty-year-old culinary genius Fletcher had hired six months ago, she was basting two succulent ducks with a garlic plum marinade, all her attention consumed by the movements of her creative hand.

Before Albert could offer any objections, Noh pulled Mercedes through the kitchen and out a swinging door into a huge dining room set for a royal gathering.

Mercedes forgot her purpose there. Thoughts swam in reflections of Lalique, china and an antique Baroque chandelier that belonged on the set of Phantom of the Opera. The art hanging on forest green walls was collected from sundry galleries around the world. Most English and American tributes to realism, thick oils spread on a palette to remind diners of their rich spoils. Still lifes with fruit, dead game, fresh cheese and pearly grapes.

"Here," Noh said, slipping a key into Mercedes' hand. "Fletcher keeps her bedroom locked. It's where she used to keep the dance-card. In her vanity, top drawer to the left. Maybe there's something you can use as . . . ." Her voice stopped as a waiter brushed by carrying a huge tray of shucked oysters. "Wait until dinner, when everyone's seated. Top of the stairs, third door to the right."

Mercedes quickly dropped the key in her pant pocket. She wondered if Eva had persuaded Noh to be more cooperative or if Noh was just leading her on a wild goose chase? Her heart beat fast as they moved closer to the hub of conversation emanating from the living room.

Reading Mercedes' mind, Noh stopped at the double doors. "Samantha's not here yet."

Mercedes nodded. Noh placed the chilled bottle of champagne in her hand, wrapped a white monogrammed towel around her arm. "Now whatever you do, don't get caught upstairs. It won't be nice." Noh gave her a weak smile and opened the door.

Her entrance into the smoke-filled room, all white and gold and smelling of money brought about as much attention as a fly in a zoo. No one noticed. No one that is except a middle-aged matron who'd had one too many glasses of champagne.

"Be a dear, dearie, pour me some of that," she ordered, her grating, rather hurried voice full of crushed dreams. "I hate champagne, but I love drinking." She winked at Mercedes, her eyelashes sticking together from an excess of mascara. She distended her bony hand to receive the effervescent wine with about as much distaste as a diner flagging down a waiter to complain about a dirty glass.

As Mercedes poured the expensive champagne into the woman's tulip-shaped flute, her eyes scanned the room, stopping at a trio of heavies. There they were: Fletcher, Max and Regan, the big combo, a prominent study in composition—Queen, King and Joker, dealing out looks to the guests like so many cards across a gaming table.

"Hey, watch out, guy." The woman dabbed the bottom of her glass with a linen napkin, drying the champagne that dribbled down the side.

"Sorry," Mercedes said, dropping her voice three octaves.

"No shit, Sherlock. All over my new dress." The woman stood up, precariously balanced on a pair of blue shoes too small for her size nines. She left a trail of poor taste in her wake as she crushed through the crowd in the room.

Mercedes moved closer to the combo, closer to the thick of the action where she could overhear some meaningful conversation.

Fletcher's good hand waved her over. Her glass was empty. An essay in simplicity, her black dress was no doubt some Parisian import trimmed with the close-cropped fur of a Persian lamb. Her bruised arm was still in a sling, designer, no doubt. Two carat diamonds dangled from small lobes and her hair was coifed like Ivana Trump, only not so full, or piled so high.

"Who are you?" Fletcher asked, the smell of her pungent civet perfume wafting over to Mercedes like a smoke signal.

"Nick," Mercedes replied, avoiding Regan's curious eyes. Regan was the most down-dressed in a pair of black slacks and matching turtle neck.

"Nick," Fletcher repeated, the fleck of the name sharp like a talon on steel. "I need a refill."

Mercedes poured the champagne, careful this time not to cause another accident. Max extended his arm in her direction, his glass half full, his suit some Japanese import with chartreuse stitching along the sleeves and lapels. Mickey Mouse suspenders peeked from underneath where a simple white Gap v-neck t-shirt covered his hairless chest.

"What's he doing here?" Fletcher asked, gritting her teeth. Mercedes looked over and saw Pinkerton cutting through the crowd in a camel coat and burgundy borsalino hat.

"It's a party, relax. Maybe he has some information for us." Max smiled at Fletcher as she rolled her eyes, then looked over at Regan and scowled. Her annoyance was as transparent as Saran Wrap.

Mercedes moved off to clear away a table, keeping within earshot of the big combo, the threesome, now a foursome. She wondered where Mallory was, but more importantly, she wondered how fashionably late Samantha would be.

Pinkerton smiled that supercilious smile and joined in the evening's festivities. He accepted a Scotch from a waiter and handed the servant his coat in exchange. The hat he left on his head. Max and

Pinkerton seemed fixated with each other, it was evident in the cross-fire of their eyes. Were they falling in love (a little homoeroticism under the guise of an "after hours" three-way the other night?) or plotting someone's murder? Perhaps Fletcher's? Perhaps hers?

Mercedes' imagination was taking a turn for the worse. The party was having that effect on her. No wonder Mona Lisa got lost beneath the ritzy veneer of these "high society" crooks. All this bad influence, money, food, champagne. An environment more phony than most of her movies. Would Mercedes have succumbed?

She scanned the remainder of the crowd, intermittently pouring champagne. The snatches of dialogue that reached Mercedes was nothing but party banter. Several of Fletcher's guests seemed DOA, as if they stepped out of the pages of the Tibetan Book of the Dead. Especially the tight-faced woman with the patinated complexion, smooth and shiny like calf liver. Did women like her pay for Mona Lisa's services? Or was it the dyke in the corner with the short-cropped hair and faint moustache who looked like a poor imitation of Gertrude Stein? Or the sexy femme with the black pumps who kept smiling at the sequined matron lost behind the pall of her husband's cigar smoke?

The last drop of champagne reached someone's glass just as the double doors opened. The crowd suddenly parted as ice floes on a lake. Mallory made her grand entrance decked out in a quilted white cloche jacket and satin pouffed skirt, her blonde hair as soft as a whisper, her eyes taking in the room, yet taking in nothing. But as soon as she spotted Fletcher, Mercedes noticed a thick glaze of indifference—or was it hate—douse the light in her eyes.

"A nice little slice of lemon meringue," someone cattily remarked.

Mercedes had never seen Mallory. Now she knew what all the fuss was about.

"Her longest to date. But mark my words, this affair will turn out worse than the others. Her temper . . . ." The two gossips fell into a whispered hush.

Mercedes looked over at the antique vases on Fletcher's mantle. More like canopic jars, elegant receptacles which contained the entrails of former habitues, lovers, you name it, faithful members of Fletcher's coterie, now blackballed to the underworld of the snub-nosed. Which guest would be next, or would Mallory eventually earn a place on her mantle?

Mercedes needed a breath of fresh air. She was just about to open the door when the door opened for her. Standing there in front of her, their noses practically Eskimo kissing, was Samantha. Dressed like midnight without the promise of morning, she wore a butter-thin leather dress the color of eggplant that folded like rich pudding over her well-kept body. Blood red garnets hung on her lobes and the full lips were made even fuller with an Indian Red matte.

Mercedes tore her eyes away, praying Samantha wouldn't recognize her. It was only then she noticed there was a woman behind Samantha. A woman she'd seen before. Fire raged in Mercedes' veins. She almost crushed the empty champagne bottle in her hand.

Mercedes would know that face anywhere, not to mention the breasts which, sans bra, were barely covered by a veil of black lace. It was the señorita with the modest bathrobe in Samantha's room at the Chateau Marmont.

The two women moved into the room, the siren's arm clinging onto Samantha's as protectively as chaps on a cowboy. As they passed Mercedes, a paralysis of the utmost acuteness rendered her motionless.

The hand was complete. The Ace had arrived.

SKATING ON THIN ICE

Beyond the protective shield of Fletcher's coterie, Regan felt edgy. She knew Mallory wouldn't try to get her attention with Fletcher at her heels, so it made perfect sense to stick as close to her employer as possible.

Regan had tried to convince herself that the letter Mallory had slipped into her hand in the privacy of her bedroom was nothing but schoolgirl gibberish. The girl rambled on about how Fletcher was killing her a little each day. And how she needed someone like Regan to take care of her. As if Regan didn't have enough trouble these days. She didn't want to fall into Mallory's trap.

Still, those eyes were dangerous. Her kiss lethal. After their secret meeting Regan dreamt about having sex with Mallory. And just before the dream's climax, Fletcher stormed into the picture, a knife in hand. Regan woke up in a cold sweat and knew the girl had gotten under her skin.

Regan always backed the favorites and stealing Mallory away from Fletcher without any fatal repercussions was a long shot.

Walking among the crowd of guests, some who would stay on for dinner, others who would leave to join parties or meet at restaurants (Fletcher liked to let her guests know exactly who was the most regarded by sending invitations and indicating whether or not supper would be served), Regan wondered how much longer she could hack working for Fletcher.

She, of course, was staying for dinner, but not because Fletcher regarded her as one of the social elite. It was because Fletcher was plagued with suspicions that someone was really after her. She had toyed with the idea of a bodyguard, but Regan assured her that she was all that was needed.

Regan wondered whether Fletcher was on the brink of menopause or just going daffy because of Mallory? Maybe a bit of both.

Stuffing her hands in her pant pockets, Regan checked out the rooms to make sure no one was loitering. Fancy crowds made her uncomfortable, self-conscious. She didn't understand their mind-frames, nor did she want to.

Society darlings and wanna-bees and a few token artists, one of whom had recently completed an original for Fletcher that Regan thought ridiculous. Spending money for something that looked like the insides of an animal made no sense to her. People wasted fortunes in search of the remote. Next they'd be taking trips to the moon just to see it wasn't made of cheese.

Regan passed an eight foot tall grandfather clock on her way to the library. When she opened the door, she discovered Mallory making an appearance from the northern entrance. Call it a coincidence, Regan wondered for all of a second if Mallory had followed her. She looked so fetching, defenseless and lost, Regan didn't even stop to weigh the repercussions of the random encounter. She gathered Mallory in her arms.

In the soft glow of candlelight, Mallory shimmered like a lake in moonlight. And Regan was in the mood for a boat ride. Denial had fallen overboard as soon as the fresh scent of Mallory's skin drifted to her nose.

Little tears of melodrama spilled down Mallory's cheeks. She needed a strong shoulder to lean on.

Regan had two.

The sobs subsided. Regan pulled her closer. She could feel everything that was meant to be hidden. Then she kissed her salty lips stained with tears. Kissed her in a place that didn't belong to her. It made sense, Mallory didn't belong to her. But now she did.

Had Regan understood Latin, she would have seen "*caveat emptor*" written all over Mallory, but the only economics that made sense to her were sitting on Mallory's ears. They were a pair of gold and diamond earrings Fletcher had given her when the dance-card was stolen. With the money Regan would be able to fetch for them, they could leave town for awhile until the heat died down.

Mallory must have read her mind. She took off the earrings and put them in the palm of Regan's hand. "You'll do it, won't you?"

Regan rolled the earrings in her hand like a pair of dice.

"Take me away from here," she shouted.

Regan clasped a hand around her mouth. That's all she needed was Fletcher storming in here. She could feel the bullet in her back, feel the hot heat of the metal as it ripped through her body. She unconsciously touched the scar on her chest where a bullet had entered and exited, clean as a whistle. A stupid accident during target practice at the Academy.

"I need time," Regan said. She looked toward the door. No doubt the guests would be making their way into the dining room. Fletcher would be looking for Mallory. It was a big house, but not big enough.

"You don't understand," Mallory gasped, the sobs coming on again like the hiccups. "She makes me . . . she makes me do these things . . . and I can't . . . ." She caught a gulp of air and started choking.

Regan rubbed her back. "Shush . . . get hold of yourself." She pulled out a handkerchief and tried to wipe the mascara from the girl's cheeks, but Mallory pulled away.

Regan grabbed her arm. "Things. What things?"

Mallory bit her lip and shook her head.

Regan shook her, pressing her thumbs into Mallory's flesh until she winced.

"You won't like me if I tell you..." she dropped her head, ashamed.

Regan's face was red. She didn't understand why she was so angry, she just was. "Things. She makes you do *things*?" A spray of spit escaped passed clenched teeth.

Mallory nodded, her eyes as vulnerable as tinder in a roaring fire.

"And how *hard* do you say no?"

Mallory's head snapped back. "This hard." She slapped Regan across the face.

Regan took the blow. "Don't ever slap me again."

This time Mallory whacked her hard across the other cheek. "You'll take it. Just like I took it . . . and like it . . . like everything about me. . . ."

Regan muffled Mallory's words with her hot tongue. It was wild, crazy and all for nothing, but it felt like a million bucks.

The hinges from a door creaked. The two lovers split apart like a deer cleaved in half with a machete.

Regan checked to see if anyone was there. The door remained open about ten inches, wide enough for someone to hear and see. The corridor was empty. Had a hunter entered their forest of dangerous pleasure?

"I better go." Mallory straightened her hair and smoothed her dress. She took a deep breath, smiled wanly and left to rejoin the party.

Whoever it was, Regan thought as she downed a shot of Fletcher's brandy, had better be on her side, otherwise she was a dead duck.

FOOD FOR THOUGHT

Most of the little nucleus were seated, soldiers lined along a thirty-foot table with hungry eyes and sharpened tongues ready to cut into their victims of gossip as salaciously as they were about to devour the warm *foie gras* and chilled lobsters set before them by tuxedoed waiters.

Mercedes stood behind a harried Fletcher and a cool Max preparing to make their grand entrance.

"Looks like you've been tearing at someone's throat," he chided.

"I'm about to." Her black mood made the lines around her lips appear to be etched with dark pencil. Fletcher turned her head in the direction of Regan, seated across the table from Mallory.

Both Mercedes and Max followed her gaze. Mallory was smiling at Regan as she toyed with her napkin.

Regan, on the other hand, was fidgeting with her knife while trying to make small talk with a bald man whose obscenely large head made him look like E.T. His jaw was small, lost in that overbearing cranium and he wore a black eye patch across his left eye.

"Looks like your Cinderella may have found her slipper." Max's voice had lost its jocular tone. He was dead serious.

"Damn you." Fletcher's good hand griped her expensive skirt, then relaxed.

Max extended his arm, led her to the opposite end of the table where he pulled out a chair for her. As she sat down, a hush fell and everyone nodded in her direction, acknowledging the diva's arrival.

Fletcher cast a cold smile out across the table as a fisherman throws a net out to sea. Conversation started, someone laughed and soon knives flayed the *foie gras*, clinking against the china and forks found their way into mouths as Mercedes moved around the table pouring the latest shipment of Nouveau Beaujoulais.

The room was a hothouse of scents, but the most provocative was the musky, heady fragrance of Samantha. Seated next to Carmen Miranda, Samantha held out her glass while Mercedes poured her wine, trying with difficulty not to stare.

Not only did she look more beautiful than Mercedes had last seen her, she appeared to be having quite an enjoyable time. For someone who purportedly despised Fletcher and her ilk, Samantha had no trouble fitting in. Nor did she have to muster too much effort to flirt with her companion.

Mercedes was seething about the ruse Samantha had pulled at the Marmont. Perhaps Samantha was hiding in the closet when she stormed into the room. She bet the two woman had had a good laugh. Mercedes was tempted to pour the bottle of wine in Samantha's leather-clad lap, but she managed to control her urge.

Mercedes was just about to leave the room when Fletcher's chilling voice pierced the din of the guests. Mercedes dallied by the serving tray, pretending to tend to the creamed dill and lime sauce heating in a silver chafing dish.

"Darling, your diamond earrings, where are they?"

Mallory turned the color of the half-eaten lobster on her plate. She touched her ears and giggled. "I must have left them upstairs."

Fletcher didn't take her eyes off Mallory and Mallory couldn't pull her attention away from her plate.

Mercedes wondered where this was leading to.

"I'll run upstairs and get them. You look so naked and vulnerable without them," Fletcher laughed. A few guests followed her cue and forced a chuckle.

Mallory jumped up. "Don't be silly, I'll get them."

Fletcher watched Regan's face. "No, stay here with me."

Mallory sat back down. She seemed relieved. Regan shifted uncomfortably in her seat. Mercedes knew something was up. She'd better take care of her own business before things got completely out of hand.

*   *   *

Mercedes had no trouble finding Fletcher's bedroom. The double doors were painted with rococo cherubs and the room was magnificent. Fit for an empress. A combination of French and Asian decor, it reflected Fletcher's haughtiness and her love of order.

Her closet was about as large as Mercedes' entire bedroom. Massive, probably a former room converted to a storage compartment, it was filled with designer clothes, color coordinated with rows and rows of shoes and dozens of handbags.

On Fletcher's vanity were a variety of elegant bottles filled with imported perfumes. Mercedes checked out her appearance in the mirror. She wet two fingers and slicked back a few strands of hair that were out of place.

She opened the drawer. Inside were a number of letters addressed to Fletcher from someone with the initials D.L. in London. There was a faded black and white photo of a little girl with curls and a white frilly dress. Mercedes recognized the eyes, even at that age. It was Fletcher before she was corrupted in a no-doubt short-lived age of innocence. Mercedes wondered what events had led to turning this little girl into a such a vengeful, wicked woman?

Mercedes heard a noise outside the door. She stopped breathing. The door handle turned. Mercedes quickly closed the drawer and dashed behind a *shoji* screen blocking the bay window. Whoever was trying to break in, certainly had no business being there. The footsteps receded and disappeared. She started breathing again.

An antique clock ticked on a mantle over the fireplace. Could Noh have come across something herself? Why was she so convinced that there would be something of value to Mercedes in this drawer?

A burgundy velour jewelry case, just large enough to house the dance-card was stuffed in the back of the deep drawer. Mercedes pulled it out and snapped it open. Inside lay an article from *ARTnews*. It was yellowed and frayed and dated July 1982. Mercedes carefully opened it. Her eyes scanned the paper. It didn't take long to uncover some more dirt.

The article detailed the investigative work of INTERPOL in locating a number of precious artifacts that had mysteriously disappeared from private estates and museums. It turned out that the Josef Hoffman dance-card had been one of the most treasured items from the Vienna art scene. Lloyd's of London had recently sold a similar piece and it brought in a cool $2.1 million.

Formerly in the possession of a Sardinian King who had bestowed it upon his mistress, the dance-card appeared to rue disaster to the owners.

After the King's wife discovered such a lavish gift had been given to a common, but uncommonly beautiful woman, the mistress mysteriously disappeared, along with the dance-card. The mistress was never found, but the dance-card surfaced again in the early '70s. Lloyd's of London was the sales agent.

It went on to enumerate that Mr. and Mrs. Cartwright, a wealthy Bostonian family with assets in the billions, had settled in London and acquired the antique from an auction spearheaded by Lloyd's for the purchase price of $1.1 million. It was then given to their daughter, the lovely Winnifer Cartwright in honor of her "coming out" at an exclusive and much ballyhooed ball of the season.

The event caused quite a stir. Not only for the lavish party and the coterie of well-known attendees, but because that night, after dancing to Ms. Cartwright's heart's content, one eligible bachelor after the next filling up her dance-card, the debutante and card disappeared without a trace. Two months later the poor girl's body was found buried in a barn in Cornwall. Her hands had inexplicably been severed and buried several feet away. The authorities had arrested one of Ms. Cartwright's admirers that night who had recorded over six dances in the victim's card. Apparently, Johnny Withey had one prior arrest for breaking a prostitute's arm, but the charges of first degree murder were eventually dropped on the Cartwright case when no evidence could be produced. The investigation was ongoing.

Mercedes' hands were shaking. Not only because she was trespassing in Fletcher's room, but because the dance-card, which was something she'd treasured and cared for, seemed to be cursed with misfortunes.

The antique clock appeared to tick tock, tick tock, doom. Her hope sank like a weathered rowboat at sea and for the first time, she lost faith of ever seeing Mona Lisa again.

Mercedes replaced the article and closed the drawer. She would be missed downstairs. She walked to the door and checked the corridor before exiting Fletcher's bedroom. Until she figured out this mystery, until she returned the dance-card to its rightful owner—whomever that might be—she too was in serious danger. She shuddered.

As Mercedes made her way down the dimly lit corridor, a shadow crossed the plush carpet. Someone was exiting a room. There was nowhere to hide. Mercedes pulled herself back against the wall, hoping the person would pass without noticing. It didn't work.

The shadow became a form. "I like this new look of yours."

Samantha stood before Mercedes and smiled. "You looking for something?" Her eyes had the deadpan innocence of a child.

Mercedes could feel her body tighten. A wall rose up between them. She seethed with anger. "Get out of my way."

Samantha opened her arms as if she'd been crucified. "Am I in your way, Mercedes?" Those eyes again, as playful as a shark's.

Mercedes pushed past, but Samantha caught her suit sleeve. She pulled Mercedes close and kissed her on the cheek, then whispered, "I haven't made love to a man in more years than I care to remember, but the prospect of making love to you, tonight, dressed like that, excites me."

Mercedes laughed. She couldn't help but marvel over Samantha's defiant and egotistical attitude. After blatantly parading Carmen Miranda in front of her all evening—knowing full well Mercedes was there in drag—Samantha had the nerve to try to seduce her. "You've got balls, you really have."

"You're the one wearing the pants." Samantha pressed a hot palm on Mercedes' thigh. Her lip curled into a sinister smile.

Mercedes pushed Samantha's hand from her body. "What were you doing at Sayonara with Pinkerton?"

Samantha lifted her hand, as if these questions were too amateurish for her to deign to answer, but she managed. "Same thing you were doing there—and here—private dick. Pinkerton was sniffing around under orders from Max and I was there to find out what the hell happened to Mona Lisa. I thought I was doing you a favor."

Mercedes laughed. "Yeah, well, don't do me any."

Voices came from the end of the corridor. Samantha pulled Mercedes farther down the hall to a small closet. She opened the door and pushed Mercedes inside. When the door closed behind her, Samantha switched on a small dim light. Hanging on a rack were the carcasses of skinned fox, mink, and leopard. Fletcher had quite a collection of fur coats.

"Listen, you think this is a game? Well, you're wrong. Fletcher's nuts. And Max is prepared to do anything, and I mean anything, to get back that dance-card. And I think you have it and either they get it from you or I do, in which case you get to live to tell the story."

"Don't threaten me. I know what I'm up against."

Samantha pushed her further into the closet. She brushed up against a warm, furry, full-length coat.

"You don't know anything. Trust me. I don't want you hurt . . . I happen to care about you."

"Your `care' has been hanging on your arm all night" Mercedes sneered. "The two of you must have had a nice laugh at my expense after I left the hotel."

Samantha's eyes twinkled. "Is that a little jealousy I detect?"

"I don't like being played for a fool."

"I'm not playing, not with you. With her, maybe. But not you."

"You're a liar."

"So spank me." Samantha's directive was in earnest.

Before Mercedes could even take her up on her offer, she delivered the next blow.

"You're lying to me about not having the dance-card."

Samantha had the most annoying way of corralling the conversation round to suit her needs. The anger rose in Mercedes like a tempest. "Fuck you." She lifted her hand to swipe Samantha against the cheek, but instead slammed her fist against the wall. She thought she heard the crunch of bone; her hand throbbed with pain, but it felt good. It took her mind off other things.

"Go ahead," Samantha said raising her dress along her firm thighs. "Get rid of that anger. Here in the closet." Her eyes were all cold pleasure.

Mercedes' breathing was heavy, the air compressed and confined and her heart felt like five sticks of dynamite ready to explode. Mercedes clenched her fist, then opened it, as if flexing her fingers would stave off this white hot craving.

Samantha's perfume had that heady scent of "no trespass" while her skin glistened with murderous invitation. She inched her leather dress farther up her thighs. She wasn't wearing panties.

Mercedes stopped breathing. There wasn't any air left to breath. "You think I'm easy to be had?" Mercedes' voice was deep and raspy, as if she'd just smoked a pack of cigarettes and drank a bottle of Sheep Dip whiskey. Her hand opened and closed, opened and closed and the veins in her arm grew strong and plump with the surplus of blood.

"Not easy. Hard." Samantha grabbed Mercedes' crotch and her lips curled into a full smile. "Look at me."

Mercedes was backed up against the fur of some dead animal. She fought hard not to look down at Samantha's half-naked body, but it was as if ten pound weights were sewn on her lids. A shiver ran down her spine like a trickle of water, the way an ice cube leaves a residue when teased along warm flesh. And between her legs there was this raw, red hot throb she had no control over. Her breasts pushed out of their binding. She grabbed Samantha's dress and tried to yank it down over her nakedness, but the material wouldn't cooperate. Samantha's thighs smoldered and the leather was stuck to her flesh.

"I've really missed you." Samantha took hold of Mercedes hand and put it between her legs. She was wet.

An involuntary moan escaped from Mercedes. She looked at Samantha. Their eyes locked and dialogued as if hours of down-and-dirty conversation passed in the blink of an eye. And still she couldn't remove her hand, there in between Samantha's thighs, stuck just like the leather on this sweet-cheat's flesh.

Mercedes knew the kiss was coming even before Samantha grabbed her face in her hands and their lips met. She swooned and the small room swirled with the expensive coats like midnight ghosts in a haunted mansion. And everywhere there was this heat and the swell of music from downstairs and in the air was the acrid whiff of danger and suddenly the dynamite detonated and the shards of resistance were ruptured like a torn ligament.

Samantha broke away. She looked at Mercedes as if seeing her for the first time and as quickly as a flash of lightning, without warning, something passed across the eyes and settled in as if a final verdict had just been read in Supreme Court.

Mercedes wasn't sure about the fear she suddenly felt, but she knew that when Samantha removed her hand and pulled down her skirt, something fatal had passed between them.

Samantha pulled out a key and pressed it into the palm of Mercedes' hand. "You come to me, but only if you want to." She examined Mercedes' flushed face. "I need you."

* * *

By the time Mercedes returned to the dining room, the party was in full swing, no one appeared to notice her missing.   The scant remains of half a dozen legs of lamb were being removed and a salmon *mousse* covered in a coffin of puff pastry molded in the shape of a large fish was being passed from guest to guest as if in a ceremonial rite inherited from generation to generation.

Mercedes poured a light Pinot Grigio to complement the fish. The table was spotted with food stains, spilled red wine and soiled linen napkins. The guests were even more raucous, the food and wine having eased the tensions.

Mercedes avoided Samantha's eyes as she poured some wine for Max.

"Just heard from Waterson," Max said to Pinkerton. "He's going for the deal. I've invited him to the Halloween party. Plan on being there."

Pinkerton stuck a fingernail in between his tooth and extracted a sliver of meat. "I have every intention of being there."

Mercedes was all ears. She'd have to find out about this party.

"And the little matter of the dance-card?" Pinkerton looked over at Fletcher as he talked.

Max scowled. "With Xuan out of the way . . . one down and one more to go."

Mercedes poured some wine for Pinkerton. He looked up at her. She smiled weakly. For a second he seemed to be trying to place her in his memory, but was too engrossed in his *tête à tête* with Max to pursue it any further.

"But can you get to Martini?"

Mercedes stopped cold. Her name coming from Pinkerton sounded as chewed and masticated as the discarded meat he'd just plucked from his teeth.

"There's never been a woman I couldn't get to." Max grinned at Pinkerton and the steel on his teeth reminded Mercedes of thick staples. Pinkerton chuckled and the two men enjoyed the privacy of their joke.

Their mirth was interrupted when Fletcher stood up to make an announcement. She was wobbling on her feet, no doubt drunk. "Friends, I've gathered my dearest to share some good news."

A buzz went around the table like a swarm of killer bees. Everyone stopped eating, not wanting to break their concentration.

Fletcher placed a hand on Mallory's shoulder. "It's no secret to anyone here in this room, that I've been completely overwhelmed by this darling creature. And to show my affection, I want you to understand why I feel it necessary to run off, to leave this town."

A quick shock delivered to the ears of her listeners, they were speechless and then a collective gasp, and a chorus of "Oh no's" drowned out the music.

"How long?" someone shouted, reluctant, no doubt, to give up Fletcher's lavish parties for too long.

"Months, a year, perhaps. I've discovered this wonderful island off the coast of Malta. We'll be very happy there."

Mallory's face turned ashen. She gripped her linen napkin in her small hands. Max's eyes were frosty. He twirled an unlit cigar in his fingers, his mind mulling over implications of Fletcher's stupid decision. Regan opened the top button of her shirt, her forehead mopped with sweat.

Fletcher leveled a deadly glance at Regan more menacing than a cockatrice, then smiled. "Mallory's tired of sharing me with the world. It will do us good to be alone, just the two of us." She squeezed Mallory's shoulder so hard, the girl grimaced.

Regan pushed her chair out and stood up. Just then the lights went out. A gun shot resonated, the echo from the blast caroming off the four walls. And from the ceiling, having been confined in a papier mache sculpted angel, triggered by some electronic device, iridescent, day-glow confetti exploded like colored snowflakes over the guests.

As "ohs" and "ahs" escaped from the delighted spectators, Mercedes gripped onto Regan, who tried to lunge for Fletcher.

Music filled the room, majestic, heavy on the bass and organ. Three waiters marched into the darkened room carrying trays of baked Alaska and pears *flambe*. It was just enough diversion for Regan to get hold of herself and leave the room unnoticed.

The party wasn't nearly over, but Mercedes had had enough for one night. Her head was swimming. She needed a drink herself. And she needed to get as far away from Samantha as possible.

TERMINAL CONTOUR

An electric kaleidoscope of neon and traffic lights gyrated against the ebony backdrop of night as Mercedes drove along Sunset Boulevard. The hard shapes and contours of the streets seemed to meld into the mirage of a woman. A stone-hearted siren who went by the name of Samantha.

Mercedes pulled into the driveway of the Chateau Marmont and left the old Ford with the valet. Her gait was steady, her purpose clear. As she slipped the key in the door, Mercedes knew why she'd come back to Samantha.

Samantha knew too. She was standing in front of the open window, smoking a cigarette. Her eyes were covered by a pair of designer sunglasses.

"I've been standing here, wondering whether you'd come, and I realized for the first time that I wanted you here with me, more than I've wanted anything."

Mercedes walked to the window and stared out at the city. "And your date?"

"She had a plane to catch." A 747 cut across the moon.

"You said you needed me?"

"I've never needed anything before, until now." Samantha turned away from the window.

Mercedes tingled inside. "I still don't think I'm more important than the dance-card."

Samantha smiled. "You're all business, aren't you?"

Mercedes poured herself a cognac. She swallowed the shot. Her mouth and her eyes watered. "No, but I am here to find out what's going on. Fletcher seemed to be in a rare mood tonight."

"You don't know the half of it. You're lucky you got out of there when you did. Fletcher's onto Regan. And Regan's onto Mallory. It doesn't look pretty."

Mercedes was puzzled. "Why would Regan jeopardize everything she's worked so hard for by moving in on Fletcher's girlfriend?"

Samantha ground out her cigarette and joined Mercedes in a drink. "Because Fletcher's crazy. She probably threatened Mallory, she's done it before with others. She's so goddamn jealous. And Regan likes playing hero. That's all any of this is, isn't it? Games."

"I'm not playing."

"You're still sore, aren't you?"

"I'll get over it." Mercedes poured herself another shot.

Samantha lit a cigarette and gave it to Mercedes. "That's what I'm afraid of . . . you see I had every intention of conning you into giving me the dance-card."

"But I don't have it."

Samantha removed her sunglasses and turned to Mercedes.

Mercedes gasped. Samantha's left eye was bruised, swollen, a large purple and red welt singed her cheekbone.

"What the hell happened?" Mercedes reached out to touch Samantha's face, but Samantha pulled away and put the glasses back on.

"Slow motion suicide. I knew this would happen as soon as I stepped foot in L.A. It's hard to go straight in a town like this—no pun intended."

"Was it Max?"

Samantha didn't reply. "It all goes back to the source—Fletcher. She wants that dance-card, I said I would get it back. And I haven't. This is just a warning. So you see . . . ."

"I see that your feelings for me may have more to do with your own survival." Mercedes was getting the full picture.

"You're good with words, aren't you?" Samantha walked over to Mercedes. "But I like you even better when you keep quiet." Samantha pulled Mercedes to her and kissed her.

Mercedes tried to pull away from her grip, but it was impossible. A terminal contour of flesh, blood and bones, Samantha's strength grew in proportion to her anger.

Samantha pushed Mercedes away as if she'd gotten hold of something beyond her control. She downed her drink.

"Are you telling me your life depends on getting hold of the antique?"

"No. My life depends on getting hold of you."

Mercedes laughed and opened her arms, needling her. "Come on, you wouldn't know how even if you wanted to."

Samantha was to determined to prove her wrong. She wrapped her arms around Mercedes and kissed her again, then pulled her over to the bed.

Mercedes sunk into the plush down comforter and watched as Samantha dropped her dress on the floor and kicked off her heels. She wore nothing but a deep purple corset that made her look like a queen of midnight on a dirty French postcard.

"If I let you keep the dance-card, I'll have to go away again."

"I'll wait," she said, pulling Samantha down on top of her.

Samantha threw her glasses on the floor and bit Mercedes' earlobe. Her hand tortured Mercedes between the legs. Her fingers were warm, velvet smooth and played a slow, unyielding riff.

Mercedes felt Samantha's pent-up anger smolder and burn like a fire out of control. Her eyes locked on the bruise and dried blood caked in the corner of her lover's eye. She knew it didn't come from the whack of Max's palm. More likely a blunt instrument, the handle of a gun.

Mercedes touched Samantha's wound. The palm of her hand stung with pain. She had absorbed the suffering and internalized the brutality and knew she too could be lost in the riveting, hard-boiled landscape of crime.

The tenacious pressure of Samantha's hand exacerbated her fears, but there was no going back. The fury of desire, this Medean vengeance, lured her away from Mona Lisa and the dance-card. She felt herself sink into a quicksand of pleasure as Samantha baited her over the edge into a dark abyss. She was hovering over a precipice and gasping when she heard a click. Her eyes flew open. The shock pulled her out of her erotic quagmire.

A .38 derringer was pointed at her temple.

Mercedes was as stiff as a steel beam. Her eyes raged and still this fatal attraction moved on top of her as if nothing had come between them. As if the gun meant no more than some toy picked up at the Pleasure Chest.

"You're not serious?" Mercedes gasped for breath.

"I'm always serious," Samantha replied, removing her corset

with her free hand. The gun was aimed straight at Mercedes' heart. "Give me the dance-card." Samantha didn't move a muscle or skip a beat.

Mercedes was paralyzed, Samantha's strong legs pinioned her to the bed. The woman's breasts glistened in the dim orange light of the room, the nipples hard as bullets. "No."

Samantha leveled the derringer. "The world's safest handgun." She then emptied the double barreled pistol of its ammunition. Bullets dropped like gold coins on the down comforter. Samantha flung the gun across the room. It shattered a vase on the dresser, shards of glass landing everywhere. Water dripped on the carpet.

Mercedes twisted her body hard, knocking Samantha off the bed. She headed for the door, but Samantha grabbed her leg and pulled her down.

Both women tumbled on the floor, rolling on the carpet like two angry schoolgirls embroiled in a catfight. Curses shot through the room. Samantha pinned Mercedes' arms to her side and straddled her. Mercedes thrashed about. "Are you crazy?"

"Yeah, crazy about you. Crazy enough to let you go, only next time it won't be me who's pointing a pistol at you. So you better learn how to use one. Remember I won't be around."

Mercedes felt as if her head were splitting open. Samantha kissed her hard on the lips. Their sweat tasted metallic like blood. Their bodies steamrolled into one and instead of trying to pull apart, their flesh melded.

Breathless, Mercedes ripped off her shirt and unwrapped the Ace bandage around her chest. She wound it tight around Samantha's wrists, tight enough to gouge the flesh and then she tied it in a knot.

Samantha didn't like it. She tried to yank free, but it only lacerated her skin.

Sweat poured from Mercedes' forehead. The room was hot. With Samantha bound, Mercedes felt safer. She didn't have to worry about her lover pulling out a knife, an UZI or a bow and arrow.

Mercedes removed her pants and crawled on all fours like a cat toward Samantha. Her face was white as bone against the bruise tinged with sweat and blood like the juice of a pomegranate. From toe to head, her body brushed up against Samantha's, their bodies two pieces of kindling.

Hours later, when Mercedes lifted her head from the floor, the room was red hot, glowing, bathed in a hellish light. Samantha was straddled against her back as they lay there on the rug, breathing heavy, a wheeze escaping as her fingers disappeared inside Mercedes.

The room imploded one last time before the specter of night crushed them in its arms.

M.O.N.A.

It was past eight when Mercedes slipped out of the hotel. Samantha was still sleeping, curled in a ball like a little girl. Mercedes took the .38 and the bullets as a souvenir of their evening.

She didn't trust Samantha, in fact, she didn't trust anyone. Regan wasn't answering her phone, there wasn't a word from Mona Lisa and Mercedes knew she was taking a big chance bringing the dance-card to the Museum of Neon Art as the note had instructed.

Mercedes called Good Friday and told him she wouldn't make dinner at the Pantry. She failed to tell him why. "Listen," she said, "in case something happens to me, you know, I want you to take care of my things."

"What you talkin' 'bout? Now here you go worrin' me 'fore I get off the phone. I'm coming over."

"No, please. I'm fine, it's just that I can't get over Mona Lisa's disappearance and it's given me the spooks, you know how it is."

"Umm. Well listen, I just got word that Redlite told Malone someone was in the room with him at Club Sayonara when Xuan got shot. He gave him your name, but Malone didn't believe him."

"How do you know all this?"

"I got some buddies on the force. I told you I'd keep snooping around for you."

Mercedes wondered why the police hadn't contacted her. There were no messages on her machine. She thanked Good Friday.

"Don't thank me, just stay in one piece, for God's sake and if you need me, call, no matter what time."

Mercedes hung up, took the dance-card and crawled into bed. It was ten in the morning and she felt as if she slept all of half an hour last night. Thoughts of Samantha crept into her mind, but she shut them out. She needed to keep things in perspective. Her body still tingled from their lovemaking. It would take everything she had to be sensible about this affair. She fingered the three muses. She knew every intricate detail of the antique by heart. After reading the article in *ARTnews*, she was now privy to the history behind the antique. Poor Ms. Cartwright. What had happened to the King's mistress? Of all the things to steal from Fletcher, Mona Lisa had to take this. She slipped the antique under her pillow, downed three tylenol to stop the hammering in her head and stave off a migraine. She pulled the covers over her and tried to rest before her assignation at M.O.N.A.

Tomorrow she'd sort out her relationship with Samantha. She felt that throb between her legs. She punched her pillow to crush out the image of Samantha. Who was she kidding? She could no more half-way be in love with this enigmatic woman than she could forget how much her friendship with Mona Lisa meant.

*   *   *

She opened her eyes. The room was filled with dark shadows. A window flapped against the house. The Santa Anas were picking up, the wind howling outside. A metal garbage can scraped against the pavement. And then she heard a noise.

Mercedes bolted up in bed. Someone was walking up the stairs. She grabbed the gun on the night table and tried to steady her hand. She laid down, slipped the gun under the blanket and pretended to be asleep.

Heavy footsteps moved toward her. Her heart felt as if it were stuck in her mouth and her hands were clammy with sweat. Suddenly a gloved tentacle grabbed her around the neck. Her eyes flew open and standing before her was a figure, no eyes, no nose, no mouth, just a big man, his evil eyes now evident through narrow slits in the cotton mask.

Mercedes screamed, her heart hammering against her ribs. He laughed and squeezed tighter around her jugular. She whipped her hand out from the blanket and before he knew what hit him, she stuck the short barrel in his chest and pulled the trigger.

The eyes were wild. She felt a warm, wet ooze on her hands. Still he didn't loosen his grip. Mercedes shot again and this time he fell back. She pushed him off the bed. He felt as heavy as a two hundred pound sack of grain.

He hit the floor, gasped his last mouthful of oxygen; his head dropped to his side. He was dead. Mercedes crouched beside him and removed the mask.

She screamed. There, laying on the floor was Samantha. Her face no longer bruised, a serenity like a shroud over her beautiful face.

Mercedes sobbed so hard she woke herself up. The wind was howling, the trees scraping against the shingles on the house. And while the moon wasn't shining, enough of the city light had filtered into the bedroom. She was disoriented, filled with a consuming nervous energy that even the comfort of her home couldn't dissipate. The nightmare was so powerful, Samantha's face so real, that Mercedes couldn't stop crying. Just what she needed to build her confidence for this evening's rendezvous.

It was seven in the evening. The showdown was only three hours away.

* * *

Mercedes parked her car a block away from Traction where the museum was lodged between a deserted warehouse and a brick studio. She had on a pair of flat black boots, spandex pants and a bomber jacket. The wind practically swept her down the deserted block.

Above the door, DaVinci's smiling neon lady flashed as if to warn her not to trespass. She walked around the side, down a narrow alley lined with trash bins filled with refuse. The side door was locked. It was exactly ten.

A cat meowed in the distance. Mercedes jumped up on a crate under a dirty window. She peered in. A dim light was on in the room, but she couldn't make out anything. No shadows moving to and fro.

"What 'chu peeping at?" A man growled below her.

Mercedes gripped the pistol in her pocket and turned around just as a strong hand clutched her ankle. She nearly lost her balance.

She turned and saw a derelict, his hair matted like Brillo to his head, his face covered with soot. "A puppy in the middle of the cemetery. Were you having fun, or what?" he shouted. There was a nasty gleam in his eye.

Mercedes jumped down. He hopped after her, smiling, three of his upper teeth missing in action. "Come, try the back door. It's as easy as finding hell." He laughed again.

Mercedes followed him. Sure enough there was a back door and it opened. She dug in her pocket and pulled out a dollar bill. He snatched it from her, sniffed the currency, held it to his forehead and hopped off, laughing like a hyena, the wind blowing his tattered scarf up around his ears.

Inside there was plenty of neon to illuminate the room without turning on the overhead lights. She moved past assembled kinetic sculptures and a huge Van de Kamp windmill. A neon piece called *Flaming Bonsai* was contained in a case filled with sea anemones, bubbles and snakes. A ceramic hand was suspended in air holding a lavender neon string called *Slate of Hand*.

When all this was over, she'd get a tube filled with neon and string it around Mona Lisa's neck and call it *Twist of Fate*.

A door slammed shut. Footsteps followed. She gripped the handle of the gun still concealed in her pocket. Suddenly, behind one of the partitioned walls Mercedes heard the whir of a motor. It grew louder. She moved in the direction of the noise, the dance card in her dufflebag strapped around her shoulder.

Mercedes crept along the wall and turned quickly into the next room. There was no one there. No one living or breathing, that is, but someone had activated a bizarre assemblage. An old stuffed chair and black and white TV were suspended eight feet high in mid-air and rotated while a cold, lifeless dummy, hair the color of weak coffee, sat catatonic in the chair.

"Put it on the floor," a man's voice rang out in the room. Mercedes looked around. There was no one there. She could feel the icy sweat pour down her back.

"Where's Mona Lisa?"

"Put it on the fucking floor before I blow a hole in your chest and then you'll never see your friend again."

Mercedes tried to place the voice. It could be Max, but then again she wasn't sure. If she took out her gun, he would see it. She could be killed. She had no options. She took the dance-card from her bag, and laid it on the floor as if placing a beautiful flower on a tombstone.

"Good," a voice said, this time directly behind her. She turned to

get a look, but before she could identify her assailant, a hand shot out
and covered her face with a cloth. It was wet with chloroform. Her
head pounded. She couldn't suck any oxygen into her lungs. Her
arms attacked air. She was losing her strength. The smell made her
sick. She gagged, coughing up phlegm. Her eyes stung and all
around flashes of neon exploded against the darkened room.

Her legs turned to rubber and her body deflated like a blow-up
doll. Two strong hands clamped her ankles, dragged her useless
body across the floor and dumped her under a pink neon sign. Letters
swam overhead like pink angels and just before sinking into that all-
too-familiar darkness, Mercedes made out two words, *Blessed Oblivion*.

*   *   *

*The music of the twelve piece jazz band Maiden Voyage swelled like the
egos in the room. It was a Saturday night and Girl Bar was hopping with
cocktail loungers. Gray smoke hovered in dark corners. The women were
elegant and cool, the room half and half, the way Mercedes liked it. Half
pants and half skirts and plenty of fine looking legs and slicked back coifs.
Good-looking women wearing fine perfume sported plenty of cleavage. Dykes
lit cigarettes and tried to outdistance each other with their hard looks.*

*Mercedes looked sharp in a pair of tailored silk pants, a double-breasted
white jacket with nothing but body cream underneath. Her hair matched her
flame red lips.*

*She moved to the bar, taking in all eyes with her. She struck a pose, one
foot elevated on the railing, a cigarette in hand. There were enough flashes
of light around to smoke out the National Forest, but only one that lit her
stick. Hers.*

*She was drinking a Calistoga with a double twist of lime. She would
have preferred a double martini, but she was on duty. Canvassing the club,
marking her target, playing dick in a room full of janes.*

*The music was Artie Shaw, no matter it wasn't Madonna, it was all
mischief, the horns blaring a South American carioca, a jazzy little number
that got the girls on their heels, swaying by the fake palm trees and beveled
mirrors.*

*Mercedes had a job to do. She was there to see a woman, not that kind
of woman. This was business. In five minutes she'd meet the notorious
Samantha Mann in the back room. She moved across the floor and ducked*

into a room marked PRIVATE.

There they were waiting for her around the operating table, those sacred cows of the Hippocratic oath, self-serving piranhas of the heart, dressed in white gowns, gloves and hats. They moved aside to make room for Mercedes.

"Dr. Mann. Detective Martini. Mercedes Martini."

White didn't suit Samantha. It made her look decent and respectable and clean. Mercedes glanced down at the lump under the table, hoping it would move, but it didn't. "She's not a doctor. She's a high-binder, a confidence trickster, a swindler."

Gasps escaped from the women around the table. Fingers pointed disapprovingly as Samantha shrugged off the insult. She was calm on the surface, a real Jekyll and Hyde.

"Stay and watch, if you'd like," she snapped with confidence.

Samantha threw off the white sheet and there laying on the cold, steel gurney was Mona Lisa. At least what was left of her. Some slap-happy surgeon had rearranged the features of her face. She looked like one of Picasso's Demoiselles D'Avignon. In other words, she looked a mess.

"What have you done to her?" Mercedes was in a state of shock. The inert body lay before her.

"I've saved her life," Samantha proudly stated as a nurse handed her a sharp scalpel. The nurse looked familiar, even in a dress and make-up. It was Detective Pinkerton, the black beret gave him away. He looked pretty damn good for a cross-dresser.

With one quick jerk of the hand, Samantha slashed Mona Lisa across her chest with a five-inch hunter's knife. The incision was deep. The blood wasn't red, it was purple. Mercedes turned away, sickened. When she got the courage to look again, Samantha, the high-priestess, was holding up Mona Lisa's heart for inspection.

"It's still beating," Mercedes said weakly.

"Of course it is," Samantha replied, a savage glee in her green eyes. I've got her life in my hands."

Mercedes knees excused themselves from her body. She fell back and hit her head on something hard and cold.

Her eyes bolted opened. An eerie light filled the room and her head throbbed with pain. She tried to focus, but everything was fuzzy. A head seemed to be swimming in neon before her. She pushed herself up off the cold floor and came face to face with Mona Lisa.

She screamed. A chill played hopscotch along her spine. She blinked her eyes and focused on a holograph. It was a holograph of Mona Lisa encased in a black Lucite box. The resemblance was eerie. It was as if her friend's head were floating in formaldehyde.

Mercedes clutched her stomach. She was going to vomit. She bent down and saw her dufflebag. She swallowed hard, her mouth filling with saliva as she tried to stave off her nausea. She grabbed it. The dance-card was gone. She backed away and tripped over a sand bag, only this sand bag groaned. Mercedes muffled a scream.

Max Pitts laid at her feet, a trickle of blood dribbling down his face. She kicked him. He didn't move. She kicked him again. She checked his pockets. They were empty except for a crumpled invitation to his Halloween party.

If Max sent the flowers, then who took the dance-card and knocked him out? Mercedes needed air. She stumbled to the front door and opened it. An alarm blared louder than the trumpets of the four horsemen of the Apocalypse.

She ran outside. The Santa Ana winds slapped her face, restoring the color to her white skin. She gulped the air greedily, then turned to make sure Max was still out. He was. The neon glared and sizzled, no doubt having a hoot of a time, her head pounded as she raced to her car and peeled off, the sun a sliver of winter orange on the horizon.

FRAMED BY YOU

It was seven in the morning by the time Mercedes got home. She pulled into the driveway and caught sight of Regan's bike and then she caught sight of Regan, standing by a tall oak, smoking a cigarette.

Regan looked worse than Mercedes. Her face was bruised, her arm bandaged in a sling and her fingers appeared to have been mangled in a car door.

As soon as they entered the house, Mercedes drew the blinds, put on a light and poured them both a drink.

"You should get to the hospital."

Regan groaned. "Fletcher doesn't provide insurance for her employees, especially not me."

"What happened?" Mercedes tore off her leather jacket, soiled and rumpled from the night's activities. She threw her empty duffle bag on the sofa and collapsed on the sofa. Depression knit inside her. The dance-card was gone. She could feel the emptiness in the house.

"I was dumping some garbage in the trash at the end of the hall when I heard footsteps behind me. I didn't have time to turn around. Someone pulled a blackjack and hit me on the head. I fell. The bastard was wearing a hood and a pair of thick soled boots." Regan rubbed her face and grimaced. "The arm's not broken but it's sprained and hurts like hell." Regan looked over at Mercedes. "You don't look so good yourself."

Mercedes buried her head in her hands. Everything seemed so hopeless now. She looked over at Regan and gave her a thumbnail sketch of her activities. The more she went over it, the more angry she got. She jumped up and paced. The dance-card was gone. Could someone have followed Max to the museum? Could that someone have been Samantha? She shook the thought from her head. But it came back and socked her between the eyes.

"You should have told me you had the dance-card."

"I should have done a lot of things, but now it doesn't matter, does it?" She felt the tears pour down her hot cheeks.

Regan pulled out a handkerchief and handed it to her. Mercedes tore it from her hands and dabbed her tears. She railed at Regan. "And you. What did you expect Fletcher to do? Dock your pay? You're fucking around with her girlfriend. She's crazy. You heard her. She's planning to kidnap that kid and hide her away on some God-forsaken island . . . and still. . . ."

Regan's brow furrowed. "How the hell did you get this information?"

Mercedes lit a cigarette. It tasted like a dusty road. "Because I was there, dressed in drag. The cute little waiter who kept pouring too much champagne in everyone's glass."

Regan grinned. "So you're the one who stopped me from choking Fletcher? I'm impressed, but that was pretty dangerous, wasn't it? You took a real chance. If anyone had discovered what you were up to, you might look worse than me." Regan massaged her aching jaw.

The drink made Mercedes feel sick. She needed to put something in her stomach. "Don't worry, I'm retired. I'm hanging up my cloak and dagger. I've lost my best friend, the dance-card's gone and. . . ."

"And you're in love."

Mercedes frowned. She'd get over it, like she'd have to get over everything else that had happened. A few weeks of therapy, a little processing, a couple of lectures in the Course in Miracles . . . who was she kidding?

"Listen, I need to hide-out for awhile. I can't go back to my place. I thought maybe I could stay here. Now that the dance-card's gone, the heat'll be off you."

"The heat'll be off," echoed in Mercedes' head. Did she want the heat to be off? Did she want to go back to her quiet, sane life where happier endings capped off her stories? She studied Regan. Funny how a few weeks of romantic *Sturm und Drang* had taken the edge off their attraction toward each other, or at least kept it a bay.

Regan pulled out a .38 revolver. "This time I won't be so stupid, believe me. But listen, the real reason I came here," Regan tried to get

up, but she couldn't. Mercedes helped her. "I've got some bad
news."

Mercedes saw that Regan meant business. She clutched her
stomach, the residue of the chloroform still lingered in her system.
She held on to the chair, prepared for the worse, but not prepared for
what Regan was about to tell her. "Go on."

Regan downed her drink and poured another shot. "A woman's
body was found, two blocks from Sayonara. Behind a trash dumpster."

The room started to swim. Mercedes took some deep breaths and
watched Regan's lips as they moved.

"Her face was . . . ."

"Her face was what?" Mercedes whispered, her dry lips sticking
together, making words impossible.

"It was smashed beyond recognition. She had nothing on her for
identification. She was completely naked, bruises all over her body.
Her hair was blonde and matted to her head."

Mercedes couldn't hold back any longer. She ran to the bathroom,
stuck her head in the toilet bowl and vomited. The taste of brandy
mixed with the taste of bile. She coughed up chunks of food, her
stomach heaving up the details of Regan's description. Her eyes were
wet with tears. She sobbed into the bowl until Regan pulled her up.

Regan wiped Mercedes' face with a wet washcloth. Mercedes
was trembling. "It can't be her. It's not . . . not her. I've got to see for
myself."

Regan sighed. "Let me make a call."

* * *

By the time the sun was coming up, Regan and Mercedes were on
their way downtown. Mercedes couldn't say anything. She just kept
repeating to herself that the body wasn't Mona Lisa's. It wasn't.
There were probably hundreds of murders committed each week,
hell, probably every night. No. Mona Lisa was hiding out somewhere
in Mexico. She was sure of it.

The Los Angeles County Morgue was on North Mission and
Daly, adjacent to the Golden State Freeway, north of Boyle Heights.
Regan pulled into the parking lot and helped Mercedes out of the car.

The place was pretty empty. Mercedes didn't like the smell, nor did she like the look of it. Gray walls and gray floors and gray men in tired clothes who'd rather be anywhere but there.

A cop came over to Regan. The two shook hands. "Mercedes meet Detective Hansen. He's the one who called me. I told him to keep an eye out, just in case."

Hansen was a good-looking black man about six feet tall with the carriage of a football player and the confidence of youth. He made Mercedes feel safe. They walked down a clean corridor, past rows of unmarked and marked doors. Their footsteps echoed off the walls. It was just like in the movies and Mercedes wished she were in the audience right now, Mona Lisa beside her, eating popcorn and junk, giggling like kids. But she wasn't.

"Now this ain't gonna be pretty and it won't be easy on your stomach. We don't have any prints on Mona Lisa, so printing the victim won't do us any good." Hansen opened the door. A man in a white gown nodded his head.

Hansen moved over to a wall housing steel compartments, all coded with numbers. "CASE 3579." The attendant nodded. He moved over and pulled out the requested compartment.

Mercedes held her breath. A white sheet was draped over the corpse. Regan clutched Mercedes' arm.

"Are you ready?" Hansen asked.

Mercedes looked at Regan. Regan seemed to have regained her confidence. Maybe she was being strong for Mercedes. No matter.

Mercedes nodded her head. The attendant pulled back the sheet. She bit her lip so hard she could taste the blood. The face was battered beyond recognition. Blue and purple welts formed a crisscross on the gray skin. Mercedes clutched Regan's hand tighter, and then she let go.

She looked over at the two men watching. She nodded for the attendant to pull down the sheet so she could examine the body. The body was badly bruised, but not like the face. Whoever did it knew the victim. It had to be an act of personal hate.

The body could have been Mona Lisa's. The breasts were about the same size and so were the dimensions of the body. Even the pubic hair was as dark as Mona Lisa's and close-cropped. Mercedes had seen her friend naked often enough. They'd sun-bathed in the nude plenty of times and they'd gone to Beverly Hot Springs for mineral soaks and saunas.

Mercedes felt the tears welling. She held back. This wasn't real. It wasn't happening. It was merely one of her goddamn nightmares. And then, suddenly, Mercedes had a flash. A butterfly. A small, yellow and blue butterfly. "A symbol of freedom," Mercedes mumbled.

Hansen looked at Regan. She shrugged.

Mercedes looked up at them. "Please, turn her over. Mona Lisa had a small butterfly tattooed on her . . . ."

Mercedes held her breath as the attendant turned her over for further inspection. The victim's buttocks were covered with whip lashes, but nowhere on her flesh did they see a butterfly.

Mercedes heart leapt. She was hopeful again. "This isn't her," she said, almost shouting. "It isn't her," she repeated, putting her arms around Regan and hugging her.

Hansen nodded to the attendant. He covered the sheet over the unfortunate, nameless victim and returned her to the frozen vault.

*   *   *

Detective Hansen joined them for breakfast at Vickman's, an L.A. staple since the days of the Depression. An old-fashioned cafeteria with wood booths and short-order cooks and a full breakfast, eggs, bacon, sausage, toast, butter, jam, coffee and pastry for $2.95.

Mercedes didn't think she could eat, but she was ravenous. She was on her second piece of toast, her stomach returning to normal and her faith restored that soon she'd be seeing Mona Lisa, when Regan delivered the final blow.

"Hansen stuck around when all the shit went down two years ago. He's OK," Regan smiled.

Hansen finished off his coffee. "There's nothing more I'd like to see than that son of a bitch Malone get what's coming to him. Not only for what he did to your friend here," Hansen pointed in Regan's direction, "but what he's done to me, personally." Hansen toyed with his eggs. "I've taken enough shit from him and his redneck cronies."

Mercedes liked Hansen. He was nothing like Pinkerton, but then again as a detective, Pinkerton was definitely in a class by himself. Hansen's hands were soft and the fingers carefully manicured, unusual for a man in his line of work. And the hazel eyes bore into you inquisitively, as if he needed to extract every bit of information. At first she was concerned about a cop knowing as much as he did about Mona Lisa, but for a number of reasons, Mercedes felt she could trust him to keep quiet.

"I'm gay and that don't sit well with Captain Malone, although he's never said it to my face in front of anyone, but he's made his opinions known and I won't put up with his homophobic shit."

"I had no choice," Regan said bitterly. "He used me. I set up Xuan, had her arrested and then when he got what he wanted, he slammed on a pair of handcuffs on me and booked me on some stupid technicality. Something that had nothing to do with the Sayonara raid."

No wonder Regan and Hansen got on so well. The two underdogs of the force. As if racism and sexism weren't enough to battle, they got hit with a triple whammy. A macho cop, handsome and imposing, not fitting any queer stereotype, having to mask his sexual identity. And a cop who had "dyke" written all over her, who couldn't fake her sexual inclinations even if she tried.

"What does this have to do with me?" Mercedes asked.

"Hansen's involved in investigating the murder of Xuan. He thinks something's not kosher. That Malone could have set up the murder."

"But why? Why bother with some dance-club hostess when the whole city's drowning in crime?"

Regan looked at Mercedes. "That's what you're gonna find out."

"Me?"

"Captain Malone got your name from Redlite. He's still in the county jail. When I heard what was going down, I told Regan. You may get a visit from him or one of his boys. Me, he's keeping on the desk, just to get my goat. He's not a nice man and he's fucking intimidating, so be careful." Hansen finished his coffee.

Mercedes' stomach churned in a knot. If she was interrogated by the Malone, what would she tell him?

Mercedes paid for breakfast. "I've got a stop to make before I head to work," she said to Regan. She handed Regan her house key.

Regan smiled. "Thanks."

Mercedes shook Hansen's hand. She left the two behind, got in her car and drove to the Museum of Neon Art.

* * *

The museum wasn't opened yet, but Mercedes convinced the manager to let her in. She explained her business there and headed straight for the holograph of Mona Lisa. On a small placard underneath the piece was the name, MONA LISA SELAVY, 1992. The artist was S.P. Phelan.

Mercedes stared at a spot on the floor. She knew it was a blood stain, no doubt from Max. "I was visiting a friend last night, down the block, heard the alarm go off. What happened?"

The manager shrugged. "Who knows. Someone broke in, but there wasn't any damage. The police just left. Could have been someone who just wanted to get off the streets."

Apparently Max had come to before the police arrived and got out of there in time. "I need to talk to the artist. Can you give me her number?"

"You're looking at her." Phelan smiled. Her teeth were white and perfectly shaped and her eyes a deep blue set against a reservoir of sleepless nights. Her hair was buzzed on the sides and stuck up on her head like blades of cinnamon grass. She dug into a bag of Planter's Peanuts and popped a few nuts in her mouth.

"When did you do it?"

"About four months ago. I work in many mediums. I've just started experimenting with three-dimensional forms. Everything the camera can capture, her reality is there."

"It's incredible."

"It's for sale." Again the white smile.

"How much?"

"Three thousand. Mona Lisa already paid me a thousand as a deposit, but she never came back for it. I'm surprised. She was so desperate to have it done, as if she were going away and wouldn't return. As if she wanted to be immortalized."

"I'll see about getting you the rest of the money."

Phelan looked Mercedes over. "Sure. In the meantime, I'm keeping it on sale. Whoever comes up with an offer. I hate to sell it, but I've got supplies to buy."

Mercedes nodded her head. "Did she say anything out of the

ordinary to you. Anything at all you could remember?"

Phelan stuck a pencil behind her ear. "Yeah, come to think of it, she said that in a few months time, her face would make history . . . no, not exactly . . . would be history. Something like that." I assumed she was about to get her lucky break. Either that or it was just wishful thinking."

"Funny," Mercedes said, looking into the artist's pretty face. "Funny how little you really know about the people you love."

"Ain't it a crying shame." Phelan finished a cold cup of coffee, crumbled her empty bag of peanuts and stared at her creation.

Mercedes had a hard time leaving the holograph behind. It was the only tangible thing connecting her to Mona Lisa. She sighed, thanked Phelan for her help and walked out into the daylight.

FOUR

THE BLIND LEADING THE BLIND

The Santa Anas were sloppy winds. They had left a mess behind. The streets were covered with palm fronds, wrappers and soot. Mercedes looked at the sky, dotted with clouds. It felt as if the sun were stolen. People hid in the comfort of their collars, scarfs wrapped around their necks, hands in pockets, eyes shifting back and forth, back and forth like metronomes. The entire city was guilty of premeditated crimes yet to be committed.

Mercedes hurried into the Conservancy, grabbed the latest batch of info-news and was just about to hide in the safe confines of her office, get some work done for the St. James fundraiser and get back on track, when something stood in her way.

He was about six foot four inches of solid mass. A shock of white hair matched a shock of eyebrows that offset, like an awning, dark circles under cold eyes. He was dressed in navy blue and he wore his uniform as if he never took it off.

"Ms. Martini?" His voice was colder than his eyes.

"Yes."

"I'm Captain Miles Malone. I'm here investigating the allegations of John Shimabukuro, a.k.a. Redlite, regarding your presence at Club Sayonara the night of Xuan Kishimoto's death."

Mercedes opened her door. Captain Malone invited himself in, waited for her to enter and then slammed the door.

"I'm not sure I know what you're talking about," Mercedes said. She knew she had to keep calm. Play it dumb. Redlite had no proof. There were no witnesses, none that is, except Marci. Mercedes wondered if the taxi-dancer could be trusted if interrogated. Did Malone already do his dirty work?

"Where were you Saturday night, October 2nd?" Malone walked

to the window and peered out.

Mercedes could smell his cologne. It was Aqua Velva. She bristled. He was standing too close for comfort. She paused as if thinking. She couldn't let anything show. "Home."

"Alone?" He didn't take his eyes from the window. The voice had a familiar ring to it and, like a note that introduces a theme, Captain Malone's baritone words were a harsh recitative Mercedes had heard before. But where?

"Yes."

Captain Malone turned around. There was a skeptical frown on his face. He looked at Mercedes' desk, then he looked her over. "Sit down, Ms. Martini. This might take some time."

"Listen, you must have the wrong party. I've got a lot of work I need to do and . . . ."

"And I've got a lot of work to do as well." Malone cracked his knuckles, came around the desk and sat directly across from Mercedes.

His lizardlike skin was etched with years of service on the force. Up close, Mercedes noticed clumps of his hair had yellowed, probably from an excess of VO5 tonic. His teeth were stained from thousands of cups of black coffee and his fingernails were splintered with dirt. He wheezed when he breathed and Mercedes could smell the nicotine and the residue of his morning's breakfast.

Captain Malone opened and closed his huge fist as if he were getting ready to jab his vein with a needle. "Why were you in the room?"

"I don't know what you're talking about."

"You can tell me here, now, or you can come down to the station. I'd be happy to take your statement, under oath."

"Fine. Let's get this over with. Just show me a warrant for my arrest, and I'll be happy to comply."

Malone slammed his chunky fist on her desk. The small art nouveau lamp toppled over on the floor. The bulb shattered. Malone strapped his body across her desk, his face a vicious German shepherd. Spittle seeped from the sides of his lips. "You're playing with the wrong party, missy. You haven't seen the last of me."

On his way out, Malone kicked the lamp across the floor. Mercedes was shaking so hard she could barely move. The door slammed and within minutes the rank air cleared. She grabbed the phone, called

Regan at her house and told her what had happened.

"You did good, girlfriend. Detective Hansen's working on a list of witnesses, cross-examining them. By the time you come home and fix dinner, I might have some more news."

Mercedes hung up the phone, grabbed her coat and ran out the door.

Dinner?

* * *

Maybe it was Captain Malone who had given her the jitters, but Mercedes had the funniest feeling that someone was following her. Everytime she turned around, she would catch some shadowy figure run into a store or hide behind a newsstand. But then again, maybe it was just her imagination getting the better of her.

The walk today was the Theater District between Third and Ninth streets on South Broadway. The entire strip down to the Million Dollar Theater with its discount stores and bridal wear venues brought in more money per square foot than ritzy Rodeo Drive. She liked the full throttle feel of the neighborhood, loved to catch a blast of cumbia from record stores and smell greasy beef and pork grilling in storefront windows. Today she had a full group. Around twenty eager tourists and architecture aficionados, none without a camera.

It was outside the Rialto Theatre that she felt a pair of eyes on her. The streets were crowded. It was noon and hundreds of workers streamed out of buildings to grab some lunch. It could be anyone, or it could just be her imagination. It could also be someone Captain Malone assigned to tail her.

She tried to concentrate on work, but she knew her memorized repertoire was pretty bloodless. It was hard to muster any enthusiasm for brick, terra cotta and busts peeking from cornices.

She moved the group over to the Tower Theater on the corner of Ninth where a portion of "Mambo Kings" was filmed. The first theater to be mechanically refrigerated with a primitive form of air-conditioning, this movie venue heralded Spanish Baroque influences and boasted sculptures of clothed male directors (with hand-held cameras lodged on their shoulders) and naked female stars of the screen. Mercedes interjected pre-Depression anecdotes of stage and screen. Charlie Chaplin. Theda Bara. Lillian Gish. Rudolf Valentino.

"You look like hell." Mercedes turned around. Good Friday

didn't look so good himself. He was trying hard to steady his body with his cane, but it wasn't working.

Mercedes didn't like the way his eyes drooped and his skin was peppered with perspiration.

"Nothin' to worry 'bout. Just a goddamn flu."

"You should be home in bed." Mercedes linked her arm in Good Friday's as they moved down the street toward the Palace, the oldest surviving Orpheum Theater, a mock French Renaissance decor lending luster to the now dingy movie house.

"I was damn worried about you. You never called. I know you got something cooking and you won't rest till you find Mona Lisa. So I'm here to help you out."

Good Friday was heavy. His weight seemed to be concentrated in his arm as he tried to steady himself by holding onto Mercedes. "Goddamn weather's killing my bones, they feel like termites been at 'em."

Mercedes ushered the group inside the warmth of the theater. She sat Good Friday down, got him a cup of hot chocolate and continued her lecture. This time Good Friday interrupted.

"Most of you are too young to remember any of this, but I got to see Charlie Chaplin's *City Lights* opening night. Folks across the street on bread lines and me huddled in the corner watching this silly man on screen."

From out of the women's restroom, Mercedes saw a figure emerge. It wasn't someone she recognized, nor was it someone she knew. But there was something about her that gave Mercedes the chills. Somehow she just knew this was the person she felt burning a hole in her back.

Mercedes watched the figure dart out of the theater. She was wearing a red leather jacket with a fiery dragon on the back, the same jacket Mona Lisa had hanging in her closet. And her head was covered with a bolero hat.

Leaving Good Friday in mid-stream, she dashed outside. A sea of hard faces assailed her. Nowhere did she see the red jacket. She ran to the sidewalk and looked across the street. There, the red jacket. Mercedes weaved through the hordes of people crossing Broadway. Her eyes stayed peeled on the figure, who broke out into a run and disappeared inside the Western Jewelry Mart.

Mercedes narrowly avoided being hit by a bus. She pushed past street vendors selling head bands and faux Dior handbags and entered the Jewelry Mart. The place was jammed with customers trying to chisel vendors and everywhere there were endless counters of precious stones, diamonds, gold, silver, watches. Mercedes ran down a flight of stairs into the next level of sparkling jewels.

A flash of red exploded on the scene, but this time the enigmatic figure was unaware of Mercedes' presence. She was just about ready to shout for the stranger to stop when a old man collapsed in front of her. Mercedes looked down and saw him writhing on the floor, apparently in the throes of an epileptic seizure. "Help, someone please help," Mercedes yelled as a few vendors came over to the man's assistance.

It was all Mercedes could do to stop herself from leaping over the prostrate man, so she ran around him just in time to catch the mysterious figure in red departing from a side door.

Once outside, Mercedes looked to the left and right. Down the street was the Alexandria Hotel, its neon sign flashing like so much poor taste on this gray afternoon. Nicknamed the "Alex" in its heyday, Sarah Bernhardt, Fred Astaire and Humphrey Bogart all laid their heads in one of the rooms.

She took her chances and darted into a crimson lobby covered in crushed velveteen and dotted with Victorian sofas and arm chairs. It smelled like the inside of an old movie theater, old and musty, and about as appetizing as rancid butter.

The red leather jacket seemed to have disappeared into the clover-leafed wallpaper. Mercedes checked the restored Palm Court where a Tiffany stained-glass ceiling hinted at the hotel's former splendor. The room was nearly empty. She waited a few minutes, her fingernails bitten to pieces. It was unlikely there were two jackets like that. Someone must have stolen Mona Lisa's jacket from her closet. And that someone must be following her, but why? It didn't make any sense.

Mercedes ran around the block once just to make sure the red jacket wasn't lurking behind a newsstand. She hurried back to the theater only to find the group seated around Good Friday in rapt attention, hanging onto every word of his story.

She smiled at him. He winked. It was nice to know that she

could at least count on some friends to be there when she needed
them.

*   *   *

Racing west along Sunset Boulevard, it took Mercedes less than
thirty minutes to get to Mona Lisa's apartment. She parked at the end
of High Tower Drive and went straight to the manager's apartment.

After four knocks the door opened. This time the manager was
without the Kabuki make-up. Replacing the dramatic layers of
Revlon's finest was a seaweed and kelp mud mask, the sinewy strands
of the latest health fad plastered on her skin. The peroxide hair was
thankfully buried beneath a polyester scarf covered with parrots.

"I need to get into Mona Lisa's apartment."

The manager eyed her suspiciously. "Weren't you here before?"

"Yes, I paid her rent."

"Umm. Now what?"

"Now I need to know if anybody's been to the apartment?"

The manager looked inside her place as a blast from the television
set caught her attention. "Her cousin came last week. Cleaned the
place out. It's already rented so if you're interested . . . ."

"Cousin? She doesn't have a cousin."

The manager looked very bored. "Look the rent was paid, I
needed to dump the stuff anyway. She came and that's that."

"What'd she look like?"

The manager eyed Mercedes carefully, puckered her lips which
were glazed with Vitamin E oil. "Plain, nondescript, didn't say much.
Was outta here in a few hours. She had a small U-Haul and that's the
last I seen of her."

"Can I see the apartment?"

The manager sighed. She turned around, grabbed a set of keys
and gave her one. "Hurry back. I need to jump in the shower." The
door slammed in Mercedes' face.

Mona Lisa's apartment was empty. Water stains streaked the
walls, paint peeled from the ceiling. The closet was bare. All the
clothes and shoes and paraphernalia gone. Even the bottle of *Stoli* had
disappeared from the refrigerator.

The starkness of the vacant room hit her hard—as if Mona Lisa's
past was being stripped away, layer by layer by some mysterious
force. The only thing anchoring Mercedes to her friend now was the
diary.

FAR EAST CAFE

As cafes go, the Far East on First Street, directly across from the Japanese Village Plaza Mall, a retro-fifties eaterie with a vertical neon sign flashing *CHOP SUEY*, seemed an appropriate spot for Mercedes to feed Good Friday a steaming bowl of egg drop soup.

The wooden-boothed restaurant had managed to stick around for decades, downscaling the slicker, trendy Asian fast food establishments serving *shabu shabu* and popular sushi bars such as the functional R23. Mercedes toyed with a crispy fried noodle and watched Good Friday sip some jasmine tea.

"So now what?" Good Friday picked up a spoon and slurped a mouthful of soup. "Umm." He mopped his sweaty brow.

"Now I get your sick butt to bed."

Good Friday scowled. "I got a cold and you got one hell of a headache. We've got to set our priorities."

"Priority number one is getting Captain Malone off my back. Bad enough I've got Max pulling surprise appearances and Samantha bowing in and out of my life, I don't need to be under someone else's thumb."

"Well you're gonna be under more than his thumb if you don't find out who killed Xuan." Good Friday stuck a minted toothpick between his teeth.

Mercedes stared into her cup of tea, hoping the leaves at the bottom would give her an answer. They didn't. The mysterious voice inside Xuan's office was one she seemed to have heard somewhere. And how could she establish any proof, even if she recognized the voice for certain?

"Now why do you suppose some big shot police captain with a

hell of a lot more important things to do in this city would take the time out of his day to visit you? Don't make sense."

Mercedes took a sip of hot ginseng tea to clear her head.

"No sense at all." Good Friday stuck a spare rib in his mouth and tore off a lean morsel of meat.

"That's it." Mercedes pounded the wooden table with her fist. "You said it."

"I said what?" Good Friday, mumbled, his mouth full of the marinated pork.

"Malone . . . you hit it on the head. Why the hell come to me when he could have sent Detective Hansen? I thought I recognized that voice. He probably wanted to see my reaction, to see if I could get a fix on his voice."

"Whoa," Good Friday said, licking his lips. "You lost me."

Mercedes got up, pulled some money from her pocket and threw it on the table. "It's Malone. I bet you that was Captain Malone in the club. He shot Xuan."

Good Friday groaned as he wiped his greasy mouth with a napkin. "Come on, you're stepping in fire."

"Now all I have to do is find out why."

Good Friday took one more sip of his soup, then lifted himself out of the booth.

"You know where Marci lives?" Mercedes hoped Mona Lisa's fellow taxi-dancer would help to unravel some of this puzzle.

Good Friday looked embarrassed. "Yeah, I dropped her home that night after you left the Biltmore, made sure she got in safe, you know," he said, grabbing a spare rib for the road.

Mercedes grinned. "Yeah, I know."

                              *   *   *

Marci lived in a four story imitation brownstone apartment on Birch off Olympic that smelled like it had been washed down with lysol and left out in the sun to dry. It was a place that tried hard to be clean, but somehow the crawling vermin made you think you'd checked into the roach motel.

For such a dump, Marci's place was all lace, plastic flowers from the five & dime and pink frill. Her studio was larger than a hat box and as about as fancy as a Stouffer's frozen dinner. Still, it was home.

Mercedes sat in a lumpy worn yellow armchair with white lace doilies on the arms. Good Friday sat sheepishly on the sofa, Marci next to him.

"So what brings you to the neighborhood?" Marci dragged on a cigarette and winked at Good Friday.

"Marci, we need your help."

A look of pleasure swept across her face. She smiled. "Sure."

"Did you see Captain Malone of the 77th Precinct the night of Xuan's murder?"

The pleasure washed from her face and fear shot out like a marble in a pinball machine.

"Miles Malone." Her voice was less than a whisper.

Mercedes looked at Good Friday. He put his hand up. She better take it slow.

"I don't remember."

Mercedes knew she was onto something. "Listen, Marci. I know you're afraid, I don't blame you. Redlite told Malone I was in the room the night Xuan was shot. He may be trying to pin the rap on me, crazy as that might sound. I have some friends on the police force who would all sleep easier at night if they could finger Malone. I promise you protection."

Marci looked at Good Friday. He nodded his head and patted the girl's knee. She took a deep breath. "I don't want trouble with that man."

Mercedes could sense that Marci had more than once come up against Malone. "Please, is there something you can tell me about him, anything, even if it doesn't seem significant?"

Marci ground out her cigarette. "About two weeks before Xuan was shot, I was cleaning up in the restroom. You know what it's like on a Saturday night when you ain't got a man to go home to and there's no john worth talking to all night?"

Mercedes hadn't a clue, but she nodded in agreement.

"I had nothing to do and no place to go. So I was takin' my sweet and happened to pass Xuan's office, when I heard yelling. Seeing nobody was around, I listened. Some guy was grilling Xuan real hard. He kept asking, "Where is she?" But she wouldn't answer. Then I heard him slap her.

Marci jumped up and played out the scene for them. "`Where is she,' he asked again. Shit, my knees were shaking. I was afraid for her and I was never afraid for Xuan, believe me. She handled the worst of them. Then I heard a crack. And I thought perhaps he had hit her with a club or something. But then I heard Xuan say, `Over my dead body.' Sent chills up my spine, 'cause I knew she meant it. `I'll find her,' he said, `and then I'm coming back for you.'"

The taxi dancer sat down, her performance over. She grabbed a pillow with a sequined sailboat sewn on the fabric, and placed it in her lap.

Mercedes nodded her head to continue.

"I heard footsteps and hid behind the curtain by the exit. When the door opened, I peeked and there barreling out of the office was Captain Malone. He wasn't in uniform. He had on this red lumber jacket and heavy boots. His face matched his jacket and his eyes were so angry, believe me, I remembered that look."

"Are you sure?"

Marci's face tightened. Her eyes had the far away glaze of an ugly memory struggling not to surface. "I'm sure. One night, when I was leaving the club, he pulled me into his car . . . you know . . . asking fucking questions that had nothing to do with nothing . . . then he drove me around . . . and pulled into a deserted parking lot on Hill . . . and . . . well, you know the rest . . . ."

"Son of a bitch," Good Friday said, holding Marci's little hand in his.

Mercedes knew Malone had spent his career covering his tracks and making new ones. Regan was just one victim gunned down by his malice and she was sure Detective Hansen could tell a few stories of his own.

"The night of Xuan's murder. Did you see Malone go into Xuan's office?"

Marci rolled her eyes. "Yeah, he was coming out of Xuan's office after I heard the gun shot. I just didn't tell you guys 'cause, shit, I don't need that bastard breathing down my neck."

Mercedes got up, slipped two twenty dollar bills from her wallet, all she had, and gave it to Marci. "Thanks, Marci."

She hesitated, then took the bills. "I don't take money from friends," she said sincerely, "but business sucks lately, this goddamn economy. I could use the dough."

Mercedes smiled. "I'll send Detective Hansen around to get your statement. He'll make sure you have protection. In the meantime, stay away from the Club."

Marci nodded her head. "I'm working Club Paradise now."

"And I'm gonna get this man home to bed and see that he stays there," Mercedes said, helping Good Friday up off the sofa. His skin looked gray and soggy.

"Hey, they call me Florence Nightingale. I'll take him."

Mercedes looked at Good Friday. He smiled weakly. "I'll be fine, don't you worry 'bout me."

Mercedes let Marci take over. She had one more stop to make before she went home to tell Regan the news.

MILES MALONE

A tall gray building, a monolith, as cold and impersonal as any in Orwell's *1984* loomed before Mercedes, two large griffins standing guard on each end.

The Hall of Records, a cement and brick vault, housed thousands of the city's vital statistics: births, deaths, marriages, car registrations and civil suits. Mercedes stepped inside.

Upon first impression she felt like Dorothy visiting the Wizard of Oz. The huge corridor seemed to shrink-wrap her and the halls smelled of ancient tomes covered with dust and filled with yellowed paper, moldy with time. She glanced around sitting rooms where people poured through catalogues and files or scanned microfilm to locate paper footprints of the past.

Mercedes was given a registry by a bored desk clerk that she carried to small table with an even smaller lamp. She sat down and scanned the book for Xuan's last name. There were dozens of Kishimoto's listed, but only ten dated back a quarter of a century. If Noh were the same age as Mona Lisa, then her year of birth would be 1965.

The place was stuffy. A dour-faced young man was seated at an adjacent table. He scratched his head nervously as he poured through a huge tome, his thick glasses obscuring his little eyes. An avalanche of dandruff sat on his leathered shoulders.

Mercedes wanted a cigarette and a steaming cup of cappucino, but no such luck. Her fingers scaled the page until she caught sight of Noh's name. Her heart fluttered.

Noh Kishimoto. Date of Birth: June 14th. Place: Good Samaritan Hospital. Mother: Xuan Kishimoto. Father: Miles Malone.

"Shit," Mercedes said out loud. The young man looked up,

annoyed that she had interrupted his painstaking scrutiny.

Mercedes shot him a sour look and leaned back in her chair. So Miles Malone was Noh's father. He was searching for his daughter and Xuan wouldn't give her up, not for anything in the world. Miles Malone shot the mother of his child in cold blood and nobody knew it.

Nobody, that is, except her. Mercedes left the book opened, tore out of the building and, as she ran down the steps, wished she could fly away on the eagle wings of the griffin. Instead she headed to the Conservancy, got her car from the garage and hit the freeway.

* * *

Mercedes pulled up in front of Jezebel's Gin Mill. It had only taken her twenty minutes to get to the beach. She wanted to break the news to Noh before the police did and as soon as Eva saw Mercedes' face she knew something was wrong.

"You didn't come here for a drink."

"No. But I'll take a cappucino. I need to speak to Noh."

Eva looked at Mercedes. She went off to fetch the drink and her lover. Luckily the restaurant was pretty empty. It was still early and the club wouldn't fill for another hour or so.

Noh walked in and sat down. "Hi," she said simply. Eva placed the drink in front of Mercedes and sat down. She took Noh's hand in hers and the two women waited for Mercedes to break the news.

Mercedes didn't know how to do it other than get straight to the point. "I found out who murdered your mother."

Noh's eyes fluttered like the wings of a captive butterfly. "Go on."

"Captain Miles Malone."

"A policeman?"

Mercedes nodded her head and took a sip of the hot, foamy drink.

"But why?"

The why part was always the hardest. "Because your mother refused to give him some information. Information that could have been detrimental to her daughter."

Noh's face was as still and white as a geisha's. "I think I know everything about my mother's business."

"Business, maybe, but not her personal life."

Noh stiffened. "What do you mean?"

"Miles Malone . . . is your father."

Eva gasped, but Noh sat quietly, the swampy darkness behind her eyes teaming with water moccasins.

"My father?" Noh took a few seconds to digest the information, but she couldn't program the reality.

"Isn't this a job for the police?" Eva asked.

Mercedes laughed. "Yeah, I'll take it straight to Malone. Don't worry. I've got a few friends on the force and by tomorrow Malone will have some explaining to do."

Eva was angry. "Don't be too sure."

"Miles Malone," Noh muttered as if trying the name on for size. "Does he have a family?"

"Regan told me his wife died a year ago. His three kids live out of state."

Noh nodded.

"Do you want to see him?" Mercedes sensed the girl was curious to know everything she could about this phantom father.

Noh got up. "No. I never want to see him."

*　*　*

Mercedes was tired, face drawn and pale. Regan greeted her at the door. She was disappointed that Mercedes' arms weren't loaded with groceries. There'd be no down-home cooking tonight, but when Mercedes filled her in on the news, Regan salivated.

"That bastard." Regan looked at Mercedes and smiled. "I think we got the makings of a P.I. here, Detective Martini."

"Bullshit. We got the makings of a woman whose life's been turned upside down and inside out. I've been a pawn and a stooge. My house has been vandalized along with my heart. The dance-card's been stolen and I'm no closer to finding my friend than I was seven weeks ago." Mercedes sunk into an arm chair and watched the logs crackle in the fireplace.

Regan grinned. "You just sit there. I'm gonna call Detective Hansen, see what he proposes to do about this."

Mercedes didn't argue. She must have dozed off because the next thing she felt was Regan tapping her on the shoulder.

"You look like you're about to pass out."

Mercedes tried to get up, but she couldn't. "What'd he say?"

"He wants us to meet him. He knows where Malone hangs. We're paying him a visit. Are you up to it?"

Mercedes wasn't up to anything but a hot bath and a thousand hours of sleep, but she nodded yes, took a deep breath and sprang into action.

* * *

The Shamrock on Western was one of those bars time forgot. A brick, neighborhood watering hole, it serviced the mid-Wilshire district. It was dark and as intimate as a jail cell and smelled like it needed to be closed for repairs. A lifetime's worth of repairs. Miles Malone probably felt comfortable here because it was as hopeless as his soul.

Mercedes followed Regan into the bar dotted with faces plowed down by hard work and alcohol, customers who knew how to mind their business and keep their tongues in their mouths. They had no better place to go to share their misery. She spotted Malone's white head of hair. He was the biggest guy in the place.

Regan moved over to him and tapped him on the back. He took a few seconds to turn around as if he somehow knew this wasn't going to be pleasant. Mercedes watched as he stared at Regan, his eyebrows like antennae picking up the signals in her eyes and what they read, no doubt, caught him off guard.

"Look what the sewer washed in," Malone grunted, popping a few peanuts in his mouth, stalling for time.

Regan slipped into the seat next to his and ordered a beer. Malone started to grab his and move to another part of the bar, but Regan clenched his thick arm and wouldn't let go.

"I know who killed Xuan."

Mercedes stood behind Malone, he still not aware of her presence. She could see his body stiffen like a corpse in the earliest visit of rigor mortis.

It was then he must have sensed someone behind him. When he whipped around and caught sight of Mercedes, his face was a candy-cane of emotion. The eyes white with rage, the face red with anger. "What the fuck you think you're doing?"

Mercedes enjoyed the set-up even though she was frozen with fear.

Regan winked at her and took a sip of beer. This was a golden moment for her. One she'd been waiting now for three years, ever since Malone kicked her off the force.

"Looks like we have a witness. You've met Mercedes Martini, haven't you, Captain?" Regan spit out his name like a discarded peanut shell.

"Witness, my ass. I think you got your story mixed up. I've got enough information from a reliable witness of my own, says Martini here killed Xuan."

Regan laughed.

Mercedes wasn't sure this frame-up would work out. "I had no motive, but you had plenty. Xuan wouldn't let you see your daughter Noh, so you killed her."

Malone knotted his fingers in a fist. His eyes were two slits, as if a knife had cut into the surface of his skin.

He tried to laugh off the accusation, but the mirth wouldn't come out. "Bullshit." His voice was desperate and dry.

"You killed Xuan. Mercedes recognized your voice and one of Xuan's girls caught you leaving the joint."

Captain Malone sneered, trying hard to recover from the blow. "Who'd ya pay?" He pressed his face up against Regan's. "You'd do anything to get even, wouldn't you?" Malone pulled away, got up off the stool, whipped around and pushed Regan hard. Her hand slipped and the beer bottle went sliding across the bar and shattered on the floor.

Malone grabbed Regan's jacket and yanked her off the stool. Regan tried to pull away, but the Captain was stronger than a lumberjack. He kicked over her stool, pushed her toward the bar and slammed her face on the cold surface. She clawed wildly, but to no avail.

Mercedes panicked, her skin tightened in goose flesh. And then she heard a woman screaming and her vision was blurred and the scream got louder and louder until it was gone and she realized she was the one screaming.

Malone pounded Regan's head against the bar. "So I fucking killed the worthless bitch. You got proof, dyke?"

Mercedes grabbed his arm to stop him, but he was raging mad. He back-swiped her and she went flying to the filthy floor. Sawdust flew in her face and got caught in her nostrils. She coughed. Her fingers dug into the splintered wood and she tried to pull herself up. Then she heard a whistle and the stomping of feet. Someone helped her to her feet and, as she looked over, Detective Hansen was slapping a pair of handcuffs on Captain Malone.

Regan's face was red, her lip split open, the blood pouring out like tap water from a faucet.

"What are you, nuts?" Malone barked at Detective Hansen.

Detective Hansen smiled. "Yeah, motherfucker." He pulled out a small wire recorder from Regan's breast pocket and shoved Malone across the floor with such ferocity the big man lost his bearing and fell flat on his back, the broken beer bottle crunching underneath him like cereal.

Detective Hansen was about to stomp the Captain in the face, but Regan was quick enough to hold him back. "Don't man, it ain't worth it."

Detective Hansen was breathing heavy.

Regan's leg shot out and kicked Malone's face like a football. His head snapped, rolled to the side and a spittle of blood poured from his mouth.

Mercedes peered down at Noh's father and was glad the girl didn't want to know anything about him.

Detective Hansen looked at Regan, surprised. She shrugged her shoulders playfully. "*I'm* not in uniform. What goes around, comes around, ain't that right, Captain?" Regan asked.

Malone spit in Regan's direction.

"Ain't that the truth." Detective Hansen slapped Regan on the back.

Two plainclothes planted in the Shamrock picked up the Captain and pushed him outside.

CARNIVAL OF MASKS

For the last week or so, Mercedes had received several mysterious calls, but as soon as she answered the phone the caller hung up. There were plenty of clicks on her machine as well. It was obvious someone wanted to hear her voice, but didn't want to say anything.

At first Mercedes thought it was Samantha, but it didn't seem to be her *modus operandi*. Samantha wasn't the sentimental type. Besides, Mercedes wasn't sure she wanted to see her again. Especially if she took the dance-card. Life was starting to settle back to normal and, but for the mystery behind Mona Lisa's disappearance, Mercedes tried to convince herself that she preferred to put the past two months behind her.

"I'm telling you, she's off to South America again. With the dance-card. Trust me," Regan said.

The remark hurt, cut deep into Mercedes, in a place she thought no one could go.

Regan ventured that Samantha must have followed Mercedes to the museum, somehow getting wind of what Max was up to. And since Samantha had disappeared without a word to anyone, her theory was corroborated. Mallory had told Regan that Fletcher was furious with Max. They had a screaming match and Fletcher accused him of botching the whole thing.

Mercedes thought she had expected nothing from Samantha, but knowing she stole the dance-card killed everything. She felt betrayed. And because the antique was so inextricably tied to her feelings for Mona Lisa and in a way hitherto unclear to her, symbolized the richness of romance and love, she was doubly crushed. She toyed with her dinner. She had no appetite for food.

She watched Regan dig her fork into a huge plate of linguini swimming in a broth of olive oil, fresh garlic, parsley, white wine and Little Neck clams. Mercedes knew Regan had enjoyed the home-cooking and personal caretaking and she liked the company. She knew Regan was really there to keep an eye on her, to make sure Fletcher's thugs didn't hurt her. In a way, Regan filled a gap left by Samantha. The first day or so, it was a little awkward between them. The sexual energy between them had always been there, but after what had happened to both of them with their respective lovers, there was less inclination to complicate things further.

Mercedes was having this recurring nightmare. In the dream she was stalking a phantom figure who left behind a trail of Must de Cartier. She was convinced the woman was Mona Lisa, but when she finally got up close and the figure turned around, she was face to face with a corpse. The eyes all hollowed out, worms swimming in and out of skeletal cavities.

Mercedes shivered and tried to shake the memory. She had an eerie feeling that the calls could be from Mona Lisa. But why didn't she want to talk to her? Was she hiding out somewhere, injured? It was useless. No matter how hard she tried to chuck out the past few weeks, no matter how emphatic she was about moving forward, she was compelled to dig further until she hit dirt bottom.

Regan pulled her out of her musing. "Now I can't tell you all the details," Regan said in between mouthfuls," but there'll be some heavy action goin' down at Max's tonight. I might need you, so stick close."

Mercedes took a sip of Pinot Grigio, her favorite Italian wine. She had finally come round to trusting Regan and so far she hadn't been disappointed.

Tonight they'd be attending Max's Halloween costume party at his Janus Gallery. Both, of course, would be costumed beyond recognition. Mercedes had put together a black and white Pierrot satin outfit with demi-mask and a white Restoration beehive wig to hide her red hair. A large white Rembrandt collar and black boots would complete the ensemble.

Regan was going as a fox. "Suits my game plan," she said, scooping the remainder of the tender clams on her tablespoon. "We need to arrive separately. As soon as Fletcher sticks her neck in with

Mallory, get to Mallory without drawing anyone's attention and tell
her to meet me in the back of the gallery at midnight."

"And how do you propose I lure the cub from mama bear?"
Mercedes had already tried to dissuade Regan from her ludicrous
scheme, but no one was as stubborn as Regan.

Regan shrugged her shoulders. "You've got the degree, not me."

"It's in art history . . . ."

"Then be artful . . . ."

A smile smeared Regan's face. "I'm crazy, I know, but what the
hell, I'm nuts about her."

'What we do for love,' Mercedes thought as she cleared the table.
She brewed a fresh pot of coffee while Regan went upstairs to take a
shower.

She caught sight of her face in a silver-framed mirror she'd picked
up in Mexico. She seemed older than her thirty years. In a strange
way, she knew that the dance-card had anchored her to a world of
mystery and intrigue. A dark and dangerous lifestyle anathema to
the one she was used to leading. And it was a link, tenuous at best,
to Mona Lisa and now she felt everything slipping away from her as
quickly as sand in a hourglass.

Mercedes rinsed the dishes, the smell of espresso roast filling the
kitchen. She wondered what Samantha would have done if Max
wasn't at the neon museum? Would she have knocked Mercedes out?
Or would she have begged for the two of them to run off to Rio,
dance-card in hand—*hers, no doubt.*

The phone rang. Mercedes stiffened. She guessed no one would
be on the other end. She picked up the extension in the kitchen.

"Hello?" She watched her face in the mirror, catching the agitation.

Silence. She hated the silence. It was like fingernails on a
chalkboard.

"Mona Lisa?" She bared her teeth and a blue orange flame
burned in her eyes. "Please, who is this?" Her voice sounded
desperate.

Silence. And then the unmistakable sound of breathing as if she
could feel the warm breath brush against her hot cheek. For a second
she thought she even caught a whiff of Must de Cartier, but then the
click and mindless drone of dial tone broke their connection.

Mercedes threw the phone across the kitchen. It hit the bread box and tumbled onto the small white-tiled folding table.

Regan rushed into the kitchen, a towel around her wet head, a Q-tip sticking out of her ear. "Another phantom phone call?"

Mercedes nodded her head. "I just know it's Mona Lisa. I can feel it."

Regan came up and put her hands on Mercedes' shoulders. She massaged the taut muscles aching from lack of attention. Mercedes' head dropped forward. Regan's fingers kneaded her neck. "You can still file a missing report. Let the coppers do what they're paid for."

Mercedes snapped to attention. "No. No yet. She didn't want me to. I'm still hoping . . . ." Mercedes voice faded out as she grabbed her cup of coffee and headed upstairs to get ready.

*   *   *

West Hollywood was a city born to celebrate Halloween. Thousands paraded like a battalion of soldiers up and down Hollywood Boulevard. But it was along Santa Monica that *la creme de la creme* strutted their stuff to revelers on the prowl for a little trick or treat.

The "girls" were out in full force with their sequined gowns, smooth legs, high heels and beehive wigs. Some shaved their chests, other left them nice and hairy. Sailor boys stomped the traffic-less streets cat-calling and whistling to the skirts. A costumed homeless in tattered clothes held up a huge sign that read, "I'll work for sex."

The glitterati rubbed elbows with the polyester makeshifts and the bars were teeming with rabble rousers, the music pounding from clubs like Revolver, Mickey's and Rage.

Mercedes was lucky to find a parking space on Holloway. She walked down to the Boulevard, a black cape around her costume. She had promised to meet Snapshot, who had called earlier.

"I've got this picture I want you to look at," she said on the phone. "What is it?"

"You tell me, I'm not quite sure."

Mercedes didn't know what to make of the conversation, but Snapshot said she thought it could be important.

Luckily, Little Frieda's wasn't that packed and Mercedes spotted her six foot friend shooting a game of pool with a dyke dressed as a construction worker. Very original.

Snapshot pulled Mercedes over to a table where her jacket was thrown on a chair. "You want a coffee?"

"No. I've got a party to go to."

"You look great. I wouldn't recognize you if you didn't take off the mask."

"That's the idea," Mercedes said, smiling.

Snapshot handed a picture to Mercedes. It was a picture of a woman in a red leather jacket. The jacket had a dragon on the back and she was darting into the Alexandria Hotel. Mercedes looked over at Snapshot.

"Take a look at this." Snapshot pulled out another, this one a blow-up of the first. Mercedes could barely make out the woman's features. Her head was covered with a scarf and she had on a bolero hat. Mercedes felt a chill run down her spine.

"She's the same person I saw that day, but it's not Noh. I just don't recognize her."

"Lucky for you, I was running around taking some pictures on my break when I spotted the jacket. I would never have thought anything out of the ordinary had you not told me, so I got this shot. I followed her inside the hotel, but she wasn't in the lobby or the bar. She just vanished."

Mercedes sat down. The woman who cleaned out Mona Lisa's apartment was running around town with her clothes on. It had to be someone Mona Lisa knew, but who?

Snapshot bit into a huge brownie. Just then a beautiful, young honey blonde walked into the coffee house. She went straight past Mercedes and Snapshot leaving behind a trail of sandalwood and jasmine. At the back room she peeled off her expensive leather coat. Underneath, she wore a flesh-colored body stocking, which at a glance, gave the illusion of total nudity. She wore black spike heels like a pro. A girl like that went through life without a run in her stockings. The seams would be straight. They'd be Givenchy and happy to be there. She chalked a stick and bent down to hit the eight ball.

"Excuse me," Snapshot said, unable to take her eyes off the newcomer as she plopped the half-eaten brownie in Mercedes' hand. "But my distraction for the evening just arrived."

Mercedes smiled, dumped the brownie, pocketed the pictures and left.

*   *   *

There had always been something magical and mysterious about Halloween, even when Mercedes was a kid dressed as Little Lulu or Morticia. She liked playacting, pretending she was someone she wasn't. On some level, she supposed Mona Lisa enjoyed shedding her own skin to become someone else each time she performed. It was just too bad she confused her own reality for everyone else's fiction.

Mercedes turned on the radio. Carmen's show, "Dames" blared as she made her way down La Cienega. Tough and dry as Death Valley, Carmen introduced the evening's segment.

"Ghoulish eve, dykes and dames from queertown as you stomp down the boulevard or party with friends. Just a reminder. Tomorrow Dark City Productions is holding an open casting call for the lead in the upcoming remake of 'Double Indemnity.' A classic film noir that everyone I'm sure has forgotten. And now tonight, for a little noir intrigue, let's pick up where Felony left off last night."

"Felony's client wasn't gun shy, she was crazy. Not the crazy that comes from a mental breakdown, and not the crazy that comes from the excesses of a fine life. The French call it 'l'amour fou.' In Pueblo de la Nuestro Senora de Reina, we call it 'loco.'"

Mercedes smiled. She pulled up to the valet in front of the Melrose Gallery, put on her mask and got out of her car. She handed a security guard her invitation, which Regan had gotten, and crushed through the crowd of people inside.

It was eleven o'clock and the party was in full gear. Mutant ants and heavily made-up gameshow hosts, queens in drag with long legs and gold lame cocktail dresses two sizes too small. Three gorgeous sisters of darkness who looked as if they stepped out of Coppola's *Dracula*. There were keystone cops and real coppers to keep the rabble from stealing the art.

Mercedes pushed her way to the bar, passing alien lounge lizards who held exotic cocktails in their hands, their faces painted green and purple. She spotted a great Gertrude Stein and Alice B., replete with requisite moustaches. A rotund man about four feet two inches was dressed as Toulouse Lautrec and on a small platform a haunting shadow play of the *Rape Of The Sabines* was in progress.

A waiter dressed in a Roman toga handed her a glass of champagne which she gratefully drank. Geisha darlings with names like Ed, Mark and Sylvester swished by and winked at no one in particular.

She looked around for Regan, but didn't spot her. And she didn't see Mallory anywhere, but then again she could be disguised beyond recognition. As she took a sip of her champagne, something caught her eye.

It was a green creature. Mercedes was fascinated by bugs. Crickets, grasshoppers and locusts. There was something equally beautiful and repugnant about those slick colored insects of the kingdom. One summer she caught a bug in a Mason jar. It kept her awake at night because she knew that by keeping it in the jar, she'd eventually kill it. She kept it trapped. She wanted it to die because the formidable predator frightened her. That insect was a praying mantis.

And so was Fletcher. Her hair was dyed a deep green and tiny antennae sprouted from her head; her face was covered with a shiny green mask and she wore a dark green lycra body stocking. Mercedes almost expected her to swivel her head around, she looked so authentic.

A few feet away, Mercedes spotted Mallory. Dressed in a glittery white elegant tunic with *haute couture* hat, her hair was drawn back in a chignon and she looked stunning. Now all Mercedes had to do was draw her away from Fletcher and give her the message.

She moved by Pinkerton who was dressed as Bogart. Sporting an oversized two piece pin-stripped suit and a black fedora, he was absorbed in talking to a girl dressed as a satellite dish. The words STATE OF THE ART stenciled on her forehead. By the time Mercedes made it over to where Mallory had been standing, the girl was gone.

Mercedes grabbed another glass of champagne from a passing tray.

"Looking for someone?" A voice growled in her ear.

Mercedes turned around. The body was tall and lean, the face mean and pierced with bristles of hair. The snout was ugly and black, the eye's beady and vicious, the teeth, stainless steel cutlery. Brown hair cascaded over pointed ears and fell on broad shoulders. White tufts of soft fur covered his body. Max was dressed as a wolf in sheep's clothing. How *apropos*.

He grabbed her arm and pulled her close. His hot breath brushed her face like a windshield wiper and his wet lips touched her ear. "You know what I do to party crashers?"

"You do have quite a clutch there," Mercedes said, breaking free. She dodged into the thick of the crowd and smacked into a three-eyed wallflower with a bad case of acne. She turned to see if Max was pursuing her, but he wasn't. He was conferring with Fletcher. They looked over at her, then moved to a door marked PRIVATE and entered. Mallory was by the bar, unattended. Perfect timing.

She tapped Mallory on the shoulder. The girl turned around and smiled at Mercedes. "Listen, there's not much time, but Regan wants you to meet her outside at midnight."

Mallory's eyes lit up. "Where is she?"

Mercedes looked at her watch. "She'll be here any minute. She's dressed as a fox."

Mallory squeezed Mercedes' hand. "Thanks."

Mercedes moved off. A woman wearing a gown Mercedes recognized wafted past and headed for the back room. The dress had been hanging in Mona Lisa's closet. It was silver lame with matching sequins, a little too Vegas showy for Mercedes' taste, but something that Mona Lisa, no doubt, looked stunning in.

She followed the figure who wore a full silver mask, two tiny slits for eyes. Like an eerie angel of death, she floated through the hallway, opened a door and exited.

By the time Mercedes could push through the throng, the woman had disappeared up a flight of steps. Mercedes followed. The passageway was dark, but she continued, her heart beating fast. She opened a door at the top of the stairs and walked out on the roof.

Two huge aluminum air ducts blocked her view. The wind howled and the moon illuminated the top of the brick building. She ran over to the edge of the roof where the claws of a ladder were attached to the rim of the roof's awning.

Below, escaping down an alleyway, was the mysterious woman. "Hey, stop, please," Mercedes shouted.

The figure froze for a second, turned around and looked up. Then she took off and retreated behind the adjacent building.

Was someone following Mercedes? Who was this mysterious woman? Could she be the same person who wore Mona Lisa's jacket or was that too far-fetched?

Footsteps stomped behind her. Mercedes swung around. Max grabbed her around the neck and squeezed tight. Mercedes gasped for breath.

"The Venetians like to get rid of what's old and useless during Carnival. So do we here in Hollywood. Tossing you off the roof would be an appropriate gesture, wouldn't you say?" He tightened his grip.

Mercedes kneed him in the groin. He let go momentarily, then his hand shot out and got hold of the belt around her waist. She tried to struggle free, but he was strong. "What do you want?"

Max whipped off his wolf head. The latex mask had made his face hot and sweaty. "Where's Samantha's hiding?"

"I don't know." Clouds rolled in and a damp mist hovered above the building.

Max arched her over the low wall, she was about eight stories from the cold, hard pavement. If she didn't fall, her spine would snap in half.

"And I won't know who pushed you over, bitch." In his eyes hate formed and hardened like a crystal. The metal braces on his teeth moved closer to her face.

She winced and moved further away, but she was backed against the ledge as far as she could go.

"Let go of the girl," a voice cried out.

Max froze. He swung around. There was Pinkerton holding a .38. He was accompanied by two cops. Max pushed Mercedes aside.

She moved off a few feet and tried to steady herself. When she looked over, she was just as startled as Max. His buddy Pinkerton had double-crossed him.

Max wheezed as this blizzard of emotion overtook him. "What the fuck's going on?" He started to walk toward Pinkerton, but Pinkerton cocked the trigger.

"You're under arrest Max." The words poured out like cream from a pitcher.

"Arrest?" Max laughed.

"Reginald Waterson knows you sold him a doozy of a buckeye. "After the Hunt" is a fake, you told me so yourself. All you had to do was complete the sale, which you did yesterday. I've the assignment right here." Pinkerton waved the bill of goods in front of his face.

Max turned and lunged for Mercedes, hoping to use her as a shield to make his escape, but a bullet tore into his ankle and he fell to the floor. Blood oozed from his wound and stained the pant leg of his white, fleecy costume.

He howled in pain and ground his teeth furiously as if he were chewing on a doughy substance. "You set me up."

"You've set yourself up, chouser. We've confiscated the evidence in your office and have enough dirt to put you out of commission for quite a while."

Pinkerton moved closer to Mercedes to make sure she wasn't hurt. "And assault with a deadly weapon. I'm sure the lady plans to press charges."

Mercedes starred at Pinkerton who had garnered some instant respect in her eyes.

"I want my attorney," Max yelled, as the police picked him off the floor and hauled him downstairs.

Another shot rang out somewhere outside the gallery, accompanied by screams. Mercedes followed the group downstairs. She pushed through the back exit and ran outside. She was just in time to see Regan, her fox's head in hand, a leather jacket covering her costume, seated on her Harley. Behind her, Mallory held on for life as they crashed through the alley and disappeared down the street. Mallory's veil and a trail of smoke was all that was left behind.

Fletcher, garbed in her ridiculous praying mantis costume, her eyes black with rage, bugging out as if suffering from a thyroid condition, held a smoking .38 in hand. A cop grabbed the weapon and pushed her into the gallery.

Mercedes had no idea if Fletcher had hit Regan. Her head was still spinning from the attack on the roof. She looked up in the sky. The moon above seemed full of cheese and the crowd inside was packed with satyrs and wizards and demons, the noise at a fevered pitch. She had to get out of there before she got sucked into hell.

What seemed like hours later, she got in her car and drove off. A lurid tapestry of Halloween costumes swam in her head, but most haunting of all was the memory of the enigmatic woman in silver as she fled down the alley.

ART DEALER PLEADS NO CONTEST

Three days after the Halloween fiasco, Pinkerton paid a visit to Fletcher at home. He was led to the greenhouse where she was tending to her plants.

Fletcher's face had the glazed patina of mannequin with about as much emotion behind her eyes as a store dummy's. "Amazing these carnivorous curiosities, these meat-eating plants."

Pinkerton was down-dressed in herringbone pants, a white shirt and plaid vest. He cast a glance at the large flytraps with their white and pink flowers and winced. The image of Fletcher standing outside Max's club dressed as a praying mantis with a smoking gun in her hand hit his funny bone. He tried not to smirk and, even if he did, Fletcher was too absorbed by her hobby.

Her gloved hand scooped up a garden variety of live insects. "These little bugs take the place of nitrogen lacking in the soil. Just watch. It's lovely, really."

Pinkerton hated bugs. They made him sick.

"A fluid is secreted. The plant will slowly digest its prey." Fletcher was as proud as any mother and the all black get-up gave the appearance she was in mourning.

"I'd love to stay and watch, but I need to get to the point of my visit."

"And that point?" Fletcher leveled at look at Pinkerton that coiled around his throat.

"You could be under arrest for assault with a deadly weapon."

Fletcher laughed. "You sound like some canned detective on a television show. It was self-defense. I've got a license for my gun."

"You shot Regan in the shoulder. She could press charges. You're lucky she isn't dead."

"No I'm not," Fletcher said, her lips tightening like a vise. Her eyelids fluttered up and down as if she were suffering from some sort of epileptic seizure.

"You hit one of my operatives and I don't like it."

"Operatives?" Fletcher was incredulous. "Are you telling me Regan Hawk's a dick? I hired a private eye to spy on my own operation?"

"And a pretty healthy operation at that. Tell me something." Pinkerton lit up a cigarette. "You've got enough money to keep you happy for the rest of your life so what's with the pimping?"

Fletcher flung a handful of dirt crawling with insects at Pinkerton, soiling his white shirt.

Pinkerton winced and almost lost his head. His skin tightened. He down-swiped the dirt and plucked off a squirming earthworm as if it were a killer wasp and nearly threw it in Fletcher's evil face, but instead, he mercifully tossed it to the ground.

"You think you played this one smart, didn't you? Setting up Max. He trusted you."

"My heart's bleeding." Pinkerton blew a cloud of smoke in the direction of the feasting flytraps. He hoped it would kill their appetites. "He got what he deserved." He looked down at his dirty shirt and scowled. He'd just bought it at Traffic on Sunset.

"And how much did Waterson pay you?"

"That's none of your business. I was in on this with INTERPOL. Max was just one guy we have our eyes on."

"How much money do you want?" Fletcher removed her gloves.

"You're pathetic, Fletcher. I want you to leave Regan and Mallory alone. They won't press charges."

At the mention of Mallory's name, Fletcher started chewing her lower lip. She moved closer to the largest of flytraps and came so close to sticking her index finger inside, her flesh brushed against the trigger hairs.

Pinkerton whacked her hand away and she looked up at him as if she hadn't even remembered him arriving.

"You need help. I'd suggest you and Max blow town for awhile. About half a century."

An ebony flame burned in her eyes briefly and then went out. "Sure," she said, resignedly. "I just need to get some things in order."

Pinkerton walked to the door and took one last look at Fletcher. "By the way, the leaves on those flytraps die when they've had enough to eat. There's a lesson in that for all of us."

* * *

Mercedes observed Pinkerton as he dug into his bowl of chili smothered with chopped red onions and grated cheese. It was hard to reconcile this image of him with the man she spied on in the Bradbury Building that night as he made it with his secretary while Max watched. She guessed that's what gave him the edge with Max. Who'd ever suspect he'd turn around and arrest his bosom buddy?

Regan nursed a beer, her arm in a sling. They were seated in an orange booth at Canter's deli on Fairfax. Mercedes toyed with her corned beef sandwich, the phantom lady dressed in silver still haunting her.

Pinkerton had told them about his visit to Fletcher and filled them in on the back story of the counterfeit hoax.

"You see I had this tip from a buddy of mine who worked for INTERPOL, an international agency that recovers stolen art. *After The Hunt* was a little piece of Americana painted by William Harnett. You know, rabbit feet, dead ducks, partridges and oil cans strung on a wooden door. He was master of trompe l'oeil. You'd never know it was a buckeye."

Mercedes was amused by Pinkerton's ability to mingle his street slang with artsy foreign phrases. He was a wealth of information. She was surprised to discover that art swindles were the second largest illegal business in the country, the first being narcotics. That was something never mentioned in her years of graduate study.

"What happens to Max?" Mercedes took a bite of the juicy corn beef.

"Max got what's coming to him. He had to return Waterson's money, he'll be fined and his gallery just went black . . . and he'll be off his foot for a few months." Pinkerton slurped a spoonful of chili in his mouth. "But here's the *piece de resistance*. Waterson hires a pro to investigate the identity of the forger, most likely a cloner who had mastered the masters and couldn't make on dime on his own stuff—and lo and behold, they discover that underneath the counterfeit canvas is an original Rembrandt self-portrait. The piece is priceless."

Mercedes stopped chewing. An admirer of the Dutch school of painting, she was especially keen on Rembrandt and felt that he, more than any other seventeenth century painter, had left behind a remarkable *corps* of self-portraits, which like any autobiography rich in authentic details, allowed future generations to not only see the progression of his talents, but experience the artist as a man.

She had read an article in *ARTnews* about paintings—one in particular, another Dutch master, this one a Vermeer—that was smuggled out of the country with an overlaid canvas covering the original. There were even cases where special paints were used to camouflage the original surface of the priceless canvas for export.

She shared this information with Pinkerton. He nodded.

"Max had made a lot of money from his counterfeit sales. It's relatively clean work, you don't have to a carry a gun and, for the most part, no one turns up dead."

Regan winced. She popped two vicodins in her mouth and washed it down with beer. She addressed Mercedes. "What do you want us to do about Mona Lisa?"

Mercedes took a sip of her coffee. She looked at Pinkerton. He was starting to grow on her. And, after her initial run-in with him at the Bradbury Building, she never thought she'd feel this way. She was glad to discover that Regan had a legitimate job, well as legitimate as could be under the circumstances. She knew Regan was offering their services *gratis* in return for putting her up and helping her get Mallory away from Fletcher.

"I've given up on finding her." Mercedes was startled to hear the words pour out of her mouth. Her lower lip trembled. She got up.

Pinkerton looked at Regan and nodded his head. He scraped the bottom of his bowl with a piece of sourdough bread. "You've done pretty good for an amateur. You never know how things work out in the end."

Regan got up and put a hand on Mercedes back. "You OK?"
Mercedes nodded.

"Well, I'm outta here. My shoulder hurts like hell."

Mercedes helped her to the door and Pinkerton paid the bill. He grabbed a toothpick, stuck it between his teeth and escorted the women outside.

* * *

From four tables away, separated by an opaque amber partition, seated in a booth all alone, a woman with large, dark sunglasses and a leopard scarf tied round her head, got up and moved to the table Mercedes, Pinkerton and Regan had just occupied.

She sat down in exactly the same spot Mercedes had sat and fingered her coffee cup. There seemed to be a thousand miles of rough road tracked like mud in her sad expression. Every flea-bag motel, tattered coffee shop and one pump gasoline station were reflected in her clear eyes. Her finger continued to caress the cup as if she were trying to wipe away a smudge of lipstick that just wasn't there.

The waitress came by and grabbed her tip from the table. She threw the woman a suspicious look, having noticed her vacant stare when she served her on the other side. The waitress didn't budge.

Annoyed, the woman jumped up. "You'll see."

The waitress had waited on tables at Canter's now for fifteen years and had seen and heard everything worth seeing and hearing. Strange behavior was par for every course, but something about the woman's off-the-wall threat left a chill in her bones not even the matzo-ball soup could warm. She watched the leopard-scarfed woman leave the deli and disappear across the street.

LOVE'S ONE WAY TO PARADISE

Mercedes lay on her bed, the cityscape outside her window seemed to lure her out into the night. She was tempted to go. "Haunted Heart", a bluesy, romantic tune from 1947 played on her CD. It was nearly midnight and she was just tired enough to blow out the candle and go to sleep and just restless enough to put on her leather jacket and drown her sorrows at Girl Bar on Robertson.

A knock on her door detained her decision. "Come in."

Regan stuck her head in. "We're leaving."

Mercedes got off the bed. The door opened and in walked Regan and Mallory. Both were carrying an overnight bag. Mallory wore a hunter green pantsuit with padded shoulders and tiny bugle beads like candied sprinkles.

"Leaving?"

"Enseñada. For a couple of weeks. Until Fletcher gets the hell out of town. Until things die down."

Mercedes watched Mallory who looked as young and innocent as a teen. She didn't quite understand why Regan was saddling herself with all this responsibility, but then again she wasn't the one in love with Mallory.

They went downstairs. Mercedes prepared some coffee and made a few sandwiches for the trip.

Regan kissed Mercedes on the cheek. "You'd make a great wife. You're wasting away here all alone."

"And what about you? Running off to Mexico."

"I wasn't counting on leaving town, but Pinkerton insisted I needed a vacation."

"And I wasn't counting on you double-crossing me," an icy,

uninvited voice said from the doorway.

Mercedes and Regan turned around. From out of the shadows, Flora Fletcher walked into the kitchen, a nasty blue steel pistol in her hand. The stance was all confidence. The black wool suit was lacerated with crimson suede and the lashes were heavy with mascara and ill will. "Where's Mallory?"

Regan stalled. "Cut the shit, Fletcher. You're not going to get away with this."

Fletcher looked over at Mercedes. "Thanks for leaving the door opened. You made my job easier than I expected."

They all heard the scream at the same time. Fletcher turned around. Mallory stood at the end of the hallway, trembling, her little make-up case in hand.

Fletcher studied the girl. Her eyes softened, then hardened like obsidian. "Let's move into the living room."

*   *   *

The last thing Mercedes had wanted at this hour was company. She stood by the window, while Regan and Mallory sat on the sofa. Fletcher was by the fireplace, the gun pointed at Regan.

"I've come to claim what's mine. Mallory shouldn't be left alone."

"She's with me. Get the picture?" Regan's jeans were torn at the knees and her fist clamped by her side.

"First is first and second is nobody," Fletcher snapped. "She needs me." The declaration was a whine, more of a plea than a point of fact.

"She needs you like she needs the mumps." Regan massaged her bad arm.

Mallory moved closer to Regan. Fletcher winced. "She's ill."

"Cut the bullshit."

"No really, she doesn't even know it herself."

Mallory looked over at Regan and shook her head.

"What are you saying?" Mercedes' curiosity was piqued. She had no idea where Fletcher was going with this.

"No one knows. For awhile I didn't even, but then I realized there was something rather odd about her cognitive powers. People she'd be introduced to one minute, she'd forget the next." Fletcher laughed demoniacally. "Sometimes when I'd come into her room, she'd act as if she didn't even recognize me."

Regan grinned. "She didn't have to try too hard to forget."

Fletcher's lips tightened, the surface of her skin resembling that of an earthworm.

Mercedes peered out the window, hoping Pinkerton would show up or at least one of the security guards he was supposed to have covering her home.

"Mallory suffers from a tricky little malady called prosopagnosia." Fletcher pushed a few strands of hair from her eyes.

Regan looked at Mercedes who shrugged her shoulders. "Quit the psycho-lingo, Fletcher, I left my medical dictionary at home."

"In layman's terms Mallory can't recognize faces. It could be congenital. So, you see, I'm certain that with this awful disability she thinks you're me." Fletcher laughed madly as if she'd heard a very dirty joke.

Mercedes knew the woman was very close to the edge. In fact, she just may have jumped over. Fletcher lost her balance. She seemed a little drunk or high or both. Her eyes were the glazed points of the insomniac who hadn't slept in days.

"You're off your rocker," Regan snapped, getting up from the sofa. "Mallory doesn't want to go with you."

"What does she know what she wants? When I found her she was nothing. I made her what she is. I gave her everything, including the pair of diamond earrings I know she gave you. I want them back as well."

Regan looked over at Mallory. She was trembling uncontrollably. "She doesn't belong to anyone, Fletcher. You're just getting old, lonely and pathetic."

Mercedes moved away from the window. "Fletcher, let's be reasonable. She'll only leave you in the end."

Fletcher aimed the gun in Mercedes' direction. "I'll take my chances." She looked at Mallory. "Come here."

The girl froze. Her pink skin was as delicate as fissures on a ripe fruit.

"If you don't come, I'm going to put a bullet right through Regan's heart."

Mallory started to cry. Tears spilled down her face. Her upper lip quivered like a leaf in the wind.

"Dry your eyes, baby. It's out of character." Fletcher looked at her watch. "I've got a car waiting outside. Tickets for a nice long vacation."

Mallory jumped up and was about to run over to Fletcher, but Regan held her back. Mercedes tried to inch closer to Fletcher, without drawing too much attention.

"One . . . two . . . ."

Regan held on to Mallory who whimpered like a lost child. Suddenly a gun shot rang out. Mallory screamed and buried her face in Regan's chest. Fletcher whipped around, fired her gun into the darkened hallway, but it was as impotent a gesture as trying to kidnap Mallory.

Mercedes ran up behind the crazed woman, locked her body against hers and grabbed Fletcher's gun hand, swinging it toward the dining room. Fletcher pulled the trigger. A huge ceramic vase shattered and water gushed over the dining room table. Kicking her foot in between Fletcher's legs, Mercedes threw the woman off balance and swung her left arm around Fletcher's neck and squeezed until she heard a desperate gurgle escape from her throat. It seemed minutes before Fletcher gave in, her face a sick shade of blue as she dropped the gun on the carpet.

Regan scooped up the weapon, jumped back a few steps and pointed in the direction of the hallway. "Out in the open."

Samantha walked into the room and lit a cigarette.

"How many times do I have to tell you to lock your door?" Samantha grinned at Mercedes. "But I'm glad you didn't listen."

A tremor hit Mercedes in the stomach and worked its way to a seven on the emotional Richter scale.

"You," Fletcher growled. "Where's the dance-card?"

Samantha shrugged her shoulders. Fletcher lunged for her, her fingers arched like a tiger's claws; she got hold of Samantha's leather jacket and yanked so hard on the lapels the material ripped.

Samantha side-swiped Fletcher across the face with the back of her hand. Fletcher fell into a chair. Her face displayed the insufferable lunacy of the poor rake in her Hogarth painting.

Mercedes almost felt sorry for her.

"You bitch," Fletcher screamed, her eyes glowering with an

acetylene-torch intensity. "You palmed the dance-card. You're nothing but a two-bit thief."

"And you're no angel cake yourself." Samantha tucked the ripped material in her pocket.

Mallory buried herself in Regan's arm as she led her out of the room to call the police. Fletcher watched, uttering a groan that had no edge.

Samantha gazed at Mercedes. The two women seemed connected by an invisible string, as tenuous as gossamer and yet there was the possibility of a union as powerful as any alchemical transmutation.

Mercedes shivered. She tried to register what she was feeling, that onrush of adrenaline more potent than any smart drug concoction. It was hard to separate Fletcher's drama with her own reaction when Samantha had walked into the room.

"So?" Samantha started to move closer.

There would be no escape, unless Mercedes demanded one. There was no way to go back to the beginning, to the phone call she'd gotten in the middle of the night from Mona Lisa. She'd seen and experienced too much to return to a state of innocence. If she took those few steps forward, she might never look back.

Outside, sirens cut the silence. A police car pulled up, flood lights went on in neighbor's yards and the sleepy lifted their heads from down pillows and soft dreams.

The fuzziness around the edges of Mercedes' brain started to clear. In the moonlight, she could see Samantha for what she was. The random parts of her added up to a thousand nights of furious lovemaking. Fear crept into her heart and that ache in her loins burned like a fever out of control. Samantha Mann was gorgeous, seductive and dangerous.

What more could a girl ask for?

EVERY TIME YOU SAY GOODBYE, I DIE

"Pour yourself a drink. You look like you could use one." Samantha stood by the fireplace, her composure offset with enough nervous energy to give away her purpose. The house seemed deathly still. It was just the two of them. The final showdown. The cops had left. Regan and Mallory were on their way to Ensenada, Fletcher had been hauled off and Pinkerton called to wrap up the mess.

The early morning smell of the new day was about two hours away and before the darkness began to fade at the window, Mercedes knew she'd have to make a decision. She had that drink. "Why did you come back?"

"I'd say I arrived just in the nick of time."

Mercedes wondered what would have happened if Samantha hadn't arrived. "Yes, you do have an knack for showing up when least expected."

"I came back because I have some unfinished business."

Mercedes laughed. "Another heist?"

Samantha came up and grabbed Mercedes' arm. "I came back because of you."

"What did you do with the dance-card?" Mercedes waited for her response. Samantha didn't flinch. Mercedes tried to keep her temper in check.

Samantha let go of her arm and stared into her eyes. "Come to Rio with me." The invitation was less a demand than a plea.

Mercedes was speechless. This was not at all what she expected. Let's go away for a weekend, let's go steady, let's go out and blow the money I got for the dance-card, but not let's run away. She sat down.

"Rio?"

"Yeah," Samantha said, kneeling in front of Mercedes.   "To a place where none of this matters. A place where the sand is white and the water clean and the evening all ours. You'll understand me better."

"I think I understand you quite well. You're the thief who left me out cold in the museum and you want me to give up my job, take off like that and go away . . . ."

"Indefinitely."

Mercedes felt choked by the lack of oxygen in her lungs. She had to open a window, but she couldn't move. Swimming before her was Samantha's face lined with the earnest declaration of her invitation.

What was she supposed to do? Leave her life behind and put her hands in the care of Samantha, an art thief, a woman who lived on the lam and didn't know from paying rent, washing clothes or buying groceries. A woman who probably never paid taxes, or owned a library card or spent the day gardening in her yard. A woman who auctioned her nights at cafes dragging on Gitanes and cruising for all the disobedience the night had to offer. To live with someone who never knew where the money'd come from to pay the hotel bills, who scammed dinners from bored, rich playgirls on the market to pepper their days with a beautiful rake.

A sudden rush coursed through her veins and a life on the run flashed before her. Mercedes felt the old Virgo fortress start to crumble, to give way to the secret fantasy of breaking loose and living life on the edge of the world with nothing to stop her.

Samantha laid her head in Mercedes' lap and waited. "I'm sorry, really."

Mercedes could feel the woman's need as it heated her legs like a sunlamp and all of a sudden she felt the tropic breeze of Brazil's 4,603 miles of Atlantic coastline as it blew into the room. She sucked in the clean air and as oxygen rushed to her brain she started to think clearly. "If I could ever get the bit between your teeth, I'd know how to handle you, but I can't."

Samantha lifted her head and placed her chin in her hands. "You can try."

"I'm not up to it."

A wrack of disappointment clouded Samantha's face. "Women have skated in and out of my life on ice. Sure, that's the way it's been

. . . until I met you."

Mercedes wished she'd stop dropping all these lines she would have given up her first born to hear.

Samantha slithered up Mercedes and kissed her. "You want it all, I'm giving it to you. Only don't expect more than I can give."

"You're too busy taking."

Samantha grabbed Mercedes' shirt. "Who was the person who made you so sour about falling in love?"

Mercedes yanked her shirt free. She'd hit a nerve. So her heart had been stomped on a few dozen times. Pain built character, didn't it?

Mercedes refused to answer the question. Why dredge up the past? She shrugged her shoulders. "I don't trust you." Her lip quavered.

Samantha laughed. "You're scared. You're scared to death to fall in love with me."

Mercedes grimaced. "For chrissakes, we're so different, our lifestyles, I just can't pick up and leave like you."

"Yes you can. You're just afraid. You'd rather be stuck here for the rest of your life walking around dead buildings, listening for echoes of a silent past. Come on, you did it and now it's time to move on."

The words were delivered like the blows of an expert boxer. Mercedes tried to get up, but Samantha's body was lead. "You're jealous of me, I know it. You want what I have."

Mercedes was fuming. "And what's that?"

"Freedom." She cooed. *"Venga con migo, mijita."*

Why did she have to sound so damn sexy? "You call a life of crime, freedom? Try making a living and then we'll talk."

"Cut the shit. You know that's not what I'm about and never will be. Take me as I am, God knows you did before . . . and loved every minute of it."

She was right. Mercedes felt that warm ooze between her legs. That stab of pleasure that tasted as sweet as a summer melon. She looked down at Samantha's hands, those hands that held a gun as comfortably as another woman would hold a baby. Mercedes fit neither mold. And she would be insane to place her future in Samantha's hands, no matter how much at this very moment it seemed the smartest, most exciting proposition on the face of this earth.

"Fuck you."

Samantha grabbed Mercedes and pulled her down on the floor. They tumbled there like two lions, each trying to protect the offspring of their own interests as fiercely as any jungle beast.

Samantha was on top and her hand clutched Mercedes' neck.

Their lips together were an oasis of heat. A roiling, hot furnace that liquefied the metal of resistance like the blue white intensity of a welder's arc fusing their dissimilar elements into a unique alloy as powerful as plutonium. Their bodies found a motion that broke through a centrifugal force of emotional gravity. But the contact wasn't enough.

Samantha tore her lips from Mercedes'. "Are you coming with me?" The voice was raw, her eyes birds of paradise in flight.

Mercedes felt her stomach twitch with this incontestable spasm. "Will you give me back the dance-card?"

Samantha wasn't expecting the request. She jumped up and straightened her hair. "I can't."

Mercedes waited a moment before getting up. "Then I can't go."

The sun streaked across the sky and the chirping of blue jays broke the silence between them. A garbage truck clanked up the street like some mechanical beast and soon the sounds of the real world assaulted them.

Mercedes studied Samantha in the natural light as she would a Dutch painting. A haunting *chiaroscuro* of light and dark, she was clarity and color, stormy temptation, a raven-haired cutthroat hiding in the shadow of night.

Samantha picked up her jacket. "I laid my cards on the table and you walked all over me. Next time take off your heels. It won't hurt so much."

Mercedes heard the door slam and then the shrill whistle of the start of a new day. She looked out the window and watched Samantha drive away in the black Jeep. Her heart tugged and she held back the tears. Suddenly, the future looked and tasted as dull as a water cracker.

FIVE

ABOUT FACE

Christmas in Los Angeles was about as phony as a wooden nickel. Thanksgiving was hardly over and already the white lights twinkled on lamp posts in Beverly Hills and the gold and silver decorations in Hermes and Gucci and I. Magnin sparkled with the lure of money. The holiday felt like a beautifully wrapped, empty box.

But maybe that's because Mercedes wasn't in the best of moods. To temper her "bah hum-bug" attitude, she had spent Thanksgiving at the Union Rescue Mission helping to feed the homeless. Snapshot tore herself away from her civic duties as a member of the Public Safety Commission and Good Friday tied a red scarf around his neck and they joined in to help.

A sea of hungry faces lined tableclothed benches, some eyes filled with a glint of hope, others stitched closed by the weariness of sleeping on street corners. They wore the vagrant's inheritance of a doomed existence on their faces like a tattoo. They'd been offed the shuffleboard of life and for all but three percent, ninety-seven would never get back on and play.

Mercedes poured herself into her work with a vengeance. She organized the entire Conservancy West fundraiser practically singlehanded. Sleep was something she had no time for. The less sleep, in fact, the better. For it was in her sleep she felt Samantha's kisses and woke up in the middle of the night dreaming of South America and a lost paradise that could have been hers.

She'd gotten a postcard from Regan and Mallory. They were laying low, playing *touristas*, never staying in one town too long. Fletcher returned to an icy climed London, where she planned to open a restaurant with Max. It was called Lost Angel and would serve California cuisine, which meant it offered a bit of everything that wasn't kidney pie or English trifle. It would be several seasons, maybe even years, before they could show their faces in Los Angeles again.

There was, of course, no postcard from Samantha. And the phone calls suddenly stopped and the mysterious lady had all but disappeared. But Mercedes had not given up on Mona Lisa. She had to hold onto something to get her through the year.

Under the pretense of needing an actress to introduce "What Price Hollywood" to the sold-out event at the Million Dollar Theater before the party at the St. James Hotel, Mercedes called Carla Simpson, the cooler-than-cool agent at Favored Artists and set up a meeting.

Carla Simpson only kept Mercedes waiting an hour and a half before she was led into a large office with a view overlooking Century City to the south and the Hollywood Hills to the north. Her office was decorated in Bauhaus and American Craftsman. It wasn't pretentious, yet it was stylish and confirmed to the visitor that the woman behind the twelve foot long Stickley desk was a woman to be taken as seriously as her art, an art that reflected a simple workman's ethic, *do or die trying.*

Mercedes was seated in a forest green leather chair that faced the desk and matched another leather chair next to hers. Carla was on the phone as Mercedes waited.

An attractive young woman with smart hazel eyes and shoulder-length hair in a no-nonsense cut, she had a silk scarf tied around her neck and tucked into the stiff white collar of her shirt. The tailored pant suit looked like an Armani and the shoes underneath the table were Joan & David. Mercedes guessed the entire outfit to be worth approximately six weeks of her salary at the Conservancy.

When Carla slammed down the phone Mercedes knew it was imperative to get straight to the point. She told her about the event, which Carla approved without much enthusiasm, and read her a list of clients who would be happy to appear (the fee for their appearance to be negotiated later).

Mercedes decided on an actress whose father had made a big name in all the black and white films of the forties and fifties. She knew the actress would be a draw and there was history behind the screen persona as well. That matter cleared, Mercedes turned the conversation around to her own private agenda.

"Mona Lisa . . . ."

"Mona Lisa?" The words came out of Carla's mouth like two bullets. She reached for her Marlboro Lights. There was a flicker of discomfort at the mention of her client's name that was quickly extinguished behind the curtain of professionalism.

"Yes, she's a friend of mine and I know you were planning to sign her months ago. In fact we . . . ."

Carla shot up out of her chair. "Yes, we did talk. Well, I'm really quite busy."

Mercedes stood up. "Did you sign her?"

Carla weighed her remark. "In a manner of speaking, no."

Mercedes was starting to lose her patience. "Well, have you talked to Mona Lisa recently?"

"I haven't spoken to Mona Lisa in weeks. Now if you'll excuse me."

The door opened and an anemic secretary with round glasses entered. "Geneva's here. Mr. Shepherd's in the board room and everyone's ready."

Carla picked up a notepad, nodded to Mercedes and left the room. Mercedes followed her out into the reception area and before she could ask any more questions, Carla disappeared down a long important-looking corridor.

Mercedes must have appeared exasperated because the receptionist called her over. "Don't take it personally, actually she's really a nice kid, not like the other . . . ."

An agent flew by in a navy blue suit and threw a few envelopes on the desk. "Mail them, pronto."

"Assholes in this place." The receptionist finished her sentence, left dangling in mid-air. She was a pretty black woman in her mid-thirties. Her hair was plaited and pulled back in a ponytail. She had three gold hoops in her left ear.

Mercedes smiled. "So what's all the fuss about?"

The receptionist looked around to make sure no one was listening. "They just got this hot new talent signed to do the remake of *Double Indemnity*. They're out to directors now. I hear Barbet Schroeder's top on the list, but then again Jennifer Lynch has a good shot."

Mercedes nodded. "Who is she?"

The girl smiled, puckered her lips. "Her name's Gena Geneva and she looks like Gene Tierney, you remember her, only prettier."

God, you think they'd just discovered a cure for cancer or AIDS the way they got excited about putting together a package. Mercedes thanked the receptionist for the tip and started to leave, but stopped. "Have I seen this Gena Geneva in anything?"

"Umm, probably not and if you did, you wouldn't recognize her." She put up her hand and covered the side of her mouth and whispered, "Fat farm, you know how it goes in this town." She winked.

Mercedes nodded. She wondered whether it was Roseanne Arnold or Kathy Bates?

* * *

Mercedes had tried calling Mona Lisa's mother a few times, but no one had answered. She decided to try again, but this time the phone had been disconnected and there was no forwarding number.

She prepared a bath, took Mona Lisa's diary and got into the tub with a glass of Merlot. Billie Holiday crooned on the CD. The house was quiet, quieter than it had been in quite some time.

The hot water felt good. The eucalyptus oil made her skin tingle and smelled clean and refreshing. Mercedes opened the diary and started to read the mystifying journal for the tenth time. Each time she read it she gleaned something different about her friend, but search as she might, there was nothing there that would decipher her game plan and point to her whereabouts.

Three blind mice, see how they run, boy am I having fun. Myron thinks I'm getting some heat, wants to sign me for another three. Catch me if you can baby. If my plan works, and it will, I'll be able to slam the door in a few faces this time around.

The first time, the sex was really good. Hot. I liked being tied like that. Carmen didn't go in for that stuff, but I did. Gotta hand it to Fletcher, she knows her business.

He said my eyes cut through rooms, then I told him my body wasn't for hire and he laughed. I could see his teeth way back in his mouth and there was a hole where one was missing and I thought what a good place to hide something and then I thought of Marathon Man *and shivered. I'd show him a good time, I would.*

God, I almost blew it. Nearly leaned over and kissed her. I had to really hold back, but she looked so pretty and a little sad like. She needs someone wonderful in her life, I just wish it could be me.

It's the black and whites I like the best. I know how to do it now, it's simple really. Bring back the stars, I say, cut a figure, stand out and Hollywood'll take notice.

Mercedes lay the book on the tray and closed her eyes. It was obvious Mona Lisa had some plan. Whether she'd carried it out was uncertain. Who was this mystery woman who had captured Mona Lisa's affections? So many unanswered questions. She tried to picture Mona Lisa in her mind's eye, but it was impossible. She seemed a million light years away.

The phone rang. Mercedes wasn't about to get up. She took a loofah and started to scrub her arms when a voice rang out on the answering machine. It was a voice she recognized, only this time something was different.

"It's me Mercedes. I need to see you. I'm sorry about—"

Mercedes jumped out of the tub and grabbed a towel.

"Tonight at the Orpheum. They're screening *Dark Passage*. Please be there."

Mercedes ran for the phone, tripped over her throw rug and went sailing across the bed. She grabbed the receiver.

"Mona Lisa?" Too late. Nothing but dial tone.

"Shit." She slammed the phone down and played back the message. It was Mona Lisa's voice all right, but it wasn't the same as she'd remembered. There was something more mature in the tone, and although it was sexier and more seductive, she detected an underlying sorrow in the resonance.

Mercedes curled up on the bed, her wet hair matted to her head. Finally her friend made connection. Her stomach churned with excitement. But why meet after all this time in a movie theater? And why "Dark Passage?"

Mercedes opened her dresser drawer. She had saved the piece of rice paper she'd found in the dance-card. *red little fish, I kill you with the three-bladed knife that there may be an end to the silent circling of the past. This dark passage will be my guiding light.*

Dark passage again. Lauren Bacall and Humphrey Bogart. What did the movie have to do with Mona Lisa? She guessed she was about to find out.

* * *

It was six and the screening was at seven. With an hour to kill and to stave off the jitters, Mercedes drove her car up and down the dark streets. She didn't remember it ever being so cold in Los Angeles. Forty degrees with strong winds.

Hard-working citizens, part of over one million blue-collar workers, stood shivering on bus lines waiting for fat, stale houses of transportation to arrive, filled with tired employees, hungry and eager to be home, out of the cold, their faces expressionless. *Sing the traffic of never getting there.* Mercedes couldn't get Mona Lisa's diary out of her head.

Mercedes knew the person she'd been searching for these last few months didn't really exist as she had known her. *Under the Brooklyn Bridge a girl lost the only thing she had to give one night to a man who was mean and ugly and sharp. The lights mocked the girl with her skirt up over her face like a mask.*

A man who was mean and ugly and sharp. Her father?

Outside the Greyhound Bus station, people carried frayed suitcases ready to go off for the holidays or just disappear to smaller cities. A black man dressed as Santa Claus with a tattered red outfit and white beard hawked bell peppers and bags of oranges from a crate while another dude hustled stolen belts.

A woman with a sleeping baby bundled in her arms, darted across the street, stopping traffic, horns honked and in seconds mother and child disappeared down an alley, lost from sight.

Everywhere she looked, phantom men and women drifted through this concrete urban jungle, trying to find a place to just be. A councilman suggested they be put on ferries in the Harbor. A watery way station to get rid of a big headache, a little like sweeping dirt under the carpet to avoid vacuuming.

Mercedes' head was pounding. *I am the grand coquette living in the towel of babel, babel, babel* . . . . She went past all her familiar haunts: Clifton's, Vickman's, The Pantry, and drove by the Metropolitan Detention Center, one of six jails within three miles of City Hall, where Redlite was probably being served his dinner at this very moment. She cruised by the Clark, Alexandria and Biltmore Hotels, down along Fifth Street's ten block stretch of outdoor lodges for several thousand homeless.

An ambulance wailed, cars pulled over like automatons to let it pass. No one seemed to really pay attention or care. *The hot air rises from the belly of the city. . . .* A city where workers were in the midst of excavating a home for an enormously expensive 3.5 billion dollar Metro Rail system that wouldn't be completed for another decade.

Above ground, cleaning crews would soon arrive to sweep away the day's work, picking up the crumpled faxes and xeroxed copies of letters, contracts and failed mergers.

Mercedes cruised the nether world of the warehouse district next to the Los Angeles River, a cement sewer the Army Corps of Engineers had transformed in the 1950s. The shallow of heart with their thin hopes hung outside the cubbyhole bar, Campers Corner, innoculated against the cold with the prospect of a twenty-five dollar trick. *I sleep in the bed of one night stands . . . sew me a new life . . . a new life.*

I am an imitation of a perverted imitation of a work of art. DaVinci's *Mona Lisa.* Probably the most significant and recognizable painting in the world. Mona Lisa had adopted a pretty difficult namesake to live up to.

*   *   *

The Orpheum was between the Tower and United Artist's theaters on Broadway. Mercedes parked her car a half block away, zipped her leather jacket and walked toward the theater.

There were footsteps behind her. The unmistakable click of high heels. Mercedes turned around. An attractive woman brushed past. Her hair was covered with a leopard scarf, wrapped around her head in a very dramatic fashion. A pair of horn-rimmed glasses speckled with *faux* diamonds covered most of her eyes. A black wool coat with beaded buttons fit like it was custom made for her shapely figure. She was wearing a very strong perfume, a scent Mercedes had never smelled before.

Something in the woman's gait caught Mercedes' attention. She followed behind her. The woman stopped beneath the Orpheum's marquee, purchased a ticket and entered. Despite the cold, a thin trickle of sweat dripped down Mercedes' back.

She bought a ticket. A sign read, *"Teatro Orpheum . . . con titolos en Espanol."* Tonight there would be less of a Latino crowd with the week's film noir revival co-sponsored by the American Film Institute and the Association of Theater Chains.

Mercedes scanned the French Baroque lobby with its iconoclastic vending machines and video games. Mona Lisa was nowhere in sight. She felt a pair of eyes on her, turned around and caught the brunette give her a long look before disappearing up a flight of steps to the balcony.

It was the way she swept up the staircase that gave her away. Mercedes followed the woman just as she had tailed her the night of Max's Halloween party. It took a few minutes to adjust to the dim interior before she spotted the woman seated next to the aisle near the exit. They locked eyes.

Mercedes walked over to her. "Have we met?"

The woman shook her head. It was obvious she wasn't interested in making conversation.

Mercedes felt uncomfortable. She moved to the edge of the balcony and scanned the area below for Mona Lisa's blonde hair. The house was less than a quarter filled. On the gold-leafed ceiling above, five spectacular chandeliers dimmed. She took a seat a few rows down from the attractive stranger.

The theater darkened and the curtains parted on screen. Something scary tugged at her like a child who tries to bring an impending danger to its mother's attention. She picked at her cuticles.

She had never seen *Dark Passage* before. The credits rolled and Mercedes took a deep breath, not sure what to expect. A gun shot, some lunatic woman running across the stage, a fire. She thought she was prepared for anything, but nothing could have prepped her for what she was about to see.

Sixty minutes into the film directed by Delmar Davies, it hit and hit hard. In order to escape his awful predicament, Bogart secures the services of some crank doctor to undergo radical plastic surgery. It's only after the bandages are removed and he's healed that we finally get to see the protagonist's face.

Mercedes heard Mona Lisa's phone machine record in her head, drowning out the dialogue on screen. *"This is Eileen Woo. Your appointment with Dr. Flesch has been confirmed."*

"This dark passage will be my guiding light." Mercedes got the full picture. She jumped up, but the strong scent of perfume, like a fog behind her, made her freeze. A woman's hand reached out and touched her back.

"I'm sorry it had to be this way, Mercedes. I've missed you."

Mercedes turned around slowly and there seated behind her was the mysterious brunette. She had a beautiful, cold, remorseful face that lit up when a faint smile drifted across her young, smooth complexion. Mercedes sunk back in her seat.

A hundred images of women swam before Mercedes' eyes, blondes, brunettes, redheads, shaved heads. Faces heavily made up like Madonna, Michael Jackson, and Elizabeth Taylor. Noses, eyes, and lips rotated in circles like a kaleidoscope of features. Garbled voices screeched in her ears.

"Mercedes, are you okay?"

Mercedes blinked and tried to focus. A flicker of light from the screen flashed on the stranger's face again. And that's when it slugged her in the gut.

The woman looked nothing like Mona Lisa, in fact only a trace of her remained in the voice. Stunned, Mercedes recoiled with shock. Anger rose in her like an old wound tearing the surface of a scar.

The laugh that escaped Mercedes' lips was hard and bitter. She glanced around the theater. What else could have been expected?

In the intimacy of this relic, an appropriate venue for a clever denouement, she realized that Mona Lisa had indeed been killed and, in more ways than one, she had really lost her friend.

GENA GENEVA

Mercedes could barely hold the cigarette in her hand. She tapped it against the glass ashtray with the restaurant's logo several times even though there were no ashes to relinquish, and waited for Mona Lisa's monologue.

Coming out of the theater, Mercedes had experienced her own dark passage into the bowels of Los Angeles. Dazed, almost hypnotized, she felt the night had become nothing but a vast black landscape with endless questions rapping on her consciousness like the hard angry fists of workers striking against white-collar management.

Mona Lisa had to lead her by the arm. She had no recollection of getting in a car or a taxi, all she remembered was walking past the Lalique glass panels adorning the entrance of Rex II, a stunning renovated eatery in the lavish art deco Oviatt Building on South Olive Street, a few blocks from the Orpheum.

They were seated in the nightclub upstairs overlooking the expensive restaurant below. A few diners remained. A four-piece combo played romantic tunes and four couples danced on a small patch of black and white tiles.

Mercedes threw back the amber liquid in her glass and examined her friend's face as if seeing it for the very first time. She had the carriage and air of a movie-star from the forties. Her persona was as black and white as the dance floor. The way she walked, the way she held her head in a semi-frozen position, the Jungle Red nails, the eyeliner, the soft, delicate features, the amplified curves poured into a lovely Chanel dress, the purse, the gloves, the scarf, even the horn-rimmed glasses that she had removed. The nose was smart and haughty, pinched above each nostril in the exact spot like a dimple. The eyes were no longer hazel, but deep green with a forest of mystery as thick as Nottingham.

But it was the name, the icing on top of this perfectly designed cake, that completed the signature reincarnation of a movie star with all its inherent ramifications.

"It's Gena Geneva," she said, lowering her long, mascared eyelashes, the crisscross of shadow, miniature venetian blinds slashing her smooth, white complexion.

"Gena Geneva?" Mercedes furrowed her brows. The name was familiar. Very familiar. And suddenly the bizarre plot took shape in her brain. The effect was similar to viewing Chandler's *The Big Sleep*. How all the pieces fit was a mystery, but who could deny the chemistry of Bogart and Bacall? Who cared if little made sense? The story was tough and as hard-boiled as they came and it all wrapped around your gut and kept you in its clutches.

"Yes." She paused for effect. "I'm Mona Lisa's better half." She held onto her glass for support. She didn't look at Mercedes. It was too soon to get approval or acceptance. Either that would come or it wouldn't.

Her hair, without the bonnet of the leopard scarf to hide it, was parted on the left side; a thick and shiny cascade of honey brown silk, the cut was marcelled to her broad shoulders.

"Gena Geneva." Mercedes repeated the words again as if trying them on for size. It was difficult. The new look, the new voice, the new name. Any minute now, she prayed the old Mona Lisa would step out from the shadows of this reincarnation and say it was all some bizarre, crazy joke. April fool's. Ha. Ha. But Mona Lisa never appeared and no one was laughing.

"It'll take some time getting used to." She fingered her glass nervously. The keyed-up tension between them was so thick you couldn't cut it with a hatchet.

A waiter came over. "Excuse me, Ms. Geneva, but there's a call. Mr. Yamamoto. He said he's ready."

"Yes, of course. I'll be right there." ,

Mercedes watched the woman seated across from her talking as if in a dream.

The waiter moved away and headed for the bar.

"Mr. Yamamoto?"

Gena smiled. "I take it you've heard of him?"

"Yes, in fact I've heard just about everything there is to know about you, and then some. Why didn't you confide in me? Maybe it would have been easier to take all this in." The words flew out of Mercedes' mouth.

"I think it was better you found it out yourself."

Mercedes shook her head. "You should have been straight with me."

A faint smile creased Gena's face. "Several times I tried to tell you, but you live such a goddamn rosy life, I felt . . . cheated." Contempt crept into Gena's voice, but it quickly disappeared. "I didn't want to spoil things between us."

Mercedes was taken back. She never realized her friend could be jealous. "So this was some lesson you were teaching me?" Mercedes had a particularly difficult time with this.

"I didn't intend for it to be that way."

Mercedes was angry and tempted to storm out of there, but something held her back. Maybe there was a little truth in Gena's statement.

Gena crossed her silk-stockinged legs. Her voice was soft and serious, her eyes probing. "I know what you went through. You didn't go to the police, that would have ruined everything. You didn't let me down."

"I stood up for you when everyone stomped all over your name." Mercedes sounded defensive.

Gena leaned across the table and placed her hand over Mercedes'. "I know. Her voice was sad and came from a past the two of them had shared. "That's why it's gone. Mona Lisa no longer exists." She straightened her back and smoothed her hair. "Don't you like the way I look?"

Mercedes' flesh burned like hot metal from the close contact. She snapped her hand out from under her friend's. "You look swell. Just like Gene Tierney in "Laura." But tell me something, who will you look like next year, or the year after?"

She shrugged her shoulders and the ends of the mouth curled into a bud of a smile. The hair brushed across her face. "Does it matter?"

Mercedes flew up in her seat. "Yes, goddamn right it matters. It matters to me and maybe that's not good enough for you."

Gena jumped up and pulled Mercedes along a red-carpeted alcove where a few people finished up their drinks. She pushed Mercedes into the women's restroom with its dark mahogany walls and gilt fixtures.

She slammed Mercedes against the door. Her strength, surprising.

"It's good enough, believe me. It's the only thing I cared about, but living in this town, it's never fucking enough." Gena slapped the door with the palm of her hand for emphasis, then turned and paced in front of the individual wood stalls like a nervous Scottish terrier. The thick soled high heels were retro forties and no doubt purchased at Maxfield's on Melrose.

"I've got your diary."

Gena stopped. Her hand clutched at the expensive material of her dress. "So then you do know everything." The words came out like a sigh of relief.

"Yeah, everything and nothing." A bitterness underscored the declaration. "So that was you downtown in the red jacket and in the silver gown at Max's party?"

"Yes. I had to see you, but I wasn't ready yet for the unveiling. It took longer than I expected to get up the nerve. You see changing my name wasn't enough this time. I had to go all the way. You don't know, you just don't know."

"No, I don't, do I?" Mercedes turned on the faucet and let the cold water run over her hands. She thought she saw steam rise from the fingers.

"Xuan did the make-over. But she didn't do it right. She kept the old way of life right along with the new face."

"And now she's dead." Mercedes pushed her hair out of her eyes.

Gena showed no sign of remorse on her face. "I had a second chance to do it right. It wasn't only the dance-card and the money, it was something I'd been planning, something I knew I'd do, I think, since the day I was born." Gena smoothed her hair back. "I've altered my birth certificate. All the documents of my identity have been falsified. I don't have an accountable history. Even my mother's gone."

"Gone?"

"Yes. I've sent her away. She always dreamed of living in the south of France. It's best for both of us."

"How much does your agent Carla know about her client?"

Gena looked at Mercedes with admiration. "I'm impressed." Gena unbuttoned her Eisenhower-styled jacket. "She knows very little. Certainly nothing about my past. You're the only one who knows everything . . . and I'm counting on you to keep it that way."

She leveled a look at Mercedes that was loaded with threat, but within seconds it disappeared behind the foliage of her gorgeous green eyes. Gena slowly removed her jacket and dropped it on the small cushioned seat. Then she undid the gold buttons of her dress, deliberately dragging the action along like a striptease.

She wasn't wearing a bra. Her breasts were two sizes larger than they used to be, maybe three. And firm, as firm as summer fruit plucked from the vine. Her surgeon, Dr. Flesch, had done an excellent job.

Mercedes steadied herself on the sink. She groaned softly, watching in utter fascination.

"Pretty spectacular, huh? The kind we'd always dreamed about owning, like the convertible red Mercedes I drive now."

While Mercedes' eyes were glued to Gena's breasts, as exposed as her old friend's fabricated existence, she heard the details of the gruesome surgeries and post-op care: rhinoplasty, cheek implantations, eye lift, cleft in chin, liposuction, (tummy, neck and buttocks), Zyderm collagen injections in the lips, breast augmentation, colored contact lenses, elocution lessons (not to mention a crash course in Spanish while she spent most of the time recovering in Mexico).

Gena grabbed Mercedes' hand and placed it on her breast. It was soft, but firm and the nipple hardened to the touch. Gena then took Mercedes' face in her hands and leaned in and kissed her on the lips. Their bodies touched and it was as if all the dynamite in the world was packed in that kiss.

Mercedes pulled away, stunned. Gena had a look in her eye as stultifying as any femme fatale. Mercedes got it. She got it so hard she felt socked between the eyes. It was crazy. They didn't say anything for what seemed to be a few years and then Gena spoke.

"It was you," Gena said, growing as distant as a retreating storm. She fastened the buttons of her jacket. "I wanted you. But I could never tell you. Not after all I'd done. I couldn't lie, so I never told you the truth. I had a better chance at keeping you my best friend than I would have had as a lover." Her voice broke.

Mercedes gripped the sink for support.

Gena closed the final button. "And now I'm not sure I have either." Gena lifted Mercedes' face with her fingers. Her breath was sweet and warm and inviting. "I won't ever give up hope." The words stopped.

Mercedes' head was reeling. Suddenly she felt drunk, as stoned as if she'd had five Scotches instead of one. She slumped against the sink. Gena's performance was a living example of the best *trompe l'oeil*, she had fooled Mercedes like any good counterfeit. And she was good. Really good. The voice had grown husky and deep, the edges aggravated with just enough tension to make you believe she'd suffered and that she was going to share that suffering with you. The eyes were lost in the third act of a tragedy yet to be written and the movement of her hands and her body was syncopated with the delivery of her dialogue.

Mercedes avoided the implication of Gena's last remark. She wanted to change the subject, to buy time to sort this all out, to process her feelings. "The dance-card's been stolen."

Gena shrugged her shoulders. "It got me what I needed to get started. A means to an end, it meant nothing to me."

"Nothing?" Mercedes boiled with anger. "I nearly got killed."

Gena lit a cigarette, her hand was shaking. The smoke wafted between them like a huge fissure in the earth's surface. "Look, I had no idea, I'm so sorry." Suddenly the cigarette tasted foul. She threw it in the sink and turned on the water.

Mercedes felt a sharp stab, hard in the belly. She closed her eyes and it was dark, as black as the inside of a coal mine. The air was thick, insufferably difficult to suck into her lungs. How could she say that about the dance-card?

Mercedes saw the three women on her beloved antique, each with the precious ruby in place of their hearts as they whirled around in a circle and then the dancers had faces she recognized and when she focused harder she could make out Gena's face and then there was Samantha, eyes stone cold, and in the middle, was Mercedes and she was being pulled to the right and left by these two women, these two women who had kept her spinning around in circles, waltzing and twisting and hip-hopping like some crazy dervish.

Her eyes flashed open. Gena was holding her in her arms. Mercedes tossed her off like a bad penny.

Gena stood there, her lower lip trembling. She reached out for Mercedes again. "Please."

In the mirror Mercedes caught a glimpse of the two of them. Gena was crying, hot wet tears spilled down her new face. The room seemed to spin out of control and for a minute they were back at Two Bunch Palms, back in time where ignorance was bliss and no one could see disaster lurking in the wings of the theater like a nasty critic.

Gena wouldn't give up. "Please," she implored.

Mercedes relented. Gena buried her face in the protective fold of her friend. They stayed like that until the lights in the bathroom dimmed and it was time to leave.

* * *

The Oviatt Building used to be one of the most elegant haberdasheries in town. A place Clark Gable and John Barrymore came to be attired and accessorized. It was built by a man with vision, a man by the name of James Oviatt, who had discovered the girl of dreams working as a common shopgirl in his store and married her. Amidst twenty or so tons of imported Lalique glass, he added a sumptuous penthouse where a small swimming pool and private elevator housed his little family.

It was in this elevator that Mercedes traveled as she watched the silent Gena Geneva. They reached the penthouse, the doors opened and they stepped out into a luxurious interior. The green fixtures were imported and the rugs were plush and complemented the art nouveau decor.

Gena opened a pair of double doors, Mercedes at her heels. Inside the living room everything was a swathe of white, gold and amber against carved wood and onyx.

Mercedes stopped following Gena. There seated on the sofa, a pair of demi-reading glasses on his nose, was a large man with a kind, pleasant face. He closed his book. Next to him, showcased on a lacquered end table, was the holograph of Mona Lisa. The effect on Mercedes was as startling as finding a decapitated head floating in a huge pickle jar in her refrigerator.

Gena put a hand on his shoulder and looked over at Mercedes. "This is Mr. Yamamoto," she said. "He too knew Mona Lisa."

Mercedes pried her eyes off the piece of art. She looked at Gena, puzzled.

Gena winked at Mercedes.

"Call me John. No need for formality." The man got up and walked over to Mercedes, his hand outstretched. "I've heard much about you."

Mercedes shook his hand and allowed herself to be led to an upholstered chair that welcomed her exhausted body. So this was the mysterious Yamamoto. She glanced at the book he was reading. It was the *Tales of Genji* by Lady Murasaki.

"Can I get you a drink?" The suit he wore was dark blue silk and the brown alligator shoes must have cost five hundred dollars and change.

Mercedes nodded. "Some cognac."

John smiled and looked over at Gena. "You, darling?"

"Perrier. Twist of lime."

"Right away," he said, nodding to Mercedes.

When he left the room, Gena put on Cole Porter's "Night and Day" and gazed out the huge window in front of the baby grand piano. The setting was perfect.

"He's really very nice. I stay here on occasions. You know his real estate company purchased this building ten years ago for over thirteen million. He loves Los Angeles, as much as you do."

Mercedes sank back in the chair. She knew when Mr. Oviatt had died in 1977, the building was sold for a mere $400,000. Developers had sunk millions to restore it to its former grandeur and now Mr. Yamamoto had taken over.

Gena invited Mercedes to join her by the window. "You see, I told him I met his Mona Lisa down in Mexico and she asked me to look him up. At first he was disappointed she never returned. He was crazy about her, but then, I took over and that was the end of it." Gena looked over at the holograph. "He bought that for me."

"Why didn't you just ask him for the money?"

Gena smiled. "You mean instead of stealing the dance-card?"

Mercedes nodded.

"That would have been highly improper. He was very generous and to ask would have demeaned me in his eyes."

"What about your butterfly tattoo?"

Gena smiled. She touched Mercedes' shoulder. "It's still there. I said I copied it. It impressed him. He's a lepidopterist. He's got quite a collection of rare butterflies."

They stared at the city still clutching onto the last hours of night like a baby its favorite blanket. A plane crossed the sky and somewhere not too far in the distance a fire burned and black smoke billowed against the sky like a huge bat's wing.

Gena reached for her purse. She opened it, pulled out an envelope and handed it to Mercedes. "I know you paid my rent. My landlady told me."

Inside the envelope was five crisp, one thousand dollar bills. Mercedes removed one bill and returned the rest to Gena.

Gena shrugged her shoulders and stashed the envelope in her purse. She hummed along with the music.

Mercedes studied Gena's reflection in the glass. A beautiful victim of her own image-repertoire, she was guilty of reinventing herself. A Brooklyn nobody suddenly takes on the pedigree of a Bostonian and the second class actress who did little more than extra work turns into a classy glamour girl soon-to-be plastered on billboards along Sunset Boulevard. She had taken cosmetic surgery to she-devil proportions and would no doubt grab Hollywood around the throat and squeeze until she landed herself an Oscar.

Mercedes surveyed the city's medley of steel, reflective glass, terra cotta, brick, chrome and iron. It too had reinvented itself. New architecture had drawn and quartered a past people hoped to bury. Transformed into a town of blue, green and chartreuse mini-malls, nobodies could walk in fly-by-night stores and come out a star.

Gena lit a cigarette. "Yamamoto just bought Orion's library. He's renaming the studio. The first picture they're doing is—"

"*Double Indemnity.*" Mercedes heard her own voice and for some reason it sounded older, wiser, sharper than the voice she'd awakened with that morning.

Gena Geneva did a double take. "My, you really did do your homework."

She moved away from the window and leaned on the piano. She

looked grand in the shaft of moonlight, prettier than she ever possibly could as her old self, but something was missing.

"It all worked out rather nice, didn't it? John is wonderful, not like the others. You see we have this understanding, this arrangement, that's just the way it goes. He has a wife, kids, the whole nine yards, don't they all, they get it all, believe me, Mercedes, I know."

She laughed. "You remember that scene in *The Player* when Tim Robbins returns home to his wife and she's pregnant and glowing with love on that pretty face of hers for her big Hollywood executive husband? And we all know he's literally gotten away with murder, but he's got his happy little Eden and soon he'll have some mistress on the side. Live and learn, I say. Well here's my dream. I've got it all and nobody can take it away from me." She tapped her polished fingernails on the lacquered piano for emphasis.

It hit Mercedes like a two-fisted punch. She realized what Gena was missing as she looked around at all the flash, the pomp and circumstance.

She had lost her soul.

One phone call in the middle of the night. A precious dance-card. A gorgeous black widow and one prosthetic star.

THE NIGHT WAS FULL OF SIRENS

When the St. James Club was founded in England nearly one hundred and forty years ago, women carried dance-cards. It was a civilized social custom. A girl whose dance-card was full would certainly be the most popular girl in the room. A blank card could mean disgrace. A wallflower was not a pretty sight.

Mercedes stepped out of a white stretch limousine that had pulled up in front of the St. James, the multi-million dollar art deco masterpiece, a real cliff-hanger on the edge of Sunset Boulevard. She turned to smile at her companion getting out behind her.

Good Friday looked dapper in a suit she had rented for him despite his protestations. In fact, he looked so good and had gotten so much attention from widowed Conservancy donors that he told Mercedes he was going to go out and buy one. "Yessiree, they do say clothes make a man."

The Million Dollar Theater never looked better filled to capacity. The screening of *What Price Hollywood* was a success. And unlike Constance Bennett who played the lead ingenue, a Hollywood hopeful who finds that prosperity in tinseltown does not necessarily bring happiness, Gena Geneva's career was skyrocketing and that smile on her face was as ubiquitous as DaVinci's *Mona Lisa*.

Scott E. Schwimer, a sharp entertainment attorney, who had built his industry reputation on discovering a stable of raw talent, nabbed Gena as a client and her movie was on the fast track at the newly named Capricorn Pictures. The media were picking up all the scraps they could find on this latest star on the horizon. There was gossip in the local tabloids about the heated affair of her *Double Indemnity* co-star, Alec Baldwin. Already she was outpacing Barbara Stanwyck, the queen bee of noir.

That was the rumor mill for you. Managed by Michaels & Wolfe, Gena Geneva was taken under wing by an aggressive young publicist, Staci Wolfe, who saw to it that Gena was on the cover of every magazine. There was a picture of Gena, Carla and Staci at a Hollywood gala in *Movieline*, Gena's hair outrageously styled by the chic Milange salon.

Mercedes wore an elegant black cocktail dress with antique bugle beads in a deco swirl on her chest. Her sheer seamed stockings disappeared into a pair of suede black high heels. Good Friday crooked his arm in hers as they moved past white Christmas tree lights twinkling in potted Jacaranda on each side of revolving copper doors. Men wearing pillbox hats, navy blue suits, black patent leather shoes and white socks escorted them inside the St. James.

Georgia Press, the Conservancy's director, couldn't contain her excitement as she made a beeline for Mercedes, pulling her husband along. "Mercedes, I can't tell you what a terrific job you did. Everyone is raving. We've more than met our expectations for the fundraiser." She looked over at her husband who wore a very drab suit and a tie dotted with green hens, or some sort of fowl. He nodded his head in agreement.

Mercedes was pleased. Besides keeping the theaters in shape, a portion of the money raised was targeted for the renovation of the Streamline Moderne Thomas Jefferson High School, designed by Stiles O. Clements in 1936 on Central Avenue. This delighted Good Friday since he had attended school there in the fifties.

"That's my girl," Friday beamed with pride.

Georgia smiled at Good Friday. They had been introduced at the theater and still behind the eyes, it was evident Georgia couldn't quite figure out what Mercedes was doing with this older man. "Webster couldn't make it to the theater, but he'll be here shortly. I do so want the two of you to talk, you know."

Mercedes broke away as soon as she could and darted past a sea of faces and the swoosh of taffeta, silk, the smell of expensive perfume and imported cigars till she got to the bar. "Champagne, make that two."

Everything was cool gray and Lalique glass, wrought-iron balconies, Limoge china and black deco chairs against chestnut wood paneling. The dance floor three steps below the intimate bar area was filled with tables and diners who had paid $250 a seat for the evening. Against the dramatic wall of a window, the city spread out to the ocean and sparkled like thousands of diamonds against a clear, velvety night.

Good Friday lit up a thin cigar and examined the crowd like a general looking out over his guests in his palatial home. "Damn good cigar," he said out of the side of his mouth.

Mercedes handed him a glass of champagne. He looked at her as if she'd lost her mind.

"That's perfumed bath water." He turned to the bartender and ordered a Glenlivet, straight up.

He clicked his glass against her delicate champagne flute. "To friends."

"To friends," Mercedes repeated. A strange sort of sadness swept over her, but she took comfort in knowing that people like Good Friday were in her life.

"Hey, what's with the long face?"

Mercedes looked over at Snapshot, her camera strapped around her. She'd hired her as the photographer for the Conservancy newsletter. There's nothing more donors liked than seeing their pictures in print.

"The long face is so Georgia's brother will think I'm ugly and won't bother to introduce himself," Mercedes teased.

"I'll take care of him."

"No, believe me, I think I can handle him."

Snapshot pulled Mercedes aside. "Any word yet about Mona Lisa?"

Mercedes looked at her friend and shook her head. "No, nothing. I guess she's gone for good." Mercedes was telling the truth about that.

"This town bleeds everyone dry. Hell, chin up, knowing Mona Lisa, she's probably on an ocean liner right now sipping champagne, having a hell of a time."

Mercedes smiled. "I bet you're right." Mercedes hadn't told anyone the real story. While Gena wasn't sure she could count on Mercedes to remain a friend, she knew, at least, she could count on her to keep her secret.

Snapshot pulled out a pack of cigarettes and offered one to Mercedes.

"I quit. Really quit this time."

Snapshot grinned. "Great. Happy New Year, kid."

Mercedes hugged Snapshot, then walked off into the crowd of men and women, past the buffet table laden with *foie gras*, *sevruga* caviar, stuffed eggs and duck canopies, and through a glass door outside onto the large patio where a rectangular pool shimmered against the white lights dotting fake palms along the deco railing. Down below was nothing but a two hundred foot drop to the sidewalk.

She could hear the swell of the crowd, the eight piece orchestra playing a medley of tunes from the forties and fifties. Songs to tug at the heart. She took a deep breath and a peace settled over her. The last few months had indeed been one rollercoaster ride to hell and back, a real eye-opener, but Mercedes knew she had emerged stronger, wiser and just a bit more realistic about human nature.

"Looks like you don't need a light, beautiful." A voice rang out behind her.

Mercedes stopped breathing. The air was cold and suddenly it was as if a huge icicle had pierced her heart. She'd had no intention of staying outside this long and now she was frozen to the spot. The voice she recognized all too well.

Samantha stood beside her. She wore a black Ungaro tuxedo, her eggplant-colored hair slicked back off her face. The lips were pale mauve and the eyes pools of kohl around her long, thick lashes. She was sunburned and looked like a million dollars worth of gold in the moonlight.

The chromatics were stunning. Mercedes shivered. Samantha put an arm around her and pulled her close.

Mercedes inhaled the jungle perfume, a verdant, wild, intoxicating scent that would forever haunt her. She tried to move away, but Samantha clutched her arms.

"Don't. I came back to give you something."

Mercedes wasn't prepared for this. Not in her wildest dreams.

Samantha reached inside her coat pocket and removed a black velvet pouch. She put it in Mercedes' hand and waited for a reaction.

It must have been five hours, but then again it couldn't have been more than a minute. Mercedes loosened the draw string and dropped the contents in the palm of her hand.

The dance-card shimmered in the artificial lights. She gazed down at the three Muses, their faces were lost in the beating of her heart and the roaring of blood in her ears. She looked up at Samantha.

A second later, they were kissing and the heat of their lips burned like a Roman candle and the St. James was merely a prop, one big expensive backdrop to a passionate drama in the foreground.

Mercedes forgot where she was. Time was a broken watch sent out for repair. Sparks and embers flew between them and for a second their lovemaking was a beautiful freeze frame against a haunting cityscape. Mercedes pulled away.

She looked at Samantha and realized how much the woman really loved her. To come all this way, to return what had been stolen from her. To make amends.

Mercedes looked back at the people inside the hotel ready to ring in the New Year. "I've got to take care of something."

Before Samantha could stop her, she hurried inside, back to the party. She didn't give a damn if a few people spotted her there by the pool. It made no difference anymore. She had no intention of donning a disguise. If Georgia tried to fix her up with Webster, she'd tell him she was into women and that would shut him up, good and fast.

Mercedes pushed open the heavy door of the restroom and flew inside. All marble and mirrors, the room was empty. She opened one of the two stalls and hid in the privacy of the toilet. She was shaking so hard she could barely hold the dance-card in her hand.

She took several deep breaths and then she unclutched her hand and examined her beloved dance-card. The ache she felt in her stomach was a slow, sick burn, a fever that starts with a few dots of sweat and within the hour turns into a blazing, shivering heat, water pouring from your head like rain.

She held it close to her face. She ran her finger around every curve, opened it, closed it, even tried to cool her burning cheeks with the metal. But it was hopeless.

Mercedes sat on the toilet, the dance-card on her lap, her fist pounded the walls and she let out a cry. Tears streamed down her face and any residue of naivete evaporated into thin air.

She dried her eyes and then exited the stall. No one was there. There was a big commotion outside. It was five minutes before midnight. She took one more look at the dance-card, then flung it in the gray receptacle and left the bathroom.

Mercedes caught a glimpse of Samantha leaning over the railing, smoking a cigarette. Part of her wanted to run out and push her over the small bluff, the other part wanted to get a room upstairs, forget the deception and make love to her.

She did neither. She got her coat and walked out into the cold night, people counting down the seconds in unison behind her as the year slipped away like a dream.

Samantha was a fake, a counterfeit, just like the dance-card. Mercedes wasn't about to be duped again. She knew every inch of that "passion piece" and while it was an admirable replica, it wasn't the real McCoy. It was a good show, a brave act and it almost worked, but she could no more live with Samantha than she could have back her old friendship with Mona Lisa.

Squeals, noisemakers and honking horns rang in the New Year as Mercedes walked west into the wind, her eyes watering, her heels clicking along Sunset, refrains from "Auld Lang Syne" filtering on to the boulevard where dreams are made and dreams are broken.

The thin scream of sirens in the distance gathered in full force as an ambulance tore its way along this major artery, growing louder and louder and more insistent, wailing and screeching, making itself heard over the din of traffic and merrymaking till it dragged past Mercedes and the whirling red turret was like blood against the canvas of night.

ABOUT THE AUTHOR

Lynette Prucha is an active figure in Los Angeles literary circles. A novelist, screenwriter and short fiction author, her first novel, *Smokescreen* was inspired by her interest in the classic noir films of the 1940s.   She currently works in the film industry.

Clothespin Fever Books

655 4th Ave., Suite 34, San Diego, CA 92101
(619) 234-2656

A Dyke's Bike Repair Handbook, a motorcycle repair book
by Jill Taylor $8.95

*Are You Girls Traveling Alone? Adventures in Lesbianic
Logic* by Marilyn Murphy $10.95

Black Slip, poems by Terry Wolverton $7.95

Crazy , a novel by Carolyn Weathers $8.95

Dangerous Ideas, a mystery by Janet Graham $10.95

Dirty Money, a mystery by Pele Plante $9.95

Getting Away With Murder , a suspense novel by Pele Plante
$9.95

In A Different Light: an anthology of Lesbian writers edited by
Jenny Wrenn and Carolyn Weathers $9.95

Island of Floating Women, short stories by Batya Weinbaum $9.95

*Loss of the Ground-Note: women writing about the loss of their
mothers* edited by Helen Vozenilek $12.95

Portraits: Sapphic Zest for Life , poems by Teresita Bosch $8.95

Shitkickers & Other Texas Stories by Carolyn Weathers $7.95